Advance Praise for *The Secret of the Nightingale Palace*

"In this unconventional road-trip tale about a grandmother and granddaughter crossing America to return a precious Japanese artifact obtained during WWII, Dana Sachs offers a graceful exploration of the human heart. With her signature elegance, she examines the burden of family secrets and how the complexities of culture can both divide and unite at the same time. The many nuanced moments of this hypnotic, satisfying novel will linger in your thoughts long after you finish the last page."

—Kim Fay, author of *The Map of Lost Memories*

"*The Secret of the Nightingale Palace* delightfully expands the route of the American road-trip novel. Old-fashioned in the best of ways, this story of a grandmother and granddaughter—revisiting the past in order to chart the future—has all the romantic elegance of the '62 Silver Cloud in which they zoom across the country."

—Michael Lowenthal, author of *The Paternity Test* and *Charity Girl*

"Dana Sachs's beautifully written novel, *The Secret of the Nightingale Palace*, is so pitch perfect that you'll be sad when it's over. A gifted storyteller, Sachs has created a multigenerational page-turner that will keep you reading late into the night. Brilliant!"

—Celia Rivenbark, author of *New York Times* bestseller *You Don't Sweat Much for a Fat Girl*

"Dana Sachs plunges us into the taut glamour of 1940s prewar San Francisco, where Goldie Rubin's relentless scrabble up from poverty unfolds a complex, unforgettable character: fearless, outrageous, and wise. Sixty-five years later, as Goldie spars with her gifted, grief-stricken granddaughter in a cross-country road trip, Sachs takes us from fury to laughter and loss to healing as the true value of a Japanese treasure is finally revealed."

—Pamela Schoenewaldt, author of *When We Were Strangers*

Also by Dana Sachs

If You Lived Here

The Life We Were Given: Operation Babylift,
International Adoption, and the Children of the War in Vietnam

The House on Dream Street:
Memoir of an American Woman in Vietnam

Two Cakes Fit for a King: Folktales from Vietnam
(with Nguyen Nguyet Cam and Bui Hoai Mai)

The
SECRET
of the
NIGHTINGALE
PALACE

DANA SACHS

wm

WILLIAM MORROW

An Imprint of HarperCollins*Publishers*

Grateful acknowledgment is given for permission to use the epigraph from *Arthur & George* by Julian Barnes published in 2006 by Knopf, an imprint of Random House.

HarperCollins books may be purchased for educational, business, or sales promotional use. For information please write: Special Markets Department, Harper-Collins Publishers, 10 East 53rd Street, New York, NY 10022.

FIRST EDITION

Designed by Diahann Sturge

Library of Congress Cataloging-in-Publication Data has been applied for.

ISBN 978-0-06-220103-4

13 14 15 16 17   OV/RRD   10 9 8 7 6 5 4 3 2 1

For Todd

Does every marriage have its own damn secret? Is there never anything straightforward at the heart of it all?

—Julian Barnes, *Arthur & George*

The

SECRET

of the

NIGHTINGALE
PALACE

Part One

1

Summons

*O*ne Sunday in the spring of her thirty-fifth year, Anna Rosenthal opened her eyes, sniffed at the air, and stepped back into the world after being away for a long, long time. Later she would describe May 29, 2005, as the day she "emerged from hibernation." Such phrasing implies that Anna initiated the change herself, which was not the case. If the phone had not rung that morning, she would not have left her little house on Waynoka Avenue. And if she had known that it was her grandmother calling, she would not have answered at all.

At first glance, the day did not seem to herald anything dramatic. A storm had moved through Memphis the previous evening, and outside Anna's bedroom window, sticks and leaves lay scattered across the yard. The stems of waterlogged phlox, planted so conscientiously by her husband, were already popping back up in the morning sun, and the new leaves on the elm tree seemed to have doubled in size overnight. But these were the typical miracles of spring, sometimes tardy but always expected.

Not so expected was the voice on the other end of the line. Still groggy from sleep, Anna had not bothered to check the caller ID. "Hello?" she answered.

Her grandmother, Goldie Rubin Feld Rosenthal, was calling from New York City. "I need you to come up here," she announced. Acquaintances often marveled that, despite having left Memphis more than six decades earlier, Goldie had retained her southern drawl. Anna never heard it as southern, however. To her, it was her grandmother's voice, grating as the screech of a garbage truck.

"To New York?" Anna asked, not bothering to sound friendly. She and Goldie had been particularly close throughout her childhood, but they had not spoken in five years. The reason lay in an ordinary family drama: despite Goldie's disapproval, Anna had chosen to marry Ford Pierce, a university librarian with, as Goldie saw it, "a nothing job, a nothing income, and a nothing life." The breach led to a period of almost complete estrangement. Even when Ford died of leukemia three years after the wedding, all that passed between them was a brief phone conversation followed by a formal condolence letter from Goldie and Anna's reply with one of those printed acknowledgment cards that convey appreciation and nothing more.

"Well, of course New York. You think I'm in Alaska?"

Anna wished, as she often did, that a glass of orange juice would somehow materialize on her nightstand. Because it didn't, she pulled herself out of bed and, carrying the phone, walked barefoot into the dining room, which she used as her studio. Her drawing table sat by the window, its surface angled so that she could see her work as soon as she walked through the door. The sound of her grandmother's voice unsettled her, and she took comfort in looking at the six new panels of the comic she illustrated, which she had completed between the hours of 10 P.M. and 3 A.M. the night before. Graphically, she considered them ineffective—unfortunately, a long time had passed since Anna was able to appreciate the quality of her own work—but she continued to draw, almost manically, nonetheless.

"Are you sick?" she asked Goldie. She picked up an eraser to work away a stray pencil mark left in a corner of sky.

"No, I'm not *sick*." Goldie's tone was acid, and filled with recrimination. "I need you to come up to New York and then accompany me somewhere."

"Where?"

Goldie paused for only a second, but the delay undermined the urgency of her demand. Perhaps as a hedge, she sounded even more belligerent. "Is that important right now?"

Anna didn't bother to answer, as she had no intention of going anywhere with Goldie. "What about Dad?"

"He's fine."

"Why can't he go with you?"

"Are you out of your mind? He'd be hopeless."

Anna had to agree that whatever Goldie needed, her father couldn't supply it. He cared about his mother, but he didn't have many practical skills.

"What is this about?" Anna penciled in some cross-hatching on a stand of trees that suddenly struck her as thin and unformed.

"I haven't asked you for a single thing in five years. More than five years. I would have thought you'd be willing to do something for your own grandmother."

It surprised Anna that Goldie knew so precisely how long it had been since their relationship had ruptured. Somehow the realization touched her.

"I don't need you to take care of me," Goldie continued. "I'm perfectly capable of taking care of myself. I just need your help with something. And you can spend a little time at your sister's before we go."

Anna thought about the apartment of her older sister, Sadie, in Manhattan. It had carpets that felt like cashmere and a living room view that at certain times of the year put the full moon directly above the Empire State Building. Anna leaned down and brushed the grit off her feet. It had been Ford, not Anna, who said they needed hard-wood floors. Every time she walked barefoot, she resented it.

Goldie said, "After everything I've done for you—"

For a moment, Anna had felt herself begin to soften, but Goldie's tone reminded her of how much they disliked each other. She cut her off. "It's impossible. I'm on deadline after deadline. Sadie knows that." Anna and her sister worked as a team to produce their comic, *Shaina Bright, Danger Ranger.*

"According to Sadie, you've finished five books ahead of schedule already." Goldie sounded like she was accusing Anna of smoking crack. "I have no idea what that means, but your sister manages much more than you do, and she still has a life."

"I have a life," Anna said. It was true that while Anna's sole work responsibility centered on *Shaina Bright,* Sadie managed to write that comic and oversee the production of five others while at the same time building her business, Zing Girl House, into an increasingly promising publishing operation. It was also true that Sadie and her girlfriend, Diane, were having a baby this year and had recently invested in a downtown restaurant *and* gone backpacking in Greece. But none of that proved that Anna had no life.

"Sadie thinks you're a workaholic," said Goldie.

"Sadie's a workaholic."

"She used that exact word."

If her sister had been present at that moment, Anna might have jabbed her with a pencil. For years now, Anna had managed the crises of her life with steady grace—someone had actually written "steady grace" on a condolence card. She was the one who, faced with a choice of caskets for her thirty-four-year-old husband (her *thirty-four-year-old husband*!), walked calmly through the funeral home showroom while every other person in the family stood frozen in the doorway, wiping away tears. And now they were calling her a workaholic, as if she had a mental problem?

Something shifted for Anna then. In the two years since Ford died, she had tried to put the pieces of her life back together in a way that made sense. Did people see her, then, as failing at it? "I'm sorry. It's impossible," she said, interested in nothing now except getting off the phone. Perhaps Goldie heard, across the miles and the years, the despair in Anna's voice. Perhaps she didn't. In any case, Anna felt a sudden, almost suffocating compression in her lungs, as if some massive unjust force had suddenly sucked away the oxygen she needed to sustain her.

After taking a few minutes to compose herself, Anna called her sister in New York. "What do you mean by calling me a 'workaholic'?"

"What are you talking about?" Sadie asked.

"Thanks for all your support. Thanks for telling Nana I don't have my life in order." She couldn't literally jab her sister with a sharpened pencil, so she tried something similar with words.

"Oh." Sadie finally put it together. "She said she might call you."

Anna was still sitting on her drawing chair in her nightgown. She had pulled out her soft-leaded pencils and was adding foreboding shadows to a gathering of clouds. "Why didn't you warn me?"

"I didn't think she'd do it. She's always threatening to call you. Anyway, she just asked me how you're doing, and I gave my honest opinion."

"You didn't *have* to give her your honest opinion. And why was that your honest opinion?"

Now it was Sadie's turn to sound irritated. "Have you decided it's my fault that she called you, then?"

"I can't believe you think I don't have my life together."

"I didn't say that, Anna."

"Not in so many words but, essentially, yes. You did say that. To Nana, too. Why would you say that?"

In the pause that followed, Anna concluded that her sister was smoking a cigarette. Sadie, four months into her pregnancy, had thus far failed to quit, and she often lied about it. She must have thought that Anna couldn't tell, but the extended lag in her responses—just enough to signal the satisfaction of a slow exhale—always betrayed her, especially since Sadie was, in every other aspect of her life, quite speedy. "It's probably not the best word, *workaholic*," she finally said. "What I meant was, you put all your energy into drawing these comics, and you don't even like *Shaina Bright*. It doesn't seem worth the effort, really."

Anna had gotten up and wandered into the kitchen. "I do like *Shaina Bright*." The comic, which was geared toward an audience of ten-year-old girls, depicted the adventures of a coffee-swilling, ukulele-playing forest ranger (the eponymous Shaina), whom Anna drew as a cross between Josie (of *Josie and the Pussycats*) and Princess Leia. "And anyway, if you feel my 'effort' isn't valuable, then fire me."

"I'm not saying your work isn't valuable. It's just that—"

"What, then?" Anna pulled last night's takeout Chinese from the refrigerator. She dug around in it with her finger, stuffed a piece of broccoli in her mouth, then quickly spit it out. It was too cold.

"Two years have passed since Ford died, and you don't do anything but work and sleep."

"And eat!" Anna said, shoving the to-go box into the microwave. During Ford's three weeks of hospice, Anna had lost ten pounds. Since then, she had gained it all back and then some. These days she felt pretty chubby.

"I know this sounds corny," Sadie said, "but I think you're ready to blossom a little."

The microwave pinged. Anna fished out a piece of beef and began to eat it. She wasn't completely blind to the limits of her current existence, but she believed she had found a routine that worked for her.

Privately, she tried to convince herself that her increased heft was a sign that she was coming back to life, despite feeling chubby. Sadie, of all people, should have understood how well she was doing. Sadie was Anna's boss. And thousands of fans loved their comic.

"Aren't you going to say anything?" Sadie sounded worried now.

"I'm chewing."

Sadie waited. Anna decided that it was safest, at that moment, to focus on the oddness of Goldie's invitation. "We've barely spoken in five years, and now she wants me to 'accompany' her somewhere. Is she feeling sorry for me?" Anna asked.

Her sister laughed. "Pity doesn't motivate her."

"Is she feeling guilty for how she acted?"

"Guilt doesn't motivate her, either."

"Well, why, then?" Anna was losing her patience.

"Maybe she misses you."

"Me?" Anna tossed the empty takeout box into the trash, then picked up a sponge and wiped a half-moon of oyster sauce off the counter. "She doesn't act like it."

This time the lag in Sadie's answer suggested that even if she was taking a drag on a cigarette, she was also giving Anna's question serious thought. "I think she does miss you, even if she tries to hide it. And maybe she sees herself as the old widow reaching out to the young one?"

"I don't believe it," Anna said.

For a long moment, both of them were silent. Then Sadie said, "I really don't get it, to be honest."

The phone rang again an hour or so later. Anna had showered and dressed and even brewed some coffee before settling down again at her desk. With the window open, she could hear, from some stretch of nearby backyard, the whooping of children enjoying the first sunshine after days of rain. What was wrong with all this? Who was Sadie to judge it? And who was Goldie to say anything at all?

When she heard the telephone, Anna assumed at first that another member of her family was calling to express some new worry. Perhaps as a defense, she answered in a tone that was particularly effervescent: "Good morning!"

It was a relief to hear the voice of Pierre de Rosset, one of Ford's old friends. "Come over," he said. "I'm having a pancake fiesta."

Anna tried to gauge the time by glancing through the window toward the sky. The whole morning seemed to have slipped by already. "Isn't it kind of late?" she asked.

"This is *brunch*," Pierre said, as if introducing a new word. "It can last all day. And anyway, I've got bacon." Despite the evidence of French ancestry in his name, Pierre de Rosset was, in tone and manner, pure, well-bred Mississippi. When Anna met him ten or so years earlier, he owned a restaurant/gallery/movie theater off Oxford's square. Not long after Ford died, Pierre sold the place and moved to Memphis. These days he ran a firm that promoted southern specialty foods, like pickled okra, Charleston benne biscuits, and muscadine wine. The bacon, which Anna loved, came from a pig farmer in Holly Springs whose rashers, by comparison, made any other bacon seem tasteless and insubstantial.

"Sounds perfect," Anna said. "I'll be right over."

"Really?" Although Pierre always invited Anna to his parties, she rarely made an effort to attend. Most times, if he wanted to see her, he dropped by her house with a bottle of wine, and if she was willing to put down her pencils for the whole evening, they'd watch old movies on DVD.

"Really," Anna told him.

When she arrived around two, Pierre was standing at the stove in the center of the loft with ten or twelve guests arrayed in a semicircle around him. "You have to commune with the pancake," he explained, glancing at Anna only long enough to raise his chin in a fleeting hello. "You pour in the batter, and then you watch her. Let her tell you when she needs to be flipped." He bent down, staring at the little discs beginning to bubble, then gently turning them one by one. "You treat her with respect and grace." He sniffed at the air above the pan. "You take in her perfume."

Finally, a guy in the back said, "This is getting X-rated."

Without acknowledging his heckler, Pierre took his spatula, gave one of the pancakes a tiny nudge, flipped it into the air, and caught it with the pan. "This is the language of love," he announced. "Syrup and butter are on the table."

Pierre's gathering offered the perfect occasion for Anna to prove, to herself at least, that she lived a full life. She had changed out of her shorts and pulled on a sundress and a pair of pretty sandals she hadn't worn in years. Over the course of the afternoon, she tried to talk to everybody. She ate a lot, too—five or six pancakes and she didn't even know how much bacon. Generally, Pierre was only a mediocre cook, but he always had the best ingredients. His pancakes, which were nothing special on their own, became sublime with the addition of top grade New Hampshire maple syrup (judged superior by *Yankee* magazine) and butter from France. Under these conditions, people became ravenous. The African steel drum music and the coffee laced with Cuban rum certainly didn't hurt.

Anna had just finished a conversation about Argentinian tango when she heard Pierre call her name. He was standing at the stove, motioning to her with a tip of his head.

Anna walked over. "Are you feeling like a slave over here?" she asked.

Pierre, tall and broad shouldered, wore a long goatee that made him look, against all evidence to the contrary, like an ascetic. He was actually the most social person Anna knew. Now he leaned closer to her ear and whispered, "I like having a task. If I have to flit around and talk to everyone, I become cross and overwhelmed." He was agile at the stove, moving swiftly on the balls of his feet, like someone playing Ping-Pong. He flipped a couple of pancakes.

Anna opened the microwave and stuck her coffee mug inside. "It's gotten a little cold. Do you mind?" she asked.

"I'm surprised you didn't do that earlier," Pierre replied. All Anna's family and friends knew that she was particular about what she put in her mouth. She called herself "discriminating"—she had one place for Chinese takeout, one café for coffee, one brand of pasta she deigned to buy—but others used less generous terms. Ford had called her "fussy," and he had eventually refused to eat at Chi Chi's with her because she sent her burritos back to the kitchen so many times.

"Stop it." Anna whacked Pierre gently on the arm. When the microwave stopped, she pulled out her mug and took a sip. "Now it's perfect."

Pierre grinned at her. "How are you doing?"

She appreciated that he wanted to check on her. "I'm being the life of the party," she told him. She felt good in her dress, and despite her time away from society, she was finding herself nimble enough, and even a little witty. "I was talking about Sartre."

"Really?" Pierre's Mississippi was all plantations and bourbon, old money, cotton. His accent was so melodious and refined that it sounded, to Anna, almost British. When he said, "Faulkner," it came out as "Faulknuh." And when he said, "Are you bragging?" as he did right now, it sounded like "Ah you bragon?"

Pierre had a sharp, angular nose, thin lips, and a long, narrow face. Each feature alone seemed slightly off balance, but somehow they combined to give him a look that was pleasing, though not quite handsome. "I'm not bragging," Anna said. "I'm just happy because I'm so"—she hesitated to admit it—"out of practice." Maybe her sister was right. It helped, after all, to get out of the house.

"What did you say about Sartre, anyway?"

"I said he broke Simone de Beauvoir's heart."

"That's not talking about Sartre. If I started talking about Einstein's relationship with Marilyn Monroe, I wouldn't be discussing physics."

Anna pulled a last piece of bacon off of a platter by the stove and took a bite. "I didn't say I was talking about philosophy," she told him. "I said I was talking about *Sartre*."

Pierre set the spatula down on the counter and lifted a finger to brush a stray curl away from Anna's cheek. He said, "Show-off."

Pierre's parties evolved into laid-back marathons of food, music, and conversation. Today, his Argentinian friends showed a rough cut of their documentary about Memphis blues. The guests, made sleepy from the pancakes and bacon and rum, lay sprawled across the sofas and the floor, some nodding off on their pillows. Anna remained near the stove. Pierre stood behind her, his hands resting on her shoulders in the easy affection that had, over the past few years, become natural to them. While Anna's husband was healthy, her relationship with Pierre had been merely tangential. It deepened when Ford got sick, though, and Pierre, unlike some of their other friends, continued to visit them. Now, two years after Ford's death, Anna considered Pierre an important presence in her life, though she always felt that the bond between them had a tear in the middle of it, where her husband used to be. When she was with Pierre, especially, she often found herself conjuring Ford. If he were here, would he have liked the film? He had always loved the blues, but would he have agreed with Anna that the movie was totally boring?

Oddly, it was in part the thought of Ford that made Anna reach up at that moment and take Pierre's hand. She felt a sense of inevitability, too, combined with certain looks that over the past few months had let her know that Pierre was there for her. It was Goldie's call as well, and Sadie's worry. It was the gauziness of her sundress, and the fact that looking at herself in the mirror that day, Anna had really, really liked what she saw. It was a recognition that her compulsion to conjure Ford didn't help her feel better in any measurable way, and it was a fear that she could spend the rest of her life circling back to the same low-grade sadness. It was all of these reasons that compelled her just then to pick up Pierre de Rosset's hand, slide it along her cheek toward her mouth, and kiss it. And by doing so, everything between them shifted.

Over the past few months, Anna had contemplated the wisdom of allowing more to happen with Pierre. She could imagine herself with him, yes, if circumstances had been different—her own widow-hood less raw, Pierre's social life less, well, *social*. In the years that she had known him, she had watched him pass through several serious, though "not quite right" relationships, plus various passionate and brief affairs that had given his life a theatrical intensity. Anna had quite enjoyed her role as friend and impartial observer. She felt like a person with a front-row seat at the circus, able to watch heart-stopping feats without actually putting herself in any danger.

With one gesture, kissing Pierre's hand, then, Anna pushed herself into the ring. On the television in front of them, a grandniece was recounting her memories of W. C. Handy, Father of the Blues. Anna felt Pierre's body step closer behind her, and though there was nothing terribly different in the way they might have appeared to others, the change felt so portentous that Anna was glad to be standing at the back of the room, where no one could see them. Pierre pulled her toward him, letting his chin settle onto the top of her head. He sighed. She didn't hear it so much as feel it, full of heat and promise. Anna could not have said if the rest of the documentary was boring, because, though she kept her eyes on the screen, she didn't see it.

When the film ended, at around seven, an uncomfortable moment passed during which the filmmakers seemed ready to take questions. A few polite viewers offered vague compliments, but within minutes the guests were carrying the sticky dishes to the sink and looking for their backpacks and purses. Soon, everyone had left but Anna, who helped Pierre clean up while at the same time fighting a sudden urge to flee. Outside the window the sun had begun to set, turning the sky a dusky pink and the woods across the river gray. Anna faced Pierre in the empty loft. "Maybe I should head home, too," she offered.

She didn't have to mention the complications here. They were longtime friends, and between them lay the no-longer-pertinent but still awkward fact that it was Anna's husband who had introduced them. On top of that, Anna was out of practice. Not only had it been years since she had kissed anyone, but a decade had passed since she had experienced a moment like this one. Her last first kiss had been a singularly important one—something or other with Ford, the memory of which, unfortunately, had grown hazy over time. She worried that *this* first kiss, in relation to *that* one, would somehow upset her. She felt, too, a tumult of conflicting emotions: In addition to the welcome surge of sexual excitement and the enormous relief that came with the sense that something new, finally, was happening, she also felt apprehensive about so great a change. Two years had passed, but was she ready?

Still, she felt that she should try. It was Pierre who walked over, took her arm, and led her to the sofa, but it was Anna who pulled him close in a way that was so open and eager that it represented a different category entirely from the dozens of hugs they'd exchanged in the past. He nuzzled his face into her neck and inhaled deeply, seeming to absorb everything—her smell, the feel of her skin against his, her solid substance within his arms. Then he pulled back and gazed at her, reaching toward her face to weave his fingers through her hair. "I've always wanted to do this. You may not know it, but I love"—his voice broke off—"your curls." Anna laughed, tipping her ear down to brush against his fingers.

It all seemed sweet and right to her, until they kissed. One can never know what to expect from that moment when two people, and two bodies, tentatively begin to explore each other. Pierre and Anna started slowly, with a few brief rubs of lip across cheek, down to chin, the scratch of goatee, then lip to mouth. Hesitant nibbles. Lip pressed lip, then, finally, that opening and tongue to lip, lip to tongue, then tongue to tongue. Considered intellectually, the process sounds entirely unappealing, but people like it. Lovers crave it. Anna herself had liked it very much in the past, which made it even more upsetting to discover that now, Pierre's tongue in her mouth disgusted her. It felt like a snake trapped in a bag. Her own tongue, repelled, slithered away. Was she a coward? Summoning her courage, she moved forward one more time and, at the bottom of his mouth, she discovered a pool of saliva, thick and still, lukewarm. Anna's tongue jerked back. The suddenness of the move caused Pierre to tilt his head. His jaw lifted and their teeth crashed against each other. Anna's eyes shot open. From this angle, she could see the pores spreading in a fine mesh across his nose. She couldn't breathe. She pulled away from him.

They fell against the sofa, each in their own private universe, staring at anything besides each other. The last few pinkish slips of sun were visible out the window, and the lights of the Memphis-Arkansas Bridge had already begun to twinkle.

Anna said, "I'm so sorry. I thought I could do this, but I can't." She picked up his hand and held it lightly. She didn't want him to feel rejected by her entirely.

Pierre contemplated Ford's wedding band, which Anna kept on her right thumb. "You don't wear your own wedding ring anymore, but you wear his. Your left hand says, 'I'm a single woman now.' And your right hand says, 'I'm still kind of married.' It's like your two hands are debating each other."

Anna welcomed the change of tone, but she didn't appreciate this dissection of her psyche. "Don't get overly analytical."

"Maybe you're still in love with him."

Hardly, Anna thought. She didn't want to get into that subject, so she just looked down at the ring and tried to offer her own reasonable explanation. "They asked me what I wanted to do with it, you know, before the funeral. It didn't seem right to bury it, so I just stuck it on my hand." Wearing Ford's ring had seemed the right thing to do at the time, but she hadn't anticipated the open-ended nature of the gesture. At what point would she take it off?

Pierre dropped Anna's hand to rub at his eyes. His breathing sounded much less robust than it had before. "I guess it's me, then."

"No!" She wasn't just trying to make him feel better. She had grown attached to Pierre, and she had even begun to think that eventually they might end up together. How could he be the problem, really? More likely, romantic feeling remained completely unavailable to her, not just with him, but with anybody. "I'm flat," she explained. "Empty. Finished. *Finissimo.*"

"That's nonsense," he said, but not emphatically. Pierre was a realist, not a masochist. He seemed willing to believe that her rejection was universal, not specific. He eased back into the sofa, and when he spoke again his words were confessional, but also detached. "I might have fallen in love with you," he said.

Anna had seen evidence of Pierre's feelings toward her over the years in many unspoken ways, so she believed him. It seemed unkind to acknowledge it, though. She patted his knee. "You fall in love too easily."

He wasn't really listening. "You're pretty, funny, so much smarter than I am. I always felt like Ford was so lucky." It only took a moment for them both to register the absurdity of that statement. He put his fingers to his forehead and shook his head. "That's not right. *Lucky* is the wrong word."

"No, not lucky."

"You know what I mean."

Down below, a barge slipped past, its lonely horn like the notes of "Old Man River." Anna watched as the hulk of metal faded into the darkness of the water around it, one shadow sliding into another. After a while, Pierre picked up Anna's hand and gently moved it off his knee. She felt a weary discouragement and anger at herself for having raced down a path that, in the end, was so embarrassing and potentially destructive to their friendship.

She said, "I guess I'm kind of flailing here. I'm sorry."

For a while they just sat, staring out toward the river and the fringe of woods on the other side. "It's not the end of the world," Pierre said. There was a forced lightness to his tone, but he didn't sound angry.

Anna knew that she should leave, that Pierre would be relieved to see her go, but she couldn't bring herself to get up from the sofa. The prospect of returning to her house, all emptiness and mess, immobilized her. It was at that moment that Anna's thoughts, like birds disturbed from their nest, somehow settled on Goldie. "My grandmother called this morning and asked me to go up to New York."

Pierre looked at her. When, years earlier, Goldie had denounced Anna's decision to marry Ford, the couple's friends and family, including Pierre, had rallied around them, calling Goldie everything from "hateful" to "toxic." Anna had a vague memory of Pierre himself using the word *bitch*. Now, though, he just seemed surprised. "Are you going?" he asked.

"No," said Anna, but she really wasn't sure. Talking to Goldie on the phone that morning, Anna had found support and comfort in the familiarity of her own home. But now, at night, and considered from a distance, the thought of her little bungalow—with its dusty floor, its neglected garden, its solitary toothbrush tipped against the edge of a University of Memphis mug—only made her feel more lonely.

Pierre turned toward her on the couch, pulling his leg up so that there was a bony knee between them now. "Maybe you should," he said. She detected in his tone some sense of relief that, after tonight's embarrassing interaction, she might leave Memphis, but his demeanor also retained enough of his old warmth and friendliness that she was curious to hear what he had to say.

"Why?" she asked.

"You need a break. You work too hard."

"You sound like my sister. And you're ignoring the fact that my grandmother has been horrible to me."

"It could be bracing."

Pierre was the only person Anna knew who would use that word, in any context. "You sound like we're talking about a trip to the Arctic."

But Pierre wasn't moved. "You need a change," he said.

And there it was. Anna realized, with a clarity that seemed all the more absolute for being so unexpected, that he was right. She needed a change. The thought of seeing Goldie again raised her anxiety in every way, but at the same time she suddenly felt an enormous sense of relief and possibility. She let her head fall back against the couch and, without making any overt signal of acquiescence, moved on to the next logical question. "How am I going to survive such a thing?"

But Pierre could never abide self-pity. He gave a thoughtful tug at his goatee and said, in his most syrupy drawl, "Well, darlin', I expect that woman will eat you for dinner."

Anna's expression had turned dreamy, but her eyes shot open now. "Stop!" she said, and it was with this sudden sense of laughter and fear that finally she propelled herself off the sofa.

Pierre stood up beside her. "I'm joking," he told her, taking firm hold of her shoulders. "You're going to be fine." And when he pulled her into a hug, it did feel awkward, but not as awkward as they might have expected.

Four days later, Anna's plane touched down at LaGuardia Airport at three o'clock in the afternoon. By four thirty, she had gotten the key from the doorman downstairs and was pulling her suitcase into her sister Sadie's apartment. By four forty-five, just as she was brewing herself a cup of tea, her cell phone rang.

It was Sadie. "I'm ridiculously late. The color on the *Super Kitten* proofs is all fucked up. Pink looks red. Red looks brown. It's giving me a heart attack."

"I can imagine," said Anna, who had officially taken a leave of absence from *Shaina Bright*.

Long, tobacco-infused pause. "Listen, are you okay there?" Sadie asked. "I know this is the last thing you need, given everything. I said I'd be there, and now I'm not."

"What do you mean, 'given everything'?" Anna asked. "I'm fine. I'm going to drink your pomegranate tea. I'm going to eat all your Carr's crackers."

"You only just got here. And now I'm not even home to help you get settled."

The big-sister thing made Sadie slightly crazy sometimes. "Will you get off it?" Anna asked.

Finally, carrying the tea and what was left of the crackers, Anna made her way into the living room, with its clean lines, luxurious rugs, and expansive views, which, because this was a corner apartment, stretched down Eleventh Street and up Fifth Avenue. A sense of optimism had accompanied Anna from the airport, but Sadie's overwrought concern had thrown her off. As she sat down on the sofa, she felt her excitement evaporate like the little puffs of steam rising from her mug of tea. For how much longer would Sadie continue to think of her as the grieving widow? It seemed to Anna that that one word, *widow*, with its sad but somehow spidery connotation, had become tangled with the way that people thought of her these days. In her own mind, though, it wasn't Ford's death that weighed most heavily. It was two other facts that, even after two years had passed, caused the most lingering damage. These were the facts that buzzed around her head in the middle of the night, keeping her from falling asleep.

Fact One: By the time Ford died, he hated her. You could detect it in everything he said to her, in every look and sigh. Sometimes, in a fit of frustration, he would call her a "cunt" or, on days when he felt creative, a "dirty cunt." He told his parents that she had cheated on him (she had not), told his friends that she stole his money (she did not). Most people ignored such remarks, or gave Anna's hand an extra squeeze when they said their good-byes after a visit. Those who did acknowledge Ford's fury explained it away as an understandable, though unanticipated, result of his illness. He wouldn't be so angry if he were healthy, Anna's mother said, offering, too, the theory that Ford was having a weird reaction to the drugs. Sadie, who had her own explanation, would pull her frantic sister aside and comment, in the manner of a grade school schemer, that Ford was a "dope" who had "lost his marbles." But Ford's aversion toward Anna became a thick smog, despite others' attempts to brush it away. It floated through their home, making it impossible to breathe when the two of them were together.

During the worst of this period, it helped Anna to recall healthier times, like the weekend they drove to New Orleans on a whim, or the year (it took an entire year) they read *Middlemarch* aloud to each other before going to sleep, or how, on Sunday mornings, Ford brought freshly squeezed orange juice, along with the morning paper, to Anna in bed. But these memories came to be like money in the bank. She returned to them so often that eventually she used them up.

As the end approached, Ford receded deeper into his illness and need. It had been months already since he'd "retired" from his job at the University of Memphis libraries—"retired" being the most delicate way to phrase the fact that a thirty-three-year-old rising star archivist was too sick to work and would not recover. Anna, who worked from home, began taking her drawing materials to cafés just to get some distance. Eventually, though, she and Sadie put *Shaina Bright* on "indefinite hiatus," which meant that for the rest of Ford's life, she was bound to him without relief. Ford demanded her constant attention, and no matter what she did, she failed him. He wanted the cup on the table. No! On the floor. He craved eggs, but he wouldn't eat the egg salad, deviled eggs, scrambled eggs, poached eggs, fried eggs, or boiled eggs she brought him. He craved brownies, but he rejected the brownies with nuts, brownies without nuts, cheesecake brownies, blondie brownies, and butterscotch brownies she baked (though not the marijuana brownies, thank God, which eased his nausea, a little). Why was she baking all the time, anyway? Why did everything taste so bad? Why all the smells? Why so much food? Why so little? Too much! Too little! Too much! Too little! And why did she keep asking questions?

"Make your own decision," he cried once, when she asked him for the second time that day if he wanted noodles or rice in his chicken soup.

"Sometimes you change your mind," she replied. The house had filled with the aroma of the stock, "built," as the recipe described it, by simmering over the course of an afternoon three pounds of chicken bones, two heads of garlic, and an entire onion, tossed in whole. Anna worried that the resulting flavor might be more than he could take. "I can't always know."

"Well, you should by now." He slumped further into the cushions of the couch, the newspaper spread across his stomach, his face, yellowy and cracked, stained by frustration and despair. Sometimes she could still make out his healthy face in this sick one. The color of his eyes, for example, never changed. (Long ago, in a fit of sentiment, she had described the shade of brown as "the color of melted Kisses." Ford, in reply, had called it, "Pepsi in a Dixie cup left out on somebody's porch too long.") It made no difference what color his eyes were. They were glowering at Anna now. "How long have we been married?" he asked. "Bitch!"

She turned away from him, out of anger, yes, and also out of pity, because she did hear the agony in his voice. But mostly she turned away from him because she had come to find him so ugly, so awful. As a girl, she had cried through *Love Story* and *Brian's Song*, and she could remember how at the very end of those films, death became quite lovely. When would Ford's death become lovely, too? As his health deteriorated, Anna experienced no uplifting moments, no wise words.

Here was Fact Two, the most salient truth in her story and the one that she would not confess: By the time her husband died, Anna Rosenthal suspected that she had married the wrong man, that they had never been right for each other and never would have been right had he lived. That knowledge subverted the emotions of loss and grief that logic told her she should experience. She felt very little, actually, except an emptiness and uncertainty about the future. This was the emotion that she had failed, on that difficult evening with Pierre, to adequately explain. Empty, finished, *finissimo*, she had said. What she didn't say, and what she hadn't said to anyone, was that in the last few months of Ford's life, he and Anna had, essentially, split up.

The next time the phone rang, it woke Anna. For a moment, she couldn't remember where she was. Then she saw, in a corner of the living room, the boxes of brand-new baby equipment stacked like fancy modern sculpture and thought, *Oh, yes, Sadie.*

And it was Sadie, again, on the phone. "I'm just a catastrophe," she screeched. "I have to meet you at Nana's. I might even be late."

This news fully woke Anna. "Are you kidding? You're going to make me see her for the first time by myself?"

"I'm sorry. Open the Malbec on the counter and have a glass of wine before you go. Diane bought it just to torture me."

Until this very moment, Anna's anxiety about seeing her grandmother had simmered, ignored. Now it boiled over. "So you're not drinking at all these days?" She didn't have to come right out and accuse her sister of smoking cigarettes. A casual but well-placed remark would achieve the same effect.

"Of course not. I'm pregnant." Sadie sounded hurt, suspicious.

"I didn't think you were the type to eliminate things that give you pleasure."

This time there was no lag in the response at all. "You think I want to damage my baby?"

Sadie's voice carried so much tortured anguish that it was as if the entire failed effort to quit smoking revealed itself in a single instant—the guilty furtive drags; the cycle of buying packs, then throwing them away, then mooching cigarettes off strangers; the sense of doom over her prospects as a mother—and Anna rushed to comfort her sister. "No! You're going to be a great mom. The best mom ever!"

Anna took the elevator up to the seventh floor of the Sherry-Netherland, walked down the hall to the door marked 721, and rang the bell. The front desk must have phoned from downstairs, because she heard Goldie's voice immediately. "Just a minute! I'm coming," she called, as if, at eighty-five, she understood that a delay in answering the door might lead whoever had rung the bell—the housekeeper, the maintenance man, her son, her granddaughters—to think her ill or worse, simply because she took so long to move across a room. And so, without actually announcing that she was still alive, she had taken to narrating her progress: "I'll be right there. I'm on my way." She had become like a sportscaster on TV, except that she was athlete and commentator both. "Here I am!"

Goldie opened the door and peered out. Her hair, pulled back into its smooth bun, had thinned at the top and turned from silvery gray to faded ivory. Her body seemed more hunched and fragile, but Anna saw that her grandmother still looked fabulous. Today she had on a midnight blue pin-striped suit, charcoal turtleneck, three heavy strands of thimble-shaped beads in shades of royal blue, and of course the ever-present inch-wide clip-on gold hoop earrings, which Anna could remember trying on at two and seven and thirteen years old, over the course of her entire life, really.

"Well, hello," Goldie said. The words sounded friendly enough, but Anna saw the range of emotions flash across her grandmother's face—joy followed by a recollection of the chill between them, followed by wariness. She assessed Anna, then opened the door wider.

"How are you?" asked Anna. They kissed formally, like acquaintances at a charity ball.

"Fine. I remember that jacket." Goldie looked at her granddaughter. "It's a Gautier I got in Paris."

"That's right." Anna had found the long-forgotten jacket in a closet in her front hall. All the other clothes she had gotten from Goldie—the sweaters from Bergdorf, the brassy alligator belts, the leather skirts—had been packed into boxes in the attic by Ford, probably out of spite toward Goldie. Anyway, they did take up a lot of space, and Anna had never worn them.

Goldie surveyed her granddaughter. "You didn't get fat," she remarked.

Anna refused to respond, though she felt a measurable relief (Goldie's accusations about weight could have the effect of nuclear missiles when deployed at certain moments). Instead she drifted, focusing on the peach chintz pattern on the sofa, the tassels dangling from the cabinet doors, and the neatly stacked copies of *Architectural Digest*, each one marked at a certain page by an Italian leather bookmark. Anna had not grown up in this kind of opulence herself. Her parents had simple tastes. They joined book clubs and covered their sofas in flannel and chenille. As a child, though, Anna had been fas-

cinated by Goldie's possessions, and the two shared a love of beauty
that had drawn them together for years. Sometime between discov-
ering the Sex Pistols in high school and reading *The Communist Mani-
festo* in college, however, Anna's tastes had changed. She had come to
consider Goldie both bourgeois and overbearing.

"There's not even a pillow that's different in here," Anna said.
She picked up one of the trio of Japanese netsuke that had sat on
her grandmother's coffee table for as long as she could remember: an
ivory dancer in a kimono; a pair of puppies, tumbling over each other;
a carved-wood apricot with three dainty leaves.

"A pillow?" asked Goldie, somehow offended. "How about a
pencil? How about a piece of string? The room has been perfect for
twenty-five years. Why should I change it now?" It shouldn't have
surprised Anna that the place hadn't changed. An elderly widow
caused very little wear and tear, especially when she spent half the
year in Palm Beach. And Goldie was especially careful, too. Her sofa
had enormous overstuffed silk pillows on it, each of which she kept
firm and perfectly creased by employing a karate chop across the
spine whenever it threatened to droop. The artificial flowers on her
coffee table, a delicate arrangement of pinks and peaches and yellows, looked authentic—dusted regularly, Anna guessed, by BiBi,
the Dominican maid that the hotel assigned to the apartment. Even
the fake ficus in the corner looked thriving and real, just as it had
looked thriving and real the last time Anna had visited this apartment five years earlier.

With some sense that she was bolstering her courage, Anna finally
turned her attention to the portrait of Goldie that hung on the wall.
Goldie's second husband, Saul Rosenthal, had commissioned the
painting on the occasion of their tenth wedding anniversary. Goldie
must have been in her late thirties then. In the painting her face retained the freshness of youth, but it also revealed early signs of that
steeliness around the eyes that would become her most dominant

feature. After only a few seconds, Anna had to look away, not because the portrait reminded her of her grandmother's uglier traits (though it did), but because she remembered that Ford had looked at Goldie's portrait and seen so much of Anna there.

Anna felt her grandmother's eyes following her across the room. Finally, Goldie insisted on attention. "Did I get fat?" she wanted to know.

Anna turned and looked at Goldie. "No, you didn't get fat."

Apparently satisfied, Goldie lowered herself into a chair. "As soon as that late sister of yours gets here, we can go have our dinner." Anna had arrived exactly on time, which meant that Sadie was now lagging by two minutes.

The phone rang, and with an exasperated tip of the head, Goldie motioned for Anna to go answer it. "That'll be your sister."

Anna picked up the phone that sat by the chaise in the corner. "Hello?"

"I'm stuck in a cab on First Avenue," Sadie said. "Let me just meet you at JoJo."

"Tell her to forget it. Just forget it. Don't come." Goldie stared at Anna, but spoke to Sadie directly.

"She's stuck in traffic. She'll meet us at the restaurant."

Goldie stood up, walked over to the bench by the wall, and picked up her evening bag and jacket. "Honestly," she muttered. "That girl will be late for her own funeral."

Sadie apparently heard the word *funeral* through the phone line. "Goddamn it," she said. "Can't she have a little tact?"

Anna had to laugh. "Sadie!" she said. After two years, did her sister really consider her as fragile as that?

All this passed in the course of a few seconds, with Anna still on the phone, Goldie mumbling to herself, and Sadie no doubt staring at her watch in the back of a cab somewhere downtown, wishing that a light would change. "Just hurry," Anna told her.

Anna and Goldie walked down the hallway toward the elevator. In
the past, Anna had taken care with her grandmother, walking with
a hand on her arm to help her balance. She wasn't willing to do that
now, but she remained slightly behind, ready to catch Goldie in the
event that some snag in the carpet might cause her to fall. Anna did
not experience the intense dislike, or even resentment, she might
have expected to feel toward Goldie, but she felt no warmth, either.
Mostly she savored the sense of relief that seemed to have swept
through her body since she'd arrived in New York. Within that context, Goldie's reappearance in Anna's life seemed almost incidental.
When they arrived at the bank of elevators, Goldie sat down in an
armchair and smoothed out the creases in her trousers. Anna pressed
the DOWN button, then stood in front of the mirror, pulling a piece of
hair off her face and resecuring her barrette.

They were seated at Goldie's regular table at JoJo, upstairs by the
window, when Sadie arrived. "I should have just taken the subway,"
she said, giving her sister a breathless hug and her grandmother a
hurried kiss before dropping into her seat. Anna had not yet seen
her sister pregnant, and even though Sadie wasn't exactly showing
yet, her small, wiry body did look more substantial. Tonight she was
wearing a coffee-colored belted suede shirtdress, the kind of outfit
one sees on women lunching at Barney's but not on comic book publishers who operate out of Williamsburg lofts. In other words, it was a
hand-me-down from Goldie. The dress fit Sadie well, especially with
her newly abundant figure, and she had accessorized just the way her
grandmother liked, with a big beaded "statement" necklace, a Pierre
Deux scarf, and her hair pulled back into a French twist. If the strain
of getting to the Upper East Side from Brooklyn in Friday evening
traffic gave her a look that was less sophistication and more exasperation, she rallied surprisingly well. She had no sooner unfolded her

napkin than she leaned across the table to take a keen look at the beads around Goldie's neck. "Those are fantastic," she said.

The compliment mollified Goldie. "I bought these in Shanghai, and I put them on you when you wore that black Karl Lagerfeld jacket," she said, running a finger along one of the strands. "How could you not remember? They're worth two thousand dollars, at least."

Sadie sighed. Anna patted her sister's knee under the table. "Of course I remember," Sadie said, her smile only slightly strained. She looked around the restaurant and said, "I could really use a seltzer."

"You think I would forget to order drinks?" Goldie raised a finger to catch the attention of their server.

A moment later the woman arrived at their table. Blond and leggy in a short black dress, she squatted down to face Goldie eye to eye. "What can I get you, sweetie pie?"

"Melora, darling, bring us a bottle of that Gewürztraminer I like," Goldie said. "And this one's pregnant, so she'll just have seltzer. And water for all of us, mine without ice."

Melora flashed her big blank smile at them. "Wonderful! And you like tap water, not bottled, right?"

Goldie smiled contentedly. As if to point out the contrast between the server and her family, she said, "You know me so well. I'm not going to spend my money on bottled water when I can get Mr. Bloomberg's water for free."

Anna hadn't been to JoJo in five years, but she remembered Melora. She remembered the comment about the water, though it had been "Mr. Giuliani's water" then. She remembered her last meal here, too, in this salon of twinkling chandeliers, velvet-upholstered chairs, a celebrity owner, and a famous molten chocolate cake. The last time she was here, she and Ford had recently become engaged. They came north so that he could meet Goldie, but the weekend had gone badly. It was Ford's first visit to New York City, and the provinciality of this Memphis boy offended Goldie and, in truth, embarrassed Anna a little, too. During that trip, Goldie took them to restaurants she called "the most exclusive in New York." Anna didn't know if that assessment was accurate or not, but with each meal Anna grew more irritable, Goldie more haughty, and Ford more frantic and insecure. Though they chatted aimlessly, the real conversation was communicated without words. Every move Goldie made telegraphed her incredulity to Anna: "You plan to marry a *librarian* who doesn't even own a proper suit?" Ford, who could be charming with friends, proved himself incapable of even looking Goldie in the eye. Anna noticed for the first time that her fiancé held his knife in his fist, and she found herself galled by the fact that instead of just confessing his ignorance of certain dishes on a menu, he flailed around and made ridiculous choices. At La Grenouille, he had ordered "potage" as a first course and followed that with lamb stew.

Anna stood up. "Excuse me," she said. Whenever she felt stifled by the grand excess of these Upper East Side dining rooms, she made for the toilets. She appreciated their imperfection, the fact that they were uniformly tiny and grim, and the managements' strained attempts to spruce them up with fancy lotions and candles. She locked the door and splashed water on her face, wondering why she couldn't feel calmer now. Not only had seeing Goldie transported her back to the disastrous weekend with Ford, but it also pulled at her muddle of feelings about their marriage in general. Anna always tried to tell herself that she had done her very best for Ford. For the duration of his illness, she had functioned responsibly, managing his decline with the balance of composure and resolve for which observers— imagining they couldn't do the same themselves—continually commended her. Anna became expert at handling insurance claims, at convincing doctors to communicate with each other, at updating the family Listserv with clear-sighted and sometimes even witty news of her husband's condition. The whole family had behaved with sensitivity, stepping in with support, stepping away to give them privacy. They all passed around a tattered copy of *Dying Well,* and they tried to convince themselves that they could somehow find peace in this experience.

By the time they reached those last few days of Ford's life, the family was primed like actors on opening night, and still they faltered. In the kitchen, they huddled over old pizza and the cakes that acquaintances left at the doorstep. In the bedrooms, they tried to nap. In the dining room, two weeks' worth of the Sunday *Times* sat scattered across the table, only fitfully perused. And there in the living room lay Ford, gray and bloated in some places, raw and bony in others, stretched out on the hospice bed, facing the dogwoods. By this point he alternated between unconsciousness and rage, making the thoughtful placement of the bed seem like a measly consolation for what he had to endure. Whoever was sitting beside him, holding his hand, would have to face the truth then. There wasn't any beauty here. No peace, either.

Anna didn't want to think about injustice, but she couldn't help it. Not just the trauma of the illness itself, or the years that Ford would never spend on this planet, the restaurant menus he would never try to decipher, the novels he would never read, the cities he would never visit, the music he would never hear, the children he would never help conceive, or raise, or love for even a single second. There was more. The dull, relentless queasiness of chemo, the sour sting and pull of shots, the nastiness of food, which felt like betrayal by an old and trusted friend. None of this surprised them, though. Even the oncologists handing out their thoughtful little primers mentioned the daily "challenges" that made Ford and Anna's tragedy so perfectly mundane. No, it was that one unexpected final indignity, which grew in size until it dominated all their interactions with each other, that hurt the worst. They had to live with all that loss and, at the same time, feel the bond between them break apart as well.

Anna pumped some lotion onto her hand. The label said EVENING
JASMINE, but it smelled like cookie dough. She smoothed it into her
skin anyway, staring down at Ford's ring on her thumb. Then she
slipped it off. Why not now? Couldn't this trip to New York mark
the transition? In the candlelight, the simple gold band twinkled in
a friendly, less oppressive way. Anna held it over the open toilet, but
even in that moment of desperation she could recognize the sor-
didness of dropping it in. She closed the toilet seat, slipped off her
shoes, and stepped up on it. From here, she could look out a small
window onto an air shaft at the back of the building. Anna reached
up and slid her hand along the sill. It was wide and dusty, with peel-
ing paint and the stringy remains of spiderwebs. Gently she tucked
the ring into a corner on the outside of the sill. She couldn't see it,
but she could feel it there. Then she stepped down off the toilet and
put her shoes back on.

When Anna reappeared in the dining room, Goldie and Sadie, who
had seemed to be deep in conversation, stopped talking. "What?"
Anna asked, sitting back down.

But they were focused on their menus now. "I'm getting the roast
chicken," Goldie announced. "It's the most delicious roast chicken
you've tasted in your life. And the chickpea fries are out of this world.
What are you getting, Sadie?"

As if in surrender, Sadie said, "I'll get the chicken."

Anna decided on the duck.

"No one eats the duck here," Goldie said.

Anna had a vision, then, of her grandmother and her "dinner
partners" dissing JoJo's duck, dissing the crust on the pecan pie at
Swifty's, dissing the Dover sole at La Grenouille. Was this the result
of Goldie's life experience, then, an encyclopedic knowledge of cu-
linary failure, not just in New York, but in Palm Beach and London,
Paris and Rome? Did eighty-five years of fancy living in the end
amount to this?

Anna said, "I'll have the duck."

"Suit yourself," Goldie muttered. "But you're going to have to send it back."

Sadie raised her seltzer. "To all of us together again, and to Nana, because we wouldn't be here if it weren't for you."

"Well, that's obvious," Goldie said.

After the adoring Melora took their order, a busboy delivered rolls and crackers, and Goldie announced that JoJo's bread was delicious but would make you fat. She took a small piece herself, then left it on her plate unappraised. "I know you're wondering why I asked Anna to come up here," she said.

The sisters waited, but Goldie let the anticipation hang in the air for a few more seconds before saying, "I'm proposing that she and I take a trip together."

Sadie looked nervous. "Where?"

"California. I haven't been to San Francisco since I lived there."

"I thought you were going to Dubai."

"Dubai comes later. I fly there from San Francisco, so it works beautifully with my schedule."

"Maybe the two of you should try having lunch alone together first," suggested Sadie. "Just to see how you get along."

"We get along fine!" Goldie insisted.

They each looked to Anna for support, but she stared down at the bread she was buttering. Half of her attention was still focused on the fact that she had left Ford's wedding ring on a sill in JoJo's bathroom. The idea of traveling with Goldie to California was more than she could absorb.

Sadie picked up Anna's wineglass and took a swallow. "I just need a sip," she said. "It won't be healthy for the baby if I have a heart attack."

Goldie said, "I thought we'd drive. We'll take my car." She meant, of course, that Anna would drive. Goldie had never learned that skill herself.

Sadie took another gulp of Anna's wine. "Could this get any crazier?" she asked.

"I have a gorgeous car and it doesn't get nearly enough time on the road. I've decided to let Anna sell it in California—what do I need with a car these days?—and fly back home from there."

"But why drive out there?" Sadie asked. "Why not fly?" Despite the fact that they had all grown up in Memphis, they shared a nervousness about that great expanse of land between the coasts. Anna had never driven such a distance. Sadie had driven from Boston to Oregon with a Dead Head girlfriend in a dying Mazda, but more than a decade had passed since then. Goldie wouldn't even drive as far as her niece's house in New Jersey.

"You don't understand anything," Goldie said. "I need two more weeks out of New York." For nearly fifty years, Goldie had made her permanent residence in Palm Beach, but she refused to spend a single summer there. It wasn't the weather that bothered her—childhood in Memphis had adapted her to heat—but the fact that Palm Beach Society disappeared at the end of each winter. For years, Goldie had disappeared as well. While her husband was still alive, he had happily stayed in Florida, playing golf with buddies and floating lazily around the pool. Goldie, meanwhile, took rooms for two months at the Hotel de la Ville in Rome, where she ordered her fall wardrobe and practiced her Italian. That life continued after Saul died, in 1987, but when she turned eighty, in 2000, she began to spend more time at her apartment in New York, flying north every April and south again in October. She had to be careful, though. If she stayed in New York for longer than six months during a single year, the state would smack her with the tax bill of a New York resident. "I'm still short for this summer," she said. "That's why I had a meeting with myself and decided on California."

Sadie looked exasperated. "When you had your meeting with yourself, did you discuss the option of flying there?" she asked.

"You'd still be away from New York. You could spend some time in Napa or something."

A look of revulsion crossed Goldie's face. "You know how I feel about California wines. Besides, I'm carrying art, and you must be cognizant of the fact that you can't carry expensive art through security." In Goldie's opinion, airline security was a crime syndicate devised to relieve rich people of their valuables.

"Art?" Sadie looked at Anna. In their experience, their grandmother only visited museums when she was invited to a society fund-raiser.

"A very valuable portfolio of Japanese woodblock prints."

Sadie seemed completely exasperated now. "What are you talking about?"

Goldie looked at Anna. "You know what I'm talking about, don't you? The pictures."

Anna thought for a moment, and then, as if a figure were becoming clear to her through a haze, she remembered the velvet drawstring bag and the book of pictures inside it. "The Nightingale Palace," she said, pronouncing the words of a childhood game that, until this moment, she had not even remembered playing.

It all came back to her now, not only the book and the pictures, but Goldie's Palm Beach living room, the delicacy of the teacups, the way the smooth shell of an M&M turned rough as it dissolved on your tongue. When Anna and Sadie were little, their parents took them to see Goldie and Saul in Florida for spring vacation. Anna loved visiting her grandparents, but she hated going to the beach because of the jellyfish, which lay scattered in threatening knots of seaweed all along the shore. Goldie had nothing good to say about the beach, either, and sometimes she let Anna stay home with her. On those mornings, they would play a game of pretend. Anna, as "Mrs. Yves Saint Laurent," would go to visit Goldie, as "Mrs. Issey Miyake," at her mansion, "the Nightingale Palace," which was located in the most fashionable part of Japan. While they sat facing each other across the coffee table in Goldie's living room, Mrs. Issey Miyake would hover over the Sèvres tea set and perform a pretend tea ceremony with pretend tea and real M&Ms. Mrs. Yves Saint Laurent would then come around to the other side of the coffee table, climb into Mrs. Issey Miyake's lap, and carefully open the velvet drawstring bag. Inside lay a wood-bound book full of beautiful pictures. Each time, they looked at every single one.

Anna could remember little of the pictures themselves, but she did remember that she found them much more vivid and stirring than the illustrations in her books back home. She loved that her grandmother would allow her to page through the portfolio herself, run her fingertips across the velvet pouch, look as long as she liked at each image, and stick her nose close to inhale the musty scent of the paper, which Anna found rich and substantial, equating smell, as she did, with her assumption of the artwork's importance in the world. Verbally, Mrs. Issey Miyake and Mrs. Yves Saint Laurent shared their ardor for the artwork, trying to outdo each other with their praise. "Utterly enchanting!" one would exclaim, to which the other would reply, "Absolutely marvelous!" or "Superlatively divine!" On those breathless mornings, Anna imagined herself nearly adult, although she had not yet turned eight.

"I remember," Anna said. It was strange how, after all these years, the fact of the portfolio came back to her so clearly. With it, too, certain seemingly baffling aspects of her adult personality began to rearrange themselves in a way that made a little more sense. She had always loved art, for example, but hated to talk about it intellectually. And she had dropped her plan to become an oil painter, despite winning awards for her work in college. At the time, Anna had not been able to explain to herself why she had become an illustrator instead, though her public reason (she was intimidated by the competition and wanted to lead a quieter, less stressful life) and her private one (she had fallen in love with Ford by then and felt that illustration would be a better career for someone in Memphis) never seemed complete. Was there something about her early exposure to Goldie's pictures, she wondered, that had inspired her deeper love of storytelling and thus illustration?

"Of course you do!" Goldie said. An expression of tenderness swept across her face, and Anna suddenly saw how painful their estrangement had been for Goldie. Anna did not have time to consider the possibility that she had missed her grandmother as well, however, because Goldie suddenly added, "You'd have to be an idiot if you forgot."

Just then Melora, in a burst of sugary murmurs, arrived with their appetizers: salad for Sadie, tuna roll for Anna, and for Goldie, a vividly green spring pea soup. "Oh, my," Goldie said, eyeing her bowl. "If I eat all this, I'll get fat." Then, turning again to the others, she allowed a look of sadness to sweep across her face. "I had a dear, dear friend when I lived in San Francisco. She was a Japanese girl. Mayumi Nakamura."

Sadie and Anna stared at each other. Other than a few debonair gay couples and some Italians who made her clothes, Goldie didn't have exotic acquaintances. "We met when I first arrived in San Francisco," she explained, "in nineteen forty. She decorated the store windows at Feld's. She was a brilliant artist."

"So she made these pictures?" Anna asked.

Goldie closed her eyes, sighing loudly. "No! She wasn't that kind of artist at all. She designed things. She was singlehandedly responsible for the success of Feld's. People came from all over the world to see her windows."

"Like the Christmas windows at Barneys?" asked Sadie.

Goldie touched the rim of her soup bowl and carefully lifted a spoonful of the bright liquid to her mouth. "Feld's windows would make Barneys look like Penney's."

"And?" Sadie asked.

Goldie looked up. "And? What do you mean, 'And'? And the war came, and they put her away in a camp because she was Japanese." It seemed to satisfy her, for a change, to lecture to the college graduates about history. "Do you even know about that?"

"Of course," said Sadie.

"They took a real American citizen and put her in a camp like she was a foreign spy. No better than that."

"Mata Hari," said Anna, who was starting to feel suspicious about the prints.

"Her family was extremely elegant and refined. You can't even imagine. Japanese royalty. Most of what I knew at that age I learned from them. Remember," she said, veering to her own history. "I came from nothing. I dropped out of school after eighth grade. I needed guidance."

Anna and Sadie were listening closely because the conversation was quite unusual. Goldie seldom strayed from the topics right in front of them—the restaurant, your clothes, what looked good on a menu. "When the announcement came that Mayumi and her family would have to leave their home, she turned to me as her only friend. Could I keep the artwork for her?"

Anna still couldn't conjure any of the images from memory, but she had learned something about Japanese art in college. "Who was the artist?"

"You think I'd remember the names after fifty years? There are two different series. One of landscapes and one of Japanese ladies."

Sadie pressed forward. "So what happened?"

"What happened? The war happened. I had the pictures. Mayumi went to the camps. Then I married Marvin Feld, he died, I ended up in New York. What a mess!"

"And?" Sadie asked. You had to be careful with Goldie, so Sadie's more important question was implied: Why do you still have that woman's prints? And Anna knew what her sister was thinking: What had Goldie done?

Goldie seemed to understand the implication. "Don't you know what happened to me then? I almost died of poverty. Do I have to remind you of that? I was pregnant with your father. I had to keep my wits about me, save myself and my son. I could have died—like a hobo!—in the street."

Anna and Sadie gazed at each other. In front of them lay a transgression that dated back half a century already. Goldie had accepted a treasure for safekeeping and never returned it. Anna, to whom the pictures had, long ago, given so much happiness, felt implicated as well. "So you want us to take the artwork back?" she asked.

"Of course," Goldie asserted.

Though the details of this conversation filled her with concern, Anna felt a sense of excitement as well. The reappearance in her memory of the art, her grandmother's sudden, belated need to return it, and Anna's own sense of complicity stirred something unexpected in her—an awareness of knotty predicaments beyond the saga of her own widowhood. And so, in a burst of enthusiasm that would, over the coming weeks, cause her all manner of consternation, she said, "We have to return it."

Sadie looked completely agitated now. "Do you even know this woman's still alive?"

Goldie reached under the napkin on her lap, opened her evening bag, and pulled out a newspaper clipping that she had neatly folded in half. "Look at this," she said with the air of a lawyer presenting irrefutable evidence. It was an advertisement for an auction at Sotheby's, "Treasures of the Nakamura Collection." Goldie said, "I saw this in the *New York Times* the other morning, and that's how I had my great idea. Nakamura must be her brother—how should I remember his first name?—but I'm sure that's him. He established a big antique house in San Francisco. So when we get out there we'll find him and give it back." She fell silent, letting the extent of her own cleverness sink in.

"Why not just go to the auction at Sotheby's, then, and hand it over?" Sadie said. "Or ship it?"

This question made Goldie pause, but only for a moment. "Did you listen to anything I said, Sadie?"

"There are tax incentives to being out of New York," Anna reminded her sister. "Anyway, this is about more than the art. This is penance."

Luckily, Goldie didn't understand the meaning of *penance*. As a consequence, rather than taking offense, she thought that Anna was offering support. "Exactly," she said.

Sadie gave up. Anna nudged her sister's leg with her foot under the table. She appreciated her concern, but she felt inspired by the notion of chauffeuring her grandmother and a portfolio of Japanese art across the continent in a Rolls-Royce. Anna had never driven anything nicer than her mother's Volvo, had never taken a car trip of more than a few hundred miles, and had no confidence in her ability to get along with Goldie for even a day, let alone on a journey that would last several weeks. But still she felt solidly committed to the project. Compared with the worry that Anna received from the rest of her family, Goldie's indifference offered surprising relief.

Melora appeared with their dinner plates stretching ostentatiously down her arm. Sadie and Goldie's roast chicken, with its crispy skin and buttery sheen, looked like the stellar result of an exam in French cooking, its aroma forming a rich and meaty cloud above the table. Their eyes turned to Anna's duck, a set of brown slabs spread across a plate. "No one orders the duck here," Goldie said.

It was in the shuffle of putting on their jackets and picking up their purses that Anna remembered Ford's ring. What had seemed an hour earlier like a brilliant burst of problem solving, now just seemed wacky. "I have to go to the bathroom one more time," she said, already rushing down the stairs ahead of the others. What had she been thinking?

Hurrying through the dim, velvety restaurant filled with clinking glasses and muted conversation, Anna pictured the ring, dangling on the edge of the sill. A gust of wind might blow it off. Was it raining tonight? Could a buildup of moisture cause it to slide over the edge? And hadn't she considered the window of the apartment five feet across the air shaft? Any half-observant neighbor could spot Ford's ring and snag it. Anna could still appreciate the romance of having her husband's ring perched for eternity on a windowsill at JoJo, but she also knew that she'd be devastated to return here one day and find that it had disappeared.

Fortunately, the bathroom was empty. She stepped out of her shoes, dropped the toilet seat, and hoisted herself up one more time. Cautiously, she reached toward the window and slid her fingers along the edge of the sill, aware that she could dislodge the ring herself if she moved too quickly. She felt her finger go over the edge of the ring, then she tipped it up and slid it immediately back onto her thumb. Just as she was pulling her hand inside, though, she felt something tear her skin. She had scraped it along the edge of a shard of wood sticking out of the sill. Looking down at her hand, she saw blood welling up on the muscly part of her palm below Ford's ring.

Just then the door opened, and Melora the waitress stood looking up at her. "Oops, sorry," she stammered, too momentarily taken by the sight of Anna standing on the toilet seat to close the door again behind her.

Anna stepped down. "Do you have a Band-Aid or something?" At the sink, she rinsed her hand, then patted it with a paper towel. The wound wasn't much more than a scratch, but it was messy.

Melora stooped down and rummaged in the cabinet below the

sink. "We keep some first aid stuff down here." Eventually she stood up with a box of bandages in her hand, tore one open, and carefully applied it to the cut.

"I guess you think this is kind of weird," Anna said.

The waitress shook her head. "I've been doing this job for fifteen years. At this point, standing on a toilet seat with a bloody hand seems pretty tame." Her weary expression offered a complete contrast to the perky enthusiasm she expressed in the dining room. She looked so human, in fact, that Anna felt a twinge of regret for having sent her duck back to the kitchen.

"I should explain—"

"Don't worry about it," Melora said, sealing down the adhesive. She held Anna's hand for a moment longer, her attention lingering on Ford's ring, and then she said, "That's really pretty."

2

Bridget

*T*hree days later, Goldie woke Anna at just after 6 A.M. Anna had slept at the Sherry-Netherland the night before, curled up in the twin bed across from her grandmother's, so that they could leave New York by midmorning. She had forgotten, though, that Goldie was an early riser who would wake anyone who slept later than she considered proper.

"It's gray outside, and it might rain," she said to Anna, who was still asleep under the covers. "I don't want to be chilly, so I changed my mind about my suit. I'm wearing the heavier linen instead. And I'll bring my wool scarf just in case." Her voice carried the hoarseness of sleep, but it filled the room.

Anna turned over, pretending to still be sleeping. Sometime later, she heard Goldie say, "I've had my bath and I've washed my teeth."

The word *wash*—which came out as *warsh*—echoed in Anna's ears. It was one of the lingering remnants of Goldie's childhood in Memphis. Anna burrowed deeper.

"I'll wait for you for breakfast. Anyway, I only eat a couple of tablespoons of Raisin Bran." When Anna remained silent, Goldie said, "People who sleep all day never accomplish anything."

Anna sat up, knocking her pillows to the floor. Her grandmother was walking around in her knee-high stockings, but other than her lack of shoes, she was already completely dressed. Today she had chosen a dark brown suit, a brown and white striped blouse, three strands of walnut-sized tiger's eye beads, and a jaunty cream-colored handkerchief that was peeking like a little flag out of her left breast pocket. Anna took in all of this during the time it took to stomp over to the bathroom, shut the door, and lock herself inside. She sat on the toilet for several long minutes, her face in her hands, considering the fact that she had agreed to drive Goldie all the way across the continent. *Was she out of her mind?*

Anna was still feeling irritated with her grandmother at ten thirty, when they finally left the city. They had waited until after rush hour, then headed out through the Lincoln Tunnel. To Anna's surprise, she found driving in Manhattan less terrifying than she had expected. Once they were safely in New Jersey, Goldie said, "You're really smart, aren't you?" She seemed impressed by Anna's skill. A few minutes later, though, passing through Paterson, Anna veered too quickly between lanes and her grandmother announced, "I'm not going to tell you how to drive this car," as if she would have liked to do just that.

Normally Anna was an inattentive driver, but today she focused completely. Yesterday's tune-up had revealed that the forty-year-old Rolls-Royce remained in excellent condition. According to the records, it had added exactly 2.8 miles to its odometer since Anna's father, Marvie, drove it from Palm Beach to New York City three years before. In total, the car had 27,437 miles on it, or just under 700 miles a year. This information seemed to prove that other than forays to nearby restaurants and occasional cruises along South Ocean Boulevard, Goldie and Saul Rosenthal had rarely driven it in

Florida. Pete, the New York mechanic, specialized in various models of Bentley and Rolls, and because he deeply admired the '62 Silver Cloud, he volunteered to ride with Anna on a practice loop up Park Avenue and down Lexington. "She'll be a doll," he told Anna. "Treat her nice and she'll drive like a dream." Anna felt concerned that the car would break down on I–80, maybe somewhere in Indiana, but Pete gave her his cell phone number and told her to call if she had any problems.

Anna already liked this car. The carpet, a rich gray that turned shiny silver in the sun, felt luscious to her touch. "Can I drive barefoot?" she had asked Pete.

He shook his head. "Your feet sweat, and they'll slide right off the brake."

The air inside the car still smelled like new leather, and the upholstery felt as soft as an Italian glove. Shiny steel framed the windows, and the dashboard and rear of the seats had silver fixtures and rosewood molding. The backseats even had fold-down tray tables, with lace doilies on them. Best of all, though, for her purposes, the car really did drive like a dream. From the outside, it looked enormous, but you barely had to press your finger to the wheel to feel it respond to your touch. The gas pedal and brakes were equally sensitive—so sensitive that she lurched at the corner of Sixty-eighth and Park. "Hey!" Pete said. "We're not driving a Chevette here."

"I think it needs a name," Anna had told Pete as she closed the door of the car to leave it with him for its last night in New York City. Even the sound of the door shutting was substantial, more of a firm click than a loud bang.

Pete was probably in his sixties, and he had become invested in the plan of a young woman about to drive her eighty-something grandmother all the way to San Francisco. "Can't hurt," he said. "What you got in mind?"

"Chitty Chitty Bang Bang?" Anna suggested.

"You need something classy."

Anna felt stumped.

"You want a friend," said Pete. "So give her a friendly name."

"I'll name him Pete," she decided. "It's the least I can do. You gave me your cell number."

He shook his head. "She's a she. Like a boat."

"You decide."

Pete took a long, fond look at the car. "She's a beauty."

"If she does break down, can I even find someone to fix her?"

Pete gave the car a friendly little tap on the hood. "Any mechanic can fix her, especially if you give me a call. This is not the space shuttle."

Anna put her hand on the edge of the hood where it arced gently toward the driver's window. She could love this car, she thought. "Give me a name."

Pete said, "Bridget."

The next morning, although the traffic demanded attention, Anna felt calm. She could keep her eye on the road while following the driving instructions on the Post-it she'd stuck to the dashboard. She welcomed the need to concentrate, too, because it meant that she and Goldie didn't have to talk to each other. The silence gave them an opportunity to adjust to the fact that they were stuck together now.

It wasn't until Bridget reached I–80, about twenty miles out of Manhattan, that Anna felt ready to engage in conversation. She had good news for Goldie, too. Even if they couldn't see California from this distance, they could not get lost. "This road is called Interstate 80," she announced. She pointed her finger toward a blue and red sign that said 80 WEST, then explained, "This takes us all the way to California. Nearly to San Francisco."

Goldie looked at her. "You've got to be kidding," she said. "Isn't that marvelous?"

"We can thank President Eisenhower for the interstate system," said Anna. "Didn't they build it during his era?"

"That's not my area of expertise."

Pete had told Anna to keep to a maximum of seventy miles an hour. That would be tricky, because Bridget had no cruise control. She was beautiful and she had a Princess Grace glamour, but she was also old and lacked basic features you would find in a cheap rental.

Those thoughts made Anna feel disloyal, though. "You know," she said, "the mechanic told me about a famous Rolls-Royce ad that claimed that when you get up to sixty, the loudest sound is the tick-tock of the clock."

"Are we going sixty now?" Goldie asked. She had her purse in her lap and her hands clasped on top of it. She looked exactly the way she looked when she perched on the bench in her elevator at the Sherry during the seconds it took to travel to the lobby. Did she have any idea, Anna wondered, how far they had to go before they reached the West Coast?

"We're going sixty now," Anna said. "Sixty-five. Seventy." The engine hummed and, yes, just the slightest bit louder, like the clicky purr of a cat, they heard the clock. "It's kind of exhilarating," Anna admitted. For an instant, the joy of being on the road drew them together.

"Your sister was wrong," Goldie said. "We are flying to California."

Late that first afternoon, Anna pulled into a Hampton Inn in DuBois, Pennsylvania. They had been driving for five hours, plus stops for lunch and the bathroom, and though their progress was microscopic compared with the distance they had to travel, Anna felt slightly euphoric. She really could tell the difference between driving Bridget and driving her Honda back home, though she didn't think that difference was worth the cost of a Silver Cloud. More importantly, she and Goldie had been civil to each other, even kind. Maybe they'd get along just fine.

It wasn't until Anna had pushed the luggage trolley back to the car, with Goldie trailing right behind, that she considered the problem of their luggage for the first time. Anna's legs felt sore from the drive, and her back ached, too, but she could have pulled from the trunk the small items—her own little weekender, their carry-ons, the velvet drawstring bag containing the treasured artwork. She had forgotten that Goldie's method of travel harkened back to the days of wardrobes and steamer trunks, however. For this trip, she had brought two very large black Louis Vuitton suitcases, neither of which had wheels.

"I need a pulley," Anna said, gazing at the bags in the trunk. The latch was almost vertical, like the back of an SUV, and lifted to reveal a shelf on which the Sherry-Netherland bellman, Will, had managed to fit the luggage snugly.

"It's rude that they don't have a bellman here," Goldie said.

Anna put her hands against the small of her back and stretched up onto her toes, which gave her muscles a satisfying tug. "There's probably not a bellman between here and Manhattan," she said. She wanted the sound of her voice to make clear that her grandmother had brought a ridiculous amount of luggage. Theoretically speaking, you could slide each bag right out, maneuvering it slightly over the edge. Practically, though, Anna wasn't certain that she'd be able to transfer it to the luggage cart without either dropping the suitcase to the ground or causing the cart to lurch away. She considered the situation, looking at her grandmother, at the cart, then back at the luggage still sitting in the car.

"What can I do to help?" Goldie asked.

Anna rolled the luggage cart so that its upper bar was right in front of her grandmother. "Grip it," she instructed. "Don't let it roll away."

"Got it," Goldie said. She fixed the strap of her purse onto her shoulder, then grabbed the luggage cart, holding it tightly with both hands. "I've got it," she said, thrusting one of her legs backward for traction. In her designer suit and silk blouse, she looked like a very old and well-dressed athlete easing into a runner's stretch.

Anna began to jiggle the suitcase inch by inch out of the trunk until it was suspended, half inside, half outside, over the luggage cart. "Hold tight," she said. "Almost there." Suddenly the suitcase began to wobble, then it finally tipped out of the trunk and fell with a crash onto the luggage cart. As it was falling, Anna grabbed the other side of the cart, and together she and Goldie kept it from jerking away.

"We've got it!" Goldie screamed. "We got it!"

"Hallelujah," said Anna. With a few more moves, she had all the baggage piled on and was pushing the trolley toward the front door. "I need a glass of wine," she said.

Goldie was breathing heavily behind her. "Make that two. And two for me also."

In the end, though, they ate at a restaurant that lacked a liquor license. They had asked for a recommendation from the clerk at the front desk. "We want something *good*," Goldie had said, as if to set herself apart from other guests in the hotel. "What's the nicest place in town?"

The clerk was a curly-haired, dazed-looking high school boy. It didn't seem to matter if he was staring at his computer screen, running a credit card through the scanner, or making suggestions for dinner, his mouth lolled open in the same vacant way. "You could try Applebee's," he offered.

Anna asked, "Is there any place that's not a chain?"

"I don't care," Goldie said, "as long as it's clean."

The clerk didn't answer quickly. Anna wondered if he had taken a sedative. "You could try the diner," he said.

Anna looked at her grandmother. "That could be kind of fun. Old-fashioned."

Goldie put a hand to her cheek. "Could I get a milk shake?" she asked, like a flirt.

"I guess," the clerk mumbled.

The word *diner* made Anna think of sock hops and poodle skirts, and she expected that here in small-town Pennsylvania they might find some authentic relic of the past. Instead, Kirsten's Diner was a fifties-style retro establishment, probably built in the nineties, decorated with familiar mass-market photos of James Dean, Marilyn Monroe, and Elvis, but appealing to a contemporary clientele by including on its menu veggie burgers and chicken nuggets. Their waitress, a Goth girl, had a Sanskrit tattoo on her neck and two lip piercings. Goldie ordered a strawberry milk shake and liver and onions. Anna chose the meatloaf and a chocolate shake.

"Your grandfather used to live on liver and onions," Goldie said. "Remember Hamburger Heaven?"

"They had liver and onions there?" Anna had been in college when Saul Rosenthal died. She remembered him as kind and stodgy, a man of routine. He always ate at the same restaurants, and at each restaurant he ordered the same dish.

"They did a very good liver and onions. It was greasy, but he liked it."

"At the Colony, he ordered the chops."

Goldie nodded. "At Lutèce, he ordered a steak. That was a waste of money. You go to the most famous French restaurant in New York and order a steak? But that's what he wanted."

Before they left Manhattan, Anna had worried over how she and Goldie would interact on this trip. Her concern had centered less on the hours in the car—wouldn't an eighty-five-year-old nap?—and more on the time they would spend facing each other in restaurants. And she'd been right. In the car, their conversation had been light, almost breezy. Now it felt strained, as if they had both remembered the unsettled history between them. The real discussion, about *that*, was taking place entirely through gaze and gesture—a refusal to make eye contact here, a shift of glance there—while they both pretended that things were fine.

The Goth waitress arrived with their milk shakes and dinners. Goldie looked at the girl with an expression of complete distaste, then she pulled her milk shake close, put her mouth to the straw, took a sip, and said, "This is delicious."

"You're not a snob about food," Anna observed.

Goldie looked up, her mouth pinched and sour. "A snob about food? I'm not a snob about anything."

Anna said nothing.

"You think I'm a snob about something?"

Suddenly scratches appeared on the polish of the day. Anna took two more sips of her shake, then concentrated on the meatloaf in front of her. "This is good, too. When we walked in, I thought this place would be a waste of time."

"Why did you call me a snob?" Goldie demanded.

Anna knew that she should hold herself back. Goldie had offered her such a tantalizing invitation, however. "You were a snob toward Ford," she finally said. "You hated him."

It took a few seconds for Goldie to absorb this comment. "Hated him? I didn't hate him," she finally said, as if Ford hadn't deserved such intensity of feeling. "He wasn't right for you."

"Why wasn't he right for me?" Anna's own complicated feelings toward her husband receded into the background. She had to defend her choice in men.

Goldie took a bite of her liver, chewed, and swallowed before she said another word. "He trapped you in Memphis. You were young and too stupid to understand that you could find a better match."

"You don't know what you're talking about," Anna said.

Goldie ignored that comment. She kept her eyes on her plate, wrapping a piece of onion around her fork as if it were a strand of spaghetti. "The point is that you have your future to think about now," she said. "There's a whole world out here. You can get out of Memphis if you want."

Anna almost had to laugh at the breathtaking consistency of Goldie's opinions. As a young woman she had clawed her way out of Memphis, and ever since she had regarded her hometown as a place of misery and defeat. When her only child, Marvie—only Goldie called him Marvin—visited some cousins after college, fell in love with a Memphis girl, then decided to marry her and settle in the city, Goldie nearly boycotted the wedding (though eventually Anna's mother, Carol, had won her over with a mix of canny obsequiousness and actual affection). Later, Goldie pinned her hopes on her grand-daughters. After Sadie and Anna both got into good colleges in New England, Goldie celebrated not because of the impact on their education but because she imagined them leaving Memphis for good. And then Anna had fallen for a Memphis man and married him.

Anna knew she couldn't fight a loathing that stretched back a lifetime, and she knew there was no point in rehashing the old argument about Ford, but she did see an opening here, a possibility of mutual understanding. After all, Goldie had been married twice herself, and widowed twice as well. Couldn't she remember that? "You know it's not easy getting over a loss like that," Anna said. "You understand love. You remember how you felt about Poppy and Marvin Feld."

Goldie looked up from her plate. The shift in topic momentarily threw her, but she recovered soon enough. "Who could forget them?" she asked, her tone seeming to imply that her husbands merited remembrance, while Anna's did not. "Marvin Feld was a gorgeous man from an outstanding family. I had nothing back then. We were deeply in love, and I was lucky to get him. I was devastated when he died."

At another time Anna might have been offended by Goldie's undisguised dismissal of Ford, but the obviousness of her tactic just made her look silly. Across the restaurant, a toddler screamed and they both turned to look. Goldie didn't mind children in restaurants, but she expected them to behave like adults. This child was tossing French fries across the room, and as their waitress bent to pick the food off the floor, the artful rips in her neon blue stockings became pronounced. Goldie said, "You'd think the management here would maintain some standard."

Anna was still thinking, though, about what her grandmother had said. Despite the use of words like "deeply in love" and "devastated," there was a flatness to Goldie's account of her first marriage. After so many years, Goldie's appreciation of Marvin Feld had settled into something rote and offhand. "What about Poppy?" Anna asked. She had heard the Saul and Goldie Rosenthal story so many times that it felt more like legend than true history: Goldie, widowed after the death of her war hero husband, took her fatherless little boy with her when she went shopping for handbags in New York City. Haggling for a purse, she met an ambitious leather goods wholesaler who married her and adopted her child. Goldie and Saul worked hard, invested their money perfectly, and soon had apartments in Palm Beach and New York, Louis Vuitton luggage, and for Goldie, summers in Rome.

Goldie looked at her blankly. "What about him?"

Anna suddenly wasn't sure what she wanted to know. To talk about widowhood would once again draw them back to Ford. She wanted to stay away from that subject. "You remember how you felt about him," Anna said.

Goldie looked annoyed, as if Anna were questioning her loyalty in some manner. "I would have died without your Poppy." She unzipped her pocketbook and began rooting around inside it. "He saved my life."

Anna couldn't help herself. "Did your family approve of the marriage?"

"My family?" Goldie gave a dry little laugh. "What did they care? If I had died, they would have come to my funeral, but they wouldn't have paid for flowers or anything. I was absolutely on my own."

An image of the young Goldie appeared to Anna then—not the domineering grandmother, but the young widow, vulnerable and full of need. In terms of family support and material comfort, Anna had much more to keep her afloat, but still, she shared with Goldie the experience of profound loss followed by emotional chaos. The grief that had colored her days during Ford's illness had devolved after his death into something more dull and pervasive, like a low-grade flu that drained her of energy. She wondered what Goldie had done to keep herself intact, and if Goldie had, like Anna, ever suffered from tortured recollections of how the man she'd loved had slipped away.

If the young Goldie had been sitting across the table from her, Anna would have reached over and taken her hand. They could have formed a support group together, had the timing been right. But the Goldie facing Anna now had long ago left behind such agonies. She found her lipstick and compact, flipped open to the mirror, then began applying a fresh coat of color to her mouth. "I wouldn't rave about this restaurant," she said, "but it suited our purpose. We had to eat."

3

The Unexpected

Ford started losing weight in the fall of 2000. He'd gotten a promotion at the University Libraries and ran the Special Collections division. Sometimes Anna would stop by and find him sorting through postcards of Memphis in the 1930s. Other times he seemed to spend entire days in meetings discussing interlibrary loan services and expanded reference hours. In other words, sometimes he loved his job and sometimes he hated it.

At first they thought that the weight loss came from stress. The state had cut the library's budget, and now he was doing not only his own work but also that of his former assistant. He came home late at night, tired and irritated. The food lover who had once eaten three large meals a day plus snacks now found himself unable to finish a piece of grilled chicken. "I'm just not hungry," he told her. He'd go to bed, and she'd stay up watching TV and wondering if he was depressed. When she did finally get in bed with him, Ford was sleeping so soundly that her own movements on the mattress never woke him.

"I think you might have mono," she told him. On weekends he

would sleep for fifteen or sixteen hours at a stretch, and simply climbing the stairs to their porch seemed to wear him out. "You should go see Dr. Snider."

"I get a checkup every year," he told her. "I'm fine."

They had not been getting along for months, and sniping had become their natural way of interacting with each other. "Whatever," Anna replied.

So they waited, but in March the nosebleeds started. Usually they happened at the end of the day, when he was especially tired. Then he got one during a staff meeting at the library. He was giving a presentation about reorganizing the archive on the King assassination. The provost, who had a particular interest in Dr. King, was at the meeting, which made the silence especially awkward while Ford fished in his pocket for Kleenex. Eventually he had to leave the room, and though he managed to stop the bleeding and get back to his presentation within a few minutes, he had lost his concentration, and the bloodstains on his shirt embarrassed him. That afternoon he made an appointment with their doctor. "Can I come?" Anna asked.

"I'm not a kid, Anna."

"I have to know that you'll ask the right questions."

"Fine. Then come."

They visited their general practitioner, Susan Snider, on the day that their first daffodil bloomed that spring. "Hey, Ford," Dr. Snider said, barreling through the door of the examining room. She was a tall, solid woman whom Anna had known in high school and who had gone on to play volleyball for the U.S. Olympic Team. Today it took Dr. Snider a second to notice Anna in a corner of the room. Once she did, Anna saw in her face the quick deduction that the "fatigue" Ford had described to the nurse on the phone might be something more complicated. "Hey there, Anna," she said gently.

Anna managed a cheerful "Hey," but both she and the doctor were looking at Ford.

He sat on the examining table, a patient's smock pulled around his naked body. Eventually Anna would grow used to the look of exasperation on his face. Now, he sighed and cocked his head toward Anna. "She's worrying," he said. "She wanted to be here." Though the words sounded annoyed, his tone was so full of unexpected affection that it took Anna a moment to come up with a reply.

When she did, she tried to sound relaxed and easy. "I know. I'm a pain." She stared at her husband, suddenly awash in love for him.

The doctor sat down on a wheeled stool, opened her laptop, and held it on her knees, scanning the screen. "Looks to me like you're due for a regular checkup in about a month," she said, absently rolling her stool back and forth across the floor. "What's up?"

Ford shrugged. "It's really nothing. I'm just tired a lot."

"A lot of stress at work?"

"It's terrible," Ford said emphatically, as if to convince them of the cause for his malaise. "I'm at the University Libraries. Cutbacks. You know."

The doctor stood up and set her computer on the counter. "Just let me check a few things." She did the usual examination, half talking to them, half concentrating on what she was doing. Ears, throat, heart, and lungs. Then she held Ford's arm to check his pulse. "What's that bruise?" she asked.

They all looked at the inside of Ford's arm. "I don't know," he said, turning to Anna. "Do you know how I got that?"

It was a large bruise, the kind of thing that could only come from a fairly painful injury, but she, too, had to shake her head. She hadn't even noticed it. "Is it new?" she asked.

"I don't know." Ford looked as mystified as she was.

The doctor didn't say much then, but she became more focused. She found more bruises, one behind Ford's leg, another on his back. Ford said, "Are you thinking she beats me?" He was grinning, but Anna could see that he was becoming concerned. She tried to laugh.

The doctor smiled, then asked Ford, "Any other problems? Changes in your sleeping patterns? Your diet?"

"I've been sleeping a lot."

"Like what's 'a lot'?"

Ford looked at Anna. His exhaustion had created a distance between them. He went to sleep so early and woke so late that they never talked in bed these days, seldom talked at all. Now, though, she could see that he wanted her close. She couldn't, of course, know it at the time, but the look on his face at that moment, his sudden and frank expression of need, marked a shift in their relationship. With that one simple glance between them, Anna slipped right into her new role as caregiver, though it would be weeks before either of them understood that.

"Well," she told the doctor, "like on Friday night, he came home and went to bed at around eight, and then he slept until noon. He did the same thing on Saturday night. Could it be mono, maybe?" Now she suddenly wanted mono, because the bruises scared her.

"And diet?"

Ford kept his eyes on his wife. She said, "He's lost some weight."

"Anything else unusual?" the doctor asked.

Ford shook his head. "I think that's it." But when he saw Anna staring at him intently, he asked, "What?"

"The nosebleeds?" There had been a couple of occasions in recent weeks when Ford had grown furious over Anna's nagging about his health. She did her best, then, to sound gentle and uncertain, like an imbecile making random connections.

In retrospect, though, she would have preferred his anger, because the fear on his face at that moment nearly broke her heart. "Do you think that's related?" he asked.

"I'm just wondering," she said vaguely. Had Ford never considered these questions? Had he failed to notice that these days he always spit out blood when he brushed his teeth?

The doctor kept her attention focused on her computer, into which she was putting her notes. "This is all very helpful," she told them.

In the end, Dr. Snider ordered a range of blood tests and asked them to come back the next day. There was a comfort to the fact that they would have some answers very soon, but the urgency added a new reason for concern. Didn't lab tests usually take longer? In any case, Dr. Snider offered nothing in the form of hypotheses. "Do you have any ideas?" Anna asked.

"Oh, there are a lot of possibilities," she told them, offhand now. "Don't worry." She looked at Ford. "You need to get some rest, obviously. I'm not saying you should skip work, but I'd like you to take it easy until we get to the bottom of this."

Both of their mothers went with them to Dr. Snider's office the next day. Anna's mother, who drove, tried to offer cheerful commentary on everything from the possibility of rain to the opening of a new Whole Foods near her house. When no one responded, though, her voice eventually trailed off. Ford's mom was catatonic. Once they arrived at Dr. Snider's office, the mothers stayed in the waiting room while Ford and Anna filed through the door and into the maze of examining rooms and offices. This time Ford didn't have to strip off his clothes. The nurse led them into the doctor's empty office, where they sat in chairs in front of her desk and stared at pictures of her kids. The night before, Anna had asked Ford if he'd like to talk. "Why speculate?" he'd replied, before heading off to bed. Now, in the doctor's office, Anna felt like she was crossing an ocean just to reach over and take his hand.

After about ten minutes, they heard the doctor in the hall. She was laughing with a nurse about a basketball game they had both watched on TV the night before. Anna let go of Ford's hand because she could feel herself shaking and she didn't want him to sense it. Briefly, she began to talk to God. She wasn't making deals exactly.

She was simply saying, "Please, please, please." It seemed, at that instant, that her entire life had been leading up to this one moment, in these two chairs, in front of this desk.

Dr. Snider walked in. "How are you two doing?" she asked.

"Fine," said Ford.

"Fine," said Anna.

"Are those your mothers out there?" They nodded. The doctor said, "That's very sweet."

Ford said, "I think we need to know what's going on."

Now, Anna's entire body had begun to shake. She sat on her hands and tried to breathe deeply. *Please, please, please.*

Susan Snider moved some papers around on her desk, not looking up at them for such a long time that Anna realized she wasn't actually searching for anything. She was merely trying to choose her words. "I'm not going to be cagey about this," she said. "Your blood counts concern me. Your white blood count is highly elevated and your platelets are extremely low."

They waited. Ford, clearly trying to control his impatience, said, "That doesn't mean anything to us. We're not doctors."

"You're severely anemic," she told him.

"Anemia?" asked Ford.

Anna felt that she could breathe again. "Anemia," she repeated, like it was a silly punch line to a morbid joke. Didn't people take iron pills for that?

As soon as the word came out of her mouth, though, she saw by the expression on the doctor's face that they had misunderstood.

"Anemia may be a symptom of something more serious," Dr. Snider explained. She picked up a pen on her desk and wrote something on a pad of paper, then tore it out and handed it to Ford. "I'd like to make you an appointment with an excellent oncologist, Dr. Stephen Tran. He's over at UT."

"An oncologist?" Anna felt herself sliding down in the chair.

"I'm concerned that it's leukemia," Dr. Snider said.

Ford said nothing. Anna wanted to scream, but she pushed her hands into her knees and bit her lip instead. "How can you know something like that?" she demanded. "All you did was take some blood."

Dr. Snider rolled the pen back and forth on her desk. "This is not a diagnosis. My job is to recognize the symptoms and send you to a specialist."

The consultation continued for a few more minutes. They could not have accused Susan Snider of wrapping up too quickly and sending them on their way. But there was, and always would be, a chasm between the information doctors had and the information patients needed. Because the most important questions were ones that Dr. Snider could not answer, and neither could the bright and conscientious Dr. Tran, or the various other specialists they would meet along their way: How could such a thing have happened? How long would Ford live? And as Ford would demand to know in his darkest, most searching moments, Why me?

Eventually they stood up and Dr. Snider walked them to the door. She put her hand on Ford's shoulder. "We're going to do the best we can for you," she said.

Anna looked at her husband. Had he become paler and more fragile in just the last few minutes?

4

The Pictures

*A*fter their meal at Kirsten's Diner and the strained conversation that went with it, they returned to their hotel in silence. Goldie's head fell back against the seat as they drove the short distance, but as soon as they arrived, she opened her eyes, got out of the car, and scurried across the parking lot and into the building. Within minutes of returning to the room, she had changed into her nightgown, brushed her teeth, and completed the tender ritual of hanging up her clothes. Now, sitting back against the pillows on her bed, she looked at Anna and asked, "Are you going to sit there like a bump on a log all night?"

Anna was slouched in a chair by the window. She had been trying to build a ring of privacy around herself by reading a *People* magazine. Now, almost like a student unexpectedly singled out in class, she raised her eyes warily. "What?"

"The pictures? Have you completely forgotten about our plan?"

Anna had, in fact, forgotten that she and Goldie had decided to pull out the portfolio after dinner. But Goldie's tone was so harsh and accusatory that Anna had no interest in that now. Not even twelve hours had passed since they left Manhattan, and already she was having trouble remembering why she had decided to come. Something about finding purpose beyond the rut of her own dismal existence. Was that it?

But then Goldie's tone shifted. "I've never shown them to a living soul except for you when you were a little girl," she said, sounding almost wistful. "It's been years and years since I've even looked at them myself."

Anna, suddenly touched, stood up, leaving *People* on the table. "Let me get them from the closet," she said. Earlier that evening, before dinner, Goldie had called in a housekeeper to pull the spreads off their beds and cover the blankets with clean sheets. "I don't even like to think about what's been on those blankets," she had told the young woman, as if general queasiness would prove the necessity for this extra work. Goldie didn't complain about the room itself, but it disturbed her that they had only one luggage rack. Now Anna stepped around Goldie's second suitcase, which lay open on the floor against a wall, and walked over to the closet. "You never even showed it to Poppy?" she asked. It took two hands to haul the velvet bag up from the floor by Goldie's shoes. Anna carried it over to her bed, and perched on the edge, balancing it in her lap.

"Are you crazy? Have you forgotten him completely? He was a brilliant businessman. I thought you would be cognizant of the fact that he had no interest in art."

"I guess that's true," Anna said. When did the word *cognizant* take such a dominant place in her grandmother's vocabulary? Anyway, Goldie was right. Saul Rosenthal was knowledgeable about wine and partial to Italian suits, but Anna had never known him to visit a museum. Goldie, for her part, had famously exquisite taste in clothes and an excellent eye for antiques. Her preferences in art, though, ran toward the sweetly sentimental: portraits of dogs, toddlers cavorting in the sun, doe-eyed girls in pretty dresses. She had spent a good deal of money on her "collections," as she called them, and so many other wealthy patrons apparently shared her taste in puppies and frilly-clothed children that the work of these artists had increased in value significantly. The effect, of course, was that Goldie considered herself a connoisseur, even if critics derided the work that she purchased.

Readjusting the parcel on her lap, Anna began to open it. "Careful with that," Goldie said, watching Anna's hands. "Slowly. That's it. Easy. Don't do anything stupid." Her voice sounded strained, and her breath carried so much nervous tension that Anna wondered if her grandmother's anxiety was actually misplaced guilt for having kept this artwork for so long.

Anna felt some nervousness of her own, a sign of the tension between her memory of the pictures and her awareness that, after all this time, they might disappoint. She had no reason to worry, though. Almost instantly the years slipped away and she forgot everything but the object in her hands. The portfolio was a book, of sorts. It had wooden covers on the front and back, but no binding at the edges. The pages were attached to each other, accordion-like, at the sides, and though the whole thing could have been unfolded to stretch across the room, it made more sense to page through as if it were a book, perusing the pages on one side and then flipping it over to look at the images on the reverse. On one cover, in gold calligraphic writing, were the printed words *The Reverend Maurice M. Castleman, Scenes of Japanese Women*. On the other cover, in the same formal script, *The Reverend Maurice M. Castleman, Scenes of Japanese Life*.

"Who is the Reverend Maurice M. Castleman?" Anna asked.

Goldie did not even lift her eyes from the portfolio. "How should I remember? Just open it up."

Inside each cover lay a piece of yellowed stationery on which the names of the artists and the titles of the artwork had been handwritten. On the side labeled *Scenes of Japanese Life*, someone had written, "Hiroshige, 'Fifty-three Stations of the Tokkaido Road,' Tata-e Edition (vertical Tokkaido)." The other piece of stationery said, "Kunisada II, 'The Tale of Genji.'"

Anna glanced up at Goldie, but her grandmother's eyes had settled on the book, as if she, too, were filled with suspense. "You don't have to pull the whole thing open," Goldie said. "Just unfold it, a page at a time." Carefully, Anna began to examine the prints. It was really two different sets of prints, the Hiroshige landscapes on one side and the Kunisada images on the other, the thin paper of each individual print glued along the vertical edges to the ones behind it and beside it, forming the folds of the book. Anna, who had studied Asian art in college, could only vaguely remember the name of Kunisada II, but she had a clear memory of Hiroshige and the influence of his work on Impressionist painters like van Gogh and Monet. It seemed bizarre, and not quite right, to be holding something so precious while sitting on the bed of a Hampton Inn in rural Pennsylvania.

Slowly, Anna paged through the Hiroshige landscapes, a disparate range of turbulent rivers, lonely pine trees, and vast mountain ranges that often included glimpses of the iconic Mount Fuji. She had only been looking for a few minutes before Goldie, impatient, said, "Turn it over and see the other ones." Anna obliged. On the other side of the book, the Kunisada prints were a different style of art entirely, vivid domestic scenes of elegantly dressed men and women in kimonos. Above the heads of each set of figures hovered a trompe l'oeil fan, decorated in calligraphy and small motifs: a boat, a cherry tree, a burst of wild carnations. Anna loved the oddness of these delicate prints, the whimsy of the ornate fans seemingly floating over the heads of the figures. She did not feel finished with the landscapes, however. When she saw that Goldie had tipped her head against the pillow and closed her eyes, she turned the book over again.

Eventually Anna managed to look through the entire set of Hiroshige landscapes as well as the more intimate illustrations from *The Tale of Genji*. Altogether, there were nearly a hundred prints, and Anna perceived each one with a feeling of intense familiarity and pleasure. Part of her was seven again, Mrs. Yves Saint Laurent curled in the lap of Mrs. Issey Miyake. Another part of her, the adult Anna who worked as an illustrator herself, considered the images within the vast context of art history. A third Anna, the private, grieving one, found herself fascinated by the farmers, fishermen, and teahouse attendants who populated Hiroshige's landscapes. Unlike the well-dressed men and women in *The Tale of Genji* pictures, these tiny figures, struggling against the vast backdrop of mountains, oceans, earth, and sky, somehow reflected the melancholy that had become the dominant feature of Anna's days.

What would Ford have thought of all these pictures? Anna had always felt certain in her judgment about art, even though she lacked conviction in other aspects of life. Ford, in a sense, was Anna's opposite—decisive in general, but quavering when he stood in front of a painting or a sculpture. Before he got sick, the two of them had sometimes gone to the Brooks Museum or the Dixon Gallery, especially when a traveling exhibition came through Memphis. Anna really cared only about work that spoke to her emotionally. After forming an opinion about a piece of art, she would either focus her complete attention on it or walk away. She loved Goya and Vermeer, for example, but Picasso left her cold. Ford, on the other hand, needed to understand why a particular work had received so much acclaim. He would read about the artist before they went to the show, then search out the most famous pieces and stand in front of them, trying to explain to Anna why they were important. As a result, Ford always wanted to slow Anna down. And Anna, though she never expressed this feeling directly, believed her husband was too afraid of art to give any credence to his own taste. Faced with these Japanese prints, and no critical reviews of Hiroshige or Kunisada to back him up, would Ford have been able to recognize their power? She felt a wave of disappointment in him then, followed, predictably, by guilt and a profound wish that she had somehow been a better wife. As a consequence, the artwork struck her as even sadder.

She heard her grandmother's voice then. "My favorite is the one of the man looking at the girl from behind the screen. The fan has cherry blossoms on it, and when the girl sees the man, she looks surprised. She doesn't know what to do about him standing there."

Anna glanced up at Goldie. "I thought you'd fallen asleep," she said. She turned the pages of the Kunisada series until she found the cherry blossom picture. The woman, in a deep purple robe decorated with bouquets of red flowers, sat with her back to the man, holding her hands to her chest and glancing at him over her shoulder. Anna held up the book so that Goldie could see. "This one?"

Goldie nodded. "For a while, I'd pull the book out every night. I always spent a long time looking at that poor girl. She made me feel so sad." Her eyes, maybe from sleepiness, had glazed over and turned rheumy, but her attention remained completely focused. "Isn't that silly?"

"Why didn't you ever show these to anyone else?" asked Anna. It astonished her that something so precious had remained in Goldie's possession for all those years without anyone else knowing. It seemed so out of character. Goldie never held anything back. Why would she keep such a secret? "Did you forget you had them?"

"Of course not. How could I forget?" Goldie had taken the bobby pins out of her bun, and her hair stretched like a gray silk sash down the front of her nightgown. "You're too young to understand. Those pictures came from a very difficult time in my life. I learned to put sad things behind me."

Anna opened the portfolio randomly and gazed down at one of the

Hiroshige images: on the edge of a hillside, a procession of travelers filed through a solitary village at dusk. Through Anna's eyes, the view seemed almost unbearably forlorn.

After a while, she heard her grandmother say, "You think you're going to feel this way forever, but you won't."

Anna kept her eyes focused on the pictures, worried that at any second she would start to cry. "I don't," she insisted, but without any real conviction. The truth was that the emotional state that she had experienced immediately following Ford's death—she didn't know what to call it: grief? sorrow? would it help to use a nineteenth-century word like *woe*?—seemed to have evolved into a permanent condition. It didn't help, either, that stuck with her grandmother in this cramped hotel room, Anna was even more vulnerable to Goldie's attacks. She felt as if she were holding the portfolio of her own emotions.

5

A Famously Happy Marriage

Somewhere in eastern Ohio, Goldie's travel agent called. Goldie had friends all over the world (or Friends All Over the World, as Anna, Sadie, and their parents called them), and her phone rang so often that, in the car, she often sat with her pocketbook in her lap and the phone in her hand on top of it, prepared to receive calls. Anna's father, Marvie, had taught Goldie to use the cell phone years ago, and she loved everything about it, especially the caller ID and the option to press IGNORE if she didn't want to answer. She still looked rattled and perplexed every time the phone rang, however. Now, when the notes of "Mack the Knife" blared through the car—the ring tone being the result of Sadie's efforts to program something that echoed the tunes of their grandmother's youth—Goldie managed right away. "Hello?" she said. "Oh, Rhoda. Tell me again about the ship."

Anna vaguely listened to the conversation—a confirmation of Goldie's seat assignment in Emirates business class and some back-and-forth about a restaurant Rhoda recommended they try in Cleveland. Mostly, though, Goldie wanted to focus on her cruise from Dubai and specifically the ship. Her requirements were inflexible: closet space in her stateroom, elegant people, and edible food, in that order. She didn't care about the itinerary, although she had been collecting suggestions from her friends. "Everyone says I have to see the restaurant with the aquarium in it. You know that one? It's got some kind of Arab name."

Ohio was flat but green. They crossed over the Cuyahoga River on a bridge that soared so high above the ground that Anna felt like they were traveling in a low-flying plane. In Cleveland, where they stopped for three nights at the Ritz-Carlton, they went sightseeing and got their nails done. Goldie found the Rock and Roll Hall of Fame more delightful than her granddaughter did. "I'm a rock and roller," she reminded Anna, and after watching concert footage of Aerosmith, announced that she considered the band "out of this world."

"So you like Steven Tyler?" asked Anna.

"Adore him," said Goldie, her reaction just vague enough to betray the fact that she didn't connect that name to the lithe-limbed singer they'd just watched prance across a stage.

"And the Beatles?"

On this topic, Goldie showed more certainty. "Fabulous. Wonderful. I always danced to the Beatles in the nightclub of the Hotel de la Ville in Rome."

In the museum bathroom, they could hear the cheery refrain of a GoGo's hit. Goldie stood at the mirror and watched herself dance, thumbs tucked under her armpits, shoulders swaying. Anna remembered how, when she was a little girl, Goldie would lead her around the living room in Palm Beach, teaching her the Lindy Hop. "You've always been the best dancer around," Anna said now, feeling generous and full of affection.

Goldie's eyes were shining. "Everybody says that."

A couple of teenage girls in cutoffs and T-shirts had paused to wash their hands, and now they watched the well-dressed old lady getting down in front of the sinks.

"I've got the beat," Goldie informed them.

The girls nodded, but they did not seem charmed. Rather, their faces revealed a tinge of dismay, as if a geriatric's passion for rock and roll somehow diminished theirs.

Their reaction did not slip past Goldie. When the bathroom door closed again behind the girls, she caught Anna's eye. "I'd call that two pieces of trash, wouldn't you?"

Goldie's ill will swirled like a toxic vapor through the bathroom. "I didn't see anything wrong with them," Anna said, trying to deflect it. She tugged her hair out of her ponytail, then pulled it back up again, keeping her eyes on her own reflection so that she didn't have to look at her grandmother's.

But Goldie stared right at her, her anger inflamed by Anna's nonchalance. "That's because you dress like trash yourself," she said. "How are you ever going to get on with your life?" There was a note of strained desperation in Goldie's voice that, had Anna been able to hear it, might have lessened the nastiness of her words. But given the context, Anna could not hear it.

Rationally, she recognized that Goldie felt insulted by the teenagers. She also knew her grandmother believed that appearance offered a revelation of character—you *can* judge a book by its cover, Goldie would say—so there was a logic, however questionable, to her thinking. If Sadie or their parents had been in the bathroom at that moment, any of them could have concentrated on these facts and gently steered Goldie back to good humor. Anna lacked that skill. Her temper was as quick as her grandmother's, and now, her face hard, she stared at Goldie in the mirror. "So does that make you feel better?" she demanded.

"Does what make me feel better?" Goldie blinked and suddenly seemed to falter.

"Cutting strangers down and being so mean to me."

It was fortunate, perhaps, that at that moment a woman pushed into the bathroom with a screaming baby in a stroller and a runny-nosed toddler in her arms. The ensuing noise and crowding displaced Anna and Goldie from where they were standing, compelling them to leave the bathroom altogether. The tumult gave Goldie a moment to catch her breath and bolster her defenses, so that by the time Anna opened the door for her, she was able to glide past, sneering, "You're just a Pollyanna. You can only see the good in people."

"Is that so bad?" asked Anna, trailing her grandmother across the museum lobby. "Is that so bad, Nana?" But Goldie ignored her.

They had planned to buy ice cream sandwiches when they finished at the museum, and they stuck to their plan, even though they were no longer speaking to each other. They sat outside, on chairs overlooking Lake Erie. It was a bright day, but windy, and Goldie pulled her scarf tighter around her neck and buttoned her sweater. Anna, happy to feel the sun on her skin, slid off her sandals and stretched her legs in front of her. The plaza was crowded with fans of rock and roll—moony-eyed couples, a group of bikers in Harley-Davidson leather, and families balancing trays of overpriced burgers while searching for spots at the outdoor tables. Goldie looked around at all the baseball caps and Van Halen T-shirts, crew socks, sneakers, and fanny packs. She must have felt quite superior, Anna imagined, in her Armani.

Anna had not forgotten how, as a child, she had idolized Goldie. For years Anna had considered her grandmother such a perfect embodiment of style and good manners that life with her had seemed as close to royal as one could get. The elegant lady tea parties of Anna's early childhood had been only a part of that mix. In Palm Beach, Goldie let Sadie and Anna try on her clip-on gold hoop earrings and diamond necklaces, or prance in front of the mirror in full-length mink coats that bunched around their little legs, making them look like princesses draped in ermine. It was Goldie who taught them how to put on stockings. It was Goldie who allowed them to eat cold asparagus with their fingers (but required them to eat hot asparagus with a fork and knife, especially if it had Hollandaise sauce on it). It was Goldie who bought them monogrammed thank-you cards when they turned sixteen, insisting that they inscribe them with pretty words like *marvelous* instead of common words like *nice*. In retrospect, Anna could understand how all of these disparate moments of glamour and instruction delighted Goldie as much as it did the girls. How could anything more absolutely confirm the fact that she had made it in the world than her ability to let her granddaughters play with diamonds and furs or to instruct them in the ladylike virtues of manners and poise?

Anna could understand, too, Goldie's disappointment when their relationship soured. Eventually Anna and Sadie reached adolescence and began to shop at Goodwill and St. Vincent de Paul. They turned up their noses at the flowery Laura Ashley dresses that Goldie brought them from London and the beaded leather evening bags she special ordered for them in Rome. They tried to educate her about *vintage fashion*, but she rejected the term completely, declaring, "I suppose you're wearing some stranger's dirty underpants as well." The situation reached a crisis one spring when Goldie and Saul visited Memphis, and Anna paired a six-hundred-dollar Christian Dior scarf, which Goldie had given her, with pink rubber ankle boots and a 1920s flapper dress missing a strip of fringe at the hem. Anna could still remember the reaction of each member of her family when she walked into Chez Philippe. Marvie's face expressed the dread that accompanies the arrival of long-anticipated bad weather. Carol, whose own taste (much maligned by Goldie) centered on blue jean skirts and the occasional splurge at Ann Taylor, looked sick. Sadie laughed into her napkin. Saul rolled his eyes. And Goldie? She could not have responded with greater fury if Anna had literally slapped her in the face. As Anna's mother later remarked, "You should have just walked in with a megaphone and declared: 'All that stuff you tried to teach me, Nana? I don't value any of it.'"

Goldie didn't give Anna another item of clothing until she left for college, by which point Anna had given up Goodwill in favor of the Gap—not exactly high style, but Christina Herrera was wearing jeans from the Gap by then, so even Goldie kept a couple of pairs in her closet. When Anna graduated from Brown, Goldie gave her a cashmere wrap from Yves St. Laurent and a card on which she'd written, "I love you very much. Don't disappoint me this time." For a while, Anna didn't. And then she met Ford.

Goldie, tiny and hunched over in her wire chair, wiped her mouth on a paper napkin and then folded it neatly and held it in her hand, smoothing down the creases in her trousers. "Let's go," she said. It was hard to imagine that Goldie was unaffected by the words that had passed between them, but she was excellent at pretending that she didn't care. When they walked back to the car, Goldie went first, her head held high. Anna stayed a few paces behind her.

Somehow they made it through the rest of the afternoon and evening in this same atmosphere of strained silence. They ate dinner in the restaurant that Rhoda the travel agent had recommended, and though the bread was stale, the chicken was dry, and the wine was barely passable, neither of them mentioned it.

At 3:17 in the morning, Goldie decided to express herself right there in their well-appointed room at the Cleveland Ritz-Carlton. Actually, she must have decided some time earlier. It was 3:17 when Anna, pulled from her dreams, finally looked at the clock on the table while her grandmother harangued her from the opposite bed: " . . . such a bright future in front of you . . . get yourself out of this mess . . . I know a few things about life. . . ." How many long minutes had passed before Anna began to absorb these words?

"What are you talking about?" she finally asked. "Why are you saying this now?" Her voice sounded scared and plaintive, like a child's.

"What do you mean, 'saying this now'?" Goldie's words were spirited and emphatic. "When else would I say it?"

"Can't we talk in the morning?"

"No. I'm going to tell you right now: You have no sense. My mother had no sense. She married a drunk and ended up raising ten children without a man to back her up. I learned from her stupidity. I tried to make good decisions my whole life, and then you went and married a man with no prospects—"

"Nana!"

"I'm not saying I'm glad he died. Cancer's a sad death and I wouldn't wish it on anybody—but it happened. The question I'm trying to get you to think about is *What next?* Do you plan to sit around and mope for the next fifty years? I've got more sense in my little finger than you've got in your whole college-educated brain, you know that?"

Anna felt as if she were drowning. She concentrated all her attention on the graceful lines of the chandelier above their heads, imagining that its solid frame was a hand reaching down to pull her out of here. "Can't we just go to sleep?" she cried. "Can't we talk in the morning?"

But these entreaties just made things worse. "You never listen," Goldie said.

"Please, Nana."

"Are you an idiot?"

"Please!"

They both heard it. Anna's voice had reached a level of despair that even Goldie could not ignore. For a long moment, neither of them said a word. When Goldie did speak again, her tone was softer. "You're so lucky, and you don't even know it," she said. She still sounded aggrieved, but the words lacked their earlier edge.

Anna said nothing. She stared at the chandelier, counting seconds, holding her breath.

"The whole world's been handed to you on a silver platter," Goldie said. And then, a couple of minutes later, "You don't even know it," and, "You don't even know it," again, some minutes after that. Then silence. Then the soft snores of sleep.

The next morning, they drove out of Cleveland under a bank of grim clouds, the sky the same dull concrete as the road beneath them. Neither Anna nor Goldie mentioned what had happened the night before. Anna wasn't sure if Goldie even remembered, but the air between them seemed even heavier. Nothing felt resolved.

They were extremely polite. "Are you hungry?" Anna asked, somewhere beyond Toledo.

"You're the one doing all the work," Goldie responded. "I want to do whatever makes you happiest and most comfortable. I'm just a passenger here."

The day seemed interminable, one county sliding into the next. Eventually it began to rain, a desultory splatter that turned the spindly trees into dull green shadows outside the windows. Everything else was brown and gray except for the billboards imploring them from the side of the highway. Anna tried to find satisfaction in the fact that, mile by mile, they were moving closer to California, but she had no confidence that they would ever actually get there.

Despite the troubles between them, six days had passed since they left New York, and they were comfortable now with life on the road. Anna had grown adept at maneuvering the suitcases in and out of the car (though they both appreciated the bellman, Hiep, who had handled their luggage at the Ritz-Carlton). In odd homage to urban living, the communities of chain hotels along the interstate often included chain restaurants that you could reach simply by crossing a couple of parking lots on foot. As they pulled up that night to the

Hampton Inn in Angola, Indiana, they saw an Applebee's just on the other side of a Sizzler and Best Western.

"If we go to Applebee's for dinner," Anna said, "I could have a glass of wine and not have to worry about driving us back to the hotel." At this point she considered her evening glass of wine to be indispensable to her sanity.

Goldie held her hand to her eyes to make out the restaurant beneath the sharp rays of the setting sun. "What luck," she said, as if the probability of having an Applebee's near their hotel had not been something like 75 percent. "I could eat there every night."

It struck Anna as ironic that she had to travel with her grandmother, a habitué of La Grenouille and JoJo in New York, in order to familiarize herself with American chain establishments. Goldie loved restaurants and loathed staying in, even for a single evening. "That's just eating," she always said. "I *dine*, and you have to go out for that."

Oddly, Ford—the objectionable Ford—had been much more picky than Goldie, who could see the value in an occasional Big Mac. When he traveled, he carried along guidebooks that pointed the way to "authentic regional fare." He would skip lunch rather than eat fast food. When they went to New Orleans, he plotted their itinerary based on where they would stop for meals. Anna could remember buttery pillows of biscuits, and mashed potatoes as rich as whipped cream, but she could also remember a Thousand Island dressing that tasted like chunky mayonnaise with sugar mixed into it. In comparison, Anna found Applebee's palatable at least. "Well, we know what we're getting," she said. They had, after all, eaten at an Applebee's for lunch.

Later, after dinner, as Goldie started to get ready for bed, Anna said, "I'm too edgy to sleep." She felt she had suffered a wound the previous night, and a day spent with Goldie—even one that had been excessively polite—had not allowed it to heal. "I think I'll take the portfolio down to the lobby with my drawing stuff and fiddle around for a while. Do you mind?"

"I couldn't care less," Goldie replied, sitting on the edge of her bed, pulling off her knee-highs. "I'm not even going to wash my teeth." Without her stylish clothes on, she looked much older, but Anna refused to see her grandmother as vulnerable in any way. She considered Goldie's physical frailty as just a trick to put you off your guard.

And indeed, after Anna had pulled off her jeans, put on a loose cotton skirt, a T-shirt, and her espadrilles, Goldie let an expression of complete distaste cross her features. "That's what I'm talking about," she said.

Anna had hoped Goldie's politeness was a means of making nice after the attacks of the previous day. Now, though, it seemed that she wasn't finished yet.

Anna looked down at her clothes. "What do you mean?" she asked.

"What I mean is you're a pretty girl and you don't even make an effort."

"I need to make an effort to go sit in the lobby?"

"I wouldn't walk into a gas station without making an effort. All the beautiful clothes I've given you, and the way you dress you might as well wrap yourself in a roll of toilet paper. If I had looked like that, Marvin Feld never would have noticed me. I'd be a pauper lying at the bottom of a pig sty."

On another night, when she was feeling stronger, perhaps Anna could have ignored such talk. Tonight, though, she felt raw and vulnerable, worn down from all these days alone with Goldie. Worse, she heard a contempt in her grandmother's voice that reminded her of how, all those years ago, Goldie had spoken to Ford. And then, without any other thought, she cried, "I loved him!" and for that moment she felt it as deeply as she ever had in her life.

Goldie looked confused. "Loved who?"

"You know who I'm talking about. I loved Ford. Can't you understand that?"

Something shifted in Goldie's face then, some flash of understanding, perhaps, and her resolution seemed to falter. Then the moment
passed. Her expression grew hard again and she said, "That's not
even worth whatever change you keep in that ugly backpack."

For one brief moment, Anna had felt a flicker of hope that finally
the two of them might begin to understand each other. Now she
pictured the great expanse of North America looming in front of her,
an infinite line of tractor-trailers, each of which had to be passed,
like her own labor of Sisyphus, from coast to coast. Whatever shaky
support had held up the last of her civility suddenly collapsed. "Why
are you always such a fucking bitch?" she asked.

Goldie froze on the bed, her stocking halfway down her calf.
These were not words that Anna could remember ever being uttered
in her grandmother's presence. Goldie clearly understood them,
though. Anna saw the tiniest flinch in her eyes, but when she spoke,
her tone was as forceful as ever. "I am a lady," she replied.

Anna knew that she had to get out of the room as quickly as possible. She didn't want to give her grandmother the satisfaction of
seeing her in tears. She put her hand on the outside door and swung
it open. "A lady," she said, "would never act like this." Then she
stepped out into the hall, letting the door slam shut behind her.

Downstairs in the lobby, Anna sat down in the breakfast area,
set the portfolio and her drawing materials on the table, and
walked over to the hot drinks bar. Her hands were shaking as she
poured herself a cup of tea. Wouldn't this have happened eventually anyway? Putting Anna and Goldie into a car together for all
those long miles was bound to cause combustion. It would have
been more convenient, of course, if the flare-up had occurred in
Cleveland, where the large metropolitan airport could have offered
Anna an exit from life on the road (she imagined her father flying

in and taking over as chauffeur). But surely there were planes out of Indiana, too. In any case, Anna and Goldie would not be getting back into that car again. Anna felt no regret for what she had said upstairs—she actually felt a sense of exhilaration for having spoken the truth—but she didn't like that she had lost her temper, and worse, she cringed at the prospect of what lay ahead for her: return to her house on Waynoka.

Better not to think about such things. Better to sit in the lobby and draw until she could assume that Goldie had fallen asleep, then sneak upstairs and deal with it all in the morning. Anna carried the tea back to the table, sat for a moment until she began to calm down, then opened the portfolio and pulled out her pencils and sketchbook. Every few seconds she glanced toward the elevators, half expecting to see Goldie hurling herself across the lobby in her bathrobe, ready for battle. The lobby remained empty.

Feeling more at ease, Anna began to page through the Japanese prints, as she had taken to doing every night now. They calmed her after the days on the road, and she found them inspiring, too. A keen knowledge of her own limitations kept her from comparing this artwork to the illustrations she made for *Shaina Bright*, but she found that she could learn from what these long-ago artists had created. Each image, each individual subject, each alteration of perspective, taught her something new about design, or light, or color. During the crisis of Ford's illness and death, drawing had helped to distract her from her personal troubles. She knew, however, that the comics she drew these days did not approach the quality of those she had made before Ford got sick. In her earlier years of creating *Shaina Bright*, Anna had developed a style that was both minimalist and highly expressive. The slightest alteration in the profile of Shaina's neck, for example—a hard line, say, instead of a delicate curve—could indicate a drastic shift in the character's mood: under pressure from Superintendent Markley, calm and practical Shaina Bright had turned irritable and huffy. Once Anna returned from her "hiatus," though, she struggled more and yet failed to achieve the same effect. She would stare for hours at the page, or discard drawing after drawing that seemed heavy with effort but uncommunicative nonetheless. Oddly, the popularity of the comic didn't suffer. *Shaina* had developed an avid fan base. As long as new stories continued to appear, readers didn't seem to notice what had become horribly obvious to Anna, that *Shaina Bright* was little more than a collection of lines on a page. The fact that no one cared about the quality of the work bothered Anna even more.

Looking through the Japanese prints, then, reminded her of how much she loved to draw. Within a few minutes of gazing at the portfolio, she had picked up her pencils and begun to copy, taking comfort from the steady accumulation of lines and the familiar friction of pencil on paper. At first she glanced up now and then, still anxious about the possibility that Goldie would appear in the lobby to berate her. But Goldie did not appear, and little by little Anna forgot everything but Hiroshige's images in front of her.

The pictures were, in general, extremely solitary—village streets at night, isolated mountain roads, a small group of travelers paused along a rural path—and that emptiness gave them a terrible lonely quality that in Anna's present state seemed to speak directly to her. She focused most intently on an image of farmers in a field that sliced through a deep ravine. In the near distance, a few people walked along a quiet road. Still farther, two mountains emerged from a fog-covered valley. Here was the simplicity and eloquence that Anna had lost in her own work. The farmers were represented by little more than scratches of black on the page, but the *shape* of those scratches articulated the hunched back of arduous labor as precisely as anything Anna had ever seen. That these shapes could be pared down to their elements meant that the artist deeply understood the human form and the ways in which toil made itself known in the body. There was no need for extraneous detail. A line, a scratch even, could say it all.

And then, without much thought, Anna tore the copy out of her sketchbook, set it beside her on the table, and began to conceive of something new. The jumble of emotions in her mind—her fury at Goldie, her recollection of Ford, her need to draw, her fascination with these lonely Japanese pictures—suddenly coalesced into a single desire. She wanted to draw a new comic. Instead of the adventures and tribulations of a pert teenage forest ranger, Anna wanted a comic that reflected the dramas of real life. And not just any life. Her own.

She decided to draw a scene that marked a moment of intense emotion, the scene that had come to mind so vividly when she heard the contempt in Goldie's voice upstairs. The drama had taken place in Goldie's living room at the Sherry-Netherland, at the end of Anna and Ford's first and only visit to New York. Although, throughout the weekend, Goldie had remained ostentatiously civil, Anna had seen immediately that her grandmother did not approve of Ford. It was clear in the way Goldie curled her lip when she looked at his clothes, which were clean and neat but *vin ordinaire,* as Goldie would put it. And Anna heard it in the way Goldie spoke to him. No matter what her grandmother said—"You're ordering *beer* at JoJo?"—she always managed to sound appalled. By the time Anna and Ford stopped by Goldie's apartment on their way to the airport, Anna understood the complete failure of the visit. She suspected that Ford had recognized it as well, though he only mentioned Goldie one time when they were alone, saying, "You and your grandmother are more alike than anyone else in your family." Had she refused to have sex with him that night?

For her drawings, Anna envisioned three comic panels, a triptych of disaster, so to speak. The entire drama took place in about ten minutes, and now, all these years later, she found it hard to believe that a few heated words could have had such long-term and drastic consequences. In drawing it, she hoped to understand more precisely what had happened then.

Anna began with the three of them seated around the coffee table in Goldie's living room. To make clear the awkwardness of the moment, and to try to achieve the profound simplicity that she saw in the Hiroshige prints, she concentrated on a single element for each of the three human figures: the stiff line of Ford's back (he must have been heeding the words of his own grandmother, "*never slump*"); the tiny dot of Anna's mouth, around which formed all her pinched anxiety; and for Goldie, the backward tip of the head, which enabled her to look down her nose at them, even though she was the smallest person in the room.

The second panel depicted the moment the phone rang. Goldie rose and crossed behind Ford's chair to answer it. Ford had gained weight recently, and he hadn't bought clothes to cover his increased bulk. Consequently, his polo shirt rode up his back, which meant that the view for Goldie was all too clear: Ford's ass, exposed over the top of his khakis. As she drew, Anna discovered that of all the marks she put on the page, only three really mattered. The first was the fat scratch of the butt itself. The other two formed a pair: the knifelike point of Goldie's eyebrows. Anna, on the other side of the coffee table at the time, had seen the look on Goldie's face, and she had seen immediately that all was lost for Ford. Drawing the scene now, she almost laughed at the irony of employing Hiroshige's style for such a drama. Yes, a single well-placed line could change the entire mood of the image. But could Hiroshige have ever imagined that the power of a picture could revolve around the crack in a person's rear end?

Goldie had taken her time on the phone. After she hung up, she walked straight to the front door and opened it. "Young man," she had said, "I'd appreciate it if you went downstairs and let me have a few words with my granddaughter." Drawing from memory, Anna's only concern in this image was Ford. In the final panel of the triptych, he filled the page as he walked out the door, his slouch so extreme that, in Anna's drawing, no light shone between his shoulders and his ears. That vision of Ford had felt like tragedy to Anna at that moment. But years had passed, and Ford was dead. You couldn't just throw the word *tragedy* around right and left anymore.

In any case, the drawings in front of Anna now weren't *Shaina Bright,* and that felt like victory. Anna had no obligation to tell a comprehensive story here. She did not have to draw Goldie calling Ford "Porky Pig" and "Elmer Fudd," while at the same time claiming that he was a charming gold digger capable of making off with the family wealth. And she didn't have to draw herself responding with equal heat, accusing Goldie of being a "social climber" and "snitty"—which sounded close enough to *shitty* to convey that idea as well. Perhaps most importantly, she did not have to re-create the substance of the exchange, which passed in the few brief seconds before Anna finally walked out the door. Anyway, the argument wasn't all that different from what had just occurred upstairs at the Hampton Inn, except that Goldie was harping on some new issues now, and Anna's sense of her future had altered completely.

Anna remembered how, after the fight in New York, the family machinery had lurched into gear. Her father had worked the phones with the determined optimism of a diplomat mediating the rift between two warring nations. Her mother had tried to cajole Goldie, while using psychology with Anna, imploring her to relent by acknowledging that Goldie really was a bully. Sadie was less forceful, but her reaction hurt the worst. "Nana's totally out of line," she said, "but you're just as stubborn as she is." Ultimately, the urging of the family had no effect, and Anna proved her sister right by refusing to see her grandmother for the next five years.

Why did that moment in Goldie's apartment matter now anyway? So much time had passed. It mattered, though, and not because the fight with Goldie had been so final and dramatic. No, there was another reason, which Anna had never confessed to anyone. The episode in Goldie's apartment had undermined Anna's confidence in her feelings for Ford. As resolutely as Anna had resisted Goldie's criticisms, they had a noticeable effect anyway, causing her to be more seriously bothered by things that she wished she could ignore. Anna could easily dismiss the comprehensive charges that Ford was "beneath" her, for example, but she did begin to feel disturbed by smaller things that showed a lack of refinement, like the way he held his knife and fork. It embarrassed her that, standing in a room of Impressionist paintings at the Met, he pronounced the name of the French artist Cor-bett instead of Courbet. On the other hand (and this had nothing to do with Goldie's complaints), Anna also began to worry that he might be too brainy for her. He brought Marcel Proust home from the library and he actually read it. He liked to argue about philosophy, which Anna couldn't bear. She found Ford's jazz albums unbearable, too. Did they have enough in common? What would they talk about when they got old? After the weekend in New York, Anna lived with a niggling worry that she and Ford were not, in fact, quite right for each other. The anxious fights that began soon after led to more mundane conflicts about daily life: Whose turn was it to wash the dishes? Who forgot to water the plants? They married anyway, because they loved each other still. Didn't everybody fight? When she did, finally, walk down the aisle, it wasn't so much from certainty in their union as from resolve not to break up.

Anna gazed at the sketches in front of her. The act of drawing always gave her joy, but now, for the first time in so long, she could also find real satisfaction in what she had accomplished. These three panels were nothing like Hiroshige (or at least no one would ever discern the influence of one on the other), but his work had helped her to rediscover, in some small way, the expressive quality she felt she'd lost. Unwilling to put the drawings away, she fiddled for a while, adding some sheen to the coffee table here, more ruffles to Goldie's scarf there. To Anna, the catastrophe of the visit to Goldie's apartment did not feel remote. In all other aspects, her recollections of her husband were growing hazier every day. And yet, for better or worse, she could still see him so clearly, stiff backed on the chair, his pants sliding down his butt. Why did that memory, of all memories, have to remain clear?

Up at the front desk of the Hampton Inn, a new group—all flip-flops and soccer balls and teenagers with skateboards—had just arrived in a muddled flurry of noise and action, dragging Anna back into the present and reminding her that even if Goldie had fallen asleep, she was sure to wake up early and ferocious, like a screaming infant. For another minute, she idly watched the new guests check in, corral their kids, and make their way to the elevators. Her body felt tired from the day's drive, but she also felt more centered and content than she could remember feeling for years. The act of drawing the scene of that awful afternoon had forced her to recall it, but it also gave her the blessing of distance from it.

Anna stood up, stretched her achy body, and put away her drawing materials and the prints. She remembered a condolence card that a distant cousin, Mindy Steinberg, had sent after Ford's funeral. The cousin, a granddaughter of Goldie's sister Rochelle, had lost her own husband in a car accident a few years earlier. "You have a choice here," Mindy wrote. "You can be sad or you can be happy. BE HAPPY." Anna had only met Mindy once or twice (Rochelle and Goldie never got along). The advice, which Anna took as kindhearted, also seemed naive. She sent Mindy a printed acknowledgment card, but she did not respond to the message directly. Now she reconsidered Mindy's words. She remembered, too, how once, on a whim, she had asked Goldie the secret of her busy social life. "Make your own party," Goldie had answered. "Call people. Never wait for them to call you." *Would that really work?*

The clock on the wall above the microwave showed that it was nearly midnight. Anna picked up her things and hurried upstairs, focusing all her energy on the hope that Goldie was sleeping, which would spare Anna another altercation.

On the third floor, the elevator opened onto a general commotion in the hallway, testifying to the fact that the hotel's new guests had taken rooms on her floor. The teenagers were kicking a soccer ball down the hall, while one of the mothers yelled at them to be quiet. Anna caught the mother's eye and grinned sympathetically. She wanted to demonstrate that she could be an easygoing neighbor (if only to distinguish herself from her more rigid grandmother). She pulled her key card from her pocket and pushed past them, worried now. If the noise woke Goldie, then the two of them would have to deal with each other again that night.

Goldie wasn't asleep. As Anna discovered as soon as she walked through the door, Goldie wasn't even in bed. The lights were on, too.

"Nana?" Anna stepped inside.

"Anna?" The voice came from a hidden corner of the room. It sounded strained, and wrong. "What took you so long?"

It took Anna a moment to find her grandmother, who lay on the floor by the window, tangled inside one of her suitcases with the standing floor lamp on top of her. "I fell," Goldie cried. It looked as if she had stumbled, grabbed at the lamp for support, then crashed into the suitcase, bringing the lamp down with her. Anna squatted down. Goldie's left leg was pinned beneath her body, her knee wedged inside, and her peculiar position, combined with the fallen floor lamp on top of her, had made her unable to pull herself up. Somehow she had cut her arm, too. The bleeding had stopped, but dried blood had smeared across her face and hands. She looked at Anna, her face as pinched and pale as that of a terrified child. "Where were you?"

Anna felt the weight of a thousand mistakes on her shoulders—

every little way she'd erred with Ford—but she forced herself to concentrate on what she had to do right now. Hadn't she read somewhere that moving a person with a spinal injury could result in paralysis? She pulled the floor lamp off Goldie, but she didn't try to get her out of the suitcase. "I'm calling an ambulance," she said.

Goldie's eyes fluttered, then closed. Her breathing slowed. "You're—" she murmured, seemingly too exhausted to keep talking.

It took Anna a moment to punch in the right numbers on the phone because she had to dial out of the hotel before she could reach 911. "We're at Hampton Inn, Room 318," she said. "Hurry!"

She ran to the door and propped it open, then rushed back to squat on the floor next to her grandmother. "It's okay, Nana," she whispered. "I'm not leaving. I'm staying right here." She held Goldie's hand, trying to keep the sound of panic out of her voice. Goldie's eyes remained closed, as if it were all she could do to concentrate on her breathing. The pain seemed to intensify, then lessen, over and over again. Goldie's hand would relax in Anna's, then suddenly grip her fingers tightly. During those long moments, Goldie's breathing almost stopped. Then, at last, her fingers would relax and she would begin to breathe again. "This happened before," she said. "I almost died."

"You're not going to die this time, Nana," Anna said.

She gently ran her finger across Goldie's cheek, brushing off the dried blood, and found herself proposing her little deals with God again. *Please, please, please.* She didn't have the gall to ask for much. Couldn't Anna be the one to feel the pain this time? Why was it always someone else?

The ambulance seemed to take hours to arrive. She tried to keep Goldie conscious. "It's okay. You're going to be fine," she said, though that seemed impossible now.

Goldie opened her eyes. Her breathing was shallow. "I almost died last time," she said.

"You're not going to die," said Anna.

Finally they heard the siren down below. A moment later two paramedics in blue uniforms came through the door, first a tall guy with a moustache and then a woman in her fifties with a long blond braid, carrying a leather case. "Hey. I'm Robin. What's the problem?" she asked.

"My grandmother," said Anna, looking up at them. "She fell." She stood up and moved out of the way.

Instantly the paramedics squatted at Goldie's side, asking questions. "Ma'am, can you talk to me?" the woman asked. She looked at Anna. "What's her name?"

"Goldie. Goldie Rosenthal."

"Mrs. Rosenthal? Goldie, I'm going to need you to talk to me."

Goldie's lips moved slightly, but her eyes didn't open. The paramedic felt for her pulse. "We're going to have to get you out of this thing, but you might have fractures and we don't want to hurt you more," she said. "We'll lift the whole suitcase onto the bed, then we'll move you onto the stretcher. It might hurt for just a second." Anna saw Goldie's mouth pucker in fear, but her eyes didn't open. The other paramedic left the room. Within a few seconds, he rolled the stretcher inside. As Anna watched, they lifted Goldie to the bed while still inside the suitcase. Then they gently moved her out of the suitcase and onto the stretcher. The act of unknotting her body seemed to inflict whole new waves of pain, and Goldie began to scream.

"She's eighty-five!" Anna yelled at them.

"Ma'am, we're doing the best we can," grunted Robin.

Once she was on the stretcher, Goldie stopped moving. She seemed to have turned inward, as if she were concentrating entirely on the effort of getting through each moment as it passed.

"Can't you help her with the pain?" Anna asked.

Robin glanced up at her colleague. "Let's give her Dilaudid," she said.

The guy with the moustache opened the case and prepared an IV, hanging the plastic bag of medication on a hook attached to a bar above the stretcher. Robin rolled up Goldie's nightgown sleeve and slid the needle in, then attached the catheter. It all happened so quickly that Goldie hardly seemed to notice. She didn't even wince when the needle penetrated her skin.

"We're going to take her on in now," said Robin. " It's Cameron Memorial Hospital. You can meet us there." And then they wheeled Goldie out the door.

"I don't want to leave her! Can't I ride with you?" Anna called after them, but the room was empty now. She ran to the doorway and saw them disappear on their way to the elevators. Up and down the hall, other guests of the hotel—she saw some of the soccer players from a few rooms down—had opened their doors to watch. Anna turned back into her own room and shut the door behind her. Her entire body was shaking, and she sat on the bed and began to cry. It really seemed that there wasn't a person in the world who was safe with her.

Part
Two

6

Salesgirl

In the spring of 1940, Goldie Rubin traveled alone by train from Memphis to San Francisco. She was twenty years old, on her first journey, and because she could not afford to buy a berth, she spent the entire five-day trip on the observation deck, having stashed her suitcase in one of the sleeping cars. At first she subsisted on the cheese and bread she'd brought from home. When that ran out, she bought one sandwich a day, and only at station snack bars, where the prices were cheaper than on the train. She cut the sandwiches into quarters: one for breakfast, one for lunch, one for dinner, and one for emergencies.

Sometimes, too, she would amble through the club car in between seatings and scavenge bread. Despite her poverty, she dressed smartly. Her mother had taught her to buy one very good thing and supplement the rest of her wardrobe with less expensive accessories. She had a very good wool coat, for example. When she wore it, people didn't seem to notice that her dress had faded, that the leather on her shoes was cracked and thin, or that her hats were merely scraps of beautiful fabric that she tacked and darted into interesting shapes and pinned to the top of her head. During that brief ten minutes between the early and late service, she hoped that the waiters might mistake her for an actual patron, or perhaps, she thought, they were too busy to notice a young woman snatching leftover dinner rolls off the tables. In fact, nothing slipped by the railroad staff. They'd seen all the tricks and scams, from freeloaders hiding in the toilets to the furtive trysts that took place late at night behind the flimsy curtains of the cheaper berths. They noticed Goldie, of course, but she was young and pretty and they sympathized with her situation. When the dining car waiters saw her approach, they turned their backs a little, just to give her a chance.

By the time Goldie made it to California, where her married sister, Rochelle, met her at the station, she had grown weak and ill. Rochelle's first thought, upon seeing the pale-faced Goldie totter from the train, was to regret that she'd invited her to come live with her in San Francisco. Rochelle had two young children and a traveling-salesman husband who left on Monday morning and didn't return until Friday night. She had invited Goldie to live with her family in the expectation that Goldie would help around the house and provide her with some companionship. She didn't want another responsibility on top of the ones she already had. Fortunately for both of them, a big meal of brisket and potatoes revived Goldie quickly. She might have seemed on the edge of starvation, but she was also young and healthy, so she recovered amazingly well. Within a week she had found a job at Feld's Department Store. Dozens of young women had applied for the position, but Goldie impressed the manager, Mr. Blankenship, with her sense of style and her previous experience as a clerk in the hat department at Lowenstein's in Memphis. She was hired at the decent salary of twelve dollars a week, and she quickly earned a raise.

Goldie wasn't a beauty in the way that film stars of the day were beautiful, with their fair complexions, angelic smiles, and easy grace. Goldie had olive skin, thick brown hair, and dark circles around her deep-set eyes that gave her the haunted look of a waif in a silent movie. Her body, though, was elegant and curvy, her eyes bright, her expression quick, her mouth full of sultry charm. The thing about Goldie that most impressed her customers at Feld's, however, was the fact that she had an almost magical way with clothes. No matter what she put on, it looked like something out of *Harper's Bazaar*. The simplest shirt or the slimmest, plainest skirt had the look of Paris couture as soon as she slid them onto her body. The wealthy San Francisco matrons who shopped in the store recognized that quality in Goldie and wanted it for themselves. During her first week, posted in millinery, she sold seventeen hats.

It took Goldie longer than that, though, to make friends. She was younger than her colleagues, with less experience, too, and they resented that she sold merchandise so easily, and that she so greatly impressed Mr. Blankenship. So Goldie ate her lunch alone. It wasn't until Mayumi Nakamura began to work at Feld's, in April, that Goldie made a friend. Unlike Goldie, Mayumi wasn't hired as a salesgirl. She had taken design classes at the Academy of Art College, and Mr. Blankenship hired her to create the store window displays. When they pulled the paper down from Mayumi's first window, Goldie thought it was the most beautiful thing she had ever seen. Mayumi had created an ocean scene in the tiny six-by-eight-foot space. The walls and floor were aquamarine, speckled with different shades of green. Growing up from the corner, a giant coral sculpture, carved from foam and sponge, stretched like an undersea tree toward the surface. Cut-out fish of all shapes and colors—feathery purple, shiny silver, and striped in orange and yellow—hung from the ceiling. In the midst of all this, a mannequin had been reborn as a mermaid, twisting in the current, her shimmering tail making a joyous flip through the water. Only one piece of Feld's merchandise was on display in this entire scene. It was the flower-link sapphire necklace that glimmered on the mermaid's neck.

Until then, store displays had followed a model of crowding every window with as much merchandise as possible. The more you put in the window, the better chance you had of attracting customers with at least one product they might like enough to come inside and buy. Mayumi's windows were never meant to sell particular objects (though the necklace was extraordinary, it was meant to accessorize the mermaid more than anything else). Rather, Mayumi's window sold an idea of beauty and happiness that would draw people inside to choose merchandise that might satisfy their own desire for beauty and happiness.

For Goldie, Mayumi's window served as a revelation that beauty was not a quality within a particular object, but a more generalized attribute to strive for throughout life. She began to wonder about the existence of ideas greater and grander than she could yet understand, and she began to consider new possibilities for her own future. Looking at the mermaid, for example, did not kindle a desire for underwater exploration, but it did make dreams that once seemed impossible—like traveling to Paris or Rome—just a little less remote. Goldie began, then, to keep an eye on Mayumi and plotted ways to talk with her.

Mayumi, though, was difficult to know. She didn't work regular hours but would instead show up when she felt like it, perform her magic on the windows, and leave. During the time she spent in the store, she worked with serious concentration, but her movements were languid and she never seemed anxious or even concerned. Often Mayumi would simply stop whatever she was doing and sit there, on the floor or wherever she happened to be, staring into space. Did all artists work in such a dreamy way? Goldie had never met an artist before, so she couldn't know.

Goldie also noticed that Mayumi didn't act like other people. In

Goldie's experience, normal conversations followed certain cues. You might say, "How are you?" and the other person would respond, "Fine, thank you. And you?" Mayumi didn't care about those cues. If someone asked, "How are you?" Mayumi might reply, "I'm thinking of Florence all the time. I need to see the Uffizi Gallery." Or she'd say, "I think I can find a shade of red that is also black. Or black that is also red," and then she would laugh at herself because she knew she sounded silly. Goldie liked that laughter, too.

And finally, Mayumi was attractive in a way that struck Goldie as completely new. In Goldie's experience, women attracted men by using certain predictable, and fairly conventional, methods. One girl might be pretty and sweet. Another had curves in all the right places. Another might be flashy and somewhat dangerous. *Prettiness*, to Goldie, always amounted to the ability to buy the right clothes to fit that year's fashion. If you had money, you bought silk. If you didn't have money, you bought cotton or wool and kept it clean and neat. The rules were fairly simple.

In Mayumi, Goldie identified a new kind of attractiveness. Later, when it became more of a religion for her, Goldie would call it "refinement." But in 1940, she had not yet heard the word. Other women layered fabrics in showy, predictable ways—blouse tucked into skirt, matching jacket, coordinated heels and stockings, a hat and a pair of gloves. Mayumi rejected these conventions. She might pair, for example, simple black wool trousers with a lacy ivory shirt. Often she didn't even wear a hat but would instead pull her long hair into a bun and don large hoop earrings as a sort of balance.

People less attuned to fashion would have seen Mayumi, said, "She looks good," and left it at that. Goldie observed more carefully, however, and was able to see the particular sophistication with which Mayumi dressed. While others might have observed Mayumi in a green crepe dress and thought, "That's beautiful," Goldie could see that the dress was beautiful for one specific reason—a twist in the pleat of the skirt that captured and accentuated the narrow line of Mayumi's waist. As Goldie increasingly admired Mayumi for her ability to create her own style, she also began to think that she could learn from her.

Mayumi took more time to notice Goldie. What Goldie saw as a dreamy aloofness actually stemmed from nearly constant inspiration and glee. Mayumi had spent months convincing her parents to let her get a job. Once they finally did, and she found her position at Feld's, she went into a frenzy of creative activity. She had always loved making things. Now, the windows offered an outlet for every idea in her head. If Goldie was a girl adrift, Mayumi was a girl set free.

It took several weeks, then, for Mayumi to begin to notice anything beyond the paint cans and fabric and tissue paper surrounding her. And then, like someone emerging from a fog, everything around her clarified, and there was Goldie, standing in the doorway, watching her.

At first the two talked while Mayumi worked, Goldie spending her lunch break on a stool just outside the platform of the window, while Mayumi, in her apron and canvas slippers, applied wallpaper or worked on some trompe l'oeil effect on a back wall. "Who is your favorite designer?" Goldie asked. She had become partial to Elsa Schiaparelli, but worried sometimes that her designs were too fussy.

"Mainbocher," said Mayumi. She looked over to see Goldie's reaction, which, as expected, was one of surprise and dismay.

"But he doesn't even show his fashions," Goldie said. The designer, who had a studio in Paris, only allowed a small coterie of people to view, and buy, his clothes.

"It doesn't matter," said Mayumi. "I can look at photographs of his clients and learn from him."

"But what do you learn?"

"All that matters is elegance," Mayumi said. She was creating a scene of lovers at sunset, and she wasn't happy with the color pink she'd chosen for the walls. She dipped her paintbrush into the bucket of white paint and started to apply a thin topcoat to mute the intensity of SPRING ROSE.

"Not beauty?"

"Not beauty. You can have beauty without elegance, but you can't have elegance without beauty."

Goldie thought about this one. Mayumi was right. Goldie had seen a lot of beautiful trashy-looking girls. And she thought of the elegant women who occasionally came into the shop. Fate might not have given these women any natural good looks. To be honest, some of them were downright homely. But if they were elegant, they became beautiful. Wallis Simpson, for example, was nothing to look at but had become one of the most admired and attractive women in the world. Goldie knew that she herself was pretty enough, but she decided then that she wanted to be elegant even more.

When Goldie thought back on her childhood, even the periods of joy were laced with sadness. She was only thirteen when her mother died, and though she could recollect random images of her early life in Memphis—the creaky porch of her house, the chicken coop by the shed, the greasy smell of Friday's matzo ball soup—she could feel her memories of her mother growing dimmer as every year went by. The most vivid one came from a summer day when they held a party. The Jewish families in the area knew each other well, and that day many of them gathered in the dusty backyard of Goldie's house on Bullington Avenue, a shoddy, narrow street that, to Goldie's eyes, led nowhere in both directions. Goldie, the youngest of ten children, must have been about eight or nine then. Only the four youngest, all girls, remained at home, and none of them considered summer a vacation. The time away from school meant that they had to work to

earn the family extra money. Posie sewed. Eleanor cleaned a neighbor's apartment. Rochelle collected bottles. Goldie went from house
to house selling the eggs she collected from the family's hens.

Early that morning she woke to find her mother, Libke, in the
kitchen making strudel. In retrospect, she didn't remember the occasion, but imagined that it must have been a very special day. The
sight of her mother cooking at all surprised her. Libke's illness meant
that she seldom had the energy to get out of bed, much less cook
anything. More often, Posie or Eleanor would throw something together on the stove, and Goldie, Libke's favorite, would carry in soup
to her mother on a special wooden tray. This morning, though, Libke
had put on a dress and an apron, and she stood at the kitchen counter
like any other mother, making strudel.

All afternoon, people came over, not just friends and neighbors,
but the six older children, too, with their husbands and wives and
babies. There were also cousins who took the streetcar from the
Pinch, a larger Jewish neighborhood on the other side of town. The
children played at the back of the yard. The adults spoke Yiddish,
which Goldie couldn't understand. The men and women teased each
other, and the men told jokes while drinking beer and eating awful-
smelling cheese and a smoked fish that stank like rotten eggs. Late in
the day, when the air was still hot but the sun had dipped behind the
house next door, they sat in chairs pulled out into the yard. Goldie's
mother stretched across a blanket on the ground, her head and shoulders propped on pillows, and Goldie fanned her. Libke had taken off
her apron, revealing her best dress, a pale blue belted cotton with a
lace collar and white silk rose pinned just above her right breast. Her
hair hung down in little ringlets that Eleanor had helped her curl,
and she wore pink rouge and Fragrance of Paris. All across the yard,
the guests reclined on chairs and blankets in groups of three or four,
some sitting only a few feet away from Goldie's mother. Each man
tried to be cleverer than all the others. Goldie noticed that as they

told their jokes, they glanced at Libke, assessing her reaction. For as long as Goldie could remember, the men had called her mother "the Queen of Bullington Avenue," and they continued to do so even now, when she lay with a damp hand towel spread across her forehead. She didn't say a word, but if the joke was funny, you could see her mouth ease very slightly into a smile. Goldie fanned her. Libke's fingers swept across the tufts of grass at the edge of the blanket. The men told their jokes. Eventually, of course, lying on the grass became too difficult. It was Louise, the eldest of the siblings, who finally helped Libke into the house when the coughing started. Louise had never married, but everyone, even the brothers, did what she said. Now she told Goldie to stay outside, so Goldie lingered on the edge of the porch. Even there, she heard the violent sounds of her mother coughing into the old rags that they washed every day but that still retained the stains of blood. Outside, the joking stopped and the men turned to whiskey. Someone, Goldie couldn't remember who, passed the strudel. She had no memory at all of her father being there, though he must have been.

Mayumi came from a different world entirely. Her father had been born in the town of Takayama, in Gifu Prefecture in Japan. As a distant cousin of the imperial family, he enjoyed certain privileges as a child. He had visited the palace of the emperor and played with the emperor's children there. His mother had been trained in the exacting rituals of the tea ceremony, and his father had studied with the prince himself. The family had a beautiful home full of art and antiques. Mayumi's father, though, spent most of his childhood in the gardens. He wasn't interested in the family rituals. He loved the quiet of the outdoors, and most particularly he loved to watch things grow.

His parents, though, expected something more of him. They

imagined that he would marry within the imperial succession. He was smart enough, and talented, too, but he shied away from the gatherings at which he would have met such people. Instead, he stayed home, worked in his garden, and when he finally began to notice women, he fell in love with a neighbor girl who came from no lineage whatsoever. They married and decided to leave Japan, where history threatened to suffocate them and where the imbalance in their backgrounds seemed likely to trouble them forever. A few months after the wedding, they immigrated to the United States.

When Goldie discovered that her new friend was the daughter of a baron, she could hardly contain her joy. According to Mayumi, Japan had a line of royalty that dated back farther than England's. Goldie had had no idea. Nobody taught Japanese history in grade schools in Memphis, and Goldie's education had stopped there.

"You're nearly a princess," Goldie said. She was sitting on a stool by the windows during her lunch break, trying to keep the crumbs of her sandwich from getting caught in the fine weave of her skirt.

Mayumi was painting a backdrop in vertical stripes of purple and yellow. "It doesn't even mean anything in this country," she pointed out. Mayumi wasn't blind to her heritage, but she honestly couldn't see how it affected her current situation. "I'm no different than you here."

Goldie disagreed. "Your parents left everything behind to come to America, and my parents left nothing behind to come to America," she said.

"What does that mean?" Mayumi asked.

"My parents had nothing. When my mother arrived here, she had the hat on her head. My father had the shoes on his feet."

"And they made their fortune nonetheless," said Mayumi, who still believed in the American dream.

"No. They were born with nothing and they never made any more than that. They had ten children and an ugly patch of land on the outskirts of Memphis."

"Where did your parents come from?" Mayumi asked.

"Russia or Spain. Someplace like that." Goldie knew that they had traveled through Spain on their journey to the United States. Her sister Rochelle liked to say that they came from Spain, and Rochelle had even tried to study Spanish once, as if she were trying to rediscover their long-lost birth tongue. Goldie didn't quite believe it. The only thing she knew for sure was the way the scratchy weeds had tortured her feet in their yard in Memphis.

"I'm about the future," Goldie said.

"I'm about the future, too," said Mayumi. They smiled at each other, because their roots were so different, but they had flowered very much the same.

Often, after work, Goldie and Mayumi would take the bus to the Japanese Tea Garden in Golden Gate Park. Mayumi's father, Hiroshi, had created the garden for the city of San Francisco, and when Goldie met them, the family lived in a slope-roofed house on the grounds, surrounded by maple trees and pines.

Out in the avenues, the sky would fill with great banks of fog, and even in the late spring the girls bundled themselves in sweaters and scarves to keep warm. Goldie, new to town and easily disoriented, always felt lost. Mayumi knew every shortcut home. As soon as they got off the bus on Fulton Street, she would bound down a narrow path and disappear into the woods with Goldie right behind her. Both girls knew that the mud and dirt would ruin their shoes, so a few feet in from the road they would hide behind a bush and, leaning on each other for balance, slip off their heels and stockings before running, barefoot, the rest of the way through the trees.

It was a sign of how much she had come to trust Mayumi that Goldie took off her shoes at all. Goldie's feet were the one relic of poverty that she had not been able to put behind her. She had been born with extremely wide feet, and a childhood of wearing her sisters' narrow, hand-me-down shoes had deformed her toes, leaving them knotted together like a braid. It wasn't until she was fourteen years old that she finally earned enough money to buy a pair of shoes that fit. By then it was too late, though. The damage was permanent.

The first time Mayumi saw Goldie's feet, she agreed that they were ugly, but she was practical about it. "Just don't wear open-toed shoes."

"I would never wear open-toed shoes. Are you bananas?" Goldie said, but she was worried. "What about when I get married, though?"

Despite Mayumi's dreaminess, she had a practical side that gave Goldie comfort. "Just keep your shoes on. By the time you're married, he's going to be so crazy for you that you could have fur on your feet and he'd think it was beautiful."

Despite her ugly toes, Goldie could walk for miles without complaint. She never had trouble keeping up with Mayumi, and by the time they entered the tea garden gates she was always happy to plop down on the grass by the Moon Bridge and dip her feet in the stream. She loved the way the current lifted the dirt from her toes, swirled it into little pinwheels, then carried it away. The wooden Moon Bridge made Goldie feel that she was stepping back to a time when people fought with swords. If the pleasures seemed childish, particularly for a twenty-year-old woman, it was only because her own childhood had never allowed for such abandon, and consequently, she felt entitled to it.

Once they reached the garden, Goldie and Mayumi could quickly find Baron Nakamura in his overalls pruning one of his shrubs, or prowling amid the cherry trees, which needed constant care. As soon as he saw them, he would wave them over, then usher them up one path or down another, expecting them to care as much about each new bud and shoot as he did.

"Girls," he said one day, "Goldie must see our excellent development." He was small and solid. His mustache, waxed at the tips, looked like quotes around his features, which were as sharp and angular as letters chiseled in a marble frieze. Goldie could not forget that he was a baron, and she loved the quaintly formal rhythms of his accent. He might have dressed like any gardener, but to Goldie he seemed royal.

They followed him to a cluster of willow trees surrounding a fishpond. He squatted down on the rocky ledge and pointed at a giant carp the color of a peach blossom, its tail moving through the water like a swath of silk. "She is twenty-five years old," the baron said. "She arrived last week in a barrel on a boat from Japan." Goldie stood among the willow trees, staring at the fish, whose color was so different from that of the many orange or orange-and-white carp surrounding it. The idea of transporting this creature across the ocean seemed unbelievably extravagant to a girl from Memphis who owned a single pair of shoes, but it gave her a sense of possibility that made her almost giddy.

"That fish is older than me!" She laughed.

"She was swimming through a pond in Japan before we were even born," Mayumi said. She didn't share her father's love of nature, but the age of the fish, and the extent of its travels, mesmerized her, too.

The baron liked their enthusiasm. "She will live a hundred years," he told them. "Or longer. She will see your grandchildren, Mayumi."

Mayumi smiled, but she didn't enjoy this kind of talk. She liked the idea of love, but she had little interest in marriage, or raising a family, and she heard her father's words as a subtle pressure, as if he sensed her misgivings. Goldie, though, found their interactions sweet. If someone had asked what intoxicated her more—the beauty of the garden or the fact that she was talking to a *baron* in it, she would probably have claimed that the garden "enchanted" her. The truth was, however, that Goldie didn't have an eye for nature. In her experience, nature was the moody force through which you tried, and usually failed, to grow a few limp beans on a tangle of vines. The tea garden introduced her to a different kind of nature, one that seemed both tame and resplendent, but her early experience had made it hard for her to feel its charms.

The enchantment came from the Nakamuras themselves. In her forlorn youth, Goldie had dreamed of meeting a prince, but the fantasy served more as an escape from her own circumstances than from any true belief that such a thing could happen. When Rochelle invited her to California, Goldie saw it as an opportunity, not as a magical gift of fortune. She continued, even after starting her new life in San Francisco, to formulate new hopes for her future—a smart, hardworking, handsome husband; a nice house; enough money—but Goldie was also a practical person who focused on the possibilities in front of her and not on foggy notions of things beyond her grasp. In other words, she had never anticipated meeting a royal family, but the fact that she had served to expand her ideas about what was possible.

"I believe, sir, that you know every leaf in this garden," Goldie said, trying her best to sound both contemplative and poised.

The baron appreciated the comment. He liked any acknowledgment of his accomplishment on this piece of land that, many years before, the city of San Francisco had offered him. He squatted down on the path and lifted a handful of gravel, then let it sift slowly back to the ground. "Every pebble, my dear," he said. "Every pebble." Goldie recognized the overblown theatricality of the gesture, but it moved her nonetheless. In her own life, older people were sickly, lying in bed and coughing up blood. She had known plenty of young people to be sickly, too. Her mother had begun to cough up blood before she was out of her thirties. The sick and the old had the same dried-out smell of spilled medicine, unwashed clothes, and sugary perfume. Moving from Memphis to San Francisco had made Goldie conscious of her own youth and promise. Now Baron Nakamura showed her that age could be beautiful, too.

On those afternoons, they sat on the terrace overlooking the garden, amid the almost musical sounds of the stream. The house, a compact structure built of wood and stone, was so well integrated into the geography of the garden that visitors would sometimes unknowingly step up onto the terrace, not understanding that they had entered a private home. Perched on a stool, a porcelain teacup balanced on her knee, Goldie felt like an audience member chosen to sit backstage during a great performance of ballet.

The baroness, who moved with even more grace than her husband, served them sweet cakes and sugar-coated candies called Drops from the Moon. She was so serene that even a sudden noise—the roar of a truck out on Fulton, a distant baby's offended scream—wouldn't ruffle her. She rarely spoke, and when she did her voice never rose above a whisper. In comparison, Goldie felt her own voice to be piercing, her walk jarring, her body sharp, loose, and uncontrolled.

Mostly, the baron and his wife told stories about Japan. They had both grown up in Takayama, a hill town of narrow lanes and soot-dark houses. They talked of the thousand-year-old gingko tree in an ancient temple, the open hearths that warmed their homes, and visits to hot springs just outside of town. One day they spoke of Mount Fuji, to which they traveled just after their wedding, and their attempt to climb it on an early spring day that unexpectedly turned snowy.

"I only really began to know my wife," said the baron, "when we had to hurry back down the mountain together during that snowstorm. I had brought a pair of warm mittens, but she only had thin lace gloves. We held hands and stretched a single mitten around both of them, then walked like that all the way to the bottom. That's how I think of Mount Fuji."

Mayumi, sitting on a stool next to Goldie, had heard this story dozens of times. Sometimes the lace gloves were calfskin. Sometimes the snow was hail. She didn't doubt the general truth of the tale, but she had tired of it. She tried to catch Goldie's eye, to share her impatience, but she could see that Goldie found the romance stirring. Goldie had never even heard of Mount Fuji, which surprised Mayumi and reminded her that every childhood takes place in its own tiny universe.

"There are a dozen haiku poems about every possible view," Mayumi said, despite her weariness of such topics, "about every possible kind of light."

"Or, as our poet Basho wrote"—the baron paused to give the line its full effect—" 'Rising mist . . . the day when Mount Fuji can't even be seen, most intriguing!' "

The baroness added, "On warm nights, I still dream of Mount Fuji."

"She does. I hear her sighs," her husband said, turning his eyes toward the clouds and sighing, too.

Mayumi stood up then and started taking the tea things back inside. She became irritable when her parents romanticized the past. "They left Japan, didn't they?" she had once remarked to Goldie. It bothered her, in particular, that her father continued to act as if his lineage mattered here. "He should be known for the garden," she complained, "not for who his parents were."

Goldie didn't argue, but she believed that lineage mattered quite a lot. A baron remained a baron, even in Golden Gate Park. As much as she felt grateful to live in America, where anybody with gumption could make it, the old hierarchies impressed her. Goldie knew that Mayumi's parents *bestowed* their kindness on her, like a king and queen touching the tips of their scepters to a lowly subject's head, but their condescension didn't bother her. If the baron spoke to her in a particularly haughty tone ("You wouldn't understand, my dear," he might say), she felt pleased that he would speak to her at all. Once, she noticed the baroness watching her with barely masked distaste. Goldie realized that she had been holding her teacup with only one hand, while the baroness and Mayumi cradled theirs gently, making a bowl with their fingers. Instantly, Goldie lifted up her other hand and mimicked their gestures. Mayumi might cringe over her parents' ways, but Goldie saw the opportunity to learn from them. She knew her place in the social order, and she was determined to make her way up.

One afternoon, Mayumi invited Goldie to the tea garden for an occasion she would only describe as "very special." Despite Goldie's insistent questions, Mayumi refused to reveal any information. Consequently, by the time they arrived at the entrance to the garden, Goldie felt jumpy with anticipation. They walked up the path to the house, and she immediately noticed two things. First, the baroness, who usually wore Western clothes, was standing on the front terrace of the house wearing a formal kimono. The fabric itself was the color of wheat, while a heavy coffee-colored sash secured the garment tightly around her waist. Although the baroness had pulled her hair back in her usual bun, today she had also attached tiny silver ornaments to it.

The second thing Goldie noticed was the young man sitting on the edge of the terrace, his legs dangling over the side, balancing a cigarette in his mouth and an ashtray on his knee. He was watching Mayumi and Goldie's approach with curiosity and amusement.

They stopped in front of him, and Mayumi asked Goldie, "Can you guess who this is?"

Goldie looked at the young man, then back at Mayumi. When she didn't respond, Mayumi offered a hint, "Don't you see the resemblance?" She put her face in profile, closed her eyes, and pointed her nose to the sky. The young man smiled slightly and took a drag on his cigarette.

Neither Mayumi's hints nor her posing did anything for Goldie. The truth was, she couldn't easily distinguish among Japanese people. They all had those thin eyes and that straight black hair. She wouldn't have asked Mayumi directly, but she did wonder if the Japanese had trouble, sometimes, telling themselves apart.

When Goldie continued to look blank, Mayumi laughed and took a gentle swipe at her friend's arm. "Silly! It's Henry."

It took Goldie a moment to connect the sight of this stranger with the image she had developed in her mind of Mayumi's beloved older brother—from Mayumi's reckoning the kindest, smartest, most handsome man in the world. Over the months of their friendship, Goldie had often heard about Henry, so often that he had edged his way into her fantasy life, along with a debonair salesman at Feld's, a well-dressed fellow commuter on the Geary Street bus, and a teller at the bank who spoke with a European accent. Now, seeing Mayumi's brother for the first time, Goldie felt a stab of disappointment and shock at her own denseness. The man was handsome enough, but she had never visualized—stupid girl!—that Henry would also be Japanese.

"Come along!" Mayumi said, grabbing Goldie's hand, pulling her forward and up the stairs onto the terrace. "Henry, this is Goldie!" Mayumi announced, but after all the professed import of the moment, it was an offhand introduction, made by calling back to her brother over her shoulder as she and Goldie moved on. "Goldie, this is Henry."

Henry pushed himself down off the side of the terrace, then followed his sister and her friend back up the stairs. For the past three months, he had been living in Los Angeles, training at an import-export company as he made plans to open his own business in San Francisco. He had returned with a head full of profit-margin figures and sales expectations. Two containers of inventory were now following him up the coast by ship. At twenty-two, after four years of college and his months of training with a firm, Henry Nakamura felt that he had returned to San Francisco to finally begin his life.

The baron appeared on the terrace then. Like his wife, he had dressed in a kimono, though his was much simpler, and he looked less happy wearing it. He stooped down and squatted on a large mat, arranging a ceramic brazier on a low wooden table. "Children, take your places," he said. "We should go ahead and begin now."

"Is this a performance or something?" Goldie whispered to Mayumi.

Mayumi shook her head. She stepped behind Goldie and guided her friend toward the mat, where she instructed her to sit on her knees with her toes tucked underneath. "It's a Japanese tradition called tea ceremony," Mayumi said. "My mother is offering it to Henry because he's been away for so long. I wanted you to see it."

The tea ceremony began with the four "tea guests" sitting in a semicircle facing the table, with Mayumi and Henry in the middle, the baron next to his son, and Goldie on the other side. The baroness, also perched on her knees, faced them from behind the table, checking the progress of the water steaming on the brazier. The idea of a tea ceremony struck Goldie as both interesting and bizarre. She and her family had drunk tea, of course, but there was nothing ceremonial about that. Her family did have its own traditions—the typical Jewish ones, like lighting candles on Friday night (which Goldie's family had often neglected to do), and the more peculiar ones, like taking turns wiping their mother's brow, or leaning out over the porch railing at night, watching for the return of their inebriated father. It struck her that Japanese traditions were much more elegant.

When the water had boiled to the satisfaction of the baroness, she lifted a small ceramic tea bowl, took a square of fabric, and wiped out the interior. Unlike the cups in which the baroness normally served tea—dainty porcelain pieces with chrysanthemums or cherry blossoms on them—this rough-hewn ceramic bowl had a muddy brown glaze with a single swipe of gray running down one side. The baroness treated the heavy object with delicacy, though, slowly measuring out the tea, which was deep green and as fine as confectioner's sugar. Carefully she ladled boiling water into the tea and began to whisk the liquid. The tea turned frothy. Very slowly, with the cup between her fingers, she rose first onto her toes and then unfolded her knees until she was standing. With tiny steps, she walked over to her son, knelt in front of him, and placed the cup into his hands.

Henry received the tea silently, only acknowledging the offering with a subtle dip of his head. He rotated the cup in his hands, looking carefully at its markings, then drank it quickly in three swift sips. The baroness rose, returned to her table, and performed the ritual again for each of her guests, first for her husband, then Goldie, then Mayumi.

Goldie found every movement and gesture so intricate that she felt anxious over her inability to absorb it completely. She had never seen any activity completed with such a perfectly ritualized series of movements. If the Japanese focused so much effort on the simple act of making tea, then it seemed to her that they had elevated the whole breadth of human experience to something artistic and beautiful. This thought dazzled, but also confused her. How was she, as a guest, supposed to behave? Was she doing something wrong? She continually glanced back and forth between the baroness and the other guests beside her. When Mayumi lifted her sweets plate in one hand and her miniature fork in the other, then skewered the bite-size nest of sugary yellow noodles and lifted them to her mouth, Goldie did the same. The confection tasted eggy and strange, like candied spaghetti.

Mayumi leaned sideways to whisper in Goldie's ear. "Do you like it?"

"It's delicious." She had never experienced such a mixture of delicacy and earthiness, which is why she praised it so highly, even though she didn't actually care to try it again.

Each of the Nakamuras was participating in the ritual in his or her own particular way. The baroness came from a family of candy-makers, not aristocrats, and she had never had an opportunity to study the tea ceremony as a girl. Rather, she had taken it up in San Francisco, when a retired chemistry teacher from Osaka began to give lessons to earn extra money. Comparatively speaking, then, the baroness was new to this hobby, and while she was proud of her accomplishment, she also felt uneasy that her husband would see flaws in it. For his part, the baron was only half attentive. He had grown up in a family that practiced such refinements, but he found the entire enterprise dull and useless. Though he tried to look interested, he watched his wife with an impatient awareness that the afternoon was passing quickly and he had three cherry trees near the South Gate that needed pruning. Next to Goldie, Mayumi watched more closely, but she found her mother's efforts too self-conscious and pretentious. Only Henry, whose travels had renewed his appreciation for his own heritage, shared Goldie's full pleasure in the ceremony and participated wholeheartedly.

Just as the baroness was concluding her presentation, the little group on the terrace was interrupted by the sound of people approaching down the path. Something about the tenor of one particular voice alerted the baron to the fact that he had to attend to these new arrivals. He pulled himself quickly, and somewhat overeagerly, off the mat, and gave his wife and fellow guests a superficial wave of apology before darting down the steps to greet the visitors. Mayumi and Henry looked at their mother, who tipped her head with resignation, signaling that the young people should follow the baron down the steps to say hello.

Mr. Banes, the park superintendent, had arrived unexpectedly. "Nakamura!" he roared, grabbing the baron's hand. A bearish fellow, Banes was in the midst of offering a running narrative to the cluster of subordinates trailing him. "We planted that line of firs in twenty-seven," he told them. "Good growth on those beauties." To Goldie, he sounded like a truck driver delivering beer. She felt that the dream of the tea ceremony had been shattered.

"You were right about that little maple up by the gate, Naka-mura." The superintendent chewed on a battered-looking cigar, his eyes taking in the details of the garden with the pleasure and ease of someone literate in a language only a few could understand. "And the Moon Bridge is looking damn good, too." The horseshoe-shaped structure had been installed decades earlier, during the San Fran-cisco Exposition, and the baron had been overseeing its renovation for a month. "Where'd you get that idea of planting the little bonsai beside it?" he asked.

"Hiroshige," said the baron.

"Hiroshige?"

"One of the most precious Japanese artists." The baron became teacherly then. "My garden is a series of scenes." He looked at Mayumi. "What's that word?"

"Motifs," she said.

"Yes, motifs. Each turn on a path invites a new moment, a new drama. Hiroshige had this same idea about landscape. Often, a tree or even a shrub makes a person feel a particular emotion, so I planted the tree beside the Moon Bridge for the same reason that an artist intro-duces a new element to a picture—to change the feeling completely."

The superintendent puffed on his cigar, which made the air smell like prunes. "A drama?" he asked. "I think of gardens as a series of landscapes. They change, but so slowly that you can't catch it. It's the opposite of drama to me."

Mayumi's father shook his head. "A different kind of drama. Not drama like a play. Not sword fights!" He laughed, but also seemed concerned that he might be misunderstood. "I'm talking about natu-ral drama. The drama of light, a falling leaf. Do you ever see, at the ocean, the way the wind blows sand?"

"Sure."

"That kind of drama."

The superintendent looked mildly interested, as if the baron were describing an intriguing theory that he couldn't quite absorb. "I'll leave the philosophy to you, Baron," he finally said. "But if you have a problem with your cherries, you let me know. I've got fertilizer up the wazoo."

The baron looked down the path that led to the beginning of the cherry grove. "I have no problems!" he exclaimed, and his arm swept wide enough to take in not only the grove, but the entire garden, the house, the park, his newly returned son, all of California, the sky, the moon with its sugar-coated droplets, the expanse of the universe, a single leaf, a lonely pebble.

By the time the superintendent left, it was nearly dusk. The baroness had retreated to her room, explaining that she wanted to take some notes on the strengths and weaknesses of her tea ceremony performance. The baron had wandered back toward his cherry trees, anxious to make use of the remaining light. Most days, Goldie would have headed home by now, but Mayumi wasn't ready to let her go. "I want you to see something Henry brought back with him," she said, pulling at Goldie's hand. "Stay for a few more minutes."

The two young women sat down on the wicker sofa on the terrace while Henry disappeared inside the house. Kneeling on the mat had made Goldie's muscles feel like rags rung out to dry, so now that she was alone with her friend, she slipped off her shoes and turned her feet in little circles, trying to stretch.

Mayumi leaned over the plate of tea ceremony sweets that the baroness had left on the coffee table. Pointing one by one at the pink pansy-shaped disks, the pale green leaves molded from sugar, and the yellow tangles of sweet spaghetti, she said, "Flowers, new leaves, bird's nests."

"Remember that chocolate train we saw at See's Candies?" Goldie asked.

Mayumi did remember the chocolate train, but she shook her head, because she wanted Goldie to understand the difference here. "The candies don't have to be exact replicas, like that train. They're meant to introduce the idea of something." She picked up one of the pink disks and bit into it. The hard sugary shell cracked like an egg, opening to a soft center. "My mother chose these candies to evoke the changing seasons. It's the end of May, so she focused on the moment when spring turns into summer."

Goldie didn't care about the symbolism so much as the exacting attention that had gone into every detail, from the careful motion with which the baroness whisked the tea to the way the pink and green candies, arranged precisely on a plate, looked like flower blossoms nestled among leaves. "Every little thing was perfect," she said. Then, seeing Mayumi's brother reemerge onto the terrace, carrying in his arms a velvet bag, she dropped her feet to the ground and, worried that he would see her toes, thrust them back into her shoes.

Henry did not see Goldie's toes, but he did notice her quick maneuver. His sister had always been selective about her friends. Not considering it worthy of her time, she had rarely invited any of them home with her. Now he wondered why Mayumi had felt drawn to this nervous girl, who seemed sweet, but so young and undefined.

He sat on the chair across the coffee table from Mayumi and Goldie. "What did you think of the tea ceremony?" he asked Goldie. He held the bag on his lap, not quite ready to open it.

Goldie sat up straighter and folded her hands primly. "I found it very, very superlative," she said. "Supremely superlative."

"Really?" Henry and his sister exchanged a glance.

Goldie nodded, then leaned forward. "I don't understand one thing, though. Your mother has such beautiful china—I've seen it. So why did she use those rough-looking bowls?"

Mayumi watched her brother. She could see that he was assessing her friend. And because he was perfectly capable of being rude, she felt relieved that he was civil. "Well," he said, "the tea ceremony focuses on simplicity. It elevates the beauty in nature and rejects anything artificial or overly decorative, like my mother's porcelain cups."

Goldie had never heard that peculiar combination of words before. "Overly decorative?" How could something be *too* beautiful?

"Is that strange to you?" His tone was cooler now.

Goldie didn't miss the shift in Henry's manner, which seemed to underscore the chasm between her own inexperience and God knew how many centuries of Japanese tradition. For a moment she simply stared down at her hands, unsure of how to answer him. Her sense of good fortune at knowing Mayumi was always balanced against a worry that her own substantial failings—ignorance, stupidity, poverty, lack of sophistication—would eventually drive her friend away. Another girl might, at that moment, have folded, cowed by her own insecurity. But Goldie had a strong defense: blind bravery, masked as an unwavering belief in her own opinions. Thus, when she looked up to see the brother and sister gazing at her, she tossed her head and said blithely, "Well, it's just about the silliest thing I ever heard. Why would anyone reject something beautiful?"

Mayumi reached for a bright green sugar leaf and snapped it between her teeth with a satisfying crunch. She and Henry often complained about the snobbishness of their parents, but they could both be scornful, too, of people they considered beneath them. She admired Goldie for fighting back and, rushing in to bolster her friend, said, "I agree. The tea bowls are hideous, and it's pompous to claim otherwise."

Henry looked at his sister. Mayumi had never liked the tea ceremony, but normally her criticisms were light and her mind distracted. Now, she seemed unusually determined to belittle it. "I hope Mother didn't hear you say that," he told her. He was teasing, but his words sounded more petulant than he intended.

Mayumi glared at him, then turned to Goldie and said dryly, "Welcome to the Nightingale Palace."

"The Nightingale Palace?" Goldie's face conveyed such delight over the glamour of the phrase that, to Henry's mind, it hinted at how she would look if, say, Clark Gable and Vivien Leigh had suddenly joined them on the terrace.

"It's just a joke," he told her. "We made it up." Normally, he admired his sister for her frankness, but this particular disclosure felt like a betrayal of trust. The term *Nightingale Palace* had developed out of the siblings' mutual frustration over the constraints imposed on them by their parents. Why would Mayumi share such a thing with this stranger?

But Mayumi was irritated with her brother, too, so she made the story even more elaborate. "It's not a joke. Our parents named their home after Ninomaru Palace in Kyoto." She reached over and squeezed Goldie's hand. "It's very regal and mysterious, don't you think?"

Goldie was beaming now. "It's beautiful," she said.

Henry sighed, exasperated over his sister's sudden gilding of their lives. "Can we just look at the book?" he asked.

Mayumi curled her bare feet under her on the sofa, then took hold of Goldie's arm and squeezed it, leaning close against her friend. "You'll love this. My mom and dad and I are probably more excited about Henry's new business than he is. He brings home these amazing discoveries and we can't get enough of them."

"What amazing discoveries?" Goldie asked.

"Antiques. Art. We adore it all, but we're mostly motivated by the lack of them. When our parents left Japan, they could only bring a few suitcases, so Henry and I grew up hearing about all the exquisite things they left behind."

Something about Mayumi's smile struck Goldie then, and suddenly she did see a resemblance between the Nakamura siblings.

They had the same fine line of the jaw, the same delicate mouth, and the same shrewd gaze, although Mayumi's face had a kind of effervescence, while Henry looked more weighed down and sober. They moved in different ways as well. Mayumi, who could be so calm at Feld's, was quick and fluttering, like a bird, around her family. Henry observed more closely, and took his time.

Henry glanced at his watch. It was nearly four thirty. He fought against his restlessness by being even more polite. "Were your parents immigrants, too?" he asked.

Goldie nodded. "From Europe."

"Did they bring anything precious to this country with them?"

She found this question funny. "I think they felt lucky to get out alive. My mother brought a locket, but it wasn't worth anything. My father brought his tools, which weren't worth anything, either, but they were worth a lot to him." Goldie could understand her parents leaving their village. They had nothing there, and nothing to lose. But the Nakamuras had been royalty in Japan. Goldie imagined treasured furniture and jewels. "Why did your family come here?" she asked. It didn't make sense.

Out in the garden, a cardinal was weaving through the branches of a miniature maple tree, adding a burst of crimson to the late afternoon light. Mayumi said, "Our parents had more confidence in a future here, and they had too many obligations to their family in Japan." She glanced at her brother. "What do you think, Henry?"

Henry's eyes rested on the bird, which helped to ease his sense of irritation. He had often wondered about his parents. He said, "America is the place for dreamers. You must have noticed that our father is a dreamer."

Mayumi gestured toward the bag with her chin. "Show her," she said.

Henry untied the cord and pulled out an object that looked like a book with wooden covers. It was large and cumbersome, and he had to use both hands to extricate it from the bag and set it on the table between them. He turned the volume so that Goldie and Mayumi, sitting across from him, could read the lines in elaborate gold lettering on the cover: *The Reverend Maurice M. Castleman, Scenes of Japanese Women.* Henry turned the book over. The other side read, *The Reverend Maurice M. Castleman, Scenes of Japanese Life.*

"Who is Reverend Castleman?" Goldie asked.

Henry lifted his eyes toward Goldie. "I like to think of a portly older man, sipping his Scotch and looking at these pictures in his cozy library somewhere in the Midwest. You'd think, if you just looked at the cover, that he was the artist, but this was just a souvenir for him. Reverend Castleman traveled to Japan on Admiral Perry's naval expedition in the last century, the one that opened trade routes to Japan. He brought this collection back to the United States."

"How interesting," said Goldie, being polite. History bored her, and anxious to catch her bus home, she stared down at the book until, finally, Henry opened it. He began with *Scenes of Japanese Life,* revealing the first image, a landscape of a village by a riverside, narrow wooden boats slipping beneath a bridge.

"These are by the printmaker Hiroshige," Henry said. "He's the artist my father mentioned to Superintendent Banes. The series is called *Fifty-three Stations of the Tokkaido Road.*"

Henry turned the pages, and Goldie and Mayumi looked at each print. At twenty years of age, Goldie's experience of art was limited to the free calendars from the local dairy that her mother had tacked to the kitchen wall, and to the prints of cats and dogs, sold as a set in a furniture store, that Rochelle had bought to hang beside her new dining room table. Looking down at these pictures, Goldie understood that Mayumi and her brother would be expecting a reaction, but she had no idea what kinds of things a person was supposed to say. She found the pictures pretty enough, but monotonous: a village street with a craggy pine tree looming over it; farmers in empty valleys, planting their fields; a mountain road and people hauling their parcels along it.

"That's Mount Fuji," said Mayumi, pointing at a distant peak that appeared in the background of many of the images.

Here was something about which Goldie did have an opinion. She leaned in closer, then shook her head decisively. "It's too perfect," she said. "That's the kind of mountain children draw when they haven't actually seen one." Goldie had come to this knowledge through recent experience. Her own first glimpse of mountains remained vivid, having only occurred a few months earlier, when she traveled across the country from Tennessee.

The Nakamuras looked at her. "But Fuji really is a perfect mountain," Mayumi said.

"I don't believe it." Goldie felt it was important that she take a position, and her experience with mountains gave her enough confidence that, when Henry turned the page to a winter scene, she decided that she was capable of a new observation, "Look at that. Every single tree branch is covered in snow."

Henry pushed the volume a couple of inches closer, so that Goldie could see it better. "The snow isn't just white," he said. His finger hovered over the image, drawing her attention to a patch of frozen ground near a bend in a stream. "It goes from almost black, here, to soft gray, and then, up here, the shades go lighter."

"You're absolutely right," Goldie said. She felt herself to be responding more appropriately now, and she did find Henry's comments mildly interesting, if hardly worthy of extended discussion. They all three stretched to see, their heads crowded together over the book. "There's not really that much white at all," Goldie said. "The shades are so varied."

"Hiroshige designed these images," Mayumi said. "Other people did the coloring, but we have a sense that he was involved with every detail because the color in his prints is always so luscious."

Henry began to turn the pages again. Goldie stared down at them. The colors were muted, mostly soft greens and yellows balanced against the pale blue of sky and water. In these landscapes, mountains towered, seas stretched to the horizon, and the humans were tiny hunched-over figures laboring in the distance. Goldie did the best she could to act impressed. "The world seems so huge and lonely," she said, and then, finally, they reached the end of the book.

Goldie would have been happy to head home at this point. She was hungry now, tired of art, and tired from the effort required to show interest in it. As it turned out, however, she had seen only half of the pictures. By flipping the book, Henry prepared to show her *Scenes of Japanese Women,* the set of pictures on the other side. Goldie's heart sank. She scanned the sky above the tea garden, which was turning darker now. She didn't want to be rude, though. The Nakamuras had gone to such efforts for her.

"These are by Kunisada Two," Henry explained, offering more detail than Goldie wanted about this strangely named artist and the illustrations he had created from a classical Japanese novel called *The Tale of Genji.* "The Japanese themselves would never have called it *Scenes of Japanese Women.* That's like calling the Sistine Chapel *Scenes of Italy.* It sounds ridiculous."

Goldie tried to look interested. She could not remember if the bus ran every ten minutes or every fifteen minutes on Fulton Street on Sunday evenings. Worse, that line might have stopped running by this hour, which would force her to make the long trek over to Geary Street in order to catch a different bus. Her hunger and her growing concern about the time distracted her. When Henry finally opened the book, she politely leaned forward again on the sofa, but she was thinking about the Nestlé Crunch bar that lay at the bottom of her handbag.

It took long seconds, then, for Goldie to focus on the first print. When she did, her mind cleared instantly. She forgot the hour, her grumbling stomach, her unlikely chance of catching the bus. And she forgot, too, the clothes she loved, elegant shoes, the hats she admired on wealthy women, fur coats, everything she wanted. Goldie Rubin looked down at this old Japanese print and, for what felt like the first time in her life, she saw something truly beautiful.

"Oh, my," she whispered, more to herself than to them. Because here were ladies: graceful and demure, cunning, flirtatious, dressed in layers of undulating robes, their hair sculpted to their heads with banquets of ornaments, their fingers long and tapered, their mouths full, their faces beckoning. Each individual robe offered a feast of detail—clusters of goldenrod set against a crimson sky, blossoming peonies, dragonflies, hyacinths amid a field of stars. "The colors," Goldie murmured as Henry turned the pages, so dazzled was she by the pinks and purples, the yellows and greens and bright, bright blues that her voice trailed off. If someone had asked her to describe her vision of the most beautiful thing in the universe, Goldie believed she would have described the pictures that lay before her now.

Mayumi and Henry watched, astonished by the expression of wonder on Goldie's face. They had never *not* known about art, and perhaps as a result, they experienced it with their intellect, but without much emotion. Goldie's way of looking at these images was entirely different from their own, a fact that Henry realized when he turned to a picture called *Festival of the Cherry Blossoms*. Here, a young woman, poised on a mat behind a blossom-covered screen, clutched her robes to her chest while, from the other side of the screen, a man peered down at her. When Henry looked at a picture like this one, he thought about design and contrast, historical relevance, the artist's eye, the archaic style. Goldie apparently brought none of that to her experience. Instead, she seemed voracious, her eyes darting up and down the page, almost desperate, as if she were hungry and only these images could offer satisfaction.

"What are you thinking?" Mayumi finally asked.

Goldie didn't look up, though she tried to answer, her hands moving vaguely through the air. "Look at the folds of the fabric," she said. "Look at the line of her neck. And look at her face. That poor girl has no idea what to do!"

The Nakamuras both knew that of the two artists in this collection, Hiroshige had always drawn the most acclaim. It was the Tokkaido pictures, not these illustrations from *Genji*, that elevated Henry's purchase from pleasant amusement to treasure. But Goldie's reaction made both of them look at the *Genji* illustrations again. In the mixing of these two foreign elements—Goldie and these works of art—an alchemy had occurred. Henry and Mayumi were able to look more closely and see, if only as a sudden flash, the beauty that Goldie experienced so completely.

Eventually Henry reached the last page of the book. Goldie, like someone waking from sleep, looked up at him, her face radiant. "I haven't ever seen anything so beautiful before."

"They're here, any time you like," he said. He was uncomfortable to have witnessed such a private burst of feeling, but he also felt obliged to make sure that she could see the pictures again.

Mayumi, of course, was even more encouraging. "Consider our house your personal gallery," she said, squeezing Goldie's hand.

All this kindness suddenly embarrassed Goldie, who didn't know how to repay it. She searched the sky for something to say, and the darkness reminded her how much time had passed. Immediately, her expression shifted. "It must be nearly five!" she said, putting her hand on Mayumi's wrist to see her watch. "Oh, no. It's five thirty."

Goldie's mind filled then with thoughts of the cranky Rochelle, the children with their dirty noses, Buddy and his beer, the fact that she had promised to cook a stew for them. "I don't even know about the bus!" she said, jumping up.

Mayumi grabbed Goldie's hand. "Don't worry. Henry can drive the car. We'll take you home." A look of relief passed over Goldie's face, and Mayumi paused, her expression full of concern, to say to her brother, "I told you the terrible thing about Goldie's sister, didn't I?"

"No," Henry said, reaching into his pocket to make sure he had his father's keys. "What?" He looked at Goldie, but she seemed baffled, too.

Mayumi took a deep, dramatic breath. "If Goldie doesn't get home before six o'clock," she whispered, "Rochelle will eat her."

For the briefest instant, Henry observed the range of expressions that flashed across Goldie's face: surprise and confusion followed by a flutter of giggles. She turned to her friend and swatted her on the arm. "I didn't say she'd eat me, silly!"

7

New World

It annoyed Rochelle that her younger sister enjoyed such success in San Francisco. Not only had Goldie found an excellent job, but she was popular with the young men, too. Goldie had already been to the Pied Piper Bar in the Palace Hotel twice. The first time, a men's shirt wholesaler from Seattle drove her there in his robin's-egg blue Mercury Coupe. The second time, she visited with Herman Isaacson, an annuities agent who worked with Rochelle's husband, Buddy, at F. S. Wreaker & Sons Insurance. Rochelle had introduced Goldie to Herman herself, but she found it aggravating to sit home every night while gentlemen took Goldie to the most glamorous spots in San Francisco.

"You need to pull your weight around here, you know," Rochelle griped one Monday morning.

Though Goldie had spent a needy first few days in San Francisco, she had quickly found her footing. Now she had little time for Rochelle. She had her new job, her social life, and obligations to keep the house clean and help care for the children. "Rochelle," she said, holding up the hand mirror to check on the foundation below her eyes, "I'm the one scrubbing the floor in the kitchen at six A.M. while you're sleeping."

Rochelle was still in her robe, drinking coffee. The baby sat at their feet, his face a papier-mâché mask of oatmeal and the scraps of toilet tissue he had found in the bathroom. "I'm here all day," she replied, thrusting her arms into the air to encompass the scope of her disappointments. "What are you, the Queen of Post Street, out there seeing the world?"

Goldie took a bite of toast. Rochelle had always resented Goldie's close relationship with their mother, which explained her bitter equation of Goldie's success in San Francisco with the popularity of Libke—the Queen of Bullington Avenue—back home. But Goldie ignored the swipe. She had a bus to catch and eight hours of selling stockings ahead of her. She had stuffed an apple, a hunk of bread, and a couple of pieces of cheese wrapped in old newspaper into her pocketbook, and it was all she would eat between now and dinner. Rochelle, on the other hand, was a married lady who didn't work. Her day would include a trip to the park and a stop at the grocer's for soap and onions. It seemed clear, on paper, which of these two sisters was better off. Still, what lay between them was not the relative comforts and discomforts of their daily lives. It was the fact that an eager young man had taken Goldie to an expensive Italian restaurant in North Beach the night before, while Rochelle and her children ate leftover chuck roast at the cramped kitchen table.

"Rochelle," Goldie said, getting up and slipping her bag over her shoulder, "you've got a husband and I don't." Neither Rochelle nor Goldie would have been able to explain, exactly, why they were arguing. Issues of happiness had never been central to their consciousness. Are you healthy? Do you have enough to eat? Do you have money? Are you safe? Goldie and her siblings had learned to assess the quality of their lives by only these practical measures, and so they had no means by which to judge the general state of their emotions. Goldie blew a kiss to the baby, and disappeared out the door.

Although Goldie worked hard, she loved every single thing about her job—the lush textures of the wools and silks in couture, the weight of the crystal vases and bowls in domestic lifestyle, the fine little gold filigree on the necks of the atomizer bottles in fragrance, even the sheen on the silk stockings. She loved her customers' need for her attention, the respect on the face of her boss, Mr. Blankenship, when he sought her out with a question, even the businesslike clip of her heels across the marble floors. It amazed her that a girl from Memphis who had only finished eighth grade could now be earning thirteen dollars a week in San Francisco, and though she had no expectations of a long career in sales—Goldie planned eventually to get married—the idea that she could take such good care of herself gave her a sense of confidence in her own abilities that she had not previously thought possible.

Unlike shops that carried more ladies' fashions, Feld's had an idiosyncratic way of combining "manly" merchandise, like humidors and decanters, with a wide selection of very feminine offerings, like negligees and perfumes. As a result, the establishment attracted a large number of male customers, many of whom liked to purchase gifts for their mistresses, if not their wives, and who appreciated the attentions of a pretty young shopgirl. These men, as well as the men on Feld's staff, noticed Goldie right away. It wasn't that she was prettier than the other salesgirls. All the salesgirls at Feld's were pretty. Anyway, regarding Goldie by that measure put her at a disadvantage. Her face didn't have the smooth and pleasing proportions that one saw on the face of Margaret, for example, the sweet girl in the hat department. She didn't have that startled and innocent look that made Shirley, in gloves and scarves, so fetching. And she didn't have the sophistication of French Agnes, who moved like a dancer, with long limbs and graceful hands that seemed destined to model nail polish and diamond rings. Goldie, who "floated" among different departments from day to day, had attractions that were harder to describe and, for most of the men in the store, more alluring. Her body was lean but curvy, and the clothes she wore covered her in a way that was both discreet and inviting. Women's fashion called for a balance between modesty and revelation. Most women found a place of comfort that tipped the balance too far to one side or the other. Some, like Margaret, dressed with too much hesitation and ended up looking prissy. Others, like Hollis, who worked in fragrance, wore blood reds and hot pinks and allowed their necklaces to disappear into their cleavage. As a result, those girls looked loose. Goldie, though, had found her balance on the knife-sharp edge of decorum. She wore her blouses buttoned nearly to the neck, but they were formfitting and thin, and covered her breasts like the tightest of gloves. The men in the shop, both customers and fellow employees, paused to watch her move across the room. Goldie knew that men found her attractive. She had learned when she was only fifteen how to dodge their ardent hands and attempts at kisses. Their desire had sometimes surprised her, but she had never felt afraid of it. The interest of men added to her sense of control over her life, and that was exhilarating to her.

But despite her charms, Goldie's social life was not as glamorous as she might have liked. Men asked her out every day, but out of concern that they were criminals, or married, she only accepted invitations from those to whom she'd been introduced by someone she trusted. When she did go out, she didn't have a lot of fun. Herman Isaacson, the annuities agent, was jovial and doting, but his manners were crude, and he ate with his mouth open. Goldie felt no joy in dining with him, even at the famous North Beach Italian restaurant, because bits of food constantly spun from his mouth, flying at her from across the table. Stan Margolis, the shirt salesman, was also doting, but cheap. True, he had taken her to the Palace Hotel for a drink, but he had only ordered a seltzer (Goldie, who avoided alcohol, had sipped a Coca-Cola). Afterward, instead of inviting her into the hotel's fashionable restaurant, he had walked her over to Third Street, where they ate dry meatloaf at Sherman's Diner. Other men, mostly friends of Buddy's, took her out as well, but none of them interested her. Out of all these dates, the only man who really stirred her was Alan Stevenson, a Nebraskan who ran men's shoes. He had a sportsman's shoulders and, despite his childhood on the farm, wore beautiful clothes. They had been out one time, to a French restaurant on Sacramento Street that Goldie found both elegant and exotic. Alan was Christian, though, unlike her other dates, and since Goldie had never known many Christians, she had a hard time reading his emotions. He hadn't asked her out again.

Goldie most enjoyed her time with Mayumi. The girls never tired of wandering through the expensive shops around Union Square, discussing fashion and men. While Mayumi talked about "finally falling in love," Goldie was pragmatic. She wanted someone handsome and charming, but her primary concern was "a good salary and solid future." The idea of love didn't factor into her calculations.

Both girls, though, wanted to have fun. Mayumi, a native San Franciscan, became tour guide for her new friend. Though Goldie found the experience repulsive, she willingly followed Mayumi through the back alleys of Chinatown, where streams of blood drained out the doors of the butcher shops and down the sidewalks. She also hated the smells along the wharves, where men in galoshes sucked on fat cigars and hauled fish as big as they were on their soaking backs. Goldie never complained, however. Every sight and smell contributed to her education. Once, they walked to the top of Telegraph Hill and stood at the base of Coit Tower. Mayumi pointed toward a patch of silvery gray beyond the Golden Gate Bridge. It was Goldie's first glimpse of the Pacific Ocean.

"One day, I'm going to travel to Japan," Mayumi said.

Goldie replied, "I'll come with you."

Sometimes Mayumi brought Henry along as well. Because of his business, he traveled up and down the coast, buying goods in the antique markets of Los Angeles, Seattle, and Vancouver and bringing them back to sell in the fine stores of San Francisco. Often he sold merchandise to Feld's. He had exquisite Chinese wooden boxes, each with dozens of working drawers. He had Siamese ceramics in shades he described as "cerulean" and "azure" and "celadon." Goldie had never heard these words before and never seen such porcelain. He also showed her two tiny Italian chess sets that had arrived in the United States, he didn't know why, through Indonesia.

If Henry dropped by Feld's in the late afternoon, he waited until closing time so that he could ride home on the bus with his sister. Sometimes, after work, the three of them walked to a diner a couple of blocks down Market Street, where they drank coffee and, if they had time, played penny games of gin rummy. Although Mayumi had easily warmed to Goldie, Henry took longer to adapt. He had been born in the United States and had business relationships with many different kinds of people, but his personal life remained entirely Japanese. He was surprised to realize how little Goldie understood about the exclusivity of San Francisco's various communities: the Chinese didn't mix with the Japanese; the High Society on Nob Hill didn't mix with the Irish in the Mission; the Mexicans lived in their own little world. Goldie, however, only seemed to notice who interacted (or failed to interact) with the Jews, and now that she had become an ardent friend of Mayumi, she focused primarily on their similarities, not their differences. "I'm an immigrant, too," she remarked one time, stressing the parallels between their lives. Though Henry wasn't sure that Goldie fully understood the meaning of the term—they had all actually been born in this country—he had to agree that she was right. They were all outsiders here.

One afternoon Henry suggested that they take Goldie to see Japantown. She had heard of the neighborhood and had several times mentioned a desire to visit, but unless she had a date after work, she needed to be home by six thirty. "I wish I had time," she said.

Henry pushed up the sleeve of his shirt and showed her his wristwatch. "It's just five now," he said. "Japantown is on one of the bus lines that leads straight back to your house." Goldie had lived in San Francisco for three months by then, but she still didn't understand the geography of the city.

"We'll make sure you get home," Mayumi promised.

On the streetcar, Goldie felt the urge to describe her latest confounding interaction with Alan Stevenson, the Nebraskan. Mayumi had an intimate knowledge of the ups and downs of that relationship, which despite flirtations at the store had yet to lead to a second date. Because Mayumi was Japanese, the two girls did not consider the same men as potential boyfriends. Over the months of their friendship, they had each taken on a singular role in the other's life—that of an adviser who was interested but personally uninvolved. Today, Alan Stevenson demanded their entire attention, and though on another occasion Henry's presence might have kept Goldie from speaking on the subject, her emotions this afternoon so weighed on her that she felt he might, as a man, offer needed perspective.

"I was in the stockroom when he came in," she began. "He saw that we were alone, and he immediately came over to me. I was so nervous. He whispered in my ear, 'That shade of blue brings out the color of your eyes.' Those exact words." She looked at Mayumi. "Have you ever heard anything so romantic and sweet?"

The two girls sat on a long bench facing the center aisle of the streetcar. Henry, pressed among the crowd of afternoon commuters, stood above them, holding one of the metal poles that stretched between the floor and ceiling. Mayumi said, "Of course it's romantic. He's stuck on you."

Goldie liked that idea. She anticipated that another invitation—perhaps to the Pied Piper Room?—would arrive soon.

"But," said Henry, looking down at her, "your eyes aren't blue."

Mayumi scowled up at her brother. "What does that matter?"

"It's still romantic," Goldie suggested, but his comment touched on a fact that she had herself considered.

Henry seemed unconvinced.

"You don't think he meant it?" Goldie asked.

"I think it sounds stupid."

Mayumi chastised her brother. "You don't even know Alan Stevenson. He's not stupid. He's from Nebraska. And handsome. And he wants to open his own shoe shop one day. He's going to call it Stevenson's Fine Shoes." This last bit of information had come, of course, from Goldie herself, who had taken Alan's revelation of his career aspiration as a signal that he might ask her to join him in the enterprise. It had seemed somehow perfect to her that a girl with twisted toes could end up with a purveyor of beautiful shoes.

Goldie didn't join Mayumi's protestations, though. The streetcar had left the center of the city and was moving up an avenue lined with Victorian homes. San Francisco architecture delighted her with its turrets and balconies, lacy woodwork, and bay windows, each individual home like a palace. Some days Goldie felt like a princess, too, but she had not yet moved far from her real-life troubles—her father's devotion to whiskey, her mother's death, Rochelle's constant demands, and her own poverty and loneliness. It took a huge amount of focus to imagine something better, and in recent weeks, Alan Stevenson had taken hold in her mind as possibly offering that relief. She deeply wanted to believe Mayumi, but she suspected that Henry understood the situation better. Alan Stevenson, handsome and debonair, with his shoe store fantasies and excellent clothes, might have other plans besides marrying Goldie. She thought about how, in those brief moments she had spent with him alone in the stockroom that afternoon, his hand had slid around her waist in a way that wasn't proper. Now, the memory unsettled her.

"Maybe it's because I'm Jewish," she said. "Some men don't like Jewish girls."

Mayumi shook her head. "Lots of men marry Jewish girls. They don't mind at all."

Goldie continued staring at the city outside. Sometimes those beautiful homes looked so inviting; at other times they teased her. "I had never been on a date with a Christian before," she said. Back in Memphis, Jewish parents would never allow a daughter to go out with, much less marry, a non-Jewish man. But Goldie had no parents to guide her here. Rochelle might get angry, but her emotions came from irritability, not concern.

Although Mayumi and Henry had read about Jews, they knew very little about them. "You're still white," Mayumi reminded her.

"People don't like Jews," Goldie said. "They think we're thieves and greedy."

Henry looked at his sister. "It's really bad for the Jews in Europe."

Goldie had no interest in the Jews of Europe. "It's bad for the Jews right here. Rich people don't marry Jews. Unless they're Jews themselves, and then they have no choice."

Mayumi slapped her hands against her knees. "Then you have to find a rich Jew."

Goldie said, "Exactly." She looked at Henry and Mayumi. "You two can understand what it's like. You're Japanese."

Henry shook his head. "It's not the same. You can hide being a Jew. Everyone knows we're Japanese, whether we like it or not."

The streetcar lurched down the final hill. Many people had gotten off already, so Henry was able to squint down the aisle and see out the front windshield. Mayumi said, "I think he's going to ask you out again soon. He doesn't care if you're Jewish."

"One more block," Henry announced. He found their conniving interesting, but their perspective on men seemed completely naive.

"Maybe he's just saving up his money for a grand night out," he suggested. "He'll want you to think he's rich."

The streetcar stopped in Japantown, and Goldie followed her friends onto the sidewalk. The neighborhood looked much like the area where Rochelle and Buddy lived, except that the signs on the windows and awnings of the little shops were printed in Japanese. Goldie stopped to take it in. The writing looked like messy little boxes, similar to what she had seen in Chinatown. She understood that those scrawling lines constituted a language, but the fact that they carried meaning didn't enter her head at that moment. "It's so charming!" she told them.

Henry and Mayumi looked at the writing—a list of shoe-shining and dry-cleaning services—and laughed. Although Goldie had odd and fairly casual interests (she never bothered to remember any facts that they shared with her), they couldn't doubt her intelligence, curiosity, and sincerity. She had told them that she dropped out of school at thirteen because her family had no money. With so little education, she had never developed the habits you would need to build a body of knowledge. Everything was interesting for its own sake at a singular moment. If Mayumi took her to a museum, the art might make her sigh with pleasure, just as the *Tale of Genji* prints had done, but the details of the works—artists' names, schools of painting, historic contexts—struck her as completely irrelevant. Still, despite her random way of learning, she had, over the past few months, come to a fairly keen appreciation of art in the world, and perhaps most importantly for her future, she had increasingly firm opinions about beauty.

For the next half hour or so, they wandered in and out of the various stores. Compared with what they saw in the fashionable establishments around Union Square, these shops were rustic and slightly bare, full of mysterious products. Henry would raise a lid on a bin or a bucket, allowing Goldie to peek in at vegetables pickling in brine, or mounds of tiny pink dried fish, the acrid smell of which made her wince.

"Let's go to our uncle Aki's," Henry suggested, leading the girls across the road and up the block to a large store shaded by a red awning. Compared with the other shops, this one looked fairly modern, full of canned goods lining shelves, bags of candies, jewelry display cases, plates, and cups and saucers.

Uncle Aki, small and round with a missing front tooth and a wide grin, was delighted to see his nephew and niece, and even more delighted when he saw that they had brought a young white lady along with them. "She's never been to Japantown before," Henry explained in Japanese.

"Where'd she come from?" From Aki's perspective behind the counter, Goldie, standing uncertainly in the middle of the floor, looked like a Hollywood starlet.

Henry gestured toward his sister. "They work together downtown."

Aki watched her. He had opened his shop nearly thirty years earlier and felt proud of what he had accomplished. Not only did he own the biggest general merchandise shop in Japantown, but he also carried the largest selection of Japanese kimonos on the West Coast. Looking at the girl, with her slim and fashionable skirt, her smart pumps and well-coiffed hairstyle, he knew that she'd want to see the kimonos.

Henry, Mayumi, and Goldie followed Uncle Aki to a side room. Unlike the rest of the store, with its wood floor and simple cabinets, this space looked like a dress shop showroom, with thick green carpet, standing wooden mirrors, and lustrous fabrics hanging on racks along the walls. Goldie moved toward the fabrics like a bee toward a field of poppies. Mayumi followed. Henry and Aki stood in the doorway, observing.

"She's lovely," Aki said in Japanese.

Henry had warmed to Goldie over the past few weeks, but watching her now, with his uncle, forced him to acknowledge something he hadn't allowed himself to consciously consider before: Goldie really was lovely. The thought unsettled him, which may explain why, when he did respond to Aki, he tried to sound completely objective on the subject. "She's only been in San Francisco for a few months, but she's already the leading salesgirl at Feld's. Mayumi says she could sell a fish to a fishmonger."

"We should all be so lucky," his uncle said.

Over by the racks of clothes, Goldie was fingering the massive satins and silks. Every single color was lush and rich, from pink pastels to deep reds to jewel-like greens and blues. Some of the fabrics were printed. Others had intricate embroidered designs, some as large and grand as sunbursts and peacocks, others tiny and fine, like butterflies and pea-sized flowers. Goldie felt as if Henry's woodblock prints had come to life. "How do they feel on your body?" she asked Mayumi.

"When I wear one I feel like an actor in a show."

Goldie kept her eyes on the kimonos, but she put her hand on her friend's shoulder, drawing her closer. "That's how you need to feel in anything that's beautiful," she told Mayumi. "My mother used to tell me that you don't wear an outfit, you perform in it. That's our art."

Uncle Aki, hearing her, called across the room. "Let her try one, Mayumi. Let's see her perform."

Goldie picked a silk in deep green with clusters of gold and purple dragonflies racing up one side, along the back of the shoulders, and down the arm. As Mayumi helped her slip the heavy fabric over her clothes, Goldie felt a sudden, inexplicable joy and with it a sense of her own hardiness. There was so much beauty in the world, she thought. Alan Stevenson could love a girl like her. And if he didn't, she thought of Marvin Feld, the son of the owners, a merchant marine over there in Europe. People said he'd be back in San Francisco any day. And Marvin Feld was rich *and* Jewish. Goldie closed her eyes while Mayumi finished the wrapping and secured the belt behind her back. Gently, Mayumi led her to the mirror. From behind her, Goldie heard the admiring voices of the men. "Open your eyes!" Henry called. Anything can happen, Goldie thought, and then she opened them.

8

Beyond Expectations

One morning in June of 1941, Marvin Feld strolled into the store with his father, hands in the pockets of his navy trousers, jiggling change. The entire staff of Feld's watched, transfixed, as the young man moved through the showroom, shaking hands with the employees he knew from the past. More recently hired salespeople, like Goldie, had heard of Marvin, too. They knew that he had served as chief engineer on a merchant marine Liberty ship. Now, finally, he was appearing in their midst, the crown prince in an argyle sweater.

Goldie was impressed. She had no idea what a chief engineer would do, but the work must have been dangerous and important. From where she stood observing him, she decided that he had William Powell's sophistication combined with Clark Gable's good looks. A more objective observer might have quibbled with the comparison to Gable (Marvin was fair skinned and big boned rather than dark and lanky), but he did have a pencil-thin moustache, snappy clothes, and one of those grand smiles that movie star fan magazines called "ravishing."

Goldie was selling women's scarves that morning. Her position near the front of the store offered a fine perspective for viewing the young man's movements. The anticipation of Marvin Feld's arrival had, in recent weeks, thrown Goldie into something of a tizzy. Her social life, which had continued at a frenetic pace, had worn her down. In one week, she had turned down two proposals of marriage, one from a man who was so shy he could barely speak (he had resorted to mumbling when he finally made his offer, forcing her to ask him to repeat what he'd just said) and another from a man who suffered from impossibly bad breath. Both of those men were kind, and good prospects, but the idea of spending her life with either one had done nothing but depress her. Alan Stevenson had also taken her out two more times, but neither of their dates had moved them any closer toward a proposal, and consequently Goldie had begun to feel more certain that he was toying with her until he found someone better.

Marvin Feld, though, was a Jew himself, and likely to marry one. Only one other woman on the staff was Jewish, and as Irma Manheim was nearly sixty, Goldie felt that she herself had little competition in the store. She was also confident of her own charms and felt that if she could get Marvin Feld to notice her, he would surely ask her out. Many of the other salesgirls, despite being Christian, had similar ideas. All through the store, women were ducking behind cabinets and hiding behind racks of clothes, reapplying lipstick and smoothing back their hair. Goldie slid her hands inside the waist of her skirt to straighten her blouse.

"And ladies scarves is looking robust, eh?"

Having kept her eye on the two men as they wandered through the store, Goldie turned away when she saw them heading her way. She stood on her toes, lifting a hanger full of scarves up beside another. Then, just as they approached, she turned and said, as if surprised, "Well, hello, Mr. Feld."

The older Mr. Feld was a small, somewhat hesitant man who often wandered absently through the showroom. His own father, Meyer Feld, had founded the business fifty years earlier, and longtime employees suggested that Herbert Feld, who would have preferred architecture, was not so much a visionary himself as a placeholder between Meyer and his grandson. The reappearance of Marvin in San Francisco seemed to signal that the transition to the next generation had finally begun. "Hello, Miss—" Herbert looked at her questioningly.

"Goldie, sir," she said, stretching out her Memphis drawl. "Goldie Rubin." She had to hit the bull's-eye, so she emphasized both her Jewish name and her southern charms. She tucked her chin under and smiled up at Marvin.

"Ah, yes," said his father. "Marvin, this is Miss Goldie Rubin. One of our newest, and most productive, salesgirls."

"Oh, sir, you flatter me!" Goldie knew she didn't have the coloring for blushes, so she put a finger to her cheek instead.

Marvin Feld looked down at the new salesgirl standing in front of him. He had not looked forward to reappearing at the store, and just as he had expected, the staff had made an embarrassing fuss over welcoming him home. The attentions were kind and well meaning, he knew, but they only increased his uneasiness at being back at all. The truth was that Marvin had loved the thrills and independence he'd discovered in Europe, despite the fact that a war was taking place there. Perhaps more precisely, he had enjoyed the distance his year in the service had provided between himself and his parents, who had expectations for their only child that Marvin felt less and less capable of fulfilling as time went by. This young woman caught his attention, however. Miss Rubin had an accent that sounded familiar to him. Then he remembered how Hefferton, a muscular second mate, had drawled in much the same way, stretching out vowels and dropping consonants at the ends of words. "Where are you from, Miss Rubin?" he asked.

For the moment, his eyes focused on her. Goldie said, "Why, I'm from Memphis, Tennessee. Do you know Memphis?"

He shook his head. Hefferton, as he remembered, came from Mississippi. "It's an accent I recognize. I met a lot of southerners during my time overseas."

While Marvin's eyes remained on Goldie, she thought quickly about what to do next. She had learned very early how to read the attentions of men. This man, to her immediate disappointment, looked at her with a complete lack of appreciation for her physical charms. On the other hand, he seemed curious enough to pause for a moment and hear what she had to say.

"Some people consider southerners to have our own distinctive culture," she said. Goldie refrained from batting her eyelashes, because part of her skill lay in knowing where to draw the line. Anyway, he didn't seem to be the sort of man who would be moved by that technique. "I've heard so much about Europe," she said, adding, "One day I'd like to visit there myself."

"Hopefully, not while the war is going on," he said with a laugh. "The cities are beautiful, though, of course, nothing compares to our beloved San Francisco." Marvin's eyes swept the showroom as if, from inside the department store, he could look out across the hills toward the Golden Gate.

At this point, sensing that Herbert Feld was inclined to drift away, Goldie hurried forward with her plan. "Mr. Feld," she said, addressing the father. "I'm wondering if I might take a moment to speak with you about an issue in our fragrance department?"

Herbert paused. Despite his disinterest in business, he liked to follow the latest trends, and all the magazines were talking about "employee input."

"Why certainly, Miss—" He had forgotten her name again.

"Rubin."

"Miss Rubin. What's on your mind?"

"Sir, I've noticed that we've been selling an awful lot of a new scent called Pioneer. Actually, we sold more Pioneer last week than all our other perfumes combined."

"Is that so?"

"It's extremely popular." Goldie left the scarves behind and led the two men over to fragrance. There, Hollis had decided to climb a footstool and buff the brass ornaments in the center of the display, no doubt hoping that the sight of her shapely body would catch the attention of Marvin Feld.

Goldie was all business, though. It was one thing to look good— Goldie noted that Hollis had readjusted the buttons on her blouse to reveal a few more inches of chest as well—but you had to show your smarts, too. In her thoughts, Goldie said to Hollis, *I'm Jewish. He won't be interested in you.* but in manner she ignored the girl completely. She pulled open a drawer and picked up a box of Pioneer. "Do you know this scent?" she asked, looking up at the father and son.

Marvin shook his head. He didn't even like cologne.

Herbert said, "It must have just arrived."

"It's fairly new," said Goldie. In truth, they'd been carrying the product for a month already, but she didn't want to embarrass the owner of the store. She handed them the box, the front of which featured an image of a farm girl who stood, hand on her hip, blowing a little horn toward the distant fields. "It's a reproduction of a lovely painting by Winslow Homer called 'The Dinner Horn,'" Goldie explained. She was sincere in her appreciation of the artwork, though its effect on her did not compare with her profound affection for Japanese prints. "It's an American scent, so they used an American picture."

Marvin studied the box. "And you say it's providing some competition for the European brands?" he asked.

"Oh, immensely," said Goldie, who had figured that given Marvin Feld's military experience, he'd feel loyal to his country. Personally,

Goldie found Pioneer too cloying. She liked a more complex scent and believed that the French, with their experience, made a better product. In fact, the week Pioneer had first appeared on the shelves, she and Mayumi had gotten into an argument about the new perfume, and taste in general. Though neither girl liked Pioneer, they had different explanations for its popularity. "People around here like a sweet perfume," Mayumi had said. "You can't choose what you love."

"Sure you can," Goldie had replied. On this point, she felt certain. The two had been standing behind the perfume counter, comparing Pioneer with their own favorites. Up to now, Goldie had taken only French scents seriously, and she felt that the appeal of Pioneer had more to do with patriotism than anything else. "I made a conscious decision," she said. "I decided to love Madeleine Vionnet and to hate Schiaparelli," she said.

"No, you like feminine things, so you like Vionnet."

"But why do I like feminine things?" asked Goldie. "Because I *decided* that I would be a feminine lady. Your style is more Schiaparelli, and you made that choice, too."

Mayumi looked up at her. She seemed equally positive about what she was saying. "I did not," she said.

"You did."

Now, though, Goldie was ready to gush over Pioneer. She looked up at Marvin Feld. "Would you like to try the scent?" she asked. She never suggested that someone "smell" a perfume. She asked them to "try" it.

"Why not?" Marvin said.

The son was intrigued, but the father seemed ready to wander off. Now, Goldie threw out her hint in an offhand way. "It's too bad we don't have a more prominent display for this fragrance. It's such an American scent." She turned her gaze to the elder Mr. Feld. "I wish there were some occasion that we could use to promote it."

Though Herbert Feld cared nothing for the products themselves, Goldie knew from past experience that he had a passion for presentation. At Easter he had turned the display stand behind cosmetics into an arrangement of painted cardboard eggs and bunnies, which was so trite and offensive to Mayumi's aesthetic sensibility that she had told Mr. Blankenship she was tempted to quit. "What did you have in mind?" Mr. Feld asked, focusing more intently.

Goldie picked up the sample bottle. She held it in her hand for a moment, feigning contemplation. "It's the scent, they say, of 'lazy afternoons, prairie grass, and wild rose.' It's so nice. Is there some occasion that we could tie it to this summer?"

The elder Feld's eyes widened. "The Fourth of July!"

Goldie thought, *Bingo!* She said, "Mr. Feld, that's an excellent idea."

The father hurried off to find Mr. Blankenship. The son remained, waiting to sample the fragrance. Goldie sensed Hollis only a foot or two away, glaring at her, but she ignored the girl. "Let's see what you think," she said. She pumped the perfume a couple of times onto the inside of her wrist, then waved her hand through the air for a moment to let it dry. Marvin Feld watched her, thinking how pleased his parents would be if he ever became so enthused about a brand of perfume. Finally Goldie lifted her hand to his nose. He touched two fingers to the back of her wrist and inhaled.

It took three more weeks—until just before the Fourth of July—for Goldie to finally go out with Marvin Feld, and even that was not a "date." Up until that point, Goldie had tried to put herself in his presence at every opportunity without appearing to be chasing him. Conveniently, the Pioneer perfume Fourth of July promotion presented regular opportunities. Goldie and Marvin were both assigned to the team that produced it, Goldie through assisting Mayumi on the Independence Day windows and Marvin in his new position as vice president for marketing.

Marvin threw himself into the project with determination, if not with relish. Less than a month had passed since he had been wandering the streets of London. His parents seemed to have assumed that by returning to San Francisco, packing up his uniform, and changing into civilian clothes, Marvin had become once more the son they had known before he joined the service. His father, fondly mussing the young man's hair, had said, "Glad to have you back, my boy. Now we can get on with things," while his mother had surprised him with a furnished apartment on Vallejo Street, only a mile or so from his parents' house. Herbert and Madeleine Feld seemed to expect their son to slip right back into his former life, with mornings in marketing meetings at the store downtown, then afternoons at the golf club at Lake Merced. Saturdays, they would sail, and on Sunday nights they would dine at the Tadich Grill. Marvin had been gone a year, however, and he had returned from duty feeling profoundly changed. He had traveled widely, experienced moments of great fear and exhilaration, and become, he felt, a man at last. His parents didn't seem to see that. Perhaps, he thought, the success of the Pioneer perfume campaign would force them to recognize that he had grown up.

Throughout the second half of June, life for everyone involved in the promotion became a hectic jumble of activities. July Fourth fell on a Friday that year, so they would unveil their windows on the Tuesday before. Mayumi had designed three windows for the event, each one meant to evoke a sublime moment of summer. The first, based on the painting by Homer, featured a pastoral scene of green grass, wildflowers, and a blond mannequin in a simple cotton dress, holding up her little trumpet. In the second window, three male mannequins in seersucker suits rowed a pretty young woman across an expanse—the girls had bunched shimmering taffeta into rippling waves—of deep blue water. The third window, Goldie's favorite, offered a pair of lovers. The girl sat on a swing, her head thrown back in delight, while the boy stood behind, gently pushing her into the air.

The campaign demanded an immense amount of work, which meant that Goldie spent little time actually out on the showroom floor. Instead, she filled her days consulting with Mayumi, ordering and purchasing supplies, reporting back to Marvin, appeasing the petulant Rochelle at home, and most importantly, arriving at work every morning looking both fashionable and, despite her lack of sleep, well rested. Goldie found all this activity stimulating in a way that was new to her. Her memories of childhood included few moments of joy or abandon. Even here in San Francisco, her energy remained focused on her ultimate goal of finding the right man to marry. As a consequence, despite a busy social schedule, she didn't actually have much fun. Putting together the Pioneer display led Goldie to discover that she had skills and talents she had never recognized. She could help to devise and execute a complicated plan; she could work tirelessly without losing heart; she had a practical side that helped her distinguish between what was possible and what was not; she got along well with other people. And to top it all off, she loved the whole process.

They did have some technical problems, the most serious of which revolved around the challenge of making the swing in the third window actually look as if it was flying through the air. This effect demanded engineering skills beyond the capability of either Mayumi or Goldie. Consequently, the night before the windows would be revealed, they enlisted Marvin, and even Henry, to help construct an elaborate system of hooks and fishing wire that, in the end, created the illusion of defied gravity. "I feel like we're putting on a show!" Goldie exclaimed happily as all four of them congregated in the small space of the window. She remembered seeing a film in which a group of teenagers had taken over a rural barn to produce a musical review.

"Thank God the newspaper doesn't have a critic for window displays," said Marvin, who was standing on a ladder, anxiously appraising the papier-mâché sun he had just attached to the ceiling. Though he cared nothing for the perfume, he was quite worried that any little glitch would undermine his effort to establish his competency in the eyes of his parents.

The four of them had been working in the lovers' window for the past two hours. They had painted the walls a cottony blue, and bright green artificial grass now covered three-quarters of the floor. Mayumi worked ahead of Goldie, cutting the turf into squares and pressing them neatly into place. Goldie followed, securing tiny silk wildflowers into the flooring with hidden thumbtacks. In the doorway, Henry sat on a folding chair with wire and pliers, the swing upside down on his lap.

Goldie said, "If this were a movie, I'd want to play the Myrna Loy character, like in *The Thin Man*." She looked over at Mayumi. "Who are you?"

Mayumi didn't bother to look up from the grass she was cutting. "I don't exactly look like any of those girls," she reminded Goldie.

Henry said, "She'd have to play the vamp."

Goldie pushed another flower into the lawn. "You're not a vamp," she said. "You're more like the girl next door."

"You can't be the girl next door and be Japanese," Henry replied. He stopped what he was doing to look at Goldie. It continually surprised him that a girl could be so bright and at the same time so obtuse.

But Goldie barreled forward. "I forget that Mayumi is Japanese," she insisted. "There's nothing at all about her that's Japanese. That's just silly."

Henry picked up his pliers again. "Rose-colored glasses," he muttered.

"Honestly!" Goldie exclaimed.

"Honestly, Goldie," Henry replied, more firmly. "Everyone doesn't see things the way you do."

Goldie remembered Marvin then, above them on the ladder. "Do you care?" she asked. On some level, she was aware that, in her plan to snare the son of the owner of Feld's, she was asking a pertinent question. Would he, as a Jew, marry a Jew himself, or would he consider a Jew beneath him? She needed to know if she had any hope of success with him. At least that's what she told herself. Oddly, though, Goldie often forgot about Marvin altogether. Now, for example, her attention focused on Henry. She needed him to respect what she was saying and to understand that she was right and he was wrong. People could forget about heritage, or race, or money. "It's the person," she asserted, "not the background."

Marvin, who was securing the last piece of wire to a hidden nail, agreed with Goldie. "Those divisions are old-fashioned," he said. Despite his experience in a war with a very clear enemy, he prided himself on being able to judge each person as an individual. "This is nineteen forty-one. Our parents might care, but we're more modern than they are." On the whole, though, Marvin was more focused on the technical problems with the window than on this conversation. Leaning back a couple of inches to get a better look at the sun, he asked, "Do you think it's straight? Does it look a little crooked?"

Mayumi, making calculations for the next set of grass squares on a piece of scratch paper, wasn't listening to any of them. Henry glanced up. "It's fine," he said, but he couldn't focus on the sun. "Each person comes from a particular background," he told Goldie. "You can't separate yourself from that."

"Of course you can," she insisted. She had no intention of getting personal here, but her own life offered proof of her contention. Otherwise, how would a poor girl from Memphis end up spending the evening with the children of a Japanese baron and the son of the owner of a famous department store?

Henry became exasperated. "Don't you see what's going on in the world?" he asked. "People are killing each other over race. Look at what the Germans are doing to the Jews. Look at the Japanese and the Chinese. You want to just ignore that?"

Goldie looked at Henry. He seemed so serious, and she couldn't very well shrug off the destruction taking place around the world. But did the bloodshed in Asia and Europe mean that people couldn't be happy together right here? "If a German walked in here right now, do you think he'd try to kill me?" she asked.

Henry closed his eyes for a moment. He couldn't argue with Goldie in any conventional way because she never used conventional tactics. When he opened his eyes, he saw that she was looking at him quite seriously, her eyes wide open and waiting. She really wanted him to answer her.

"I don't know," he sighed. "I don't think so."

"The Japanese and Germans are allies," she said. "The Germans hate the Jews. Do the Japanese hate the Jews?" At this moment, two Jews and two Japanese were peacefully occupying one very small space.

Henry scowled. Goldie was so simplistic.

"Do they?" she asked. "Do they?"

"No!" he finally responded, feeling completely annoyed. "How should I know? I don't hate the Jews," and the admission seemed so suddenly personal and irrelevant to his larger contention that he looked down at the swing in his lap and turned his focus to it entirely.

Mayumi, who hadn't even been listening, jumped in suddenly, her satisfaction over the look of the window translating into an overall delight. "I love Jews," she said, picking up Goldie's hand and kissing it.

"That's very flattering," Marvin sighed, "but we'll be here all night and this window will still be a disaster."

At that moment, the store manager, Mr. Blankenship, opened the small wooden door that connected the display window to the store itself, and stepped inside. An Englishman, he was middle-aged, slight in stature, and so formal and well mannered that everyone, even the Feld family themselves, found him intimidating. "I'd like to see what you've accomplished after all the time you've spent in here," he said. His voice was soft, his words inconsequential. What mattered was not what he said when he walked in the door, but what he said after he'd looked around. More than anyone else involved with Feld's, Mr. Blankenship served as the arbiter of what would sell and what would not. For a long moment, he allowed his eyes to move over every detail, from the tiny flowers that Goldie had attached to the floor to the sun shining brightly now from the upper corner. Mayumi and her team of helpers waited.

Finally Mr. Blankenship turned, opened the little door, and ducked his head again to go out, but not before offering his assessment in words that were almost too flat and uninflected to be audible. "It will do," he told them.

The next morning, Mr. Blankenship proved himself correct, if perhaps guilty of understatement. The butcher paper that covered the windows came down to wild applause. People stopped on the street to look, pointing at the scenes and discussing their construction with all the serious attention that Goldie had seen among art aficionados at the museum in Golden Gate Park. At the perfume counter, Herbert Feld himself—that lover of architecture—had constructed a Pioneer display on an elaborate steel-and-wire contraption that Henry, whispering in Goldie's ear, described as "a covered wagon done in the style of the Eiffel Tower."

They sold more Pioneer that day than they had sold in the perfume's entire existence, and though Marvin had ordered ten additional cases, they quickly ran out. Inside the store, a team of salesgirls served free lemonade from punch bowls and passed around plates of sugar cookies with red, white, and blue icing. Within a couple of hours, the air for several blocks up and down Market Street would reek with the scent of lazy afternoons, prairie grass, and wild rose.

It was Herbert Feld, enjoying the role of magnanimous employer, who came up with the idea of rewarding the young people for a job well done. "Marvin," he said, "take these kids out for an afternoon on the yacht, why don't you?"

Marvin, suddenly feeling awkward, looked at the others on his team. "Is that something that would even interest you?" he asked.

Goldie had kept herself free for the evening in hopes that an invitation might be forthcoming, but she had never dreamed that she might go out on a yacht. She looked at Mayumi, who looked at her brother. Henry glanced at his watch. "What time were you thinking?" he asked.

Herbert Feld's attention had wandered toward a couple of businessmen who seemed to be admiring his covered wagon. "Take the rest of the day off, girls!" he said, already moving across the showroom floor.

Goldie had never taken a boat ride in her life, though she didn't admit it. Over the past few weeks, she had carefully measured out her revelations about her background. If Marvin Feld did turn out to seriously consider her for marriage, he would have to know that she came from nothing. On the other hand, she didn't want her poverty to put him off so completely that he would never take her seriously as a potential bride. Thus she had presented herself to him as a "southern gal who grew up on the farm," while at the same time frequently mentioning how much she had learned about fashion and good taste from her very elegant mother. When Marvin invited them out on his yacht, then, she simply replied, "That sounds lovely."

The sailboat was moored in a marina a mile or two east of the Golden Gate Bridge. Gingerly, Mayumi and Goldie, who were still in their heels, followed Marvin and Henry along the main pier and down another smaller one until they reached the boat. Goldie had imagined a boat like the ones she had seen in photographs of the duke and duchess of Windsor, who seemed to spend a lot of time drinking champagne on yachts in the Bahamas. This boat, which Marvin called a "sloop," was a simpler craft, far too small for any kind of royal party, but Goldie was still impressed. It was about twenty feet long, with cushion-covered benches lining the deck and a cabin with three round windows in it. On the back of the boat, painted in a swirling cursive, was the name *Bella Vista.*

From where they stood on the pier, Goldie could see not only the Golden Gate Bridge, but also the Marin Headlands, Alcatraz Island, and a huge swath of the city stretching across the hills behind them. "I could stay right here," she sighed, "and be happy." She did not want to admit that the idea of boarding the boat was making her nervous. She didn't see a gangplank. How would she climb on?

The others were already in motion. Marvin grabbed a rope, pulled the boat toward them, and made a graceful leap aboard. Then he tugged on another rope to bring the craft toward the pier. "Careful now," he said. Slowly, the boat moved closer. Henry stepped across and landed easily on the deck, then turned around, took his sister's hand, and helped her on board. He waited for Goldie.

Goldie pulled her sweater tighter around her shoulders. The sky was bright, but the wind blew hard, knocking the ropes against the mast. Out on the bay, would she feel even colder?

Marvin, squatting on the ground with the ropes, looked up at her. Goldie's nervousness reminded him of his own good fortune—how many young people grew up sailing on a family yacht?—which in turn gave an added gentleness to his encouragement. "Don't worry, Goldie. We've got blankets on board."

Mayumi, who had quickly gotten her footing, eagerly strode up and down the deck before ducking into the cabin and disappearing. A moment later, she reappeared. "The blankets are *fur*!" she said.

Henry and Marvin waited. Goldie looked at Marvin. This was a moment when he might reach his hand out and grasp her fingers, but he had to hold the ropes tightly to keep the boat from drifting.

"Your turn, Goldie," Henry said.

By pulling hard, Marvin could bring the boat to within inches of the pier, but just as quickly it would tip against the surge of a wave and drift away again. At some moments the gap between the boat and the pier would widen to a foot. Goldie looked down warily. The bay itself was a steely gray, but the water here looked black. "I can't swim," she said.

Marvin was patient, but holding the boat steadily against the pier put a strain on his arms. Henry said, "Goldie, first pull your shoes off. Then take my hand."

Goldie would rather have jumped in the water than pull off her shoes in front of these men, but she could hardly explain that to Henry or Marvin. Instead she stood frozen, watching the rocking boat. After a moment, it eased in closer. "Now!" Marvin said. Goldie reached out and took Henry's hand. Her left foot stepped off the pier and landed firmly on the deck. Instantly her other foot followed. "Oh, my goodness," she gasped. "I made it!" She looked down and laughed when she saw how hard she'd been gripping Henry's hand.

They sailed east toward Oakland. Marvin, who was the only one who knew how to sail, put Henry on the tiller for a couple of minutes so that he could duck down the steps and scrounge up some drinks. He came back with a tray of glasses, a flask of rum, and some bottles of Coca-Cola. "Sorry I don't have more to offer," he said. "My mother usually stocks the galley better."

"But this is divine," Goldie responded, employing an adjective that felt particularly aristocratic. She and Mayumi each accepted a cola. While the young men sat near the rudder, the girls huddled together on the cushioned bench, curled under the fur blankets, the existence of which Goldie planned to emphasize when she described her afternoon to Rochelle.

The whole city of San Francisco lay in front of them. Marvin pointed out famous sites: the Fairmont Hotel, the Bay Bridge, Coit

Tower alone on the top of Telegraph Hill. Except for the time that she had climbed that hill, Goldie had never seen such a view. "The city makes more sense from here," she said. "I can see how things relate to each other."

"Henry and I live way over that way," said Mayumi, tossing her hand through the air as if she were trying to lob a ball toward the tea garden in Golden Gate Park.

"Where do you live, Marvin?" Goldie asked. She had yet to think of Marvin when she lay in bed contemplating her future, but she expected that she would tonight. Knowing the location of his home might help to better illuminate him in her imagination.

"Up that way." He gestured vaguely toward a hill just west of downtown. "And my parents live farther in that direction." He was too modest to be specific, but Mayumi and Henry understood that he was pointing to two exclusive neighborhoods: Nob Hill and Pacific Heights.

"Where do I live?" Goldie asked.

Henry pointed up toward Marvin's parents' part of town. "You live that way, but down the hill on the other side."

"My sister Rochelle calls it 'Pacific Lows,'" Goldie told them.

Marvin Feld watched Goldie. She seemed so alive and fresh, so open to the world. He envied her ability to joke about her situation. In his own life, he felt uncomfortable about the fact that he had been born into wealth. Except for his military service, of which he was very proud, he felt he had done nothing of value with his life. As a result, he was self-conscious and at the same time annoyed at himself for caring about such things. Why couldn't he be more easygoing? Why couldn't he laugh at himself, like Goldie did?

Mayumi saw the look on Marvin's face and glanced at Henry, who had noticed, too. Riding home on the bus the night before, Mayumi had said, "He's going to fall in love with her." Henry had disputed it. He didn't have any evidence to prove his sister wrong, but he had argued with her anyway. Now he couldn't miss the expression of admiration in Marvin's face. Mayumi gazed at her brother with satisfaction. "See?" she seemed to be saying. "I told you."

Henry, irritated, ignored his sister. "Well, look over there!" he said, his tone perhaps a bit more impassioned than he intended. "Now that's an embarrassing address." After passing the big piers of Fisherman's Wharf and the Embarcadero, they had veered north to loop around Alcatraz. Henry pointed toward the island, which had thousands of sea birds soaring over it.

Goldie sat up straighter. She had heard of the famous prison but of course had never seen it so close. "That's where the gangsters live?" she asked.

"Machine Gun Kelly's in there," said Henry, who felt the need to dominate the conversation now.

"Oh!" said Goldie. "He comes from Memphis, too."

Mayumi lit up. "Really? Have you heard anything juicy about him?"

Goldie put a note of drama into her voice. "I can remember when I was about thirteen or fourteen years old. That's when they captured him. The papers had so many stories about it. He was visiting a friend, and the police surrounded the house. They had an enormous bloody shoot-out." She raised a hand to shield her eyes from the sun, then looked up toward the forbidding buildings stretched across the rock. "Now, here I am. Hello, Machine Gun!" she called, waving gaily.

Goldie was nearly as happy as she could be, but the swing around Alcatraz had put them into choppy waters. Mayumi began to look queasy. Goldie put her hand on Mayumi's cheek. "You're pale," she said.

"I think," said Mayumi, shakily standing up, "that I'm going to lie down in the cabin."

Henry and Goldie jumped up to take Mayumi's arms. "Should we head back?" Goldie asked.

Mayumi shook her head. "Absolutely not," she told them. "I'd have to be dying."

Downstairs, the space was divided into a couple of tiny bedrooms and the main cabin, which contained the kitchen area. Goldie felt a flash of disappointment over the less than opulent interior. The fabric on the seat cushions was a simple blue-and-white nautical stripe. The table was built into the wall, and the only lighting came from a row of simple sconces. Goldie had only just begun her ascent from poverty, so she had not developed an ability to read the subtler signs of great wealth—handcrafted woodwork, cotton slipcovers imported from London, antique brass fixtures purchased off the Cunard *Franconia* when it had been converted into a troop ship a few years earlier. Still, she reminded herself as she held Mayumi's arm, they were sailing on a *yacht*.

Henry and Goldie helped Mayumi onto one of the bunks, then spread a blanket over her. Henry found a wastebasket in the galley and put it next to Mayumi, "just in case." Then they closed the door behind them.

"Look!" Goldie said. From the cushion-covered bench, they could peer out through the porthole at Alcatraz. She paused there, curled up on her knees, and looked out toward the island. "It's a whole different perspective from here," she said.

Henry sat down beside her. For weeks, clusters of unfocused feelings had been fluttering through his head, and the conversation up on deck had suddenly caused them to coalesce. He felt as if his vision, once so fuzzy, had become absolutely clear. From this angle, the prison looked even more oppressive. "Sometimes the prisoners try to escape," he said. "They know they'll probably die trying, but they'd rather die than stay there."

For a long moment, neither of them said a word. Goldie imagined those angry, lonely men, up on that rock, behind those bars. "What do you suppose they think about when they're in there?" she asked.

He said, "Freedom. Love."

"They think about love?" Goldie's face nearly touched the glass.

Henry, too, pressed closer. "They're human. All humans think about love."

They think about love? For what seemed her entire life, Goldie had plotted incessantly about her future, her prospects, the material comforts that she needed from the world, but she had never thought about love. And so it was at this moment, in the expensive simplicity of the cabin of Marvin Feld's family yacht, that for the first time Goldie Rubin considered love. And it was here, too, that she knew the answer to a question she hadn't even thought to ask: Henry? Henry. The adjustment was surprisingly simple. An observer could have attributed it to the boat rising on the crest of a wave, or maybe it was something else. Indisputably, Goldie shifted the angle of her head and Henry shifted his. Their cheeks touched. At that moment, on that finely upholstered bench, the Japanese San Franciscan and the Memphis Jew froze, their warm cheeks against each other. Behind the door on the spacious bunk, Mayumi Nakamura had fallen asleep. Up on deck, Marvin Feld closed his eyes, felt the sun on his forehead, and thought of someone he'd met in Europe. Down below, Henry's hand moved up Goldie's back, slipped into her hair, and slowly turned her head toward his. They kissed.

Part
Three

9

Not a Place to Die

*C*ameron Memorial Community Hospital occupied a prominent spot in downtown Angola, Indiana, a Middle American mini-metropolis of red brick and antiques, Civil War statuary, and Wal-Mart. In architectural style, the hospital echoed the bland modernity of the Hampton Inns that Goldie and Anna had been staying in so regularly since they left New York, which might explain why Anna was sleeping so soundly on the waiting room sofa when, sometime in the night, a doctor had to wake her up.

"Ms. Rosenthal?" he asked.

She opened her eyes, remembered that her grandmother had fallen into a suitcase, and immediately sat up. "Sorry," she said. Beside her on the couch lay the scattered sketches that she had completed, in a frantic spasm of creativity, earlier in the night. Now she shuffled them together and folded them into a pile, which she stuck beneath her leg while straightening her skirt. Was it almost morning? Outside the window the sky had turned a deep violet. Hours earlier, emergency room doctors had taken X-rays, which hadn't revealed any fractures, but they had decided to check Goldie into the hospital anyway. Anna's father had been on the phone with her off and on the whole night, and he recognized that her panic, combined with her guilt about the earlier argument with Goldie, was making it hard for her to function at all. Finally, at about 3 A.M., he had counseled her to leave the hospital, drive around the block a couple of times, then come back. Somehow the change of setting had helped. When she came back inside, she completed a few more drawings before lying down on the waiting room couch and falling asleep.

This doctor was a dark-skinned Indian man, maybe in his forties, with glasses and a buzz cut. He looked down at her, his eyes tired, his expression blank. "I'm Dr. Choudary," he said. "I'm the hospital-ist taking over your grandmother's case."

The indirectness of his phrasing—her grandmother's "case" in-stead of simply her grandmother—made Anna's stomach tighten. Had something terrible happened over the past couple of hours? Anna dug into her skirt pocket for her cell phone. "Can you just wait? I need to call my dad. Shit. Where's my phone?"

"No, it's okay. Her condition is not life threatening," he told her, but though this information clearly relieved her, she remained deter-mined to find her phone. The doctor sat down on the sofa beside her, letting his head fall back and closing his eyes.

Now, with a feeling that she was holding up a busy man, Anna fumbled even more fruitlessly through her purse. She hadn't been inside an emergency room since the last time Ford became dehy-drated. Even though only a couple of years had passed, she had lost her competency in medical surroundings. She had once been good at it. Over the course of his illness, she had become so acutely at-tuned to his condition that she could know by the look in his eyes and the color of his skin that she needed to get him to the hospital. Back then, she could help him to the car, grab herself a book and a snack and her sketchbook, and have them settled in at the Method-ist emergency room within twenty minutes. Now, she couldn't even find her phone. "I'm sorry," she muttered. "I'm so out of it."

The doctor opened his eyes like someone waking from a nap. He saw that she was ready to listen. "It's not a problem," he said, sitting up. "We have phones." He looked through the notes on his clipboard. "She's lucky that she doesn't have any fractures, but we have some concern that she may have developed a condition called rhabdomyolysis, which is the deterioration of skeletal muscle."

"From falling?"

"Not so much from falling as from lying in one position for so long, unable to move. The muscles break down, and in a very short time myoglobin is released into the blood. We're watching to see how the kidneys handle it because there's a potential for some damage there."

From the opposite wall, a picture of a giant sunflower smiley face stared out at Anna, its expression full of recrimination. "She was sitting there for hours," she said.

"I'm sure it was terrifying for her."

Anna's gaze dropped to the floor. All night she had been creeping around the fact of Goldie's trauma, moving closer, then veering away from it.

Perhaps the doctor sensed her guilt, because he quickly added, "She's not in pain now, and I haven't seen evidence of any serious problem. I just want to keep her here another day to conduct more tests. Given her age, it's best to be careful."

For the first time, Anna considered the possibility that the situation might not be as dire as she had thought. "It seemed so terrible," she said, as much to herself as to him.

"She'll be sore, but assuming we don't find anything serious, she should be fine."

Anna realized now that she had fully expected Goldie to die here. Once people reached their eighties, the slightest injury seemed to rocket them toward death. "I'm having a hard time processing this," she told him. "It's a miracle."

The doctor considered this assertion, then shook his head. "You could call it that, but she's in generally excellent health. I'd call it a lesson in the results of taking good care of oneself."

Anna began to relax. She leaned back against the couch and asked, "Where are you from?"

"Queens, New York. What about you?"

"Memphis."

He shook his head and pressed on. "No," he said. "Where are you *really* from, you know?"

She laughed, realizing that a dark-skinned man in rural Indiana must have people pressing him about his ethnic roots every day. "I guess maybe Eastern Europe."

"Yeah, you look like a European."

"Sorry," she said. "I bet it drives you crazy when people ask you that."

She loved the Indian nod—a slight tipping of the head, as unconcerned as a shrug—but this doctor nodded just like she did. He put his pen back into the pocket of his jacket and said, "I've more or less grown used to it."

Then he stood up, glancing at his watch, and became harried in the way that doctors usually did after the first few minutes. "Well, Ms. Rosenthal," he said, "we'll keep her here another night for observation, and if all goes well, you can be on your way."

Anna watched him go. She thought of Goldie, and then she thought of Ford, wishing that her husband had received such an optimistic prognosis. Medicine progressed so unevenly.

"It's a miracle," Goldie said into the telephone, reclining against the pillows in her hospital bed. "A Mir. A. Cle." The sun had come up fully now, and Anna had found her telephone on the floor of the car. Now they were talking to Anna's father in Memphis. "I was extremely lucky. I could have died, you know. I got up for water, felt dizzy, and the next thing I know I'm on the floor, stuck inside a suitcase." Goldie fingered the tray that held her breakfast. The room smelled of scrambled eggs and ammonia. The coffee in its plastic cup looked like a thin broth. "I don't have any fractures, just a Band-Aid on my arm. They're doing some tests and they gave me some Tylenol and I feel like a million bucks. Can you believe it?" She paused, listening to Anna's father, then responded to a question. "Vile. Absolutely vile. But it won't hurt me to diet for a couple of days. Here, talk to Anna."

Goldie held out the phone. "Hey," Anna said to her father.

"Crisis averted," he announced.

"Well, not exactly," she said, looking around the hospital room. Goldie's face was pale, her skin almost translucent. "It's not like we missed the turnoff but still found the right road."

"What are you talking about?" asked Goldie. She was sipping some orange juice through a straw.

"But she's going to be fine, right?" asked Anna's father. Not for the first time, Anna considered how lucky she was that Goldie was her grandparent, not her parent. Marvie, who had become quite successful in his law practice, had spent his entire adult life trying to appease his mother's disappointment over his failure to leave Memphis, take up residence in a "world-class city," and just generally live a more prominent life. Anna could hear the effect of that disappointment in the peculiar mix of anxiety and optimism that crept into Marvie's voice whenever he spoke of his mother. "She fell into a suitcase," he said now. "But she's going to be fine, right?"

"Probably," Anna said, realizing that she needed to soothe him. "Don't worry, Dad. We're trying to get her up on her feet."

"Tell him I'm trying to get up on my feet," Goldie said.

"We're waiting for the physical therapist to come. They'll see how she does."

"I'm ready to get out of here," Goldie announced, loudly enough that her son would hear her. "You could die in a place like this."

Anna's father seemed relieved. "Call me after the physical therapist comes by," he said.

After Anna hung up, Goldie said, "The pain was unbearable. Un. Bear. Able. You've never been through childbirth, but this was worse than childbirth. I was asking God to let me die."

Anna felt the muscles in her throat knot up, and she blinked to keep from crying. "I'm so sorry," she said.

Goldie took her hand. "Darling. It's not your fault. I live alone. This could have happened to me in New York and I would have been stuck there all night. You saved me." She seemed to have forgotten their argument completely.

Anna pulled a Kleenex out of a box on Goldie's bedside table and blew her nose. "You don't have suitcases on the floor in New York. I was so stupid."

"I was stupid," Goldie said, smoothing down the paper napkin on her chest. "Get over it. Anyway, I want to get out of here now. It's hospitals that will kill you." She took a bite of toast. "I'm not planning to die in a hospital, but if I did, it's not going to be—what's this place called?"

"Cameron Memorial."

"Cameron Memorial. I wouldn't die here."

Anna tossed the tissue into the trash. "Do you have an idea of a better hospital? Something more appropriate?"

Goldie held up her piece of toast, looking at it skeptically. "Memorial Sloan-Kettering."

"Isn't that a cancer center?" Anna had heard about it often enough during Ford's treatment, but she'd never been there.

"I don't know what it is. How should I know? But my friends built a wing there. Did I tell you that? Not a *bench*, but a *wing*. If you're going to die in a hospital, it should be a prominent one."

"I guess," Anna said. Ford hadn't died in a hospital. He died in their little bungalow on Waynoka Avenue.

Goldie set down her toast and tried to readjust herself on the pillows. Anna took her arm to help her. "Be careful," she said. "Don't wear yourself out."

"Don't boss me around. If I want to wear myself out, I'll wear myself out." Satisfied with her new position on the bed, Goldie brushed some crumbs off her hospital gown. "Mayo Clinic. Now you wouldn't be embarrassed about dying there."

"Can we change the subject?"

"What's wrong with talking about this subject? I can talk about whatever I want. I'm eighty-five."

After another few minutes, Goldie dozed off. When she woke, she was still thinking about hospitals. "You assume I know nothing because I've been so healthy," she told Anna, "but I almost died once. An ambulance had to come get me then, too. I know more than you think."

Anna had been curled in the squeaky fake leather armchair, paging through a months-old copy of *Entertainment Weekly* she'd found in the waiting room. She had completely forgotten that the night before Goldie had mentioned another experience with an ambulance. "What happened?" she asked.

"Hand me some water," Goldie said. Anna got up, poured some ice water out of a pitcher, and gave the cup to Goldie, who took a few sips through the straw. "I feel so thirsty in here," she muttered.

Anna said, "It's good to drink."

Goldie let her head ease back onto the pillow. "I hadn't even lived yet and I almost died. I was twenty years old, almost bled to death."

"How come you never told me?"

Goldie let her fingers flutter through the air. "Why talk about it?"

Anna sat back down. She had to handle this conversation carefully. If she asked the wrong question, or seemed too avidly nosy, her grandmother would shut down completely. "Were you in an accident?" she asked, casually paging through the magazine.

"Ha! Accidentally getting involved with the wrong man."

"Oh."

"I could have died. He drugged my ginger ale. Next thing I knew, well, a few weeks later I'm in a hospital bed, my stomach cut open and needles coming out of my arms. Could have died."

"From drugging your ginger ale?"

Goldie looked at her, exasperated. "Don't you understand anything? He drugged my ginger ale. Got me pregnant. I was so young I barely understood a thing. Then I started bleeding at work. I collapsed—*collapsed!*—behind the tie display. Then I had to have surgery, and I almost died in the hospital." She paused for a moment, then apparently decided that the story offered the type of lesson she was determined to impart. "That's why I worry about you so much. I don't want you to suffer like I did."

Anna had no interest in Goldie's advice, but she was deeply curious about her history. Somehow she kept her eyes on the magazine and was able to ask, as nonchalantly as someone inquiring about the weather, "Who was it?"

"I want your life to be better than mine was."

Anna looked up. "Have I heard his name?"

She should have known that her grandmother could not be distracted into saying more than she intended. An expression of annoyance crossed her face as she seemed to realize that Anna just wanted details. "How should I remember?" she asked, then picked up the television remote, squinted down at the buttons, and said, "Come on. It's time for *Judge Judy*."

10

Haiku

*L*ate in the afternoon, Goldie told Anna to leave for a while. She wanted to nap, she said, though Anna suspected that she really wanted privacy. Anna had brought her grandmother's cell phone, and though Goldie had carefully scanned her CALLS MISSED LOG, she had thus far followed the nurses' advice to "keep activity to a minimum." The Friends All Over the World would need a report, however, and Goldie would want to make that report herself. By four o'clock, she seemed unable to resist another minute. "I need to sleep," she said. Anna pretended to believe her, but as she picked up her backpack to go, she saw that Goldie's hand was already curled around the phone.

On the road back to the Hampton Inn, Anna spotted a movie theater. It depressed her to think of sitting in the empty hotel room alone, so she pulled into the cinema parking lot and bought a ticket for *Charlie and the Chocolate Factory*. On the way inside, she stopped by the snack bar for a Diet Coke, a bucket of popcorn, and Skittles.

The theater was empty except for one person sitting a few seats in from the aisle. It was Dr. Choudary. She could not pretend she didn't see him, because they were the only two people there. Anna walked over, suddenly sheepish about the amount of food in her hands. He was holding an apple.

"I guess you keep weird hours," she said.

He bounced the hand holding the apple against his leg. "I'm a doctor."

"Right."

"Do you care to sit down?"

It would have been rude to say no, so she sat, feeling ridiculous and annoyed. What were the chances that her only acquaintance in the entire state of Indiana would have decided to see *Charlie and the Chocolate Factory* at the same time she did? "How big is this town?" she asked.

"I don't know. Maybe ten thousand people."

"You want some popcorn?" She tilted the bucket toward him.

He looked down at it. It really was an awful lot of popcorn. "No, thanks," he said.

"It's too much for one person," Anna said, though she had no doubt that, sitting by herself, she would have gone right through it.

"How is your grandmother feeling?" he asked.

"She walked down the hall three times this afternoon. Now she's resting." She put a few kernels of popcorn in her mouth. They both stared at the screen, which flashed an ad for a local chiropractor.

"Did you read this book?" he asked.

"What book?"

"Charlie and the Chocolate Factory."

"Oh. Yeah. I love Roald Dahl."

"Me, too."

"What's your favorite?"

He thought for a moment. *"James and the Giant Peach,* I suppose. And yours?"

"Maybe *The Fantastic Mr. Fox.* I liked those farmers drinking apple cider and eating goose liver."

"Boggis and Bunce and Bean." He had seemed so serious, almost severe, but then again, a Roald Dahl fan had to have some capacity for delight. They both watched the screen for a while. Finally the lights went down. An announcement appeared: "In consideration of other patrons, please silence your cell phone." Anna's cell was already set to vibrate in her pocket. The doctor reached down into his satchel and switched his off.

"Can you do that?" Anna whispered. Her grandmother might need him.

"I'm not on call," he said.

They watched a couple of trailers.

"I think I should know your first name," he said, tipping his head in her direction while his eyes remained on the screen.

"Anna."

"Nice to meet you. I'm Naveen. People here call me Nathan, but you might prefer Naveen."

"Which do you prefer?"

"Naveen."

She leaned the popcorn toward him again. He reached into the bucket.

After the film ended, they sat in the theater until the lights came up, comparing the two movie versions of the book. "Johnny Depp is pretty freaky, but I miss the humanity of Gene Wilder," he said.

"'So shines a good deed in a weary world.'" The thought of that moment in the earlier film nearly brought Anna to tears.

He looked at her and smiled. "It seems we're both old-fashioned." A teenage theater attendant appeared with a broom, and they stood up and stepped out into the aisle. As they headed toward the exit, Naveen glanced in Anna's direction, and with more feeling in his voice than she'd heard before, said, "I'm terribly sorry for your grandmother's troubles, but it was a nice surprise to see you here."

Anna stopped, and for a moment they just looked at each other.

It seemed to Anna that any positive response would somehow come across as insensitive to Goldie, but the length of her silence caused such an awkwardness that he finally said, "Well, I guess I'd better be going." He turned away, moving with such speed that he looked like he was racing through the hospital with whole wards of patients wailing for his attention. Anna had to rush to keep up.

In the parking lot, they both stopped again. "Well," Anna said. Naveen watched her. "I don't suppose you'd want to have dinner together or something? I mean, obviously I don't have any plans." Goldie had accepted Anna's proposal to return to the hospital at around seven but had refused to let her stay the night. "Neither one of us will get any sleep," Goldie had said, "and besides, I need to make phone calls." The Friends All Over the World apparently needed constant updates on the suitcase drama and Goldie's ongoing condition.

Naveen looked at his watch.

"Don't worry about it if you're busy," Anna said hurriedly. "It was just an idea."

But he was calculating. "It's not yet six o'clock. I usually cook for myself because the food in this town is terrible. I'm just wondering if I would keep you up too late if I cooked something. You'd eat better, but go to sleep later." His tone sounded professional, as if he were cautioning a patient about risky behavior, but he did seem enthusiastic. She wondered if he was lonely here.

"I have to go check on my grandmother first anyway," she said.

He pulled out a prescription pad from his pocket and drew a little map. "My house is only over here. Maybe a mile or two."

She ran off toward Bridget, and when she reached the car and turned around, she saw him still standing on the curb, apparently trying to absorb the fact that she and Goldie had driven a Rolls-Royce to Indiana.

* * *

"Are you looking for a way to get out of here?" Anna asked him later. She had brought a little potted begonia from the hospital florist, and now she was sitting on a bar stool in front of his kitchen counter, idly pulling off the dead leaves.

The doctor stood facing her from the other side, pounding spices with a mortar and pestle. He had taken off his professional clothes and put on sandals, jeans, and a cream-colored version of the long, collarless cotton shirts that men seemed to favor in India. Earlier in the day, his face had conveyed an almost impossibly narrow range of expression, basically from serious to extremely serious. Now, though, in his own home, some barrier seemed to have come down, or perhaps she was just seeing him differently. His eyes, wide and nearly as black as the peppercorns in his mortar, registered, with a simple blink and lift of the brow, a complex tangle of emotion: fatigue and resignation mixed with hope for the future. "I've been here three years," he told her. "At first I felt like I was in exile because, you know, I'm from New York. It's a very good job and I've gotten used to this place, but yeah, I can't see spending the rest of my life in Indiana." Anna revised his age down to the late thirties.

The apartment complex lay on a busy street about a mile from the hospital. It was a warren of meandering lanes, each two-story townhouse exactly like the one beside it, with the exact same bush and the exact same little patch of lawn. Inside, the decor of the condo looked like something from Extended Stay America: sturdy gray couch, white rug, glass coffee table in a stained-wood frame. "Did this apartment come furnished or something?" Anna asked. Except for one plain set of shelves packed with books, the room looked almost completely anonymous.

He looked around. "Well, yeah, almost all of it came with the place." Everything seemed very clean, but she wondered if he had ever actually noticed the furniture. He asked, "Do you think it's really awful?"

She started to shake her head, then stopped. "It's not awful, but it doesn't have any personality."

"I guess I don't really care about decorating," he said.

She looked at the bookshelf. "You're a doctor. That takes a lot of concentration."

He shook his head. "It's a certain kind of concentration. You absorb a huge amount of information, but there's nothing subtle about it."

"I've heard medicine called an art."

"Maybe for some people. I think poetry's an art." He slid spices into a pan, and as they began to sizzle, the room filled with the aromas of cinnamon, cumin, and coriander.

"Are you a poet?" she asked.

"I write poetry."

"Why the verb and not the noun? Would you say that you practice medicine, but you're not a doctor?"

He stopped, pushing his glasses higher onto his nose with the back of his hand, keeping his eyes on the stove. Behind him, steam made the lid of the rice cooker begin to jiggle. "You need to have confidence to use the noun instead of the verb," he told her, tossing onions into the pan now. "I have more confidence in the way I practice medicine. And I have a degree."

"What kind of poetry do you write?"

He was moving quickly now, dropping handfuls of cauliflower in with the onions. He looked up. "Do you mind spicy?"

She shook her head.

He threw in a few pinches of something from a jar. "It's a kind of collage poetry. I use fragments of sentences and phrases that I pick up during the day, and I try to arrange them in ways that resonate. It's a rather chaotic method. I carry a little notebook with me and write down things that I find interesting." He looked up, sort of embarrassed. "I take a lot of notes at movies, actually, but I didn't this afternoon because I didn't want you to think I was odd."

Anna realized that he was probably as disappointed to see her in the cinema as she had been to see him. "You could have missed something profound because of me."

" 'So shines a good deed in a weary world,' " he reminded her, his eyes completely on her now.

Anna wove her fingers through the begonia. "My husband used to write poetry sometimes," she said. "For a while, he liked haiku, but then he read something about haiku being a cliché of Japanese poetry, so he stopped."

"That's like saying tabla is a cliché or jazz is a cliché."

"If you're not a poet," Anna reminded him, "it's easy to feel insecure."

"That's true," Naveen admitted. He lit another burner and began a dish that contained chicken and a few heaping tablespoons of a yellow spice. "And where is your husband now?" he asked.

Anna realized that if she didn't get her hands out of the begonia, she would kill it. She reached across the counter and picked up a pencil and a piece of paper by the phone, then began to draw the plant instead. "That's kind of an existential question," she said. "He had leukemia. He died two years ago."

She glanced up quickly to see his reaction. His expression didn't change, but his focus on her seemed to soften a bit. "I'm sorry," he said. "Does that explain why you're driving your grandmother across the country in a Rolls-Royce?"

"That's not her reason. She didn't like him. But maybe it's my reason. I'm in an in-between period. What do you call that?"

"Siesta."

"No. I think *purgatory* is a better word."

He poured some coconut milk onto the chicken, adjusted the heat, and then pulled a couple of beers out of the refrigerator. "Maybe it's best to call it a transition."

While they ate, Anna talked about Ford, not because Naveen had asked but because she felt compelled to recount what had happened, or at least most of what had happened. He listened closely. She could skip all the medical explanations, which made the tale flow much more quickly. In any case, though Ford's situation had been both sudden and incomprehensible to them, it had, from a doctor's perspective, unraveled in a way that was more or less routine. In other words, Naveen knew the story already.

They did the dishes together, then he put on a piano sonata and they sat on the sofa with fresh bottles of beer. "I hope you don't think that I planned to reveal all this when I invited you to dinner," she said. It struck her as unfair, too, that though she had asked him out, he had provided all the food. "I haven't quite figured out the best way to integrate that one fact with the rest of my life."

He leaned his head against the back of the sofa and set his glasses on an end table. "I'm no expert on this issue," he said. "Only a few courses in medical school dealt with grief."

Anna might have explained that she was dealing with more than grief. She felt a lot of guilt and anger, too, but it didn't seem fair to weigh down the evening with that much revelation. She slipped off her sandals and pulled her feet under her on the ugly couch. "Grief is really boring," she told him, half apologetically.

Naveen turned his eyes to her. "I'm not bored. I just don't want to pretend that I understand something that I don't understand at all. Let me recount my own losses: A couple of grandparents died. I didn't get into the medical school I dreamed of. I wanted to live in Chicago, but I ended up in Angola, Indiana, instead. I'm divorced. I didn't tell you that one. These are disappointments—divorce is more than that—but I haven't experienced your level of grief."

"Tell me about your wife," Anna said.

"Ex-wife."

"Did you have kids?"

"No. She has two kids now."

"Why did you break up?"

"It was more like 'Why did we marry?' We both came from medical families. Both her parents were psychiatrists. Her brothers were physicians. She became an ob-gyn. My dad went into research. My mother worked in his lab. My sister is an eye surgeon. It's kind of dull after a while, isn't it?"

"Not really."

"It's not easy to explain the dissolution of a marriage."

"Do you hate her?"

"No." He rubbed at his eyes for a moment, then asked, "Do you have ex-boyfriends?"

"Yes."

"The experience is kind of like that. And then there's this other aspect, which is almost financial. You feel like you made an enormous investment in a risky venture, and then you lost it all. So you feel rather stupid as well."

The weariness in his face reminded her of the way he had looked that morning, exhausted after a night of seeing patients, but he seemed sadder now. She said, "There's just no end to all the things we can feel stupid about, is there?"

"Unfortunately, no." He picked up her hand, the one with Ford's ring on it. "Was this your husband's?"

"Yes," Anna said, and then, because she felt embarrassed, she asked, "Do I have *fucked up* written all over me?"

He laughed. "Don't we all?"

Anna held up her hand so that they both could get a good look at the ring. "I'm trying to figure out a graceful way to take it off permanently—I don't even wear my own wedding band anymore—but it seems like there should be some ceremony to it."

"I could throw it out the window with some ceremony," he offered. His tone was sweet and light, a little hesitant. When she didn't respond, he added quickly, "Or not."

"I guess not."

In the silence that followed, the individual notes of the piano music flew through the air like phrases of a conversation less awkward than theirs. When Naveen did finally speak, he seemed to have considered his wording very carefully. "I'll just be frank here. You haven't slept with anyone, then, since your husband died?"

She thought about Pierre. "I tried once, but no. I haven't. No."

"Is that what you're looking for, then?" he asked.

He was gazing at her so directly that Anna's mind went blank. "Is what what I'm looking for?"

"Sex?"

His abruptness made her laugh, but she saw that he wasn't joking. There was something guarded in his expression, and she understood that he wasn't propositioning her; he simply wanted to know the answer. She turned her eyes away and tried to focus on the only thing that had any color in this room, the bookshelf on the opposite wall. Was sex what she wanted? Well, she did yearn for a moment that would permanently separate her current existence from the years when she was married. Nothing could do that so well as the act of finally putting another man's body between hers and Ford's. Wasn't that why she had thrown herself at Pierre? And why had that ended so badly? Anna still didn't know. Was she repelled by men entirely? Or had there simply been a mismatch with Pierre? Here in Indiana, perhaps things could unfold more simply. She liked Naveen, and he seemed to like her well enough. Their lives had no other connection, and once Anna and Goldie got back on the road, they would never have to meet again. She thought it best, under such circumstances, to be completely honest. "I'm sorry," she said. "I know that's not very romantic."

"Well, at least it's on the table." She couldn't miss the shift in his tone. The warmth that had developed over the hours of their conversation veered into something more businesslike, the voice he might use while ordering a lab test or calling in a prescription. The piano music had ended, and he stood up, walked over to the CD player on the kitchen counter, and put on some new music—Johnny Cash this time. Just next to the stereo lay Anna's drawing of the begonia. Naveen noticed it and picked it up. "This is nice," he said. He glanced at her for a moment, then looked down at the paper again. "That's the first thing I noticed about you when I met you this morning. You were sleeping on the waiting room sofa and there were drawings all around you—behind your back, under your head, on the floor."

"I'm compulsive," Anna said. At the hospital that day while Goldie slept, she had drawn nearly a dozen panels. "My family and friends think I'm an addict."

He kept his eyes on the paper. "Each leaf is so precise and perfect," he said, as much to himself as to her, and then he asked, "Does drawing make you happy?"

It had been a long time since she had thought about her work in such terms. "I guess it does," she said. "And it stabilizes me. If I stopped drawing, I'd be completely unbalanced."

He looked at the begonia itself, then back at the picture of it. "In some places, the drawing is just a suggestion of nature, and in other places it's so realistic. If I could do this, I'd never stop, either."

Anna didn't know how to respond. In her need to draw, and in her concern over her inability to do much else, she had lost appreciation for her own skills. Even when Sadie gave her the monthly sales figures for *Shaina Bright*, she failed to make a connection between the comic's success and her own role in it. Now, watching Naveen look at the picture, Anna felt a sudden, unexpected surge of feeling. It began as simple relief, but then all the grief and joy of her life seemed to merge together, creating one impossible knot of hope and despair. By the time Naveen returned to the sofa, Anna was shaking with emotion. This was not the equilibrium she had meant to convey. After all, they had, only minutes earlier, defined the very practical terms of this encounter.

But Naveen saw Anna's face. His own expression, which had maintained its aloofness until just that moment, softened instantly. He knelt
beside her on the sofa and gazed into her eyes with such absorption
that she felt as if this were the first time they had actually looked at
each other. Then he unfolded her arms from around her legs and gently
pulled off her sweater. He saw the fine lines of the tattoo that spread
along her shoulder then, and like someone reading a poem, he let his
eyes move slowly across it. "That's lovely," he said. He touched his fingers to Anna's lips, and when he leaned closer and brought his mouth
to hers, Anna discovered kissing again. In one flash, she remembered
every single moment with Ford. In the next, she forgot him completely.

Given the circumstances, Goldie was in a remarkably upbeat mood
when Anna arrived the next morning at eight. "The food is vile, but
the staff couldn't be friendlier," she told Anna. She had more color in
her face this morning, and she had eaten most of her breakfast.

"That's what they say about the Midwest," Anna reminded her.
"People are apple cheeked and friendly." She had stopped at the café
in the lobby. Now she sat in the armchair, drinking coffee and breaking off pieces of scone. "Do you want some?" she asked.

Goldie looked at her granddaughter as if Anna had suggested they
buy a condo in this city. "I'm getting out of here today. Help me get
dressed."

"Did the doctor tell you that when he came in?" Anna knew very
well that Goldie could not have seen the doctor yet this morning.
The night before, they had lain in bed talking for hours. Later, after
a little sleep, he had gazed at her, smoothing back her hair with his
hand. The morning had made them formal with each other, though,
and when he got into the shower at seven thirty, she had fought
the urge to duck out without saying good-bye. Instead, she politely
knocked on the door, then peeked in.

"Um. I'm going to go on over to the hospital," she told him.

He stuck his head out between the shower curtain and the wall. "What?"

"I'm just going to go," she yelled.

Anna could not fully gauge his reaction, but he seemed unconcerned that she was leaving. Steam filled the room, and his head was covered with suds. "Okay. I'll see you there," he'd said.

Goldie pushed herself up in the bed. "He hasn't been by yet. They tell me that he'll make his rounds about nine. Even the nurse said she thought I could leave today." Her gaze fell on Anna. "You look worn out," she said. "Are you going to be able to drive?"

Anna glanced down at her skirt, which was wrinkled and dotted with stains of yellow curry. She hadn't bothered to go back to the hotel to change, which meant that she had moved into her third day in this outfit. "I thought maybe I'd do some laundry this afternoon," she offered lamely. "I didn't expect that we'd be leaving so soon."

"So soon? Are you crazy? We would be halfway to California if I hadn't ended up in that suitcase."

"We're not in a hurry."

"You might not be in a hurry, but I've got to catch a flight to Dubai, remember?"

"Let's read the paper." Anna had found a copy of *USA Today*, and she handed the front section to her grandmother. Goldie would not actually read much of the paper, but a few minutes spent absently scanning the headlines usually calmed her.

Anna must have dozed off, because Naveen's voice woke her. "Mrs. Rosenthal?" he said, stepping through the door with a nurse. Anna sat up stiffly. He looked down at his clipboard, then up at Goldie, then over to Anna. "Hello," he said politely, before turning back to Goldie. "And how are you this morning?"

"Well, I can't say I prefer this to Biarritz," said Goldie, "but we've been having a nice time, haven't we, Doris?"

The apple-cheeked nurse responded by gently squeezing Goldie's arm, proving Anna's point about the midwestern disposition. "Everyone on the floor loves Mrs. Rosenthal," she told Naveen. "My assistants argue over who's going to check on this special lady."

"Doris, you flatter me!"

The doctor smiled, but seemed to barely register the conversation. He didn't look at Anna, either. He picked up the end of his stethoscope and listened to Goldie's heart and lungs, then, apparently satisfied, moved his hands along Goldie's arm, pushing here and prodding there. "You need to tell me if any of this hurts," he said.

"Pain? I can deal with pain. Who hasn't been sore a few days of their life? I'm getting out of here today." Goldie looked defiant.

The doctor stopped and turned to her. "I don't have a problem with soreness, but if you feel an urge to scream, you let me know." He lifted the end of the sheet and took out one of Goldie's feet. Anna had always found her grandmother's deformed toes extremely disconcerting, like the shaky foundations of an otherwise formidable building. But Naveen, unaffected, gently massaged them.

Goldie seemed to relax. "You're a good doctor," she told him.

It was hard for Anna to fully absorb this conversation. The fantasy elements of the scene were like something out of *Grey's Anatomy*: sexy doctor, preoccupied patient, the patient's worn-out but turned-on granddaughter with her smudged lipstick and tousled hair. In the fantasy, the doctor and granddaughter would find an excuse to disappear together, racing down the hospital halls until they discovered an empty broom closet into which they would duck for another ten minutes of loud and heaving but somehow undetected passion.

In real life, Anna experienced none of that swelling fervor. Instead, she felt embarrassed and edgy. It would take some time before she could consider the psychic implications of what she'd done—the fact that she had now, in that most physical and intimate way, moved beyond Ford. If that realization remained too absolute for her to bear, she did allow herself to experience the normal discomfort that follows a one-night stand. Although she'd been involved in some complicated entanglements during college, she had never slept with someone she'd only met that morning. She didn't have moral problems with such behavior. Rather, sex had always seemed awkward enough to begin with; she could never fathom getting physically involved with someone she didn't even know.

And now, she had—the man standing in front of her, a divorced, bespectacled Indian New Yorker with molasses-colored skin, a fondness for Roald Dahl and poetry, and an ugly Indiana apartment. Oh, and he was examining her grandmother, too, and her grandmother was flirting with him.

"I bet you're the best doctor between New York and San Francisco," Goldie gushed, then added, "I'm fine, and I'm leaving today."

"We'll see about that," he told her, but he didn't sound dismissive. He moved around the bed and began to examine her right leg.

"You are such a nice man. Where are you from?"

"New York."

"But you seem like a person of Indian descent. Am I correct?"

"You are."

"Well, I love India. Did you ever hear of the maharani of Baroda?"

He glanced at her over his glasses. "I've heard of maharanis and I've heard of Baroda."

Goldie smiled nostalgically. "She was a dear friend. She had a gorgeous home in Palm Beach, and I was a guest at her palace in Baroda."

"Nice," Naveen said.

"She made the most divine curry out of lamb meatballs. Do you know that dish? Curried lamb meatballs?" The doctor shook his head. Goldie looked at Anna. "Did you ever make them? Remember? I sent you the recipe."

"Not yet."

"Not yet? Are you insane? I must have sent it ten years ago. Lamb meatballs. They melt in your mouth. They're divine."

The doctor turned briefly and looked at Anna. "Do you cook, Ms. Rosenthal?"

Anna kept her eyes on her grandmother. "Sometimes."

"She's a wonderful cook," Goldie said, "although she hasn't cooked for me in years. Now we just eat whatever junk we get on the road. We haven't had a decent meal since we left New York."

He looked at Anna again. "Is that so?" he asked. The cardamom-laced curry, the spicy, coriander-scented cauliflower, the aromatic basmati rice. It all lay between them.

Anna thought she'd fall apart. "We eat a lot of Applebee's. Mostly Applebee's," she said.

"And McDonald's," Goldie added.

Doris said, "Dr. Choudary is famous for his Indian samosas. He brings us samosas at Christmastime. Lamb samosas."

"Lamb! You see?" Goldie glared at her granddaughter. "Anna, you send him my meatball recipe. He's more likely to use it than you are."

The doctor slid the sheet back over Goldie's legs. "You look like you're healing well, Mrs. Rosenthal," he said.

"Then you're going to check me out of here."

He sighed. "I'm going to check you out. You're free to go, so long as you don't push yourself too hard. And next time you feel dizzy, please sit down."

Anna followed Naveen down the corridor. "Doctor? Could I have a word with you?"

He turned around. "Certainly," he said. Nothing in his eyes or expression revealed that he knew her as anything other than the relative of one of his patients. Again, the moment had all the elements of fantasy, but in fact they were moving in the opposite direction from the broom closet. Naveen wasn't pretending formality; he really was formal. He looked down at her, waiting to hear what she had to say.

"Thanks for taking such good care of her," Anna told him. "She didn't expect it, coming from New York, but you gave her excellent care."

Naveen smiled at her, and fleetingly she remembered the firmness of his hand between her legs. Anna had fallen in love with Ford quite soon after college, so it had been a long time since she'd experienced the kind of jittery excitement she felt now. Sometimes, during the uneventful years with Ford, she had missed the thrills of attraction— waiting for phone calls, unexpected meetings that seemed like gifts of fate, the giddy feeling of an "accidental" touch, and later, the hesitant pleasure brought by a first hopeful kiss—but many years had passed since she'd actually negotiated the awkward terrain of an undefined relationship. Now she felt out of practice and almost completely un-willing to consider its inherent complications. Looking back on last night, she did feel relieved that maybe, finally, she was moving back into the world. The great emotional fact of her life was, as always, Ford's death, even if the act of sex had reacquainted her with her own body. For that, she felt quite grateful to the man standing in front of her. "I guess we'll be off," she said. The nurse's station was ten feet away, so she tried to give her voice a granddaughter's expression of hardy relief, but also enough of the weight of happy satisfaction that a one-time lover would hear it as a tender good-bye.

At first Naveen didn't respond. Instead, he began searching through the charts on his clipboard, as if to telegraph to the nurses that he was answering a question. "Let me just see," he said.

For long seconds, she watched him dig around in the forms. Though he maintained his composure, she could see that he was unsure of himself and tense. Finally he said, "Your grandmother has a very strong will. Given her age, I might have expected her to be here for three or four days." His words sounded perfectly doctorlike, but—and this pleased her as it would anyone, even after the most businesslike encounter—his tone carried the slightest hint of regret that she was leaving.

Anna had nothing else to say. She felt lighter this morning and, given the circumstances, reasonably happy. Still, she hesitated to actually say good-bye. The doctor, for his part, didn't walk away immediately, either. For one moment longer than any of the nurses might have found routine, they stared at each other. Physically, there was really no difference between their expressions now and those on their faces the night before, as they lay naked in the lamplight, his hand in her hair. But Anna decided that the look between them now conveyed more amicable and practical emotions. Perhaps for that reason, the doctor said good-bye with a medical analysis. "You have very good genes," he told her.

Anna and Goldie drove along the southern tip of Lake Michigan, though they never saw the water. By now the stolid and unchanging highway had become so much a part of their lives that they barely paid attention. They each noticed particular things, though. Goldie's attention was purely within the car. She kept her eyes on Anna's clothes, for example, and noted whether or not her granddaughter had combed her hair. Anna passed the time by making mental tallies of license plates from coastal states, and she announced with some fanfare each time they entered a new county.

Mostly, Bridget moved steadily west, conveying them mile by mile closer to California. For the first few hours after they got back on the road, Anna expected her grandmother to fall asleep, but Goldie busied herself by going through her purse, counting her money, checking her glasses, and making sure that her American Express Platinum Card was in its proper slot in her wallet.

Anna knew from the map that they were now probably thirty miles south of Chicago. They had at first talked of stopping in the city for a couple of nights, but Goldie wanted to push forward now. She felt that the hospital stay had put them behind schedule, even though they had plenty of time to get to San Francisco before her flight. "I'm the type who can't relax until I take care of my business," Goldie said. Anna suspected that such a comment was meant to criticize her own, more laid-back style, but she appreciated the indication of Goldie's commitment to returning the prints to the Nakamuras.

They were traveling now through the grinding, metallic industrial belt, the world of Teamsters and smokestacks. Jimmy Hoffa. The road here never became completely rural in the way that parts of Pennsylvania and Ohio had. She longed for a tomato, pulled right off the vine. She wanted to smell a gardenia. She wished that they could make it to Iowa that night. She pictured cornfields. "I have to go to the bathroom," she told Goldie.

They pulled over at a Chevron station. Anna had become used to the half-curious, half-suspicious looks that Bridget attracted. While she waited for the tank to fill, a white-haired man with a John Deere cap called to her from the next pump. "What kind of mileage you get on that pretty baby?"

"Forty-seven miles a gallon," Anna said, picking a number that sounded impressive, if wildly implausible.

"You rebuild that engine?"

"Put in a brand-new transformer, just last year." Anna had no idea what a transformer was, or if a Rolls-Royce needed one, but the man looked convinced.

While Anna filled the tank, her grandmother went into the bathroom. Goldie always took a few pieces of Kleenex just in case. As she walked back out toward the car, a pair of truckers held the door open, then observed her as she passed. Anna understood their gaze completely. They weren't noticing Goldie because she was a very, very old lady hunched over from a bad back, two days in a hospital, and a hot June wind. And they weren't looking at her because of the fierce way she gripped her pocketbook, either. Every old lady did that at an interstate gas station in the middle of nowhere. They were looking at her because she was gorgeous, still a woman in the most definite way—elegant, beautifully coiffed, her handmade Italian shoes perfectly buffed and tied. Anna would not have been surprised to hear them whistle.

Goldie arrived at the car and gave her facilities report. "There's no soap. It's not clean, but it's not the worst we've encountered, either. What can we do about it anyway?"

Anna helped her grandmother get back into her seat. Goldie gasped slightly as she lifted her bruised legs and adjusted herself on the cushion. Though Anna would have liked to ask how she was feeling, she wasn't willing to risk the wrath that would come in response to such a question. "I'll be right back," she said, grabbing her backpack and heading inside.

Anna loved the lightness of her body when she emerged from Bridget after hours of driving. Her movements felt springy, like Tigger bounding through the Hundred Acre Wood. Even though it was only a short distance to the building, she ran, letting the backpack in her hand flop against her leg. If only for a moment, she wanted to feel the heat and inhale fresh air. Inside, she wandered around a bit, considering what snacks she might buy when she came out of the bathroom a few minutes later—the fried chicken glowing in its bright little glass-enclosed tray? A microwave burrito? On one aisle, the truckers she'd seen outside debated over a couple of boxes of herbal tea.

She found the ladies' room, a large space with a single toilet, beside the beer coolers. Just as Goldie had said, it wasn't clean, but it wasn't repulsive, either. The smell of bowel movements, urine, and toilet bowl cleaner had been masked somewhat by an After the Rain scented freshener propped in the center of a drain on the floor. Unfortunately, it wasn't until she was squatting, midpee, that she discovered the toilet paper roll was empty. She'd forgotten to bring in any Kleenex. "Shit," she said.

She stood up and, with her pants still down, waddled to her backpack hanging on a hook on the door, then dug her hand inside. Nothing. She began to go through the smaller pockets, looking for anything, even one of the pieces of toilet paper she sometimes used to wrap around a vitamin. Nothing. She unzipped the last compartment, reached in, and found some old tissue. Then she felt something else in there as well. With one hand she widened the opening of the bag and looked in, while she wiped herself with the other. There was a small package, wrapped in newspaper. She made her way back to the toilet, dropped in the tissue, flushed, pulled up her pants, and washed her hands before returning to the backpack.

The package was small and flexible, clearly a book. Anna pulled off the paper. It was an old cloth-covered collection of haiku. Inside the front cover, in pencil, it had been inscribed, "To Anna, from Naveen." Underneath was a haiku in scrawling doctor's script, and a phone number. She read the poem twice.

By the time Anna returned to the car, her hands were full of snacks—Cokes, a couple of Butterfingers, a foot-long beef jerky, some potato chips, too.

"You're going to make me so fat," Goldie said, obviously delighted, but Anna was too distracted to reply. Somewhere in the back of her mind she heard her grandmother say, "Isn't this fun? It's fun, isn't it?"

Anna decided that they would make it to Iowa that night. "Yes," she answered.

As they slid back onto the highway, she turned the words of the poem over in her mind. She knew them by heart already:

Not because of that,
Or me, I see that you, too,
Can be whole again.

11

Mrs. Yves Saint Laurent and
Mrs. Issey Miyake

By early evening they had crossed from Illinois into Iowa. In Davenport they found a Hampton Inn, and then an Applebee's, and by 9 P.M., Goldie lay under the covers, her fingers curled, like a child's, over the top of the sheet. As tired as she was, Anna wasn't ready to go to sleep. She wasn't willing to leave her grandmother alone, however. She went into the bathroom and turned on the water in the tub. "I'm going to soak for a while," she said. "Call me if you need me." Goldie was exhausted, though, and when Anna peeked out a few minutes later, she was asleep.

While the tub filled, Anna looked through the haiku book. She read Naveen's poem again, then flipped through the pages, reading more. She could remember studying the form briefly in college, but she had to count the syllables again—5–7–5—to remember its constraints. Writing a successful haiku seemed like an almost impossible feat, like etching portraits in grains of rice. But here was Naveen's, as simple and clear as a voice in her ear.

She lay the book by the sink and undressed, then stood in front of the mirror and looked at herself. For so long, the sight of her body had only made her feel more lonely. Now she found she could regard it with less emotion. At thirty-five, her breasts had begun to droop and her stomach had become flabbier. She had never liked her hips, but she felt more kindly toward them now. Her skin looked rosy and supple. Her hair fell in tangled but thick curls across her shoulders. Her shadow-circled eyes looked curious and alert. Anna thought of the abandoned house that stood on the corner of her block on Waynoka. No one had lived there for years. Boards covered the windows, and tree branches from the last ice storm lay across the roof. Still, every spring the azaleas bloomed in the front yard in a tumble of pink blossoms. It seemed that despite her own absence and neglect, Anna remained rather pretty.

When she turned off the water, she heard "Anna!" from the other room. Without thinking, she dashed naked out of the bathroom and over to Goldie's bed.

"What? What?" she said.

"Darling, could you get me some water?" The old woman's face looked pale in the light that spilled out from the bathroom.

"Oh. Okay. I thought something was wrong."

Goldie gave a little cough. "My throat's a little scratchy. I'm sorry I got you out of the bath."

Anna turned and headed back toward the sink for a glass. "No. It's okay," she began. "I just—"

But Goldie cut her off. "What in the world? What is that on your shoulder?"

Her voice, a weak whisper only a moment before, had suddenly regained its full strength.

Anna stopped, began to turn around, and then quickly retreated into the bathroom. She pulled on her silk kimono, popped off the paper lid that covered the bathroom cup, and poured her grandmother some water.

"What have you done to yourself?" Goldie demanded when Anna reappeared. She had pushed herself up in bed now. Her hair, unpinned, lay matted against her pillow.

Anna said, simply, "I've got a tattoo." She walked over to Goldie and stood by the bed.

"Let me see it."

Anna turned around and let the kimono slip off her shoulder.

Goldie switched on the bedside light.

"It's dragonflies," Anna said.

For a moment the sight rendered Goldie speechless. At last she said, "Are you some kind of tramp?"

Anna didn't have the energy to argue. "It's body art," she said. "I like it."

"Did he make you do that?"

Anna remembered Ford's reaction when she came home with the tattoo—startled and surprisingly distressed—but he'd eventually gotten used to it. "No," she said. "I did it myself."

"Did he like it?"

"Not particularly."

"It's disgusting. At least he had *some* sense."

Only a few days earlier, Anna would have protected herself through some offhand and imprecise attempt to deflect her grandmother's criticism. Now, though, the image of Goldie in the suitcase remained too fresh. She seemed so old, so deeply in need of care. "You know what?" Anna said.

"What?" Goldie sounded suspicious.

"You need to rest. You're too weak to let yourself get upset about this."

Anna pulled her robe back around her shoulder, sat down on the bed, and handed her grandmother the glass. "Drink up and go back to sleep," she said gently.

To Anna's surprise, her compassion seemed to disarm Goldie completely. She took a few sips of water, then put the glass down on the table by the bed. "You're so good to me," she sighed.

Once Goldie had closed her eyes again, Anna got in the bath. For a long time, she counted syllables against her fingers, trying to construct a three-line poem with five, then seven, then five syllables, but she was distracted now. It was, of course, unwise to have hoped that spending a night with another man would settle, once and for all, her feelings about Ford. If only one's emotional life could be so simple. Anna ducked underneath the water and held her breath, then slowly exhaled, listening to the deep rumble of the bubbles returning to the surface. She remembered lying in bed, feeling Ford's heart beat like a dependable clock against her back. How long ago was that? Five years, at least, because before he got sick he had always been the one to curl around her. After he got sick, she had always curled around him.

As they drove west the next morning, Goldie sat with her cell phone in her hand, waiting on a call from her travel agent. Despite her fall, she still planned to go to Dubai. "I'm supposed to be sore for a couple of weeks," she had reasoned at dinner the night before. "Might as well be sore on a cruise ship."

This morning, though, thoughts of the cruise were overshadowed by the revelation of Anna's tattoo. Goldie was nearly silent over breakfast, but a few miles beyond Davenport she could restrain herself no longer. "So, are you a sailor now?" she asked. They were moving through farm country, field after field of corn that, at this point in the season, stood about three feet tall. "Are you a criminal? A murderer? A thug?"

"Let's drop the subject," Anna said. The farmland spread away from them on both sides of the road, making her feel that the Rolls-Royce was a ship sailing across a vast green sea. The air smelled of dirt, manure, things that sprouted. She liked the feel of the sun on her hands as she held the smooth leather of the steering wheel.

"A tattoo is not something you can 'drop.' You're stuck with it your entire life." The harshness of Goldie's words was predictable, but Anna noticed that her tone had changed. The spite that had peppered her conversation over the first few days of their journey seemed to have dissipated now. Goldie sounded bored. She soldiered forward, though, as if she felt obligated to offer her opinions. The dragonflies tattooed up the side of Anna's shoulder reminded her, she said, of Sadie's recent decision to build bookshelves in the living room of her Manhattan apartment, which Goldie believed should be completely reserved for fancy furniture and precious knickknacks. "You girls have no sense. Next, is your sister going to put a bathtub in her living room, too?"

"Maybe she'll put in a toilet at one end of the dining room table." Anna was finding this conversation diverting at least.

But Anna's carefree manner must have been too much for Goldie. "You think it's funny," Goldie replied, her tone suddenly acid. "Well, maybe that other fellow didn't care. But what kind of man is going to marry you with a tattoo? It's not decent."

And then, despite herself, Anna began to cry. She felt as if she had lowered her defenses and that as a result she'd been stabbed. "Can you just leave it? Can you leave it for a few minutes?" She had never told anyone—not Sadie or their mother or father or, especially, Ford—that putting a tattoo on her shoulder had inexplicably helped her find balance as she watched her husband's health deteriorate. Anna certainly wasn't going to try to explain such a thing now. But the tears, in any case, silenced her grandmother.

"I know you didn't like him," Anna finally said, "but I can't hear it right now."

"I just thought he wasn't good enough for you."

"He wasn't good enough for *you*. I was lucky to have him." Oddly, despite her continuing ambivalence about Ford, Anna wasn't lying. It was as if by defending him, she saw, in a brief flash, all that she had loved about him—his affection for *Calvin and Hobbes*, his fondness for peanut butter on carrots, the way his chest hair stretched down his belly, then stopped, revealing a few tantalizing inches of bare skin. Even as she was speaking, though, she mistrusted her feelings and wondered how long they would last.

"You don't give yourself enough credit. You're a beautiful girl. You could be with any man," Goldie said, momentarily putting aside the fact of the tattoo. "You'll find another husband. You'll start your life over. I can't count the number of times I've had to start my life over. You just do it. Maybe you'll have children. You'll be happier."

Anna kept sobbing, wiping her nose with the back of her hand. Her grandmother finally opened her purse and handed Anna a handkerchief. "I don't know how you can drive in this condition."

"I can drive in this condition!" Anna cried. It helped, of course, that the road stretched straight ahead of them into infinity and she couldn't even see another car. She tried to breathe deeply. Goldie's opinion of Ford, Anna's tattoo, or even her prospects for the future meant nothing. Why should Anna care what Goldie thought? But Anna's mind was a mess of emotions, and everything, even slights about body art, could feel impossibly defeating. "He was a good man," Anna said.

"Aren't they all?" Goldie was unimpressed.

Anna blew her nose into the handkerchief. "I really loved him," she said, trying to deflect her grandmother one last time. As these words emerged from her mouth, another image of Ford came to

Anna's mind—healthy Ford, sitting on the Adirondack chair on the porch, drinking a Corona and reading *The Master and Margarita*. The jolt of love she felt at that moment almost broke her heart all over again. And then, as if she were experiencing the whole awful loss of her husband anew, she said, "We were going to grow old together."

They passed a pretty farm with a grain silo and a couple of cows in a field. A school bus, full of what looked like football players, pulled onto the highway, and the teenagers started cheering out the windows as Goldie's fancy car drove by. Finally, Goldie broke the silence. "Just because you want it doesn't make it so. I have to be honest here. You might grow old alone."

Anna sniffed, but the tone of her grandmother's voice had the strange effect of drawing her out of herself. It sounded so cynical that she almost laughed. "I probably will grow old alone," she said.

"You might not, though."

Anna had never heard her grandmother try to be comforting, and so, finally, jarred by the oddness of the moment, she began to laugh. Goldie looked surprised at first—Anna's laughter undermined Goldie's attempt to sound like a wise elder—but the change in mood brought both of them relief as well. "You never know!" Goldie said, smiling grandly now.

A while later, "Mack the Knife" broke the silence. Out of the corner of her eye, Anna watched Goldie flip open her cell phone, stare at it in a single habitual moment of bafflement, then find the right button. "Hello?"

Bridget's engine was quiet enough that Anna could hear a man's voice through the line. She couldn't understand what he was saying, though. "Who? Yes. Oh, hello there!" Goldie said. "How nice of you to call."

Anna glanced over at her, wondering.

"It's the doctor," Goldie told her.

Goldie was extremely healthy, but at eighty-five she had enough doctors in her life to make it impossible to know which one she was talking about. After Goldie landed in the hospital, they had spoken with Dr. Mitnick in New York and Dr. Damutz in Palm Beach. And of course there was Dr. Choudary in Indiana, who might have felt the urge to check in on his patient, too. "I'm feeling fine," Goldie said. "We stop every few hours and I stretch my legs, and then I get back in the car and keep going like nothing ever happened. It's very nice of you to call. I didn't expect to hear from you again."

Goldie paused, listening, then turned to Anna. "Dr. Choudary wants to know where we are."

Anna's stomach tightened. "Iowa."

"Iowa." Another pause. "The doctor says that I shouldn't be driving more than five hours a day if you can help it, but I think that's silly. Don't you think that's silly?"

Anna wasn't sure if her grandmother was speaking to her or the doctor, so she didn't respond. Then Goldie pushed the phone in her direction. "Here. He wants to talk to you."

"I can't talk. I'm driving."

Goldie pointed the phone toward the desolate highway in front of them. "You couldn't have a wreck out here if you tried." The only other vehicle on the road was the school bus, a mile or so back, just a tiny yellow blip on the horizon.

Anna took the phone. "Hello?"

"I told her I wanted to hear from you about how she's doing, and in case that didn't work, I also told her I needed the recipe for the maharani's meatball curry."

"It's in a box in my kitchen." Her nervousness made her sound like a robot.

"Anna," he said, "it's just an excuse."

"Oh." She had no idea what to say next. She did not want to talk to Naveen, even though all the way through Indiana, into Illinois, and across the green miles of Iowa, her mind had continuously drifted back in his direction. She had retraced every turn on the path of their story, from their first official encounter at the hospital, to the contours of their conversation at the movie, to their sweet, meandering lovemaking that night, and finally to their reluctant but cheerful good-bye the next morning. She had made mental lists of what she knew of him (preferences for haiku and Johnny Cash but not interior decorating), and she had pondered the differences between the emotional damage wrought by divorce, in his case, and widowhood, in hers. Thinking of Naveen gave her a pleasure that she had not experienced since she fell in love with Ford, and there was a tingly purity to it that she savored. But Anna also savored the simplicity of their encounter, the fact that it remained abbreviated, unburdened by ugliness and loss. In her mind, their "story" had ended.

But here he was, on the phone. Worse, Goldie was sitting right beside her. "My grandmother is doing really well," Anna finally stammered. "I'm not letting her push herself too hard."

"I'm glad to hear it." Then, after a pause, he asked, "Did you find the book?"

The sound of Naveen's voice gave Anna an almost woozy pleasure, which made talking even more difficult. "Yes, thanks." Did he hear the quaver in her response? And what did he expect from this exchange? She could hardly launch into a discourse on haiku poetry. Beside her, Goldie had pulled her nail file from her purse. She was working on her left thumb.

"Anna, I don't have your cell number. Could you call me sometime? I miss you."

At this point, Anna really did find it a challenge to drive. His words filled her with joy, but like a physical pain that shoots through the body unexpectedly, she also felt a sudden jolt of fear. That fear shut her down. If she could have spoken freely at that moment, she would have reminded Naveen that, by definition, their interaction had been limited to a single night. "I don't think it's a good idea," she told him.

"What's a good idea?" asked Goldie, holding up her thumb to the light.

But Naveen understood. "It's an oversimplification to call that a 'one-night stand,'" he said. His voice sounded so reasoned and exasperated that she felt as if she'd just entered a conversation that he'd been engaged in for hours, by himself.

In any case, Goldie's presence meant that Anna couldn't respond in any straightforward way. "I don't want to complicate anything," she finally told him. "She's doing fine."

He was silent for a moment, apparently trying to decipher Anna's meaning.

"Complicate what?" asked Goldie.

Anna said, "I really can't drive and talk at the same time."

"Just call me," said Naveen. Anna didn't respond, and her silence seemed to have an effect on him because, in an apparent burst of emotion, he added, "Not everyone's going to die on you, Anna!"

She slammed the phone shut in her hand and tossed it into Goldie's lap as if the metal had turned hot and burned her. "Are you out of your mind?" asked Goldie. "You hung up on the doctor? And he asked for my recipe for the maharani's meatballs."

Anna said, "I didn't hang up on him. We got disconnected."

"Oh, for heaven's sake." Goldie held the phone in her hand, waiting for Naveen to call back. When he didn't, she slid it into her purse. "Anyway, calling was the proper thing for him to do. Not all doctors would bother. The Indians are excellent doctors. I would recommend him to friends, but I don't know a living soul in Illinois. I'm no help to him at all."

"Indiana," Anna said, blowing her nose again.

"What's the difference?"

After a while, Goldie fell asleep. Anna had heard that the land-scape of Iowa was dull enough to make you crazy, but she liked the shaggy carpet of the prairie. Naveen seemed to think that Anna was afraid of death. How simplistic! No, it wasn't only Ford's death that continued to torment her; it was all the ugliness that they'd endured *before* he died as well. Even when he was still healthy, their relation-ship had troubled them. Weekends, which should have been fun, had devolved into drawn-out disagreements over how best to allocate their precious time. Should they go out and listen to jazz (Ford's inclination) or stay home and eat popcorn while watching DVDs (Anna's)? Whatever they decided led to a clash between one person's guilt and the other's resentment. Even if your marriage didn't receive a catastrophic diagnosis, was that a way to spend your life? And then, if it did, things got worse.

Anna found herself weighing, then, the joys of love against the pain it caused. Naveen had compared his divorce to losing money in a risky venture. Anna was less businesslike in her assessment. She felt the allure of romance as much as ever—and she didn't deny how much she had once loved Ford, either—but she remained focused on the complications that came with it. She didn't like the word *pessi-mist* because of the implication that *optimist* was just as valid. No, she was a pragmatist, the clarity of her understanding born of her own experience of discord and grief. She did not discount the possibility that she might fall in love again, if only because the romantic in her found the alternative too depressing, but the prospect also made her fearful and uncertain.

The sun, coming out from behind a cloud, seemed to butter the prairie. How would it feel to lie across this beautiful planet, a stem of grass in her mouth, staring at the sky? Anna pulled off the highway a few miles out of Newton, and the change in the sound of the engine made Goldie open her eyes. "We out of gas?" she asked.

"I need some grass," Anna said.

"Gas?"

"Grass." She turned down a farm road, which made her feel self-conscious in the Rolls, and let the car come to a stop on the shoulder.

"What the heck are you doing?" Goldie asked.

"I got an urge."

Goldie's face relaxed. "That's fine. Personally, I can wait and use the facilities, but I couldn't care less what you do."

Anna walked around the car, opened Goldie's door, and took her grandmother's hand. "Follow me. Just for a minute. I promise that we'll come right back to the car."

Goldie peered out toward the grassland that surrounded them. Her nose crinkled as if Anna had driven them to a hog farm, though the air smelled fresh. "What?"

"Please."

Goldie grumbled, but she let Anna help her out of the car, and together they walked hand in hand down the road and up a little farm path, only letting go when Anna took a couple of giant steps out onto the grass of the prairie. "Have you lost your mind?" Goldie asked.

Anna turned around and looked back. The grass wasn't as high here as she'd expected, nor as lush. Instead of a thick carpet, it was patchy on the ground. But she was determined. She lay down, stretching her arms and legs as far as they would go, feeling the scratchy stalks against her skin.

"Are you crazy?" Goldie stood with her hands on her hips, staring down at her.

Anna placed a hand against her forehead to block the sun from her eyes. "Haven't you ever felt the need to do anything inappropriate?" she asked.

"No," said Goldie, who had spent the first few decades of her life trying to learn the rules and the rest obsessively following them.

Anna put her hand down again and stared up at the clouds scattered across the sky. Her body felt lighter these days, so light that as the earth spun through the universe, she felt that she could fly right off. "Come join me," she said to Goldie.

"And mess up my linen pants? Not on your life."

But Goldie was laughing. Anna sat up. She grabbed a stalk of grass and stuck it in her mouth. "It's sweet," she said. "Try it."

Goldie looked wary. "I don't care for nature," she said, but she plucked a stalk and edged it between her lips anyway. Then she closed her eyes and savored it as if she were giving her attention to a new Cabernet.

Shielding her eyes from the sun, Anna watched her grandmother. At that moment a wave of beautiful, mixed-up emotion washed over her: joy over the splendor of the afternoon, happiness that Naveen still thought of her (even if she remained firm in her conviction to do nothing about it), and love—yes, love—for the old woman standing on the prairie in front of her.

Finally, Goldie said, "It's not the best thing I've ever tasted, but it's not the worst, either." Satisfied, Anna stood up, took her grandmother's hand, and helped her walk across the bumpy earth to where Bridget was waiting.

12

If Only

"I'm dead," Goldie said that night. "I'm not even going to wash my teeth." They had stopped in Grand Island, Nebraska, and it was just past nine. "Help me get my shoes off, and then you go downstairs and watch some TV."

Anna knelt down next to the bed and slipped off her grandmother's shoes. They both looked down at Goldie's toes, which she carefully wrapped in moleskin every morning to protect her skin from blisters. "I used to worry that no man would ever marry me, because of these feet," Goldie said, watching as her granddaughter gently pulled down her knee-high stockings.

"How did you get over that?" Anna asked. She could not remember Goldie ever admitting to an insecurity.

But Goldie's sympathy for herself as a young woman turned out to be no greater than her sympathy for anyone else. "I was just an idiot," she said. "Life got complicated. Who had time to worry about feet?"

Anna stood up, holding the shoes and stockings in her hands.

Goldie looked so tiny perched on the edge of the bed. "What if you need me, Nana? You could get up to go to the bathroom and fall."

"How can I fall when I'm asleep?" Goldie said. She took off her blouse and slacks, handed Anna her watch and gold hoop earrings, unsnapped her bra, then held up her arms to let Anna slip her night-gown over her shoulders. "I couldn't get up if I wanted to. I'm dead."

Still, Anna lingered. Goldie lay with her head on her pillow, the sheets pulled up to her chest, watching her granddaughter dig through her wrinkled clothes, moving them from one side of the suitcase to the other. "If you packed properly, you'd be able to find everything," she said. "In my suitcase, I could find a toothpick with a blindfold on."

"I'm just looking for the T-shirt I want to sleep in. I don't want to turn on the light when I come back in."

"You can come in with a marching band. It's not going to bother me."

Anna took her cell phone, a copy of *People*, and her sketchbook and pencils. Once she got downstairs, she made herself a cup of Earl Grey tea at the hot drinks bar, then sat down at one of the tables in the breakfast area. This Hampton Inn had a banner at the front of the lobby proclaiming that it had won a special national award for "Decorative Charm," and that charm was made obvious in the breakfast area, where a model train made a circuit through Hampton Inn Holiday Village, which was decked out for winter, although it was June.

She opened her sketchbook and looked at the drawings she had made a few nights before, during those hours when Goldie lay trapped inside the suitcase. Putting aside the guilt she felt for her part in that disaster, Anna tried to focus on the work itself. She had spent many years illustrating comics, but that night had marked her first attempt to sketch from her own life. She was pleased, then, to see that the drawings of the afternoon in Goldie's living room weren't bad. Technically speaking, she liked the textures she'd given to Goldie's fancy chairs, the enormity of the coffee table, the way the light came in sideways, through the slits between the blinds. She wasn't quite so happy with the acuity of her self-portrait, which seemed, in retrospect, imprecise. Her eyes were vague and unfocused, her ponytail too saucy (a bad habit developed from drawing so many saucy ponytails for *Shaina Bright*), and her legs too shapely. She could blame her own vanities and insecurities, not her drawing skills, for all of that. On the positive side, the pictures had achieved that fine balance of simplicity and emotional power that she felt she had lost. Goldie's eyebrows, those two thin scratches on the page, were like a treatise of scorn and recrimination.

But Anna found herself most affected by the images of Ford. Since his death, she had looked at his photographs often, but those pictures lost their power over time, becoming little more than abstract combinations of shape and color. The sketches in front of her now felt completely vivid. They were perfect. Each frame captured him just as he was—the downturn of his eyes; his shock of bangs, which fell across one side of his forehead but never the other; the gentle curve of jaw from his ears to his chin. Looking at the drawings gave Anna the unsettling feeling that she was seeing him alive again, but at a distance that made him unreachable. There, beside the twinkling lights of the Hampton Inn Holiday Village in Grand Island, Nebraska, Anna felt as if she had rediscovered something vital to her well-being and, at the same time, lost it all over again.

"Hey? Are you okay?" The hotel desk clerk, who had taken a seat at a nearby table, was peering out over the top of a book, watching Anna cry.

"Oh, yeah," Anna said. "Sometimes I just get sort of overcome." She picked up the little paper napkin she'd carried over with her tea and blew her nose. It seemed to be her fate these days to be always in need of tissues.

The clerk was in her early twenties, with spiky blond hair and sparkly gold earrings that nearly touched her shoulders. "Are you an artist or something?"

"Kind of." She felt sheepish about the tears, and so, remembering a tourist brochure she'd seen in her room, she asked, "What's with the sandhill cranes?"

"It's not the season," the clerk said. "You missed it by about a month."

"But what's the big deal?"

"The Platt River, outside of town, is a stop on their migration route. We get a couple hundred thousand birds coming through every year. It's pretty amazing if you've never seen it before. I've seen it before, so it's not that amazing."

Out of habit, Anna glanced down to see what the clerk was reading. *Claudine en ménage* by Colette. "You read French?" she asked, immediately regretting the sound of surprise in her voice.

The clerk didn't seem offended. She looked pleased that someone else would take an interest. "I spent my junior year in France last year, in Lyon. I'm a French major."

"That's cool."

"Hey, are you the one driving the Rolls-Royce?"

"Yeah. It's my grandmother's. What do you think of that book?"

"It's funny. Have you read it?" The girl must have made some connection between driving a Rolls-Royce and mastering French. She perked up at the idea that Anna could share her interest in Colette. "I've got some other ones if you need something to read while you're here."

Anna shook her head, mindful, not for the first time, that she had not taken full advantage of her excellent education. Nothing against drawing comic books, but why had she never become fluent in French? This girl had done that. And Ford, pretty much self-taught, had become a full-fledged intellectual. He used to get cranky if he finished one book and didn't have a new one waiting. When was the last time Anna read a novel? "I don't really speak French," she admitted. "I just studied it in college."

The clerk may have been disappointed in Anna's lack of language skills, but she didn't seem reluctant to chat. Her shift ran from four to midnight, she said, so she still had a few hours ahead of her. "Why are you guys driving through Nebraska?" she asked.

"My grandmother needs to be out of New York for a while because of her taxes, and she has some art that she wants to return to an old friend in San Francisco. Was it hard to leave France?"

"Terrible. I would have stayed, but I ran out of money. And now I have to take this year off from college to work."

Anna took a sip of her tea, which was lukewarm now. "Is that a drag?"

"I've got a boyfriend in Lyon," the clerk said, as if that explained everything. With her angular face and brooding eyes, she wasn't exactly the model of a Nebraska farm beauty. In France, though, she might have been a sensation. "He's actually Algerian," she continued. The opportunity to talk about love gave her face radiance. "He's studying fashion design, and we're talking about opening a dress shop. It's just kind of a dream, though."

"It sounds romantic," Anna said, flipping one of her pencils between her fingers. She was surprised to find that for the first time in ages, the idea of romance did not completely put her off. On the other hand, she felt incapable of offering the young woman much encouragement. After a while, she said, "I'd like to see the sandhill cranes."

The clerk glanced around the room as if to make sure that no one else was around to listen. "Hey, you know, if you go out that door down the hall, follow the sidewalk to the right, you'll find a little path that goes off into grass at the back of the hotel. We put a deck chair out at the end of the path. That's where we take our breaks."

Anna must have looked confused, because the young woman added, "Trust me. You'll like it." She got up, crossed over toward the hallway leading to the office, and disappeared for a moment before returning with a flashlight. "It's a new moon, so you'll need this."

"You're sure it's okay?" Anna asked, won over by this clerk who kept up with the waxing and waning of the moon.

The young woman said, "I'm supposed to offer travel tips. It's in my job description." She had also carried over with her a fat catalog: *Hampton Inns Worldwide*. "Stick this in the door so I don't have to come get you when you're locked out."

Anna went upstairs to leave her things on her bed and check on Goldie, who was sound asleep. Within five minutes, she had found her way to the trail and switched on the flashlight. It felt strange, and unsettling, to be walking down a path completely alone in the dark. Surrounded by flat prairie, though, and with the glaring lights of the Hampton Inn behind her, she could hardly get lost. The dirt path wound along a grassy slope, then followed the banks of a little creek until suddenly she came upon the chair in a patch of dirt. It was a cheap folding lounge chair that had lost a couple of bands but still looked fairly stable. She turned off the flashlight and then carefully lowered herself into the seat, stretching her legs. The chair faced away from the hotel, though she could still hear the intermittent roar of trucks on the interstate. In this direction, the flat black plain of Nebraska stretched as far as she could see. Anna was not, strictly speaking, a city girl. *City* to her meant New York, or Hong Kong, or Paris. But Memphis, too, could block the light of the galaxy. She had never in her life seen so many stars.

Once, in high school, the Honor Society had gone camping at Reelfoot Lake. The AP English teacher, Mrs. Eddington, who devoted an entire month to Wordsworth and Shelley, suggested that the stars were our lost loved ones, gazing down at us. At the time,

Anna's teenage cynicism found such a notion both sentimental and superstitious, which explained why she responded to the comment by elbowing her friend Estelle in the ribs. Who didn't want to believe that the dead stay with us? Desire couldn't make it real, though. At sixteen, Anna had only known one person who had died, and that was a Pall Mall–smoking friend of her mother, who had developed lung cancer. Could that be Irene Agnoff, looking down at them? Doubtful.

Now, though, Anna wanted it. She really wanted it. Tonight, she thought, she could see a million stars. And, surely, there were enough beyond her vision to account for all the people who had died in this world. Not just people, either. Beloved dogs and cats, birds, bees, bugs. Every aphid and butterfly, surely, could have a star of its own in this universe.

Maybe it was the kindness of the evening—the silky air, the tuneful breeze, the sweet scent of the prairie grass—that led Anna back to an afternoon some months before Ford died. They had gone outside to sit on the porch. The air had grown chilly, and they wrapped blankets around their legs to keep warm. Ford was very sick already. His illness seemed so terrible then, but it was in fact rather mild compared with what would come later. Earlier that day, Pierre had brought them a bootleg of some old Neil Young songs. Anna pulled the speakers into the doorway so that she and Ford could listen. They sat on the Adirondack chairs, Anna with the newspaper, Ford with his eyes closed, his head resting against a pillow. For a long time, they didn't talk. Then Ford said, "Fuck burning out." Anna looked up at him. He was staring at her with that worried brow, that lip tucked under, those eyes wide as open windows. It was the look that she had always taken as an expression of his love for her. If Anna had been paying attention then, she would have done something to acknowledge it.

But she wasn't paying attention to how Ford looked just then.

Love, romance, or whatever you wanted to call it had gotten buried in the daily trials of illness and debilitation. It was enough, for her, to listen to his words, to try to understand what he was saying. "What are you talking about?" she asked.

As quick as that, his expression shifted. The brow hardened, the lips pursed, the eyes clamped shut. "The song," he said, his voice a croak of irritation. " 'It's better to burn out than to fade away.' That's bullshit. And you weren't even listening."

"I was listening!" Anna had cried. And then she got angry. "Fuck you, Ford," she had screamed, not even caring that the tragic cancer couple was causing a scene within earshot of the neighbors. "Fuck you, always being the victim. Fuck you." And then she had stomped into the house, leaving the newspaper to blow wildly across the porch, like so much debris after nuclear destruction.

How had they resolved it? They had not resolved it. That moment had piled onto the other dark moments of those months and years to create the burden that Anna, alone now, had to carry with her. It was enough to make you think of life as one mistake after another.

There was nothing to be done about it, except forgive herself, which seemed completely insufficient. But she also understood now that that was all she had. And so, finally, through concentrated effort, Anna considered Ford's face again after all this time: that brow, that lip, those eyes, that impossible jumble of love and fury and sorrow. And in that momentary vision of her husband, she felt awash in love for him again.

Looking up at the universe, Anna thought, "If only . . . if only . . . if only." If only what? If only she had watched more closely. If only he had told her in actual words that he loved her. If only he had lived, or barring that, if only they could have found solace with each other before he went away.

With a sense that she was pleading now, Anna scanned the stars, searching for the man she'd loved. She reasoned that his wouldn't be a noteworthy star but a smaller one twinkling brightly from some comfortable astronomical position. "What's it like up there?" she whispered. The light from this star, of course, had begun its journey before she and Ford, their parents, Goldie and Saul, Marvin Feld, the nation, maybe even the continent itself existed. How lucky, she told herself, that she and Ford had overlapped in this world at the exact same time. They had loved each other long before the bitterness and scowls set in. And if she could remember that, then their love had lasted. For the first time, Anna began to hope that eventually it could be that emotion—love—that would stay with her.

"What if I had been born in the Middle Ages?" she asked, beginning to cry now. "What if you were George Jetson? We never would have met."

13

The Love of Your Life

They had almost crossed the country now. In Wyoming Anna discovered that her body had settled so comfortably into the groove of the machine that she understood the allure of long-distance trucking. At some moments she felt that she and Bridget were communicating telepathically. It only took the slightest pressure of her finger on the wheel to make the car respond.

Outside the window, the world changed. The grass became more sparse. At first they saw only the occasional patch of dirt. Then more bare soil and less grass, until finally Anna decided that they had officially left the prairie behind. Was this the Red Desert, which she had read about on the free Internet in the lobby of a recent Hampton Inn? The views were vast and unencumbered. No grass, no trees, just rocks and jagged plateaus in the distance. She found it exhilarating. The bare ground seemed more honest somehow, the earth revealing its truest self. Just beside the road, the color of the dirt was indeed a vibrant red. No, *rust* was more accurate. For a painter, a photographer, a printmaker, even a comic book artist, words didn't matter, though. Anna thought of the range of colors in her comics, the universe of colors in the Japanese prints. There was so much possibility in the palette, while measly *red* tried to accommodate everything from a Valentine's heart the color of blood to the arid landscape of this desert.

"Have you ever seen anything more ugly in your life?" Goldie asked.

At another time, Anna might have responded by saying, "Yes, poverty and despair," but she was feeling more kindly toward Goldie now, so she tried to be bland and diplomatic. "We see the most beautiful things and we see the most ugly."

Sometimes Goldie liked to turn philosophical, and she warmed to Anna's comment now. "I know exactly what you're talking about. I've been with the Pope and I've been with Prince Charles and I've been with the garbage man. When I was a little girl, we only ate meat on Friday nights. The rest of the week, dinner was a can of corn with some milk from our cow poured into it. Your Poppy and I had to work like fiends to make it in this world."

"I love to hear these stories," Anna said.

Goldie didn't respond for a while. Eventually she said, "It's just such a long time ago."

"Is it hard to remember?"

"Not at all. I can remember the lace on the hem of every slip I wore back then. And suffering makes you stronger. I'm as strong as an ax."

Anna considered correcting her. It was *ox,* not *ax,* but *ax* seemed right for Goldie. "You really are," Anna said.

"Thinking about it makes me tired, though. I'm eighty-five years old, and I need to conserve my energy. I need to focus on my life right now."

At lunchtime they stopped at a Subway just west of Cheyenne, and Sadie called. "Aunt Rochelle died," she told Anna. "Can you tell Nana?"

"Okay." Anna looked at her grandmother, whose attention was focused at that moment on rubbing a Handi Wipes over her fingers before she picked up her chicken sandwich. Goldie had lived with Rochelle many years ago in San Francisco, but the sisters had never gotten along. They probably hadn't spoken in a decade, though the whole family had known that Rochelle was ailing. Anna imagined that it would be difficult, no matter what, to take the news that the last of her nine siblings was gone.

Once they were back on the road, Anna put it simply. "Nana, Sadie gave me some sad news. Aunt Rochelle died."

Goldie stared out the window toward the plain of southeastern Wyoming. After a while, she said, "I can't believe it." Her posture didn't change at all. She seemed to be having a reaction that was mostly intellectual. "Someone's around your whole life, and then they're gone. Just like that."

Anna had once heard a theory that, just as dogs can't speak and horses can't fly, humans, as a species, can't understand the finality of death. "Even when you know someone's going to die," she said, "it's still baffling."

Goldie said, "I'm not going to lie to you. I didn't like Rochelle one little bit. She was mean and selfish and she never did a thing in the world for anyone else."

Anna tried to remember her Great Aunt Rochelle, but she had only a vague image of a pointy-nosed version of Goldie, sitting across a big table from her at a steakhouse somewhere.

"Not that I would ever celebrate the death of another human being," Goldie said.

Anna loved her own sister so completely that she couldn't under-stand the ill will between her grandmother and Rochelle. On the other hand, you can't force yourself to like someone. "What was the problem between the two of you?"

"She never felt anything was good enough for her. She griped," Goldie said. "Once, I took her to a wedding. My very close friend was getting married. I was a guest, and they were very nice—this was in San Francisco—and they let me bring my sister. I wanted to dance and have a glorious time, and Rochelle kept complaining. Nothing was good enough for her. The sandwiches were dry. The cakes were too sweet. I was ready to have the time of my life, but she made it impossible. For me, the entire affair was ruined. I had a miserable time. A horrible time."

"And it was Rochelle's fault?"

"All Rochelle's fault. Absolutely."

To Anna, bitching at a wedding seemed like a fairly minor infraction, surely not a thing to hold against a person for a lifetime. "Maybe she was unhappy about something," Anna suggested.

"You hit the nail on the head. Unhappy about everything."

A tractor-trailer sped by them, and then Anna had to concentrate on passing a couple of rattling pickup trucks that were driving slower than forty miles an hour. She forgot about her grandmother for a moment. Then Goldie said, "I gave her one of my Christian Dior suits, and that wasn't even enough."

Then, a while later, "I never celebrate the death of another person."

And later, "Meanness is in their bones. Like a disease."

"A mean disease," Anna said.

"Pure meanness."

Outside of Rawlins, Naveen called again. "You know," Goldie told him, "some doctors don't give you the time of day."

Anna heard only Goldie's half of the conversation, but she tried hard to follow what they were saying. "Of course, they're busy but— doctor, can I be honest here? . . . Well, yes, but I have to be honest.

When you're my age, some doctors simply don't care. They're thinking, 'She's old. Of course she's in pain.' Is that the way to treat another human being? I don't believe it. . . . I appreciate that. . . . Eighty-five years old. . . . Of course, I've seen it all. I've seen it all twice."

It amazed Anna that these two people could talk for so long—five, ten, fifteen minutes passed—particularly because Goldie, far from being a permanent patient, had only been passing through Indiana. But it was like a marathon of conversation.

"Do you know Memphis? It's in the southern part of the United States. It's a nothing town. . . . Oh, all right then. But how could I get rid of my accent when I don't even hear it myself? Well, then I lived in San Francisco. . . . You expect me to remember the name of the street? How should I know? I lived on a hill. Is that good enough for you? . . . Thank you. I lived in a very nice house on the top floor, with my sister and her family. And then, with my first husband, who was killed in the war, we lived on Nob Hill. Fabulous apartment. Out of this world. We could see almost all the way to China. . . . Then New York, then my second husband and I moved down to Palm Beach, and I've divided my time ever since. . . . No, I haven't been back to San Francisco in—" she looked at Anna. "I'm asking my granddaughter."

Anna said, "What year?"

"Nineteen forty-four. You figure it out."

Anna said, "Sixty-one years."

"Sixty-one years," Goldie said into the phone. "I loved it. Have you ever felt that way about a place? Just absolutely passionately in love with it? . . . Yes, I've been to Calcutta. . . . No, I didn't have that feeling about Calcutta."

Anna tried to picture Naveen. Would he have called from the hospital? From his soulless apartment? Would he be wearing that beautiful cotton shirt? Was he standing in his kitchen in his jeans and sandals, pounding spices? What kind of expressions would cross his face as he listened to Goldie? Anna wanted to see him.

"San Francisco was so sophisticated," Goldie continued. "I worked as a salesgirl at Feld's. Do you know Feld's? . . . Exactly. Even more elegant than Neiman Marcus. Everything I know about style I learned from a Japanese girl who worked there with me, Mayumi Nakamura. And I learned about antiques from her brother, Henry, who taught me something important every single day."

Henry, Anna thought. *Henry* Nakamura.

Naveen must have asked a question, because Goldie paused for a moment. Then she said, "Yes, Bergère. It's French. Your mother must have good taste. . . . So I married Marvin Feld, whose family owned the business. He was a war hero. A darling, gorgeous man from one of the best families in San Francisco. The cream of the crop. When I lost him, I thought my life was over."

At this point, Goldie's tone became firmer, and her words seemed to be consciously directed toward her granddaughter. Anna glanced to her right. Yes, Goldie was staring straight at her. "Life goes on," Goldie said emphatically. "You pick up the pieces. I suffered the worst broken heart that a girl can suffer. But I'm a survivor. Don't you agree?" Anna stared at the road in front of her, pretending not to be listening. What was Naveen thinking, hearing this lecture?

All the while, Anna prepared for the moment when he would ask to speak with her. She would be calmer this time, though no less firm. They could chat, a bit.

Then Goldie said, "Thanks so much for calling, Doctor. Goodbye, then!"

Anna looked at Goldie. "He didn't have any questions about your health?"

"Of course he did. I told him I'm fine."

"What about the recipe?"

Goldie had reached down to the floor to pick up her purse. "I guess he forgot."

Anna acknowledged her disappointment, then tried to talk herself out of it. She had told Naveen that she didn't want to speak to him, so it was natural that he would give up trying to convince her. Still.

Anyway, what was the point of focusing on such feelings? Anna set her attention instead on Goldie's latest revelation "His name," she said, "is Henry Nakamura!"

Goldie turned to her abruptly. "What are you talking about?" she asked.

"You'd forgotten the first name of the man we're going to see—your friend's brother. The antiques dealer." As they traveled west, Goldie's memories had become more vivid. In the past, she had never talked about her time in San Francisco. Now she seemed nostalgic for the place.

"So what?" asked Goldie.

"It's just cool that you remembered."

"There's nothing cool about it," Goldie snapped. "I just remembered. And I don't know why you keep bringing up this subject. Would you like it if I asked you a thousand questions about the saddest time of your life?"

"Maybe."

"No, you wouldn't." Goldie opened her purse, slid the phone inside, then zipped it shut and sat back in the seat, turning her face toward the window as if she actually had an interest in the landscape. "I don't like to talk about the past, and I'm sure you don't, either. People who do that are dull."

Somewhat wearily, Anna repeated the phrase she had heard her grandmother say a thousand times: "I'm all about the future."

"That's my motto: All about the future."

Outside the car the wind seemed to have picked up, and Anna could feel its resistance as she pushed Bridget forward. For a woman who had been widowed twice, Goldie did have a remarkably forward-thinking perspective. When she talked about Marvin Feld at all—and she always called him by his whole name, Marvin Feld; her beloved son was simply Marvin—her descriptions were uniformly adulatory ("darling," "gorgeous," "smart," "brave"), but also vague and wooden ("a fine man, upstanding"). The only description that gave him an actual physicality was Goldie's praise for him as a "fabulous dancer." Marvin Feld played such a negligible role in Goldie's recollections of the past, in fact, that Anna could remember how once, years ago, Goldie had described herself in San Francisco as "nothing but a piece of dust floating on the wind." Anna and Sadie had been teenagers then, visiting their grandparents for spring break. Goldie had taken them out for a "ladies' lunch" of gazpacho and shrimp cocktails at the Colony Hotel, and perhaps because Saul had stayed home, she had been willing to indulge in a bit more reminiscence than normal. It was Sadie who picked up on the incongruity of Goldie's remark. "But wasn't San Francisco where you met and married Marvin Feld? I thought that was the place you got to decorate your first apartment." Perhaps if her granddaughters had still been amenable to Goldie's dictates on fashion, she would have replied more expansively, but the visit had been tense. Anna, for one, had refused to wear any of the clothes from Goldie's wardrobe that their grandmother had laid out on their beds. As a result, Goldie was prone to attack. "What would you know about decorating?" she had asked. "You girls would rather live in a pigsty. You've got the whole world handed to you on a silver platter and you turn up your noses at it." So much for Marvin Feld.

And what about Saul Rosenthal, Husband Number Two? He had adopted Marvin, Jr., and raised the boy as his own son. Anna and Sadie had never regarded him as anything but their grandfather, just as fully imbedded in their lives as Goldie, more distant but also more solidly benign. Between themselves, Anna, Sadie, and their parents called Goldie and Saul "the Corporation"—"Is the Corporation coming for Passover this year?" "Did you send the Corporation a thank-you note?" The nickname wasn't so much a reference to the Rosenthals' financial successes, which were clearly considerable, as it was to the way in which Goldie and Saul operated as a unit, a pair of savvy business partners who happened also to be married to each other.

It was Goldie who, after five or ten minutes, suddenly broke the silence that had settled between them. Despite her assertions, she, too, seemed to have been mulling over the past. "I know what it's like to lose a husband," she said. "You think you can't love again, but you're young. You probably haven't even met the love of your life."

Anna glanced away from the road to look at her grandmother. Here was Goldie, speaking as a true principal of the Corporation: 80 percent practicality, 20 percent emotion. But in order to contemplate the future, did you have to discount the past completely? "I don't see why you can't have two loves of your life. Or maybe even more."

Goldie shook her head. "They don't call it 'the loves of your life.' They call it 'the *love* of your life.'"

"It's not that simple. There's nothing to say you can't have two. Or ten."

"You can't," Goldie said.

"Then who was the love of your life?" Anna asked. "Poppy or Marvin Feld?"

Goldie slapped her hand against her purse. "For heaven's sake. Can you just stop? This conversation is giving me a headache."

"Fine," Anna said. The land was desolate here, and she couldn't see another car in either direction. The road curved up over a hill, slid around a bend, and brought them down into a valley. On a far ridge, a line of windmills held up their arms like people rooting for the universe.

Part Four

14

The Nightingale Floors

Goldie would remember the kiss on Marvin Feld's yacht as one of the most romantic moments of her life. She discovered almost immediately, however, that it didn't help to resolve her situation in any way.

Goldie was young, inexperienced, and ignorant of social complexities. Once she and Henry had declared their affection for each other, she presumed that they would marry. Granted, during her hungry journey across the country, hunched in a club chair staring out at the churning landscape, Goldie had pictured a future husband who didn't look like him at all. Now that she loved Henry, though, he seemed the perfect match. He had an education, ran his own promising business, dressed well, and showed good manners. On top of that, she found him kind, charming, and so extremely handsome that she couldn't understand how she had failed to see him that way before. Of course she'd marry him.

Henry, though, knew better. It was the summer of 1941. The United States had not yet entered the war, but national sentiment ran against the Japanese. Henry caught the audible mutterings of "Jap" when he passed the white chess players at the cable-car turn-around near his office. He saw the rigid intensity on his father's face when the old man read the Japanese-language papers. He recognized the urgency with which his mother worked her friendships in order to complete "good Nisei matches" for her daughter and son. Life for the Japanese had never been easy in America, but it seemed to be growing more difficult every day. How could Goldie be a part of that?

Late one afternoon, Henry appeared at the perfume counter and invited her out for a soda after work. As they walked up the block, Goldie chattered nonstop about sales for Pioneer perfume, less because she cared about the fragrance than because she needed to fill the space between herself and Henry. She felt nervous to be alone with him again, but also full of happy anticipation. In the next few minutes, she believed, she would experience the light touch of his hand under the table, a bump of their knees, a declaration of love. Instead, Henry ordered two Coca-Colas and immediately launched into an explanation of why, despite their feelings, the situation between them could not continue.

"Is it because I'm a Jew?" Goldie asked.

"A Jew?" he responded. He started to laugh, but he didn't want to upset her more.

"Yes, a Jew," she said. Her tone had turned icy. People hated the Jews, but she had expected more of Henry.

"Of course not," he said, defensive now.

"I know how people feel about Jews," she told him with a toss of her head. Growing up, Goldie had learned that the world looked down on two specific groups, the Negroes and the Jews. Her only consideration of Negroes was the relief she felt that she wasn't one herself. The only discrimination she'd actually experienced was not from gentiles but from wealthier Jewish people, who had developed their own rigid caste system. Goldie was the wrong kind of Jew—not the well-off German kind (the Feld kind) who lived at the tops of the hills, owned fashionable stores, and sailed on yachts. She came from the poorer class, the scarf wearers with their shtetl accents, tattered shoes, and smelly kitchens. Henry was an outsider, though. He couldn't know about all that.

The Coca-Colas arrived, and Henry slid one across the table toward Goldie. "This has nothing to do with you being Jewish," he told her. "I'm Japanese. You're not Japanese. That's the issue."

"I don't care that you're Japanese," Goldie told him. She loved everything about him now—his steady gaze, his ivory skin, the impossible slowness of his smile. She spoke honestly, but she had an uncomfortable sense that she was cajoling him. In her relations with men, Goldie prided herself on her finesse. She might entice, but she never chased. Now, perhaps to counteract the sound of pleading in her voice, she added, "Maybe, normally, I don't like Japanese. But I don't see those things in you. Or your family." She leaned forward and pertly sipped her cola through the straw.

Henry stiffened. "What things?"

Actually, Goldie had no idea what kinds of accusations people made against the Japanese, so she mined her knowledge of what people said about her own people. "You know. Dirty, greedy, conniving," she said, then added, for good measure, the things she'd heard about the Negroes as well: "Lazy. Stupid. Ignorant. That sort of thing."

For a moment, Henry just stared at her, stunned, but then he realized that she was bluffing. He began to laugh. "You don't even know what you're talking about," he told her.

Goldie picked up her napkin and patted her lips, looking at him over the top of the folded fabric. Over the past few days, she had felt her future finally solidify into something manageable and bright. Now, though, his laughter seemed to mock her. Had he been playing with her all along? Despite her varied experiences of dating, Goldie had never felt this kind of wound. Henry might not love her. Even worse, she saw now that his scorn could cause her physical pain, which gave her a sense of absolute remorse that she had ever cared about him at all. And then, like a cornered animal, she flashed her teeth and fought back. "I most certainly do," she said, squeezing the napkin into a ball in her hand. "You can't even walk down the street in Japantown without a Jap snatching your jewelry and running away with it."

Henry froze. He heard the words coming out of her mouth, but he saw, as well, that she was flailing. Some other lover, more confident and suave, might have known exactly how to defuse such a situation, but Henry was young, equally inexperienced, and too surprised to move. At the next table, two young men stopped eating to watch. A waitress looked up from the table she was wiping. Goldie announced, "Around here, nobody likes Japs."

Everything fell silent then. Perhaps, on the other side of the room, customers continued to talk over their burgers and sundaes, but the air around Goldie and Henry became more difficult to breathe. She would not have been surprised if he had simply walked out then. But happily for both of them, Henry's mind suddenly cleared. He stood up, pulled some money out of his pocket, and dropped it on the table. "Let's go," he said.

Once outside, he headed up the block, walking so quickly that she almost had to run to keep up with him. She no longer felt angry. Rather, she felt that same sense of dread that she had experienced as a child when she flattened Rochelle with a particularly effective kick to the groin: pride in her accomplishment but worry over what would come next. In that case, Rochelle, who had four years on Goldie, had retaliated by pressing her sister's face into the gravel lot, and Goldie had run home with shards of pebble embedded in her cheek.

But what now?

She followed Henry into the Hearst Building. Goldie knew that he had his office and storerooms here, but she had never visited. Silently they rode up the elevator with its fine woodwork and filigrees. Henry stared at the numbers above the door as, one by one, they lit up. One. Two. Three. Four. Five. Six. Seven. Eight. They heard a ping, and the elevator opened onto a hallway. The lower half of the walls was plaster. Frosted glass covered the distance to the ceiling, emitting a dim blue light, which was coming through the windows of the offices on the other side. She followed Henry to the last door at the end of the hall and waited while he unlocked it. The door opened onto two connected rooms, both lined with windows. The space was bright, simply furnished with the kinds of beautiful things that Henry supplied now to Feld's and other shops across the city: a matching pair of leather armchairs, a mahogany table serving as a desk, a lampshade covered in Chinese silk, and an oriental carpet patterned with birds and flowers in bursts of red and gold and blue. An interior door opened onto another room, that one stacked floor to ceiling with boxes. From where she stood, Goldie could read some of the labels: Indonesia. Hong Kong. New Zealand. Morocco. Many bore stamps in languages she couldn't read. She had heard Henry complain about his difficulties getting new shipments into the country because of the war. These days he concentrated his trade on antiques already available within the United States. Maybe these boxes had been shipped before the war even started. She couldn't tell.

Henry opened a corner cabinet and pulled out two highball glasses and a bottle of Scotch. He poured them each a shot, then walked to a sink in the corner and added some water. Goldie hadn't moved from her spot by the door, but she accepted the drink when he handed it to her.

"You can sit down," he said. His tone was chilly.

Goldie walked across the room and lowered herself into an armchair. She sat primly, resting her glass on her knee and putting her pocketbook on the windowsill beside her. Henry stood by the window looking out. From where she was sitting, she could not see the cars below, but even in the afternoon light she could observe the activity in the offices across the street. A secretary sat at her desk typing. Two men bent over a table looking at some papers. Goldie took a sip of her drink. She had tasted Scotch once or twice, and it no longer bothered her to feel the burn of it sliding down her throat, but she remained a cautious drinker.

Still he said nothing. A clock on the wall showed that it was nearly six. Goldie would have to catch the six thirty-seven bus to be home by seven, and then she'd have to hear Rochelle complain that Goldie had failed again to help with dinner. Her awareness of the time, though, didn't trouble her as much as the need to keep silent. Talking always soothed her.

It took Henry a long time to finish his drink. When he finally did, he put his glass on the windowsill, then sat down on the armchair next to Goldie's. She set her glass beside her purse. The expression on his face was less angry than distraught, and his eyes focused on his hands, which lay clutched together in his lap. "Do you remember the day I first met you, when my mother performed the tea ceremony for all of us?" he asked.

"Of course."

"Do you remember how Mayumi called our house 'the Nightingale Palace'?"

How could she forget such a thing? "I thought it was the most beautiful name I'd ever heard."

A look of annoyance crossed Henry's face. "My sister could use a few lessons in discretion," he said, but his tone was surprisingly tender. "Anyway, we never actually explained what we meant then. My parents have never even heard that name. Mayumi and I just made it up."

"Why?" Goldie asked.

Below, on Market Street, a car screeched to a stop, and from farther away they could hear the blast of a drill engaged in some kind of destruction. For a moment Henry seemed to concentrate on these distractions, then he said, "We were frustrated with them. I don't know if this will make sense to you, but the name relates to the Ninomaru Palace in Kyoto, which dates back to the time when Shogun rulers controlled Japan. It's very elegant and has some extraordinary artwork, but the most interesting thing about it is the ingenious methods the architects devised to protect the Shogun and his family." Briefly Henry raised his eyes to Goldie, but he quickly looked away again. "In the family quarters, where the Shogun lived, they put in wooden floors that had metal plates beneath them. When anyone walked on the floors, the plates rubbed together and made a beautiful sound, like birds singing. They called them 'Nightingale Floors.' If an enemy entered the castle, the singing of these 'birds' would alert the guards to protect the ruler and his family."

"How interesting," said Goldie, who had no idea how a security system in Japan related to her.

Henry continued. "Mayumi and I started calling our house 'the Nightingale Palace' because our parents are like that. They gave up everything in order to leave Japan, but this beautiful life that they've created here is completely focused on protecting our family, protecting our culture."

"I see," said Goldie, but she didn't, really.

At this point Henry lifted his gaze again. The effort seemed terrible, as if he had to muster every ounce of energy to raise his chin and look at her. "My mother made a match for me," he said.

Now it was Goldie who turned her eyes away. She knew what "a match" meant, of course, but the pieces didn't fall together in a way that made sense to her. "What do you mean?" she asked.

"I'm going to marry a Japanese girl from Stockton."

In an office in the building across the street, a young woman in a purple suit was offering a sheaf of papers to a man at a desk. The woman laughed. The man leaned back, raised his arms to the back of his head, and watched her with what looked to Goldie like admiration. It was one thing for Henry to reveal his mother's plans, but something else entirely to express his own willingness to go along with them. Goldie felt like he'd hit her in the stomach, but she also recalled again her childhood bouts with Rochelle. After years spent wailing and screaming, she had discovered that complete indifference would drive her sister mad. "Oh?" she asked Henry. "What's her name?" The words were intended to show nonchalance, but her voice sounded unsteady.

Henry didn't notice any of Goldie's reactions. "Akemi," he said, staring at his hands again.

"Is she pretty?"

He shrugged a shoulder, completely dismissive. "Yes. I guess. Her looks mean nothing to me."

"Does she have good manners? Is she elegant?" With each word, Goldie felt as if she were slapping her own face, but she couldn't stop.

He slumped deeper into his chair. "She's elegant enough. She's very shy. I've hardly talked to her. We had one meeting, at my house, when she and her family came up to visit. I barely paid attention."

Amid the predictable pain caused by this revelation, Goldie also felt a surprising, and equally intense, emotion of jealousy toward Henry at that moment. She could imagine the scene so clearly. The mothers in their fine clothes, with their dainty teacups and tasteless sweets. The young man, distracted but polite. The girl with her intricate hair and fingernails painted that morning, no doubt, by her mother. Her eyes would be gentle and kind, her pretty face pampered. The fathers would have understood each other perfectly. The light filtering down through the tea garden trees would have settled on the scene at just the right angle. Goldie wondered how it would feel to have parents who would go to such trouble for her.

Henry obviously had no notion of his luck in that regard. Suddenly he was at Goldie's knees, his head in her lap, his arms reaching up to hold her. "I want you!" he cried, burying his face in her skirt.

His passion elated her. Gently she stroked his cheek. "My darling," she whispered, and it didn't diminish the intensity of her devotion to recognize at the very same moment that the two of them looked like lovers in a movie.

Henry lifted his eyes to her then. If it had not been for the awkward layout of their surroundings—the narrow armchairs and a picture window that made this office just as revealing to the world as the ones across the street—anything might have happened between them at that moment. Instead, he stayed where he was. Goldie would make it home in time for dinner. But first he pulled her face toward his and kissed her. A few minutes later, his hand began to move. For the first time, Goldie felt a man's fingers pull open the buttons of her blouse and begin the timid but determined journey within. All her attention focused on his hand as it crossed her satin slip, reached the lace of her brassiere, then slipped inside at the point, she thought, where her heart must be, to grasp her breast. Henry pulled away then, breaking off their kiss to absorb the details of Goldie's newly revealed body. "Oh, God," he sighed, and then he pressed his mouth against her. Goldie could remember odd moments of her childhood—sitting in an awkward position on a bicycle, or touching herself in a particular way with a washcloth in the bath—that had inspired a feeling of intense pleasure between her legs. But this was something different. She felt bursts of heat that began at the center of her body and swept outward, all the way to her fingertips. Until that moment, Goldie had thought of romance in the same way that a starry-eyed child did, as an emotion of rose petals and bridal gowns, sweet perfume and chocolates in heart-shaped boxes. Now, although it would still be months before she understood completely, she realized that there was much, much more to it than that.

Goldie didn't, however, recognize that passion and commitment were not the same thing. When finally she pulled away from Henry and looked down into his love-struck face, she whispered, as if to comfort him, "We'll find a way to be together."

But Henry only shook his head. "We can't."

15

Things Fall Apart

*O*ver the rest of that summer and through the fall, Goldie and Henry refrained from meeting privately, but they saw each other often. He came by Feld's, perhaps even more frequently than before, to meet with Mr. Blankenship or accompany his sister home. Goldie and Mayumi continued to spend their time off together, wandering the lanes and avenues around Union Square, wistfully shopping. Often, on the weekends, they made their way together out to the tea garden, where Goldie was as welcome as ever. None of the Nakamuras, not even Mayumi, showed any suspicion that anything had changed between Goldie and Henry.

One gray, gusty afternoon in early December, the two girls rode the bus out toward Golden Gate Park. Goldie hadn't worn a heavy enough coat, and she was looking forward to the cup of green tea that the baroness would offer her. The girls chattered nonstop. Mr. Feld had recently added to Marvin's title of vice president a new position, head of merchandising, and like most of the staff at Feld's, Goldie and Mayumi mulled over the duties that such a position might entail.

Marvin never spent more than an hour or two at the store on a given day, and the responsibilities of Mr. Blankenship, who was not a vice president, seemed as all encompassing as ever. They had other matters to discuss as well, like the question of where Goldie would sleep when Rochelle had her new baby. And Mayumi complained about the hideous design of the bridesmaid dress that she would have to wear at Henry's wedding, which was now only four months away. Goldie managed this topic by concentrating on weddings in a general way, pushing from her mind the fact that they were talking about Henry's, and that he was marrying someone else. Goldie did occasionally sigh too overtly, and she became quiet and distant at certain moments as well, but Mayumi, who had a fine eye for detail about fashion or art, didn't notice. Perhaps it was simply too crazy to imagine that her best friend, a Jew, could have fallen in love with her Japanese brother.

The bus dropped them off on Stanyan Street, then Goldie followed Mayumi down the path through the woods, which soon turned muddy. The girls slipped off their shoes and ran barefoot, as they always had, across the cold, soft ground. Though the path twisted and turned in front of them, the route had become familiar to Goldie now. The exertion tired her, but it also reminded her of her inherent health and strength, which Henry's rejection had undermined considerably. "I'll be all right," she said, as much to herself as to Mayumi. "I'll manage."

Mayumi called back to Goldie over her shoulder. "You're like John Muir."

Goldie didn't know anything about John Muir, but one heard the name regularly in San Francisco. "Why does everybody talk about him?"

"He was a lover of the land," Mayumi replied. "A mountain man."

"I could be John Muir," Goldie said, stepping delicately over a branch, "if they have chocolate in the mountains. And good china. And if I could wear a pretty hat."

"How about green tea and cookies?"

"That would do." Despite her protestations about hating nature, Goldie loved the tea garden. Someday, if she ever had money, she'd like to host a party there. Mayumi had told her that one of San Francisco's most fashionable families had held a dinner years ago at the Conservatory of Flowers, setting up tables among the blossoms and ferns. Mayumi said that the newspaper had described the effect as one of "unequaled delight."

They came to the end of the path, stepping out of the woods onto the road near the entrance to the tea garden. Most days, the road was quiet except for a few people strolling this way and that, but now, to their surprise, dozens of people were running by in both directions. Goldie and Mayumi, with shoes in their hands, still breathing heavily, stopped and watched them.

"Hurry!" One woman urged her little boy forward, pulling the child by the hand.

"What is it?" But no one stopped to answer Mayumi.

Finally they saw a policeman on a horse up ahead. "Officer, what's happened?" they asked. They had heard the stories of the San Francisco earthquake, followed by the fire. Was there a new disaster now?

The officer looked down at the two barefoot young women, their stockings draped over their shoulders and their pumps dangling from their hands. He focused on Mayumi. "It's the Japanese. They've attacked Hawaii. Go home and turn your radio on."

The policeman rode away. Goldie hugged Mayumi, but her friend stood motionless, staring into space as she absorbed this news. And then she suddenly came to life again, pulling away to run up to a passing couple. She grabbed the woman's arm. "Did people die? Do you know?"

The couple didn't stop. The woman pulled, disentangling herself from Mayumi's grasp, while the man sneered, "Of course they did. Are you kidding?"

More people raced by, many holding the thermoses and warm blankets they had brought along to the park, some on bicycles, a few on roller skates, mothers pushing buggies. They all shared the same expression of fear and rage and confusion, looking straight ahead or glancing briefly at Mayumi, scowling. Were they really scowling or did Mayumi just imagine it? And then the girls were alone on the road. Goldie took Mayumi's arm and could feel her friend's body shaking. "Should we go find your parents?" she asked.

But Mayumi shook her head, turned, and pulled Goldie back up the path toward Fulton Street. It would be weeks before Goldie realized something that Mayumi understood immediately. A gulf lay between them now. "I'll take you back to the bus," Mayumi said. "You need to go home to your family."

As Mayumi had anticipated, the attack on Pearl Harbor changed everything. In the post office and at the bank, posters appeared pushing war bonds and rallying support for American troops: AVENGE DECEMBER 7! Feld's filled its windows with patriotic scenes of soldiers in uniform and women filling the factories, all of which Mayumi created despite her assumption, which she confided to Goldie, that she would soon lose her job.

Henry's marriage, which had been scheduled for March, was moved up to the end of December. According to Mayumi, the Japanese in San Francisco were anxious to settle unfinished business as quickly as possible. "We're all scared," Mayumi explained. "No one knows what will happen next."

Goldie seldom paid attention to what was taking place in the wider world, but she couldn't ignore Mayumi's worries. "You're no more Japanese than I am," she insisted.

Mayumi laughed. "That's not actually true," she said.

"Anyway, you're American."

"The Jews in Germany thought they were German until the Germans burned their houses down."

It was lunch hour, and the girls had found a sunny bench in Union Square on which to eat their hot dogs. "I hardly think that's going to happen here," Goldie said. She tried to be light about that issue. She didn't often think about the Jews in Europe, partly because they were so far away and partly because the thought of them made her anxious.

"Anyway," said Mayumi, who ate with such tiny, delicate bites that she could make a hot dog look like a cucumber sandwich, "at least the wedding plans give me something fun to think about. Just wait until you see it. We're doing the most amazing things with the tables. You'll adore it."

It was at moments like this that Goldie most fervently wished that Henry had confessed to his sister his feelings for Goldie. At least it would spare her the pain of conversations like this one. "I really don't think I can make it," she said.

The smile disappeared from Mayumi's face. "You're my closest friend," she said. "You have to be there."

Goldie tried to think of an excuse. "Rochelle needs me that day, too."

"We'll invite Rochelle. Wouldn't she want to come to a wedding?"

Goldie took a last bite of her hot dog, chewing slowly to give herself time to think. She knew that Rochelle would love to be at the wedding, so she tried another tactic instead. "The two of us will be the only people there who aren't Japanese."

"Silly!" Mayumi responded, turning on the bench to face Goldie. "The wedding isn't a *Japanese* wedding at all. It's at the Methodist church. Completely American." Her tone was light, but her body had tensed and she looked, suddenly, on the verge of tears. Goldie realized then that Mayumi needed to know that her dearest friend would associate publicly with the Nakamura family.

Goldie crumpled her hot dog paper between her fingers and threw her arms around her friend. "Of course I'll be there," she told her, and then she found herself running her hand along the back of Mayumi's head, smoothing down her hair and trying her best to comfort her sobbing friend.

Several times a week, Henry Nakamura would arrive at Feld's with new acquisitions to offer Mr. Blankenship. During the late summer and early fall of 1941, the provenance of Henry's inventory had expanded. Supplies from Asia and Europe had become more difficult to acquire, but he had found ample quantities of fine wood sculpture and stonework from Mexico and Brazil. He had beaded vases, handmade Hawaiian ukuleles, a pair of Victorian kid-leather christening shoes from England that had been imported decades before. By the time the Christmas season arrived that year, everything Mr. Blankenship bought from Henry sold quickly and at a good price. Even though the atmosphere for Japanese in California was deteriorating daily, and even though his personal life filled him with increasing anxiety and despair, Henry took some consolation from the fact that Nakamura Imports had become a thriving venture.

Whenever Henry completed his business meeting, he found an excuse to drift Goldie's way. Given the relationship between Goldie and his sister, it still seemed perfectly appropriate, both to them and to everyone else, that they would talk when they saw each other. Goldie, who always spotted Henry as soon as he entered the store, had learned to calibrate perfectly the minutes he spent upstairs in Mr. Blankenship's office. She could go to the ladies' lounge, check on her hair, reapply her lipstick, and make it back inside the perfume counter, or wherever she was assigned that day, with such casual nonchalance that no one could know that she'd timed her movements to coincide with his.

"How are you?" he would ask.

"I'm just fine," she would reply, giving him a smile that was both friendly and unconcerned. He never approached when she was with a customer, but still, she tried to look busy at these moments. Suddenly the brass fixtures needed polishing. A stack of perfume boxes demanded reassembly. Every breath, every movement, every glance from her needed to say: *Nice to see you, Mayumi's brother; I care no more for you than for any other man on the planet.*

But then, without fail, Henry would pull out whatever beautiful object he had brought to the store and show it to her. Goldie would become transfixed. Carefully his slender hands would open a box, unfold a velvet wrapper, unwind a leather strap from an ivory clasp. Goldie would become almost immobile with pleasure. She could remember experiencing similar sensations when she was a child, watching her mother braid her older sisters' hair, or do needlework, her fingers piercing the fabric as rhythmically as a musician strumming a guitar. For some reason, observing the fine, precise movements of someone else's hands gave Goldie a peculiar, almost physical delight. When those hands were Henry's, though, the experience became exquisite. She might never verbally express her love for him again, or feel his intimate touch as she had that afternoon in his office, but these moments spent gazing at his hands moving across a little tea set or carved wooden box offered, for Goldie, a fleeting but almost divine consolation.

Goldie stood on one side of the counter and Henry on the other, the object of their attention resting on the glass in between. Goldie appreciated every single thing—the Russian samovar, the pair of blackamoor clips from Venice, the English silver snuffbox (hallmark 1863). Once, he brought a carved ivory chess set in a case so small it could slide easily into a man's jacket pocket.

"It's English," he said, leaning as close to Goldie as propriety allowed, "but, you see, the pieces have an Indian motif. I imagine it was made for an Englishman who lived there during the Raj."

Goldie had never heard of the Raj, but it didn't matter. She loved the sound of Henry's voice. One by one, he showed her elephants, tigers, tiny turbaned men. "Look at the rook," he said. He held the castle in the palm of his hand.

Goldie leaned closer, her arms folded on the glass display case.

"Do you see it?" Henry asked.

She stared. "What am I supposed to see?"

"The boa constrictor." With one finger, he traced a line up and around the castle wall.

The movement of his hand gave Goldie an even deeper thrill. Carefully, she looked more closely at the little castle. Beneath the tip of Henry's finger, a snake, carved from the ivory itself, climbed like a vine. "I've never seen anything so delicate," she murmured.

For an instant, they gazed directly into each other's eyes, and then, just as quickly, Henry looked away. He put the rook back in its pocket and pulled out the king. Anyone passing Goldie's perfume counter would have heard him shift into a more businesslike conversation then: "If Feld's passes on this, I'll probably take it down to Los Angeles. I've got a buyer at McAllister's who asked to see it." In truth, Henry now expected to hold on to this chess set for the rest of his life. He imagined that it would, in later years, provide him with the link to an essential memory of Goldie's face, and he wouldn't let go of something so necessary to his well-being. This sense of the sublime, though, was also why he looked away and changed his tone so firmly. Huddled close to her above the glass, he felt completely untethered, and the mention of Feld's, Los Angeles, and McAllister's served as a ballast to pull him back down. He composed himself. He took his next breath. Sometimes, when he left Goldie's side, Henry felt dizzy.

For her part, Goldie only really needed one thing from these encounters: a sign that his feelings for her had not changed. When she caught him looking at her, she felt it. If he avoided her gaze and kept up an appearance of friendly distance, she retaliated by freezing him out.

Which is what she did right now. "Thanks so much for bringing this by," she told him briskly. And with that, she set her sights on Alan Stevenson, who was buffing some loafers in men's shoes a few feet away. "Oh, Alan! Can you help me with this urn?" she said. "I'm just trying to adjust it." Then, turning to offer Henry one last dismissive wave, she saw the look of desolation on his face, which gave her exactly what she needed.

By the time of Henry's wedding, they had each become so tortured by these encounters that both of them came to hope that their impending doom would bring some relief. In short, Henry and Goldie were old enough to comprehend the finality of marriage, but too young to understand that such an event might have absolutely no effect on their emotions.

The wedding took place just before Christmas on a Saturday afternoon at the Pine United Methodist Church. Among the mostly Japanese crowd, Goldie and Rochelle stood out, not simply because they were Caucasian but because Goldie always attracted attention. She wore a slim-cut green dress with a white patent leather belt that cinched her waist into something so tiny a man could imagine stretching his fingers around it. Many of the women, Rochelle included, wore hats, most of which looked like little teacups turned upside down on their heads. Goldie went hatless. She had recently begun to wear her hair European style, pulled back into a bun, like Mayumi, and the effect, with the dress and a pair of large white geometric earrings, made her look like a visitor from Paris.

"Do you think they'll make us bow?" Rochelle asked with some concern. Her knowledge of the Japanese came from what she had seen on newsreel footage at the movies. She was six months pregnant with her third child, and bending made her queasy.

"No, they won't make us bow," Goldie responded. As the younger, unmarried sister, she continually suffered from Rochelle's comments about her ignorance. It was nice, for a change, to find herself the worldly one. "They're just like us," she said, "only Christian."

Soon, the organ struck a few notes and the congregation stood and turned toward the rear of the church. A door opened. Henry walked in with his father. For weeks, Mayumi's talk about the wedding had included discussion of Henry's suit. Goldie had some idea, then, of what he had chosen, but she was not prepared for the sight of him walking up the aisle. He wore a simple, London-style dark gray suit, but unlike the badly cut and shapeless suits that most men purchased, Henry's had the crisp lines of the clothes worn by the young industrialists she saw in photos on the society page. Goldie considered Henry almost impossibly handsome, but she had gotten used to that. What she found unbearable was the fact that now, walking gracefully down the aisle in his wedding attire, he had a manner that proclaimed, "I'm going somewhere." Of course, Goldie wanted to go with him.

Rochelle, who had never met Henry, whispered, "He's not bad looking for a Japanese."

Henry stared straight ahead, and though he saw Goldie, he didn't show it. The organ paused and, a moment later, began again with the bridal march. Mayumi appeared in the lacy pink dress that she despised, followed by three other bridesmaids and finally the bride herself, on the arm of her father. Her dress was lacy as well, with a prim collar, a shoulder-length veil, and a bouquet of carnations so large and pink and weighty that the fragile Akemi appeared in danger of toppling over with them. The girl moved slowly, eyes on the ground, and Goldie could almost believe she was counting her steps. Akemi did have a pretty face, as Henry had acknowledged, but she seemed wholly docile and without spark.

Henry, from where he stood at the front of the church, saw these qualities in his bride as well. He had never looked at Akemi from any point of view that wasn't completely objective. He didn't love her; he didn't hate her. His opinions were entirely reasoned and devoid of emotion. She was sweet and pretty enough. She would probably make an excellent wife. He didn't compare Akemi to Goldie, because he didn't consider the two in relation to each other. He loved one and he was marrying the other. From where he stood now, it seemed that the sunlight streaming in through the southern window fell like a beam directly onto Goldie's face. Henry wasn't a complete romantic, though. He maintained enough self-awareness to recognize that the effect was most likely a trick of his imagination.

The reception took place in the church social hall downstairs. The guests sat at round tables, drinking tea and punch and helping themselves to cookies and dainty sandwiches arranged in artful designs on silver trays at the center of each table. Goldie and Rochelle found themselves at one of the two tables reserved for "professional acquaintances," which was basically all the people who weren't Japanese. One table consisted of Golden Gate Park officials who worked with the baron, and the other of Feld's employees and Henry's associates in the antiques trade. A few seats remained empty, including, notably, that of the Golden Gate Park supervisor, Mr. Banes, who, as a World War I veteran, was assumed to be too patriotic to attend such an occasion.

Goldie sat between Alan Stevenson and Rochelle. Today, the qualities that had once attracted her to Alan—his exemplary sales record, his brown-haired, brown-eyed all-American good looks, his jokes about car racing and sailing—now struck her as terribly boring and indistinguishable from those of so many other San Francisco men. Rochelle, though, was delighted to have the chance to speak with a clean-cut non-Jew with excellent manners. She leaned forward on Goldie's other side, employing her rusty conversational skills to engage his attention. "And are you a habitué of weddings, Mr. Stevenson?" she asked.

"Unfortunately, never my own," he responded with a mock self-pity that made Goldie sigh audibly with irritation.

"I'm just sure you could find some lovely girl whenever you set your mind to it," said Rochelle, who had retrieved her southern accent from the same mothball-laden chest out of which she had scrounged up her best brassiere.

Alan Stevenson leaned a little closer toward Goldie now, the conversation bringing out a friskiness that he had rarely demonstrated during their lackadaisical romance. "You see, Rochelle," he said, "lovely girls don't seem to see me in the same way that I see them. I think I'm destined to be a bachelor for my entire life."

Rochelle gave him a sympathetic smile. "Oh, I doubt that. Take it from a married woman. You'll find someone. Or maybe I should say, someone will find you."

While Rochelle laughed, Goldie felt the weight of Alan Stevenson's shoulder pressing against hers. He had never been as ardent as she might have wanted, but he had continued to ask her on dates. She idly wondered if a wedding could bring out the same kind of longing in an unmarried man as it did in a single girl. She felt his fingers under the table, nimbly tapping against hers. A few months earlier, the effect might have been tremendous, but she felt annoyed by it now.

At the front of the hall, the band struck up the tune of the first song. Alan stopped talking, listened to a few notes with his eyes closed, then opened them and looked at Goldie. The song was "You'd Be So Easy to Love," and he crooned the words softly. Rochelle drummed her fingers against the table in accompaniment. Goldie turned her eyes downward and examined her nails.

Rochelle encouraged Alan. "You've got to get her out there," she said.

He took Goldie's hand. "Shall we?" he asked.

Goldie watched the dance floor. "The bride and groom take the first dance," she reminded him.

And there they were. Henry and his bride had been stolidly

moving around the hall, greeting guests at each of the tables. Now, halfway through the task, he stopped and took his new wife's hand, leading her toward the dance floor. Akemi didn't show any more vivacity than she had shown walking down the aisle, but at least she was smiling now.

"Do you think she's ever danced an American dance?" Alan asked, speaking softly enough that only Goldie and Rochelle could hear.

"I hope she doesn't trip," Rochelle said.

Goldie had no patience for this kind of chatter. "She's been living in this country since she was seven." She watched as Henry slid his arm around Akemi's waist. They danced well together, with poise and precision, but no one could miss the formality between them. His hand rested high on her back, but well below the point at which her lacy collar stopped, revealing her bare skin. His gaze floated somewhere above her head. She stared into his chest.

Rochelle said, "You could drive a truck between the two of them."

Other dancers had begun to take their places on the floor. Alan pulled Goldie along behind him, and soon she felt herself relax as she glided to the music. Whatever other emotions she might be experiencing, dancing could still give her joy. Alan moved with grace, too, and pulled her closer toward him. "It does seem a shame," he sang into her ear, "that you can't see your future with me." His hand moved down her arm, then squeezed her fingers.

"You flirt," she said, not even bothering to look at him.

Alan held her tighter. Her disdain inspired in him an interest that those earlier months of dogged conniving for his affections had never managed to secure. With a burst of drama, he twirled her. The novelty of the move surprised her and she laughed. Then, suddenly, they turned, and she found herself facing Henry directly. The two couples began to circle in each other's orbit. "It's a beautiful afternoon," Alan announced, pulling Goldie closer. "You two have started something. Romance is in the air!"

Akemi offered the same polite smile she'd been offering all afternoon. Henry looked at them, unable to say anything and equally unable to pull himself away. He made no attempt to disguise the emotion in his face. For the first time, his suffering gave Goldie no satisfaction. Instead, it nearly shattered her. And then she felt an enormous, unexpected anger well up inside. Why had he done such a thing? Why had he caused them both so much pain? Without Alan Stevenson's strong arms around her, she might have slapped Henry across the face. But Alan was holding her. She turned her eyes toward him, lifted her hand to his cheek, and gently held it there. "My sweet boy!" she exclaimed. And then, just as suddenly, the music switched tempo and he swept her away.

They were all drinking coffee when Henry and his bride finally arrived at their table. Rochelle, overcome by the sentiments of a wedding (even a Japanese one), fairly gushed over Akemi's hair, dress, and suede shoes. "They're so fetching!" she exclaimed.

Alan, too, seemed taken. "You're just as cute as a China doll," he said.

"And the gloves," Rochelle said, "they're so elegant." Akemi's giggle sounded like the tinkling of little bells. She held her fingers up shyly while Rochelle examined the gloves' intricate lacework and patterning. For once, Goldie appreciated her sister, whose exclamations were so voluble that Goldie herself didn't have to say a word.

With all this attention focused on the bride, then, Goldie and Henry found themselves standing alone. "This is really divine," she said, using her lightest tones.

He smiled, but she could hear the words coming out of his frozen lips. "I'm dying," he told her.

She laughed then, loudly, throwing her head back as if she had heard a hilarious joke. To Goldie, it sounded like a scream, but no one else appeared to notice this odd exchange between the groom and the best friend of his sister. Whose devastation was worse, she wondered, Henry's with his future sealed, or Goldie's with hers so uncertain?

After the wedding, Alan drove Rochelle home, and then he and Goldie headed south out of the city toward a little restaurant he knew in Pescadero. It was just after four o'clock. Though the sun set early in December, the sky remained so deceptively bright that it seemed the day would last forever. They rolled down the windows and turned up the radio, sending the notes of the Benny Goodman Orchestra flowing like a wake behind them on the narrow road.

"The girl from Memphis needs to see the coast," he told her as they rounded a bend and saw to their right the great expanse of the Pacific Ocean.

"I can't think of anything more perfect," Goldie said, the buoyancy of her tone reflecting, to Alan at least, her wonder over the extraordinary vista. In reality, Goldie was not so much amazed by the view as grateful to have left behind the oppressive good cheer of the wedding. Even this relief, though, remained tempered by the fact that the man she loved was married.

Alan drove with one hand, resting the other lightly on Goldie's knee. He had been making such gestures all afternoon—a hand on her leg, a finger sliding along her neck, an arm resting across her shoulders. In the past, Alan Stevenson had always balanced a strong attraction for Goldie against a fear of entanglement. Despite his statements to Rochelle, he didn't actually regard himself as a marrying kind of man, or at least not the kind to marry a charming but penniless Memphis Jew. Until now, he had taken Goldie out regularly but not very often, and never with the kind of eager attentions that would telegraph to a girl that he was in love. Lately, though, his rhythm had begun to change. Simply put, Alan Stevenson's interest increased as Goldie's waned. Her occasional requests for help at the perfume counter notwithstanding, she had neglected him, and he didn't like it. He had gone to the wedding fully intending to woo her back.

The road wound through the hills, the ocean always beside them. They rumbled past beaches and farmland, following the contours of the land to trace the edges of cliffs above the churning Pacific. "Don't be scared," Alan assured her. "Some girls get nervous on this road."

Goldie had been staring out the window without actually seeing anything. The sound of Alan's voice brought her back to the present, and she forced herself to pay attention to the landscape. "Oh, my," she said, gazing out toward the sea.

She picked up his hand from her knee and, without really thinking about what she was doing, lifted it to her mouth and kissed each finger one by one. At that moment, Goldie was only vaguely aware of Alan's presence. She understood, within the context of her own misery, that she needed him right now, which meant she had to demonstrate that she had not forgotten him entirely. Her own lack of feeling, however, caused her to seriously miscalculate the effect that a gesture like this could have on a man whose lust had grown increasingly less manageable as the day progressed. Those little taps of lip against finger left Alan Stevenson almost completely unwound. "Oh, Goldie," he sighed.

After about an hour, they turned off the highway, then followed a country road east toward Pescadero. At first Goldie saw nothing but farmland. Then, after a mile or so, the town appeared, and they pulled to a stop amid a run-down collection of buildings lining a dusty intersection. "The great restaurant is *here*?" she asked. It seemed like a long way to drive for so little.

Alan grinned and pulled the keys out of the ignition. "Trust me," he told her. Then he came around the side of the car and opened the door for her. It might have been a nothing town in Goldie's eyes, but she did notice that expensive-looking cars filled every space along the street. Alan took her hand and led her toward a door.

Inside, they walked through a carpeted vestibule and stepped down through a red velvet curtain into a large room arranged with tables set elegantly around a dance floor. Other diners already filled most of the seats. The men wore suits and smoking jackets, the women evening gowns, elbow-length gloves, high heels. Goldie still had on her outfit for the wedding, which was appropriate for a day-time ceremony and reception but made her look underdressed now. She lifted her hand to her head and smoothed down her hair.

A maître d' in a white tuxedo approached them. "Good evening, Mr. Stevenson," he said. "Your regular table?"

Alan nodded. He glanced at Goldie to see that she was impressed. They followed the maître d' to a table on the edge of the dance floor. He pulled a chair out for Goldie, then handed them menus. Goldie glanced around the room. "I don't even know the name of this res-taurant," she said.

"Maestro's Inn," he told her. "Most people just call it Maestro's." He pulled a cigarette from his silver case and struck a match. "They call it the most famous place that no one ever talks about."

Now that her eyes had adjusted to the light, Goldie could more easily observe the scene around her. The restaurant, with its white linen, twinkling crystal, and lively band, seemed much like the other fine restaurants she had visited in San Francisco, but she sensed a difference in the atmosphere here. At other establishments, each table served as its own little planet of activity, with diners focused on the people they were with. Here, people seemed equally interested in diners at the tables surrounding them. They turned to observe each new party that stepped into the room. The mood was festive, but also edgy and distracted, and this combination gave the room an energy that Goldie found unfamiliar and intriguing.

"It feels like something's about to happen here," she said. "Is there a show or something?"

"Just dancing." Alan kept his eyes on the menu. When he looked up, he leaned forward as if he were making her a tender offer. "You know, they serve lobster here. Would you like that?"

Goldie felt no loyalty to her religion, but the idea of eating pork or shellfish still repelled her. "I love a good steak," she told him.

Alan had heard that lobster made women receptive, but when he failed to convince Goldie to try one, he settled for a couple of steaks, some baked potatoes, and a bottle of champagne to "celebrate the newlyweds." The mention of the wedding made Goldie's face, which had finally grown more attentive, turn vacant again. Alan wondered if she expected his efforts tonight to lead to a proposal. The idea concerned him, but he didn't feel it necessary to alter his plans.

They danced every song. The band was only a combo, but their sound was lively and confident, and they seemed to play every melody that Goldie had ever loved. Dancing offered a kind of salvation to her then. She didn't have to think at all with Alan leading her across the floor. Together, they danced the Jitterbug, the Balboa, and the St. Louis Shag, stopping to eat only when the band took its breaks. As soon as they heard the musicians tuning up again, Goldie pulled Alan back onto the dance floor. Eventually their rainbow sherbet turned into forgotten little puddles in their crystal bowls.

At about eight o'clock, the music slowed and the band slid into "Fools Rush In." Alan pulled Goldie closer. She rested her head on his shoulder. He had taken off his jacket now, and his body, pressing against hers, gave off a heat that she found unexpectedly soothing. Goldie chided herself for her disappointment. Who had ever promised that anything wonderful would come her way? Don't think about your empty pocket, Goldie's mother had told her, think about finding that penny on the ground. Alan Stevenson was tall and handsome, Caucasian, manly, and ambitious. Every time an image of Henry floated into her mind, she resolutely pushed it away. When she felt Alan's lips against her neck, she closed her eyes and tried to focus completely.

There were times in Goldie's life when she possessed an astonishing ability to read the clues in front of her. At Feld's, she could estimate a woman's wealth by the scent of her perfume or the seam of her stockings. On dates, the way a man unfolded his napkin or buttered his bread supplied her with everything she needed to know about his background and education. She had found herself to be so consistently accurate that, in her brief adult life, she had developed an almost unflagging confidence in the sharpness of her intuition.

But tonight she was not so astute. It was perhaps too much to expect that such a young woman would remain observant at all times, particularly on a day that had nearly destroyed her. By this point, her emotions had worn her down and blinded her. Goldie failed to notice the shift in atmosphere that began to occur when the lights dimmed and the music slowed. She had not even contemplated the obvious questions about Maestro's Inn: Why would an elegant restaurant become so crowded with fashionable people at 5 P.M.? Why had these people traveled so far from the city? And why now, when it was still quite early, did it feel like the end of the night? There were other details, too, that Goldie missed entirely. For one thing, among the couples in the room, she might have noticed a predominance of gray- and white-haired men paired off with voluptuous younger women wearing magenta lipstick and thick mascara. The women's gowns, too, had necklines that dipped surprisingly low, and side slits that rose to levels that weren't quite proper. Goldie didn't notice the way the men slid their hands up and down their partner's bodies, or see the couple kissing deeply a few feet away from her. She rested her head on Alan's shoulder, keeping her eyes shut, telling herself again and again that things could get better.

Despite her obliviousness, then, it was this commitment to her future, and not her naïveté, that compelled Goldie to follow Alan out of the dining room and down a hallway that led them in the wrong direction. Later she would remember a room draped with satin curtains, a tiled bathroom, a large bed. She would remember, too, that she didn't agree, but she didn't argue, either. He was gentle enough, but driven more by urgency than care. And when, finally, she felt him slide between her legs, she wasn't completely surprised by what was happening. Instead, she pictured the smooth chairs, the lovely rug, the big window looking out onto Market Street, and the inconsolable expression on Henry's face. Now she understood that every touch, every kiss and whisper of love could, after all, have led Goldie and Henry to this. But it hadn't, and among all the emotions she would feel that night and for the days and months and years that followed, it was this sense of having missed something essential with Henry that affected her most.

By midnight, they were turning up Sacramento Street and pulling to a stop in front of Rochelle's house. Alan had held her hand for a while as they drove back up the coast, but gave that up and lit a cigarette instead. Goldie had stared out the window. Sometimes the moon lit up the hills, sometimes it seemed as though the entire world had vanished. She felt drained inside, as if she'd used up every emotion, but she sensed, too, the earliest stirrings of a deep and abiding revulsion for him.

Alan didn't get out of the car to open the door for her. He glanced at his watch. "Nobody's turning into a pumpkin tonight!" he joked, as if he'd fulfilled his princely obligations.

Goldie opened her purse and looked for her key. Was she supposed to thank him for a night like this one? "Rochelle will probably blast me about how late it is," she said. She opened the door, but before getting out she stopped, leaving it wide open, and leaned back into her seat again. "I wonder," she said, staring out the windshield in front of them. "Did I ever tell you about my sister Louise?"

"Not that I recall," he said.

"She's the oldest of the ten of us. I'd say she's nearly forty. She used to be a pretty girl, and she went on an awful lot of dates. One fellow proposed, but Louise thought she'd find a better match, so she discouraged him. Another young man moved away. My mother was sick, and my father was no kind of provider for us. We needed money, so Louise found work cleaning houses and eventually moved in with a rich family downtown. It's not easy finding a husband when you've got a job like that. Then she lost her looks. Domestic work will do that." Goldie turned to Alan. "Have you ever seen the hands of a girl who does domestic work, Alan?"

He had lit another cigarette. He didn't want to seem callous, but he saw where this was going, and he didn't want to get entangled, either. "Sure," he told her. He let the smoke sift through his lips, focusing his attention on the dim glow of the embers. The fact was, he had no intention of marrying a Jew.

"It is not a pretty sight," Goldie continued. "Your fingers get blistered and cracked. Sometimes they bleed. You spend half your time with your hands in hot water and the other half burning yourself with an iron. Poor Louise. She would have made a perfect wife." She looked at him. "You know, Alan, Louise's situation scared me. I came to San Francisco, all by myself, because I thought I'd have a better chance here."

Alan tried to laugh. "You don't have to worry about a thing like that, Goldie."

"Actually, I do."

He shifted in his seat. He'd enjoyed the evening, but he got no pleasure from her manipulation.

Goldie touched the back of her head. Earlier, in the bathroom, she had straightened her clothes again, then stared at her face for a while in the mirror. Eventually she managed to reassemble her bun so that she could return to Rochelle's looking as she had when she left. The events of the evening had caused her to lose some bobby pins, though, and now, sitting in the car, she discovered strands of hair falling out of place again. "What a mess," she muttered. One by one, she pulled out the pins and, holding them between her lips, let her hair tumble down to her shoulders before securing it again with a few deft twists and an artful replacement of the pins. "That should work," she said, before turning her attention back to Alan. "I just want you to know that this evening together meant a lot to me."

He squirmed. "Well, sure."

Goldie put her hand on his leg and leaned closer. To Alan's surprise, the gesture affected him. Despite her obvious cunning, he had enjoyed himself with her, and she remained more intoxicating than he would have liked. Perhaps he could find a way to continue to see her after all. It might be complicated, but he was smart enough to manage. Wasn't that part of the fun—the battle between the sexes? He started to pull her toward him, but Goldie moved away, preferring instead to whisper in his ear.

"Oh, Alan," she said. Her tone was deliciously soft and seductive. The sound alone excited him even more, which might explain why it took so long for him to absorb the meaning of her last few words. "I'd rather clean houses for the rest of my life," she purred, "than marry a rat like you." By the time Alan Stevenson did comprehend what Goldie had said, she was out of the car. He saw nothing but the side of her arm as she slammed the door behind her.

Goldie ran across the sidewalk and up the stairs, gripping her pocketbook in one hand and holding her hair in place with the other. At the door to the apartment, she slid her key into the lock and quickly turned the knob. Rochelle's accusations began before she'd even stepped into the hallway. For the first and last time in her entire life, the sound of her sister's voice gave Goldie comfort, so much comfort, in fact, that it brought her to tears.

16

Appendicitis

$\mathcal{G}$oldie had left school after eighth grade, and though she witnessed the progress of her sister's pregnancy, nothing in her education had taught her to read the signals her own body began to provide over the next few weeks. At first she took the exhaustion and nausea as signs of flu. She noticed the lateness of her period, but her knowledge of female fertility was vague and incomplete, and she made no connection between her current symptoms and the fact that she wasn't bleeding anymore. Goldie's mother had died before giving her any information about relations between women and men. Her sister Eleanor had at times offered advice like "Don't be alone in a room with a man" and "Keep your panties on." Once Goldie had moved from Memphis to California, Rochelle made a few distracted attempts to offer cryptic warnings—"Be careful!" and "Watch out!"—but Rochelle had been so focused on her own small children and her currently bulging belly that she didn't notice the signs of change in her sister. By now, strong smells made Goldie feel sick. She couldn't eat anything but fresh fruit and warm milk. And she felt monumentally tired. All she wanted to do was nap.

Some nights, though, she couldn't sleep. Late in the evening, she curled up on her bed, a narrow sofa in the children's room, wedged between the toddler bed and the crib. While the children slept, she moved her hands uncertainly over her body, which seemed to be failing her. Was it some strange disease? Did she have cancer? Sleepless, she could watch the crisscross pattern the moonlight threw against the wall over the baby's crib. Some nights she would lie for hours staring at it, and in the darkness, her sense of color became unsure. What color were those boxes of light on the wall? Were they yellow? Gray? Even in her worried state, she still had the presence of mind to imagine a dress in such a fabric—hazy and geometric, in night shades of black and yellowy gray—but she had come to feel so hopeless about her life that the possibility of ever having such a dress seemed no more realistic than the possibility that she would be crowned princess and get to wear a tiara.

One morning in early February, the cramps began as she stepped from the bus on her way to work. She felt some discomfort, but nothing painful, and wondered if her "monthlies," as she and Rochelle called them, had finally returned. If they had, she knew there was a box of pads and belts in a drawer in the ladies' lounge, kept there for just such emergencies. Once she arrived at Feld's, she ducked into the lounge and checked inside her underwear, but nothing had happened. It was nearly 9 A.M., so she hurried to her post at the circular tie counter, where, because she'd been feeling "under the weather," she had been assigned for the past week. The tie department was a coveted position because employees could spend most of the day on a stool. Goldie felt grateful to Mr. Blankenship for assigning her there, though he may also have noticed the increase in tie sales. When Goldie was stationed there, it seemed that every college boy in San Francisco needed a tie.

Not long after she'd stepped behind the counter, one of those very boys approached and lingered shyly near the cabinet, his gaze half on the selection inside and half, surreptitiously, on Goldie.

"Can I help you?" she asked, standing up from the stool and moving over toward the side of the counter near where the boy hovered. Because she wanted Mr. Blankenship to always see her busy, she held a rag in her hand to wipe the counters.

"I need a blue tie," the boy said. Goldie glanced down through the glass. Blue ties in every imaginable pattern lay on a tray before them, and the young man was wearing one, too. He moved closer and peered down through the glass.

Goldie might have been profoundly ignorant about the human body, but she had an intuitive understanding of her influence on men. Gently, she lifted her hand and took the edge of the boy's own tie between her fingers. "Are you looking for something like this one?" she asked him, bending closer. She knew that doing so enhanced his view of her breasts, but she didn't mind. She liked to display her body in a way that seemed thoughtless and unintentional. It made men feel that they were getting a glimpse of something private.

That was Goldie's normal approach, at least. Today, she was leaning forward in order to take the pressure off her feet. The cramping had started again, mild waves that moved up from her lower groin, then expanded out in every direction. She had to conserve her energy for the eight hours of work ahead of her. She shifted onto a different leg, but that changed nothing.

The sight of her fingers on his tie clearly distracted the young customer, and she let go because she didn't want to scare him off. He looked well dressed, and she thought perhaps that, with the right technique, she could sell him two ties, maybe three. "Um, yes, something blue," he said.

"Let me show you." She unlatched the cabinet and began to pull out a tray. Just then she felt a stabbing pain, like something suddenly slicing through her gut. "Uh!" she gasped, gripping the edge of the display. She looked around, feeling as if the earth had moved, but no one had noticed. The boy kept his eyes on the ties. He might not have even heard her.

Goldie looked down. Turning her foot, she saw a thin stream of blood moving down her lower leg and along her ankle, then disappearing into her shoe. The pain did not stop. Somehow she managed to set the tie tray on the counter. "Just a moment," she managed to say. "Let me see if I can get someone to help you."

Just then, Marvin Feld was walking by. Since the day on the boat the previous summer, Goldie's relationship with Marvin had settled into a warm and respectful acquaintance. More recent events had caused her to forget her plan to marry him, and she certainly didn't think of him as a friend. If someone had told Goldie in advance that she would face a choice at this moment, to call to Marvin Feld or die, she would have said that she would die.

Goldie's instinct for self-preservation was stronger than she knew, however. The potential for embarrassment didn't even cross her mind. "Mr. Feld," she called. "Could you help me?"

Goldie's face was white and full of strain. Marvin, seeing it, hurried over. "Miss Rubin," he said. "What is it?"

Goldie felt another stab of pain. Now she doubled over, blinded, but still aware of the customer on the other side of the counter. "I've dropped something," she groaned quietly. "Could you help me, please?" she clutched the side of the cabinet to keep herself from falling.

Swiftly, Marvin raised the hinged counter and stepped inside the display case. He saw the blood running down Goldie's leg and beginning to pool on the floor. "Oh, my," he said. Then he turned toward the young man, who seemed frozen over the selection of ties. "I'm so sorry, sir," he said. "You'll have to excuse us. Could you come back tomorrow?" Then he yelled toward French Agnes in scarves, "Call an ambulance!"

For the next several minutes, Marvin crouched in that tiny space beside Goldie, holding her hand, wiping the sweat off her forehead, whispering soothing words. The staff of Feld's had always seen Marvin as friendly enough, but disinterested and lazy. He seemed like a good-natured rich boy to them. But Marvin had spent a year on a Liberty ship in the Atlantic. He had seen his share of injury and battle. Among the dozens of staff and customers in the store at that moment, no one was better fit to sit with Goldie than Marvin Feld, who could look at the blood pooling on the floor without feeling even slightly squeamish. Marvin moved in closer, gripping Goldie's hand, and when she couldn't sit up any longer, he held her. "What's happening to me?" Goldie asked. "Am I dying?"

"Of course not," Marvin said, his voice so full of resolve that he managed to convince her, if not himself. "You'll live," he whispered again and again, until the ambulance finally arrived and took her away.

Later, Goldie would not remember the ride to the hospital. She would not remember the doctors' brief examination, the diagnosis of a ruptured ectopic pregnancy and massive internal bleeding, anything about the surgery itself, or even much about the days she spent in the hospital while she recovered from the miscarriage. She remembered the lovely vase of flowers that Marvin sent, and Rochelle's furious, repeated demand: "Who was it?" By this time, though, Goldie had figured out the details of the birds and the bees, and she refused to answer. Rochelle, as bloated and whiny as she may have been, knew enough to stop asking. Two weeks later, informing everyone within earshot that she had almost died of appendicitis, Goldie returned to work as if nothing really terrible had happened.

17

Empty Shelves

By February 1942, President Roosevelt had ordered all Japanese Americans out of the regions along the Pacific Coast. People of Japanese descent, most of whom were U.S. citizens, were told to pack up their things and report to receiving centers, from which they would later be relocated to more permanent quarters in internment camps. The Nakamura family congregated on the morning of February twenty-fourth on Post Street between Buchanan and Sutter. Henry and his new wife arrived by taxi with his mother and Mayumi. They had three trunks between them, plus a couple of duffels full of sheets, towels, and other dull but necessary household items, which took up an infuriating amount of space. Henry's father had remained at the house in Golden Gate Park for another hour or so. He had been wandering through the gardens all night. "I see no need to rush," he said. By that evening, they would be living in temporary housing at the Tanforan Racetrack, just outside the city. "We will have nothing to do when we get there, in any case."

Henry didn't argue with his father. He merely instructed him to meet the rest of the family at Uncle Aki's store, extracting a promise that the old man would show up. Henry could imagine his father now, moving slowly through the garden, taking time at each bed to offer a silent good-bye.

The rest of the family dragged their things inside the store and piled them against the wall. The shop, once so full of goods, was now nearly empty. It represented a bitter success for Uncle Aki, who had managed to winnow down his inventory so completely that he could leave behind only bare shelves instead of the vast array of items on which he had invested his entire fortune. "I've got money in my pocket," he said grimly, "but it doesn't come close to covering what I spent to buy the goods." The price slashing in Japantown had been so drastic over the past few weeks that even non-Japanese had begun to shop in their stores, attracted, finally, by the bargains.

"I had one lady in here looking at the kimonos," said Uncle Aki. "Why would she even want a kimono? But she looked so happy. 'These prices are indecent!' she exclaimed. She would never have shopped in a Japanese store if it had actually cost her money."

Henry ran his fingers across the top of an empty shelf. As always, it was free of dust and grime. Even when Uncle Aki was leaving the place, closing his shop perhaps forever, he had spent the last evening cleaning. Henry understood. He had left his office on Market Street in pristine condition, too.

"This is ridiculous," Henry muttered, but no one wanted to talk about what was happening, including him. They simply moved through the tasks of packing up and leaving.

The women went back into the storeroom with Uncle Aki to make some food. How long would they have to wait before they could again cook their own rice in their own kitchens? According to the government announcements, they would be piled into buses and taken to the racetrack on the outskirts of San Francisco, where they would live for the months it took for their "permanent" quarters to be completed in the desert. Henry walked out onto the sidewalk and sat down on the bench near his uncle's storefront. All up and down the street now, people were getting out of cabs and filing out of trucks and cars, parcels and bags in their arms. Henry had heard that the old horse stalls at Tanforan had been converted to barracks. Would he and his fellow Japanese be expected to drink out of pails and eat dried corn and the occasional apple?

About that time, Henry saw Goldie coming toward him up the street. She was wearing red heels and a slim fitted skirt with a matching jacket and white blouse. She looked so pretty and fresh that it seemed completely obvious that he could never have married her. How long would a woman like that survive in some barracks in the desert? How could she have sacrificed that much for him? As she approached, he realized that she didn't see him on the bench. He slumped deeper into his seat, hoping to let her pass. She had come to see Mayumi anyway. It would be better if she and Henry didn't talk.

But Goldie spotted him. There had been a time when she found Japanese faces indistinguishable, but that time had long since passed. Even with his unbrushed hair and wrinkled clothes, he stood out for her amid the jumble of other harried, disheveled-looking people on that sidewalk, just as he would stand out for her amid all the thousands of Japanese who were now congregating up and down the coast, preparing to be sent away. "Well, hello there!" she called, giving her voice the same easy enthusiasm it would carry if she had run into a friend shopping in Union Square. "I almost didn't see you."

Henry stood up, trying to muster whatever dignity he had left. Goldie held out her hand to him, and when he took it, her skin felt so cool and soft that he dropped it immediately. He saw a trace of disappointment cross her face, but he could do nothing about her feelings now. "How are you?" he asked. Standing close, he saw that she looked pale, thin, and somewhat shaky. Her dark eyes, always haunting to him, looked almost ghostly now. Mayumi had, not surprisingly and as she had predicted, been "let go" by Feld's, but she and Goldie had managed to get together a few times for some halfhearted shopping. Henry had heard, therefore, about the appendicitis.

"I'm just fine," Goldie replied. "Things are just fine at the store. There's been some trouble importing silk—"

"The war," he said.

"Oh, yes, of course, the war." She shrugged, and her voice trailed off. She looked around. Some of Henry's fellow future internees were leaning against the buildings smoking cigarettes. Others hunched on the piles of their belongings, trying to doze. Many watched with mild interest this awkward exchange between the depressed-looking Japanese man and the lovely, delicate Caucasian woman.

"I thought I'd come say good-bye," she said, then quickly added, "to your family."

"Mayumi will be glad. And my parents."

Goldie bowed her head, nodding. She stared at her feet, idly grinding the toe of her pump into the sidewalk. Henry thought of something then. "Goldie?"

She looked up at him, her face bereft. "Yes?"

"The book of prints. Remember it?"

"Of course."

"I have it here with me. Why don't you take it? You love those pictures."

He was trying his best to sound detached, surrounded as they were by more than fifty disconsolate people who had nothing else to do but watch. Why hadn't he thought of the prints before? She'd have something, at least, to remember him by.

"Are you sure?" she asked. "Would it look strange?"

He lifted his arms a bit, then let them drop against his sides. He didn't care what his family thought—he had given up too much for them already—but he didn't want to do anything to embarrass Goldie. "If they ask, I'll just tell them you agreed to take care of the portfolio while we're gone. But it's yours, really."

"All right." Her face filled with relief and pleasure, which gratified him at first. But then, as all sign of sadness disappeared from her face, the apparent ease of her emotions confounded him.

"So that's enough to make you happy?" he asked.

"What do you mean?"

"I mean, is it so important to be happy that you can ignore everything else?"

"What are you talking about?"

He shrugged. "Some people would rather be honest than happy. Or right than happy. Or rich than happy."

"Wouldn't being rich make you happy?" she asked, and her perfect naïveté made him laugh.

"Well, not necessarily."

It was Goldie's turn, though, to grow impatient. "Why are you asking me this question?"

"Is having those prints enough to make you happy and forget about everything else?"

"Of course it's not enough. Nothing is enough."

As their conversation became more urgent, it became more muted. Unable to hear their words clearly, the bystanders listened with heightened attention. Henry felt grateful that his family, at least, could not see them out here.

"Some people can bear anything but sadness," he said. "Heartbreak. Loneliness. Terrible loss. But they ignore it all because they just don't want to feel sad anymore."

"Is that what you think?"

"That's my observation."

"And you?"

"I think I have a deeper capacity for sadness than you."

"What are you trying to tell me, Henry?" She seemed to be angry now, but he couldn't stop himself. It was almost as if because he couldn't have her, he had to fight with her instead.

"It's not a bad thing," he said.

"What?"

"I think you'll be feeling better soon. I don't want to make myself sound pathetic, Goldie, but I won't."

"You won't what?"

"Be feeling better."

Goldie turned away from him then. She put her hand over her eyes, and he could see that she was trying to compose herself. Along the sidewalk, people were elbowing each other now. Goldie didn't seem to care, perhaps because she was not the one who would have to live with them at a racetrack for the next few months. But Henry couldn't blame her, either. He was, after all, the one who had married someone else.

Goldie finally looked at him again. "You don't know anything about what I'm feeling," she said. "You have no idea."

She was right. He didn't. "Forget what I said," he told her. "I'm upset. I don't know what I'm talking about."

Goldie's expression had hardened, though. Henry felt a surge of panic and contrition. "Maybe we should get the prints?" he asked, desperate not to say good-bye to her on such a note.

Still scowling, Goldie followed him into the store. The air was fragrant with the smell of rice. "Henry, is that you, son?" his mother called from back in the storeroom. "Come eat."

"I'll be right there," he answered. He looked at Goldie. "We'll surprise them," he whispered. "They don't know that you're here." This last fact, of course, was obvious, but neither Goldie nor Henry was able to think very clearly by then. At that moment Henry cared about nothing but taking her hand and leading her back behind the shelves. The family's bags lay piled on the floor. He squatted down

and dug through a trunk until he found the velvet case that held
the prints; then he stood up and set it on a shelf. He could hear his
family talking in the kitchen. Goldie was watching him uncertainly.
Gently, he nudged her backward until he was pressing her against
the wall. He lifted his hand to her face and slowly slid his fingers into
her mouth. Her skin was so pale, her lipstick so red. She pressed her
mouth together then.

A great deal had changed since the last time the two of them
touched. Henry had begun a dull sexual relationship with his wife.
And Goldie, in a private room in Pescadero, had learned that desire
had an end result. Now, preparing to say good-bye, maybe forever,
Henry's emotions crystallized into anguish over the difference between what he had and what he wanted. "It should be *this*," he told
himself, pressing firmly against her. Goldie, who was used to depriva-
tion, felt less a sense of injustice than Henry, but she had a clearer
sense of what she needed at that moment. She wanted Henry's touch
to replace, in her mind, the memory of Alan Stevenson's pawing.
That was something, she told herself, that she deserved. And so she
took Henry's hand from her mouth and guided it downward, helping him slip his fingers between her stomach and the waistline of
her skirt, then continue down and in between her legs. In other circumstances, he might have been surprised by her directness—in any
case, he would have a long sojourn in the desert to consider that—but
right now, sliding his fingers inside her, Henry's conscious thoughts
were very simple. He pressed his mouth against her ear. "Goldie," he
whispered, his voice more like breathing than words. She closed her
eyes and held him there.

The bells on the door rattled and they heard someone come inside.
Henry pulled away. A man's voice called into the room in Japanese.
Goldie brushed her hair off her face, tucked her blouse into her skirt.
Henry, looking flushed, managed to respond to his father. "Dad," he

said, and in what was probably the hardest phrase he would ever have to utter, he put a stop to everything: "Goldie's here."

Later, after she had said good-bye to the family, taken the prints, and gone away, Henry sat out on the sidewalk again, staring at his fingers, which her lips had stained dark red. It was a trick of his imagination, of course, but for a long time afterward he would continue to see the color there. And when he sniffed his fingers, he could still detect her scent.

For the first month or so after San Francisco's Japanese citizens were boarded onto buses and driven away, Goldie and Mayumi wrote to each other. The racetrack where the family was initially settled lay only a few miles south of the city, but Mayumi might as well have traveled to Australia considering how long the mail took to reach its destination. Most letters arrived bearing the results of censorship—a stamp saying OPENED BY EXAMINER, a black mark obscuring a sentence or phrase, even, on occasion, a paragraph clipped out entirely.

The logistical difficulties of their correspondence, however, did not present the greatest challenge. For Goldie, the act of writing to her friend, and knowing that Henry was nearby, stirred emotions she couldn't always manage. It reminded her of the thirst dreams she sometimes had—always dropping the glass of water before she had a chance to drink. For her part, Mayumi never knew what to say. Although she found it depressing to describe the experience of living with eight thousand people in rows of dusty barracks, she felt equally depressed by the prospect of ignoring her situation. Their letters, then, were stiff and pleasant, full of forced humor that neither found funny.

Goldie wrote: "I wish that you could have been with me today—I went by La Fleur d'Amour and the SALE they had going was no better than the REGULAR prices they had last month. I said to the salesgirl—'You must think we're DAFT'—and then I huffed out!!!! Seriously—their shoes are not worth half that price."

Mayumi wrote: "I have taken up needlepoint. We can't get the prettiest thread here, really, but at least I can create my own designs. I'm making little pillows with tiny birds all over them. Hummingbirds, sparrows, redbirds, and, because of the war and everything, a lot of doves. Henry says I need some cuckoos, but he's just trying to annoy me. I'll make two matched sets, a pair for you and a pair for me. We'll keep them on our sofas, and then when we visit each other we'll say, 'What darling little pillows! Wherever did you buy them?'"

Eventually both Goldie and Mayumi found this kind of banter too difficult to maintain. Their correspondence became more and more sporadic until finally, like a stream in a drought, it dried up.

18

A Sweet Life

In her later years, Goldie liked to say that Marvin Feld asked her to marry him on their first date, but their courtship did not actually transpire that quickly. They had, of course, known each other for months, collaborated together on the successful Pioneer perfume Fourth of July promotion, and spent thirteen minutes alone behind the tie counter while Goldie suffered the rupture of an ectopic pregnancy that—though she was prone to exaggeration, she was correct on this one—nearly killed her. By the time she and Marvin spent their first evening alone together, her sense of his role in her life had progressed through a series of clearly defined but unpredictable mutations: handsome prince, friendly acquaintance, lifesaver, trusted friend. Even during his princely period, she never felt the mild tingles of excitement that she had once experienced around Alan Stevenson. Anyone who knew the sequence of events that took place in Goldie's life during that period might have tried to assess her feelings for Marvin in relation to Henry as well. Goldie, however, never compared the two. "Apples and oranges," she might have said.

Anyway, it was sort of a stretch to call that meeting a date at all. Just after her lunch break one day, Marvin approached her in the hat department and asked if they could talk for a while after work. He looked both distracted and disturbed, which gave Goldie cause for concern. "Of course," she told him. He had held her in his arms while she nearly bled to death. She would do anything in the world for Marvin Feld.

It was early May, warm and breezy, and they walked down Market Street toward the bay. Goldie had imagined that he would take her for a drink somewhere, but he was so focused on his thoughts that once they headed out of the store, he didn't seem to give another thought to a destination.

"You just talk when you're ready," Goldie said. "I'm patient. I'll wait."

He lifted his arm and patted her shoulder, but otherwise didn't respond. Goldie liked walking beside a well-dressed man on a pretty day. The events of the past year had rid her of her marital ambitions, which had not only proved useless but nearly destroyed her, emotionally and physically. Compared with all that, she felt comforted by the idea of spending the rest of her life unmarried, working as a saleslady at Feld's. The job was stable and secure, and she could imagine a future of promotions. Goldie's sister Louise had nearly killed herself cleaning houses, but Goldie had discovered that domestic work wasn't the only option for a smart girl with a sense of style. She could earn her own money, buy her own clothes, and cultivate friendships with respectable people. Before too long, she planned to find herself an apartment, too, and get away from Rochelle. She had come to believe in the possibility of building a satisfying and stable life independent of the whims of men.

None of that meant, however, that she didn't enjoy the occasional walk through the city with an elegant friend. And she also enjoyed the suspense of wondering what Marvin wanted to talk with her about. Though the two of them had never formally discussed what happened the day she collapsed behind the counter, she knew that he understood everything and didn't judge her for it. One morning, visiting her in the hospital, he had looked her in the eye and said, in the manner of a teacher offering instruction, "You had a burst appendix, Goldie. Appendicitis." Two days hadn't even passed since she collapsed, and she was still absorbing the fact that a devastating episode in a private room with Alan Stevenson had resulted in swollen breasts, nausea, and ultimately, emergency surgery and a hospital stay. The realization that Marvin knew what had happened filled her with shame—it made her feel naked—but he didn't seem to regard her any differently. His concern seemed tender, almost brotherly, and nearly made her cry. A few days later, on another visit, he seemed angrier, though angry at the world in general, not at her. "Was it Henry?" he asked, out of the blue. "Was it Henry?" She reacted with heat. "No!" she screamed, and the tone of repulsion in her voice convinced Marvin that she had never thought of Henry in a romantic way at all. In truth, Goldie's passion came from a determination to exonerate the man she loved and also from the sense of regret that she had begun to experience on the night in Pescadero. As traumatized as she felt by her first experience of sexual intimacy, Goldie was perceptive enough to see that, in another context, it could offer joy. She felt it as an unspeakable loss that she and Henry would never experience that together.

Goldie loved Marvin for his kindness, then, and for the fact that he could not only forgive a fallen woman but also invite her on a walk. To the extent that he himself seemed troubled now, she resolved to help him if she could.

They crossed Steuart Street, walked up the Embarcadero toward the Ferry Building, then stopped to look back toward the Bay Bridge, which towered above them now. Other than when she first arrived in California, and the train stopped at the Oakland station, Goldie had never actually crossed the bridge—what was there for her on the other side?. She sometimes walked this way during her lunch hour, though, just to look at the way the bridge stretched, like a necklace, across the bay.

"It must be beautiful up in the Sierras now," Marvin said. "We used to take the ferry, but now we can get there in a few hours just by crossing the bridge."

Goldie was reasonably sure that the Sierras were mountains. "That's east, isn't it?" she asked. The sun set in the west, over the Pacific.

"Yes," Marvin said. Then, after another moment of silence, he turned to her. "Listen, Goldie. I want to ask you something." He still seemed bothered, but he was concentrating his attention entirely on her now.

"Ask me anything," she said, and she really meant it.

"I need to get married. It's time. And you're a great gal. What do you think?"

"Me?" she asked. Her past lay so obviously between them that it wasn't necessary for her to say more than that.

"Yes, you." He laughed. He had practical reasons for proposing to her, and he would not allow himself to believe that he was being altruistic. Still, even the best man in the world could not have seen Goldie's face at that moment without feeling, for an instant at least, like a knight in shining armor.

Marvin took her hand and led her to a bench. Her whole body was shaking now, but despite her shock, she remained composed enough to wonder if her sweaty hands might put him off. "What is going on here?" she asked.

"I'm going to be honest with you," he said. "I'm not going to lie to you, ever."

Goldie gazed at him, so completely confused about what was happening that she simply said, "I love you for that."

He put his arm around her shoulders and pulled her close, but kept his gaze turned toward the bay. "I'm a queer," he said. When Goldie didn't respond, he turned to look at her, then added, "A homosexual."

Goldie had grown used to working her way around the things she didn't know—the Sierras, mixed drinks, abstract art—but Marvin's revelation was a mystery that seemed fairly important. "A what?" she asked.

He sighed. "I was afraid of that." For the next few minutes, and in as neutral a tone as possible, he did his best to explain the vagaries of sexual orientation. He refrained from specifics about the men he had known, focusing more on the idea that a man could love a man in the same way that another man could love a woman. He tried his best to make himself sound normal, but also emphasized the need to keep this information private. Most importantly, he offered the facts—I'm homosexual; will you marry me?—but let her draw her own conclusions about how they would actually navigate a marriage. Marvin had chosen Goldie based on practicalities and some degree of feeling, too. He needed to find someone attractive enough to make the marriage pleasant, convincing, and more or less acceptable to his parents, but also constrained enough that she would doubt her chances for finding a better mate. With those two issues in mind, Goldie seemed a perfect choice. It helped, too, that she was Jewish, though Marvin suspected that his parents, with their pretensions to aristocracy, might have regarded a marriage to a wealthy gentile as something of a coup. It also helped that Marvin loved her, in his way.

Goldie needed time to absorb all this new information. The world seemed so complicated! Did Rochelle have any idea about homosexuality? Had her mother known? "Is this just something that happens in California?" she asked. "Do you think there are men like that in Memphis, too?"

"I'm sure there are," said Marvin. He was only twenty-six years old and could vividly remember the dawning realization he had had about himself. He began to sense it as a child. He was a tall boy, both strong and athletic, and he had never suffered from teasing for being "unmanly." His sense of difference had come, instead, from the unexpected attractions he felt toward other boys—not all boys, but a series of them, beginning when he was eight or nine: a boisterous redheaded child in his third-grade class; a fellow member of the high school rowing club; and then, most significantly, the teaching assistant in his college philosophy class, who had tutored him, first, in Hegel's *Science of Logic*, and later in the wide variety of ways in which two enthusiastic men could give pleasure to each other. This philosophy tutor, a Swedish graduate student named Marcus, who went by Max, had insisted that their "queerness" gave them particular insight and an ability to appreciate beauty that other people lacked. Marvin, who was not especially aesthetic, never quite believed that sexual interests could influence one's understanding of the world, but his affair with Max—which lasted four months and was cut short by the tutor's return to Europe—had lessened his sense of shame, at least. Equally significant, by the time he graduated from college, Marvin had come to believe that he could live as he wished without sacrificing the family life and social standing to which, as a Feld, he felt entitled. He just had to make wise choices and be cautious. It helped, too, that he had money.

It was a bright, windy evening, and the sidewalk along the water was full of people strolling along the Embarcadero, enjoying the fine weather. Goldie's eyes, following each of them, were filled with new curiosity and wonder. "I had no idea," she said.

Marvin found her ignorance charming. It was at moments like this one, when she demonstrated both her inexperience and her desire to learn, that he most vividly anticipated the life that they could lead together. They would have adventures. They would have fun. She would look wonderful on his arm making grand entrances at society dinners. Marvin didn't feel it impossible, either, that they could sleep together occasionally and have a child or two. He felt so optimistic that he was tempted to explain to Goldie that there were women who loved women, too (if Goldie were one of those women, he thought, with some regret, they might really have a perfect union), but he sensed that too much information might merely confuse her. "It's a subject," he told her, "that people don't talk about much."

"So you like men," Goldie finally said.

"That's a simple way to put it," Marvin responded, "but yes."

Goldie grinned broadly. "Well, I like men, too. I can't deny you the right to that."

Her statement seemed so reasonable that they both laughed. Marvin leaned closer and kissed her cheek. Though the thought of anything more intimate made him slightly squeamish, he adored playing the role of gallant lover to Goldie's bewitching girl. Had he not had a strong sense of decorum, he might have pulled her off the bench, taken her in his arms, and swung her around in a waltz (Marvin was deeply fond of Fred Astaire). Instead, he merely told her, "You're a great gal, Goldie."

And what exactly was Goldie thinking then? Throughout the conversation, she concentrated completely. She took in every word he said, considered it carefully, reevaluated what she knew of the world, and responded. She had learned that human intimacy can include not only girl loves boy and boy loves girl, but also boy loves boy. That revelation demanded a fairly comprehensive reassessment of the nature of companionship, and Goldie reshuffled her sense of the world accordingly. It was a huge thing to take in during a single afternoon, but still, this new knowledge had a minor impact in comparison to the great and simple thought that was coursing through her mind at that moment. "I'm saved," she told herself, full of unbounded relief. "I'm saved. I'm saved. I'm saved."

* * *

For the first few months of their marriage, Goldie didn't care at all that Marvin was a homosexual. Life was sweet. She moved into his apartment near the top of Nob Hill, and together they redecorated to give the bachelor lodgings more of a domesticated, honeymoon feel. They also went shopping for clothes. Marvin wanted Goldie to have a wardrobe befitting her new status as a Feld, and Goldie didn't argue. While she had gleaned a great deal about manners already through keen observation, under Marvin's careful tutelage she learned how to use all the different forks, the distinction between a dinner and a supper, and that if you weren't sure whether it was appropriate to order dessert, you should follow your hostess's lead. In short, Goldie began to learn to live like a lady. All of it thrilled her. She could drink as much orange juice as she liked. She could sleep in her own bed one night and, if she chose to, sleep in the guest bedroom the next. She could buy shoes to match her outfits, take baths every night, put lotion on her hands ten times a day. Sometimes she rolled around on the carpeted floor just for the fun of it.

Marvin's parents weren't thrilled that he had married a poor girl from Memphis, but they had picked up enough worrisome clues about his lifestyle—the lack of girlfriends, the travels with "buddies" through Mexico—that they seemed relieved, if still somewhat suspicious, about the fact that he had finally settled on a bride. Mrs. Feld, though, showed little warmth. She did her duty by inviting Goldie out for occasional lunches, having the couple over for dinner, and visiting the apartment every few weeks to offer her opinion on the new sofa or the bedroom drapes, but she never seemed to enjoy these interactions. Mr. Feld made fewer appearances than his wife, but he was warmer, in his half-attentive way, and his memory of the Pioneer perfume campaign led him to conclude that even if his son had married a shopgirl, at least he had married a smart one. The infrequency of engagements between the older and younger Felds suited everyone perfectly. Marvin found his mother suffocating and his father dull. Goldie felt nervous and awkward around both of them, and if not for propriety, would probably have avoided them altogether.

If Goldie wasn't happy, exactly, she was very satisfied with this new life. She no longer had to sleep on Rochelle's couch or worry about money. To her surprise, though, she quickly found that being in the apartment all the time made her bored and edgy. Marvin suggested that she plan a party, but Goldie only dreamed of one perfect party—in the tea garden in Golden Gate Park—and that idea had lost its luster with the removal of the Nakamura family to the desert. Within a month of their wedding, she had drifted back to Feld's. It was not appropriate for the daughter-in-law of the owner to act like a salesgirl, so Goldie rambled. Sometimes she would go into the millinery department and fluff the hats. Other times she folded sweaters. At first her former colleagues kept their distance, but they soon saw that the young Mrs. Feld could be just as friendly as the old Miss Rubin. She considered herself an employer now, and in that role she worked hard and lavished praise. The only change that she insisted upon (and this was through Marvin and thus indirect) was to make sure that Feld's got rid of Alan Stevenson as quickly and discreetly as possible. That change took place within the first week.

More than anything else, Goldie wanted to learn. The person who could teach her the most was not her father-in-law or Marvin (neither of whom, truth be told, cared about the day-to-day running of the business), but Mr. Blankenship.

"You're the one who keeps Feld's Feld's," she told him, following him into the elevator one day not long after her reappearance.

They rode together to the third floor. Mr. Blankenship hadn't complained about her return to the store, but he had made no effort to welcome her, either. Throughout the ride up, he held his hands behind his back and stared at the door. "There's no need to flatter me, Mrs. Feld," he said.

"I'm not flattering you, Mr. Blankenship," Goldie responded. "It's the simple truth." When other people addressed her now, she loved the sound of "Mrs. Feld," but with Mr. Blankenship, she felt that she needed a few years to grow into it. There wasn't much to be done about that, though. He had never called her Goldie, and she couldn't very well go back to "Miss Rubin" now.

The elevator door opened, and he stepped out into the warehouse. It was a dim, cavernous space, lit mostly by the floor-to-ceiling windows that lined the front of the building, filled with pallets of packing crates, furniture, boxes labeled FRAGILE and BILL RECIPIENT and THIS SIDE UP. Goldie would have liked to stop in front of each box and have him tell her everything about its contents, but there was no time for that now. He turned a corner and disappeared. She trotted after him, feeling more like a puppy than the new bride of the son of the owner of the store.

Mr. Blankenship ducked into his office, leaving the door open wide enough that he didn't seem rude, but not wide enough to look inviting. None of his sales staff had ever married into the family before, and Goldie's new standing presented a challenge he did not feel keen to address. For one thing, he had his suspicions about the nature of that marriage. Did she know what she was getting into? Could it last? But more pressing, how would he define his own relationship to her now? If she insisted on being on the premises, who was the boss?

He liked the girl very much. Over the period of her employment, he had come to consider her one of his "standout staff" and, like a teacher who feels invested in the future of his most promising students, had watched with optimism to see what she would make of her life. He had felt proud of her and had taken her success as a testament to his ability to find, among the dozens of sales applicants he met every year, those individuals who could bring to the floor both personal refinement and a talent for "moving the merchandise"— though he was not so uncouth as to utter such a phrase out loud. He talked, instead, about "helping our customers locate the items that satisfy their heart's desires." When he used such language, most applicants looked confused. He hired the ones who didn't.

Goldie, of course, had never seemed confused. Though her application had contained the disconcerting information that she had only completed the eighth grade, he immediately recognized certain qualities in her that would make her a fine salesgirl. She was avid to learn and, despite her lack of education, demonstrated a quickness with numbers when he administered a test. She was also good-looking, which was a particular asset given the store's clientele. And then there was that indefinable quality that made its presence known during interviews, not through the things that the applicants said but through how they held themselves, how they talked, what they wore. Goldie, Mr. Blankenship remembered, had appeared in a simple wool skirt and a white cotton blouse. Such items were hardly the height of fashion, and it was clear, of course, that she had very little money. But Mr. Blankenship met young women applicants for sales positions nearly every week. None of them had money, and most addressed that fact by purchasing cheaply made and often gaudy items that mimicked elegant style about as successfully as a rhinestone mimicked diamonds. Goldie's clothes were simpler but, he could see at a glance, of excellent quality—purchased, he guessed, with great deliberation at a secondhand store in the city. The cloth was thin and worn but finely tailored, well pressed, and immaculate. Here was a girl, he had discerned, who had good sense about style and could learn even more.

Goldie poked her head through the door. "Can I just say something?" she asked.

He looked up from his desk. At this time of the morning, the sunlight flooded the room at an angle, illuminating the dust whirling in from the warehouse in a way he found distasteful. "Go ahead." He let her see him glance at his watch.

She hesitated to come inside. "I admire you so much," she said. When he didn't respond, she added, "So, so, so, so much."

He had to smile. He twirled a paper clip between his fingers, but kept his eye on her, waiting for her to continue.

"Ever since I came here, I've wanted you to respect what I do. I've tried really hard. I mean I don't imagine that you're going to think of me as a brain or anything. But I want you to respect me."

His continued silence threw her off. "Am I making any kind of sense at all?" she asked.

"Go on," he said.

"Just because I'm not working here anymore doesn't mean I can't be helpful. I can do a lot. You can give me any job and I will do it."

"Sweeping the warehouse?" His voice carried a note of challenge, but she could see that he was taking her seriously now.

"Can I wear the maintenance uniform? I wouldn't want to get my clothes dirty."

"We could arrange that."

"Then yes. Of course. Certainly. I'll scrub the floors."

He could see that she was serious, and he was impressed, though he had no intention of having her scrub the floors. "But why?" he asked. "You are a woman of leisure now. You can go have lunch with the ladies. Have fun."

She sighed as if he didn't understand her at all. "I'm not interested in having lunch with ladies, Mr. Blankenship. This is my future. I really, truly believe that I love this place as much as you do. I love every single thing about it. I don't just mean the cashmere sweaters or the necklaces. I love the display cases and the marble floors"—he didn't seem convinced, so she gestured toward the warehouse behind her—"and those cardboard boxes, too." Then she looked directly at him. "There's a war going on, Mr. Blankenship. Honestly, I don't see Marvin or his father doing an awful lot to make sure this place survives, so I have to do what I can. If the business fails, I go straight to the bottom again. I drown."

He laughed a little, but her words unsettled him. "I don't imagine that your situation would really be so dire as that."

She responded quietly. "It feels that way. If you've been poor before, you feel it."

Mr. Blankenship couldn't argue. His own circumstances hardly compared to the Felds', but he came from a comfortable village in Leicestershire. His father had worked in a bank. He had never actually known hunger, at least not in the way that he suspected Goldie had. Among the Feld family, only Goldie truly understood the threat of failure. Certainly Marvin had no idea. The boy had a fine education and he exhibited talent enough to excel in his profession, but he seemed content to while away his time on pet projects like model ships and unnecessary inventions. Marvin's father was even worse, claiming a love of architecture and science when really he spent most of his time skiing in Tahoe or sailing on their yacht. Mrs. Feld came from a wealthy Philadelphia family—money marrying money, that one—so she had never experienced hardship, either. She had more common sense than her husband, but she considered it demeaning to involve herself in the store's affairs. Among them all, only Goldie really cared, and she had the ambition and focus to make things happen.

"Perhaps you're right."

"I just need you to take me under your wing," she said.

He gazed at her. He had never in his life seen a face that was at the same time so powerful and so forlorn. It almost frightened him.

Over the course of the next year, then, there was no one with whom Goldie spent more time than Mr. Blankenship. He was never her confidant, certainly not in the sense that Mayumi had been, or for a time Henry, or even Marvin when he was around. But he became her companion. They spent their days together at Feld's. In the evenings, he often dropped by to keep her company over a cup of tea. Every so often they would leave the store early on a Saturday afternoon and visit the antique shops of North Beach, not so much to buy things as to engage in discussions about what made one object "a thing of quality" and another object "unworthy."

"Is Mr. Blankenship a homosexual, too?" Goldie asked Marvin one night over dinner. They had walked down the hill to a steak-house called Bill's Place. Early in their marriage they had discovered, through trial and error (an undercooked chicken, a burned steak, a soggy cherry pie), that Goldie hated cooking and would never really learn. They had addressed the problem quite happily by eating out every night. Later, when she looked back on her marriage to Marvin, she realized that it was those evenings spent talking by candlelight that she had loved best. Her memories of that time almost made her believe her own stories of romance.

"Blankenship?" Marvin fingered his Scotch. He had no proof about Blankenship. He had never seen the man at any of the places he frequented around town, but like Goldie he had a hunch the man was queer. Marvin prided himself on his discretion, however. As a rule, he never speculated or revealed secrets about other men. He didn't want anyone talking about him, so he didn't go talking about other people, either. On the other hand, he could see that Blanken-ship meant a great deal to his wife. Perhaps Goldie needed to know for a reason. "What makes you think that?" Marvin asked.

"He's not married." Marvin's tutoring had led Goldie to reassess several of the men she had known—a boy in school who played with dolls, a cousin who had left Memphis to become a dancer in New York—and she had come to suspect that *lifelong bachelor* was just an-other term for *queer*.

"Some people just aren't interested in that sort of thing," Marvin said. "Taste this Green Goddess." He stabbed at the lettuce with his fork and lifted it to Goldie's lips. The thought crossed his mind, with some satisfaction, that anyone watching them from another table would believe them in love. It was a satisfying period in Marvin's life as well.

Goldie took the bite of salad and, waving her hand over her mouth, made a face of disgust. "Marvin, anchovy!"

"I couldn't taste it," he said, offering her a glass of water. "I'm so sorry, darling. I thought you wouldn't taste it, either."

Goldie took a gulp of water and then a bite of bread. Despite the terrible flavor in her mouth, she wasn't going to let the subject of this conversation get away from her. "You told me that wasn't true yourself," she said.

"What?"

"That people aren't interested in that sort of thing. You said everyone's interested in that sort of thing."

She had brought them back to a difficult subject. During those days, Goldie and Marvin were as kind to each other as they could be, and Marvin tried diligently to answer the questions that popped up regularly as his wife navigated this new, confusing phase of her life. From the perspective of his own predicament, it helped him to assert the normalcy of sexual feeling of any kind. Doing so made him feel less strange and alone. On the other hand, how could he insist that everyone felt desire and, at the same time, pay very little attention to the desires of his wife? Goldie was a beautiful young woman. He had no doubt that she felt passion, too. They had been married now for two months, and he had married her intending to have a sexual relationship with her, if not every night, then at least with enough regularity that their marriage could seem normal. But for the first few weeks after their wedding, he had relied on excuses—bad colds, headaches, fatigue—and it helped, of course, that he spent many evenings out of the house entirely, often not returning until midnight or later, by which time he had already sated his own desire and

Goldie had fallen asleep. His failure to "complete the deal," as he put it to himself, caused him to chastise himself by day and spend more and more time away at night.

Finally, with a sense that he had to pull himself together or risk destroying his marriage, he had made a trip to the library. There he found enough information on women's reproductive cycles that, along with some regular sleuthing among Goldie's underwear at home, he could get a sense of her rhythm. The entire enterprise felt despicable to him. By now, though, he was determined. He made a careful counting of days, judged the ones during which she would be most fertile, and finally, as they approached the second month of their marriage, he got into bed with her, turned out the light, and somehow managed to maintain an erection long enough to complete the act. Afterward, he sobbed from shame and relief. Goldie sobbed, too, though he was too overcome by his own emotions to ask her why.

And now, two months into their marriage, three successful episodes of intercourse behind them, she was still asking questions about sex.

"How should I know?" he demanded, unable to control the irritation in his voice.

Goldie's face clouded over. Sometimes he seemed to love her so much. Other times he hated her. Her previous experiences with men had been so much less complicated. Alan Stevenson had faked his feelings in order to do what he wished with her body. And Henry? She never knew what emotion would flame up with the memory of Henry Nakamura, and so she was pleased to experience a rush of pleasure now. He had truly loved her. Simple as that. And so, somehow, the memory of Henry's devotion led to a flash of anger in Goldie now. "You know if Mr. Blankenship is queer," she said, "so tell me."

The waiter brought their steaks. For his benefit, Goldie looked down at her plate and gave a flustered little "Oh, my." Then, once the man disappeared again, she raised her gaze to Marvin. "Tell me," she said.

Goldie hadn't realized it yet, but Marvin was beginning to see that of the two of them, she was stronger. He had not fully attended to this quality in his wife before they married, but it consistently impressed him now. He shrugged. "Okay," he said. "He's queer."

He watched Goldie to gauge her reaction, but she merely focused on her steak. The knowledge of Mr. Blankenship's private life didn't change her feelings about him in any way, but it made her feel more confident that she could understand the world, and thus she didn't feel so utterly lost within it. She picked up her fork and knife. "Goodness, if I eat all this, I'll get fat," she said. Then she cut a bite and put it in her mouth, looking happily at Marvin as she chewed.

For the first year, then, their marriage worked well in its own peculiar fashion. As the spring of 1943 arrived, however, things began to change. Marvin had gauged the pros and cons of taking a wife without factoring in the possibility that he might fall in love. In April, he did just that. The man was a sculptor, a few years older, named Thomas Raymond, and Marvin met him at a gallery opening he attended with his mother. Thomas was engaging and smart, coolly handsome, with long fingers that, when they held a cigarette, looked like art themselves. He had grown up in Sacramento, attended an experimental college in the desert called New River, spent a year studying figure drawing in Rome, then finished his degree at Yale. Now he taught at the San Francisco Art Institute and kept a little place on Russian Hill, a fifteen-minute walk from Marvin and Goldie's apartment. Within two weeks of meeting Thomas, Marvin had more or less moved in with him. Some nights he returned to Goldie by twelve or one. More often he would come home in the morning to shower and change, by which time she'd have already walked down the hill toward Feld's. She developed a habit of leaving messages on the counter in the kitchen. "Sorry I missed you!" she wrote. Or "See you tonight!" The notes served as mild communications of the fact that she noticed he was gone, without, she hoped, expressing any kind of dissatisfaction with his behavior. Goldie and Marvin had made a deal when they got married, and she planned to stick with it.

Still, the entrance of Thomas into their lives aggravated Goldie's sense of insecurity, which had not yet completely disappeared. What if Marvin ran off with Thomas? What would she do then? Those thoughts intensified her eagerness to get pregnant, which was something, she reminded herself, that Thomas could never do. Even if Marvin threw her out of the house, the Felds would never abandon a grandchild. Would they?

The more frequent Marvin's absences, the more urgent became Goldie's concern about babies. That concern, combined with boredom, loneliness, curiosity, and her own natural physical desire, meant that she began to think a great deal about sex. She experimented by herself, relying on trial and error, her own creativity, and the still-vivid recollection of her moments with Henry. Eventually she became quite adept at self-satisfaction. Various kinds of touch, she discovered, could elicit all sorts of reactions. She gave a lot of thought, too, to the male anatomy and its potential. A more interested man would have found Goldie's growing skills delightful. But Goldie faced an enormous challenge with Marvin. Ultimately, her talents helped to maintain his erection just long enough to complete the act. Neither of them enjoyed it.

Despite the disappointments, Goldie didn't begrudge Marvin his feelings of love. Thomas was tall and lithe, elegant, beautifully dressed, and could talk about anything. The three often dined together at Bill's Place, and she did notice that when Thomas joined them, she and Marvin had more fun. The man told dramatic stories about his past, describing people and places with such amusing detail that Goldie sometimes felt that she was watching a movie. His opinions often shocked her—of Franklin Roosevelt, he said, "Charming, but doesn't he look like a bit of a pig?" He called champagne, which he found disgusting, "simply a way for the rich to drink beer"—but he was so bold that he seemed to be declaring truths no one else had the courage to utter. Perhaps most appealing to Goldie, Thomas could relate to her past, not because he had grown up with chickens and a cow in his backyard, but because New River students worked as ranch hands in addition to studying.

"The dust. That's what I remember most," he said, leaning toward her across the table. He had sleepy eyes, like someone waking from a nap, which made his wit all the more surprising. "Do you remember how it felt to take a bath?"

"Do I remember?" An expression of dismay crossed Goldie's face. "Sometimes I still think I'm scrubbing the grime off my skin."

He lifted his arm and pointed to the inside of his elbow, covered now by his beautifully tailored shirt. "Right here. I'd have dark brown creases. And between my toes."

"My mother would scrub the back of my neck so hard I'd cry," Goldie told him.

Marvin had spent his childhood in Pacific Heights. His memories of rural life were limited to the farm scenes glimpsed through the car window as the family drove to their ski lodge in Tahoe. He could not, therefore, participate in this kind of banter. "You're making me feel that I've missed out on something important," he said, laughing.

"Poor you!" said Goldie, who took Marvin's hand and squeezed it.

"Poor you!" said Thomas, who would have liked to, but didn't.

These were confounding moments for all of them. Goldie and Marvin cared about each other deeply, but despite their rare occasions of sex, they were only pretending to be lovers. Marvin and Thomas really were lovers, but they were pretending that they were not. Still, from the outside, their little table in the corner, with its sparkling silver, glistening candles, and outbursts of laughter and jokes, looked like an island of conviviality: the happy newlyweds dining with their dearest friend.

By early September, dinners at Bill's Place came to an end. When

Goldie returned from the store one evening, she found Marvin sitting with his eyes closed, his arm stretched across the back of the sofa, and a glass of Scotch dangling from his hand. Marvin was almost never home at that time of the day. "What is it?" she asked, suddenly concerned. She dropped her handbag on a chair and rushed over to him.

Marvin opened his eyes to look at her but merely gestured with the glass toward an envelope on the coffee table. Goldie picked it up and saw that it contained an official government cable. The merchant marine had ordered him back to duty. He was to serve as a six-month replacement for an injured chief engineer on the SS *John Harvey*, a Liberty ship delivering military supplies between Africa and Italy. In order to meet the ship on time, he would have to sail from New York by the middle of the month.

"The middle of the month?" Goldie couldn't believe it. In less than two weeks, her husband would be transported to a war zone.

Marvin had still not moved. "That means New York by the middle of the month. I'll actually have to take the train next week from San Francisco." He related this information while staring at the ceiling.

Goldie knew a good deal about Marvin's career in the merchant marine, but she had never imagined that they could call him up again for service. The shock of this news, combined with Marvin's apparent disinterest in her own reaction to it, led her into a sudden spasm of tears. It was the tears, finally, that forced Marvin to take notice of her, and her sorrow genuinely upset him. He set his drink on the table and held her face in his hands, then pulled his handkerchief from his pocket and wiped her tears. "We'll muddle through this somehow," he said, which was pretty much what he'd been saying to Thomas all day.

Marvin had received the cable that morning, at which point, in a fit of almost complete agitation, he had rushed to the Art Institute and pulled Thomas out of class. The two had then spent an agonizing day together, alternating in episodes of tears and lovemaking, which in retrospect might have been exquisite but at that moment were hardly even bearable. If their love affair had lasted for years, they might eventually have settled into some kind of easy routine together. But they had only known each other for a few months. Unlike heterosexual lovers, to whom society provided a kind of emotional grooming for passionate love—the encouragement of teenage crushes, the acceptance of (if not active support for) kissing and petting—Marvin and Thomas had had little preparation for the intensity of their feeling for each other. As a result, though they were both nearly thirty, neither came into the affair with enough experience to adequately manage their emotions. Their interactions almost invariably devolved into fits and tears and recriminations. Who would leave the other? Who didn't *really* care? Who loved more? Who loved less? Their affection was deep and passionate, physical and spiritual, but also unpredictable, impossible to contain, and exhausting.

Marvin had never discussed with Goldie the dynamics of his new relationship. She would have been willing but had no idea how to approach such a subject. Marvin, always polite, considered it both indelicate and potentially hurtful to talk about his lover with his wife. They both might have benefited, however, from sharing their experiences of love. Marvin could have used some friendly advice, and Goldie would have had an outlet for the loss that she had suffered. By October of 1943, a year and a half had passed since Henry's departure. These days, she spent most evenings alone after Marvin went out, and she would pour herself a glass of juice and sit at the dining room table, looking through Henry's portfolio of prints. The landscape scenes were lovely and peaceful: vast mountainsides, lonely roads, limitless ocean. The lady pictures, though, with their vibrancy and drama, touched her most deeply. These scenes of Japan felt foreign to the girl from Memphis, but their mood perfectly addressed the state of her mind during that period. She felt exquisitely attuned to the beauty and possibility around her, but also adrift and completely alone. Had Henry known how she might feel? Is that why he gave her his pictures?

Goldie knew about loss, then, and so, amid the confusion of her own reaction to Marvin's departure, she sensed what he was feeling now. "And what about Thomas?" she exclaimed suddenly.

"He's handling it about like you."

Normally, Goldie drank very little, but she believed in the usefulness of spirits in times of distress. They sat for a while on the sofa, silent except for the clinking of ice in their glasses. Finally, Goldie said, "I'll go to New York with you."

Marvin answered without even a pause. "That won't work," he told her, staring at his knees.

Of course, she realized, Thomas would go. She reminded herself of her own good fortune. She had no right to feel hurt by slights like this one. But she was human, too, and not always capable of muting disappointment. "I see," she said, expressing more of it than she intended.

And so it was that Goldie and Mr. and Mrs. Feld accompanied Marvin to the station a week later. Like everything else that Marvin owned, his luggage was beautiful, a navy blue canvas set detailed in leather and monogrammed with his initials just above the brass locks. Even though he shunned the government-issue duffels, he did wear his merchant marine uniform, which, combined with his good health and stature, made him look dashing and heroic. "I'll be right back," he told Goldie, giving her a peck on the cheek. Then he dashed after the porter who was carrying his luggage up and into his private compartment.

Mr. Feld looked at his watch, then stepped closer to the train to squint up into the windows, trying to discern the whereabouts of his son. "Where's he gone off to?" he grumbled. "The train's pulling out in five minutes."

"He's just gone to supervise his luggage, dear, weren't you listening?" His wife looked at Goldie and rolled her eyes. She had still not warmed to her daughter-in-law, but she did occasionally align herself with Goldie if she felt a need for womanly solidarity.

The conductor, walking the length of the train, passed them on the platform. "All aboard, folks. All aboard."

Marvin's mother sighed. "This is the second time we've done this, you know? And now he's married. Have you ever heard of such a thing?"

Goldie shook her head. "No, Mama." Calling Mrs. Feld "Mama" had been Marvin's idea, though it never felt right to any of them. "There must be thousands of other chief engineers who could go instead of him." She rested her hand on her stomach. The night before, during the hour or so when Marvin visited her in their apartment, Goldie had confided to him the news. Under other circumstances she might have kept it to herself for a few more weeks, but he was leaving and she believed that he should know. In any case, she was certain. She was pregnant.

Mrs. Feld pulled a handkerchief out of her purse. "I'm going to cry," she announced. Then she pulled out a second one and handed it to Goldie. "You'll probably cry, too. You've only just gotten married."

Marvin appeared in the doorway of the train and hurried back to them. "I'm all set," he said quietly. He grabbed his father's hand, shook it energetically, and said, "Good-bye, Dad. I'll be back before you even notice I've been gone."

Herbert, who had continued to mutter to himself about the crowds on the platform and the recklessness of the porters, turned silent now. His son looked down at him and smiled. Finally, the father managed to speak. "Be safe, my boy," he told him.

"I always am," Marvin said, then turned his attention to his mother. With her, he showed more open affection but also adopted a lighter tone. "You're getting rid of me again," he joked, planting a kiss on each of her cheeks.

"No, no, no, no!" she exclaimed, reaching up to cradle his chin in her hand. "Your father and Goldie and I can't bear it. You, on the other hand, look absolutely happy to be leaving."

Marvin's face turned more serious. He looked at his mother. "I'm just trying to handle it as best I can."

He turned to Goldie then, stepping close and taking her hand. Other than the requisite family farewell dinners, the two had barely seen each other in the past week. When she looked at him, though, she saw anguish in his eyes. "I'm going miss you horribly," he told her.

Goldie put both her hands around his and held it tight. "Really?" she asked.

Marvin nodded. "You're the best gal in the whole world, Goldie," he told her, and she could hear simply in the tone of his voice an accounting for not only the joyful news of her pregnancy but also the surprising success of their marriage so far. "I never, ever, ever could have found a better wife."

Goldie did begin to cry. She dabbed at her eyes with the handkerchief and then, seeing that Marvin was crying as well, began to laugh while dabbing his eyes, too. He leaned down and kissed her, perhaps more firmly than he'd ever done in his life. Then he took her face in his hands and whispered, "Don't forget me."

The conductor passed again. "All aboard!" he called, and this time he meant it. The platform had begun to clear. Passengers were leaning out of the windows, waving good-bye. If Marvin had managed to run up the steps just then, Goldie's life would have unfolded in a completely different way. But he lingered for a moment too long, taking one last look at his wife's face, and that changed everything.

Because despite all his careful planning, Marvin Feld had made a terrible mistake. On the instructions he had given Thomas that morning, he had meant to write, "Board Car 3." Instead, in his distraction, he had written, "Board Car 9." Car 9 was the one in front of which Marvin, his parents, and Goldie were standing when Thomas, panting because of a late cab and a heavy garment bag, rushed across the platform to board the departing train.

"That looks like Mr. Raymond, the painter," Marvin's mother said. "Is that you, Mr. Raymond?" she called.

Goldie said, "He's a sculptor, I think."

"A sculptor," said Mrs. Feld, waving grandly. Thomas saw them and stopped. From Goldie's perspective, he looked inclined to run away. "How funny," exclaimed Mrs. Feld, "that you two would be traveling on the same train. In the same car!"

Cataclysmic as it seemed to the younger generation, the moment might have gone unheeded by the parents had Marvin addressed it with an easy greeting or even feigned surprise. But Marvin didn't manage that. His eyes turned steely. His hands became stones in his pocket. "It's a big train. There are lots of people on it," he remarked, his tone so inappropriately gruff that it sounded rude. And that was the moment when Mrs. Feld's expression of gratitude that her son would have a companion on the long journey was replaced by a look of horror, which came over her so quickly that an astute observer would have seen it as a demonstration of the fact that Madeleine Feld had had suspicions about her son's proclivities for quite a long time. "No!" she responded, stepping away from her only child. She stared at Goldie, then Thomas, then at Marvin again. "No!"

Herbert Feld took a moment longer to put the pieces together, his gaze jumping in confusion from his wife to his son to his daughter-in-law and then to the stranger who had just appeared. Goldie could almost see the realization as it moved, like an ambush, across his consciousness. His expression, normally completely flat, turned jagged. And then, in a tone so uninflected that it could have masked anything from fury to despair, he asked, "Have you been lying to us all along, then?" He looked at Goldie. "And you? Who are you?"

Marvin had frozen. "Mother. Dad," he said, his voice breaking.

But they didn't look at him. With the train's whistle blowing, the Felds only looked at each other. In all the time that Goldie had known these two, she had never seen them laugh together. Their marriage seemed based on indifference. In contrast, Goldie had flattered herself with the idea that her own marriage, despite its eccentricity, was far more successful than theirs. Now, though, at the worst time imaginable, she saw that she'd been wrong. The Felds might have shared little mutual affection, but they understood each other so perfectly that without exchanging a single word, they came to a decision that would ultimately become one of the most momentous of their lives. Mrs. Feld put her hand through her husband's arm, and like determined soldiers, they turned and walked away.

"Mother!" Marvin called.

Then the whistle blew again, and the train shook itself out of its stupor and began to move. Thomas, his bag hanging from his elbow now, grabbed Marvin's hand and pulled him up the stairs and into the train. Goldie stood on the platform, watching the windows, hoping for one last glimpse of her husband, but she didn't see him again. The train pulled away. A line of porters wandered past, dragging their empty carts behind them. Goldie let the lacey handkerchief drop to the ground. Then she spread her hands like a lattice across her belly and looked down at it. She had the strangest feeling then. The train took a long time to pass, and its rhythm reminded her of a lullaby her mother used to sing: "No one will love you, no one will love you, no one will love you," it said, "like I do."

At first she could pretend it hadn't happened. Goldie didn't hear anything from her in-laws, which gave her the courage to continue going to the store every morning as usual. If Mr. Blankenship had heard about the events at the train station, or that the family regard for Goldie had altered in any way, he didn't show it.

A couple of days after Marvin left, Goldie received a letter that he had mailed from Chicago. "Dearest Goldie," it began,

> *I've left a lot of trouble for you there. If I could say with confidence that things will turn out fine in the end, I would do so, but how can I know? At this point I can barely get myself dressed in the morning, so I'm going to be hopeless at offering guidance to you. Thomas says that the only thing to do is wait. They will come around when they see that I do love you, in my way. And after all, he says, we're giving them a baby. I have to be honest with you, Goldie. I'm not such an optimist. I know my parents, and at this point, given what I've done to them, they may not even believe that the child is mine.*
>
> *So I'll focus on the practicalities here. You've got plenty of money for the time being. I had expected that my mother would help you in a pinch—and now, with a baby coming, there will be some pinches! I don't imagine you'll want to turn to her now, though, so when I reach New York I'll transfer additional funds to our account. That way, you won't need to worry at all for the next six months. Even if my orders are extended (this is not something I anticipate, but I have to be practical here), you'll have plenty. Don't worry, Goldie!*
>
> *Write if you can. You never know how much you'll miss a person until you're gone.*
>
> *Your loving husband, Marvin*

By the time this letter arrived, however, Goldie had already taken charge of the situation herself. Though she had wandered home from the train station almost immobilized with anxiety, by dawn the next morning she was sitting at the kitchen table with her face washed and eyebrows neatly plucked, making a fastidious accounting of the bank statements, bills, and receipts dating back to the beginning of her marriage. By 9 A.M. she was hurrying down the hill to McMillan's, the furniture store, where she immediately canceled her order for a new dining room set. She walked directly to the bank and deposited the funds in her account. Later she called her tailor and put on hold her plans for two new winter jackets. She sold the pearl necklace that Marvin had bought her on Valentine's Day. She returned three pairs of brand-new shoes. She drew up a budget, cutting out beef and oranges and the fancy canned olives she liked to eat with tuna. She bought an iron and stopped sending out dry cleaning entirely. She returned to shampooing her own hair. Her long-term future no longer looked bright, but feeling more secure about the short term, she slept better.

For the first month after Marvin left, then, life continued as it had before. Because she had seen so little of her husband before his departure, his absence had little effect on her daily routines. Often, in the evenings, she and Mr. Blankenship would go to the cinema together, or he would come by her apartment for tea. She spent more time with Rochelle and Buddy, not because she particularly relished their company, but because the changes in her body made her feel she needed the contact of family. Sometimes, on a pretty day, she took the bus out to Golden Gate Park and walked through the tea garden by herself.

A few weeks after Marvin left, Goldie wrote to Mayumi. It had been a year at least since the two had corresponded, but Mr. Blankenship, who had kept in touch with Henry, knew how to reach them at the camp where they were living in the desert.

October 4, 1943—San Francisco

Dearest Mayumi,

I think of you and your family SO OFTEN—though it's been hard for me to write. You may know—from Mr. Blankenship—that I married Marvin Feld this year. He's a good man and kind to me. You can probably guess that the marriage has done A LOT to relieve all sorts of worries. It's funny, though, Mayumi. Even though I worried ALL THE TIME about money then, I think with so much fondness about the times we had together. Didn't we have fun? Remember the PIONEER WINDOWS? Remember the time on the YACHT? Wasn't that excellent? I've been on the yacht many times since then, but it's never been as wonderful as that time with you.

Sometimes I take the bus out to the park and walk through the tea garden. Can you believe that now I can FIND THE WAY through the trees from the bus stop BY MYSELF? The place is still so pretty, please tell your father for me. They changed the name from the Japanese Tea Garden to the Oriental Tea Garden. I suppose they were afraid of losing customers, but it sounds much worse to me.

I know that life is pretty rough for you out there and I want you to know that I feel for all of you. I've been having some troubles as well. Nothing bad, so don't you worry. But Marvin has gone to the war and it's lonely without him. How are you? How is your dear sweet family? I'm going to have a baby, Mayumi. What do you think of that?

Your friend, Goldie

Mayumi replied quickly.

October 10, 1943—Topaz, Utah

Dear Goldie,

I am so glad that you wrote. We're living in the camp now. They call this the desert but it looks to me like the surface of Mars. As you can imagine, it's not my kind of place at all. It's hard to know, honestly, what to put in a letter, but I think of you so often.

You're going to be a mother! This is a joy for you, I know. My mother has so many things that she wants me to tell you. Stay away from crab or lobster. Eat a lot of sardines. Don't sit with your legs crossed. Eat rice. Don't go to any funerals! I know, it's kind of funny. I laughed, too, but you might want to follow her advice, just in case.

We are all healthy. Life is very, very boring. In the summer you could die from the heat, and in the winter we freeze. My father has a little garden, but he mostly grows herbs in pots. He misses his bonsai terribly, and it was a boost for him to hear your news about the tea garden. The plants there are children to him.

I try to stay busy. I stopped sewing because we can't get good materials for that here, but I still make a lot of art. If I dig under the ground a few inches, I can find all these tiny shells. We paint them and glue them together and make jewelry in the shapes of funny things, like flowers and birds and fish. I've got a set of brooches now that look like bouquets. Compared with what you can buy at any shop in San Francisco, they're sad little trinkets, but it gives me a lot of pleasure to make them.

Do you hear about the war? We don't get much news here,

and I imagine that even this letter will be censored because I used the word "war." WAR! WAR! WAR! What do they want from us? Sometimes I think they would like to remove us from the world entirely.

I feel really sad about the Jews, by the way. It's just one thing after another these days, Goldie, don't you agree?

My family was so surprised and happy to have news of you. Did I tell you that Henry has become a wood carver? I know that's funny, but really, Goldie, we have become like a primitive people. Still no baby for Henry and Akemi.

I console myself with the notion that I will return to San Francisco and open a dress shop full of my own creations. Everything is ugly here, so I dream about silk and cotton and wool and velvet, everything beautiful.

With love to you, Goldie, Mayumi

Over the next month, the friendship became charged with new purpose, and Goldie found herself writing to Mayumi two, three, sometimes four times a week. Once, Mayumi wrote, "Mail from you keeps me going." Goldie felt the same way, but her own emotional state had become so fragile by then that she couldn't even express such feelings. Marvin, off somewhere on his Liberty ship, could only rarely post a letter, and when mail from him did finally arrive it contained so many revelations of his own anxiety about his parents that it did nothing to comfort her. Late at night, she found herself staring out at the sky, asking herself the same question: What will happen when the baby arrives?

For those few weeks, the correspondence with Mayumi served as a kind of balance to the stress created by the rest of her life. She loved writing carefree descriptions of goings-on at the store, her aching muscles and blossoming belly, her efforts to find shoes for her feet, which, always oddly shaped, were now also swollen. But this renewed contact had a way of throwing her off as well, because the letters connected her with Henry, too, and she soon needed more from them than they could provide. She would hurry home in the afternoons simply to check the post. When she did receive a letter from Mayumi, she would tear it open, skimming the contents for a capital *H*, and if she didn't find one, she would often cry. The twelve letters Goldie received from Mayumi during that period carried exactly five more mentions of the man she loved: "My father works in the kitchens and Henry works in the wood shop"; "My mother, Akemi, and I have all had colds, but Henry and my father are healthy"; "Henry borrowed *The Grapes of Wrath* and we've all been reading it. It's a sad book, but we like it"; "Henry eats all the apples"; and "Henry is the only one of us who doesn't nap." It was both more information and less information than she could bear.

Still, Goldie might have continued the correspondence anyway, if the disaster had not occurred. Goldie had not paid attention to the reports from Europe, and the fact that Marvin was over there made her even less inclined to read the newspapers now. "I just try to put it out of my mind," she told Rochelle, who often peppered their discussions with comments like "Things are really bad over there."

"I'm sure he's fine," Goldie always responded, though of course she wasn't. "He's not shooting a gun or anything," she liked to remind Rochelle. "He's on a boat."

"I'd be a wreck if I were you," Rochelle would reply.

The attack on the Italian port city of Bari took place on December 2, but the events were mired in so much secrecy and confusion that Goldie knew nothing about it until January 5. That day, Mr. Blankenship had planned to complete their accounting of the holiday sales, and by eight thirty in the morning they were already sitting together at the small table in his office. While he read through the numbers, Goldie recorded them in their accounting book. They only paused if one of them wanted to discuss a particular item that had sold well, or one that hadn't.

"I think we can go up thirty percent on our orders for the felt hats," Mr. Blankenship said with satisfaction. It was a source of continual annoyance to him when newspaper articles equated economizing with patriotism, even to the point of recommending that people refurbish their own hats. He was pleased, then, to find that Feld's customers, at least, had ignored such advice and invested in new ones.

Goldie drew a little star in the accounting book, which was her way of taking notice of a promising set of sales figures, but then she winced as she tried to readjust herself in her seat. In Mr. Blankenship's opinion a woman who was five months pregnant had no business walking down a steep hill in high heels every morning, but he felt it inappropriate to discuss such intimate matters with Goldie. He pulled a bottle from his desk drawer and, as had become their habit, handed her a couple of aspirin, which Goldie swallowed with her tea before making a couple of other notes about hat orders in her book.

At ten forty-five, the inventory clerk, Mr. Maxwell, knocked on the door and peered into the office. "Uh, there's someone here to see Mrs. Feld, sir."

Mr. Blankenship and Goldie looked up. "Send them in," Goldie said. She seldom had visitors, at home or at the store, and she felt a flush of heat as the thought flashed through her mind that Marvin had returned to surprise her. It had been weeks since she had received a letter. Part of her had worried, and part of her had decided that he was on his way home.

A handsome sailor, in formal uniform, walked into the room. Goldie and Mr. Blankenship both stood up. Goldie had heard about these men, and because she experienced a nearly constant anxiety about her husband, she knew immediately why he had come. It took Mr. Blankenship a moment longer.

"Please go," Goldie said. "You're not needed here."

"Mrs. Feld, could I speak with you a moment?" the sailor asked.

Goldie felt herself break inside. "I have no business with you," she insisted.

She never heard Mr. Blankenship move, but she felt him standing beside her. He took her hand. He turned to the sailor, and the steadiness in his voice kept Goldie from crumbling. "Give us a moment," he said. He stepped over to the little cherry cabinet in the corner and poured a brandy for Goldie. She watched him, concentrating on this image of normal human activity.

Across the room, the sailor stood motionless, his solid, handsome face a piece of marble. He stared straight ahead.

Mr. Blankenship handed the glass to Goldie. She drank it, then he poured her another. Her eyes settled on their visitor. "Give the sailor one," she said.

The young man shifted his eyes to Mr. Blankenship. "No, sir. Thank you, sir," he said.

Goldie said, "Take it."

The sailor looked at Mr. Blankenship, uncertain. Mr. Blankenship opened the decanter, poured a brandy for the sailor, and handed it to him. "Take it," he said.

The young man took the brandy and swallowed it in a single gulp. "Thank you, sir," he said. He still couldn't look at Goldie. "Thank you, ma'am," he said.

"How many of these have you done?" she asked.

"I'd rather not say, ma'am."

"How many, sailor?" she wanted to know.

"A few dozen, ma'am."

"Does it ever bother you that you're alive and they aren't, sailor?"

He shifted on his feet. His gaze remained focused on the far wall. "Every day, ma'am."

"I'll have another brandy, Mr. Blankenship," Goldie said.

He poured her another and she drank it. Then she looked at the sailor. "Go ahead," she said.

It wasn't until decades later, when her granddaughter Sadie happened to read about it while puttering around on the Internet one day, that Goldie learned about the connection between the SS *John Harvey* and the mustard gas disaster at Bari. For the first time, she heard that Marvin's ship had been secretly carrying chemical weapons and that the German attack on the port had caused the ship to explode, sending a wave of poisonous fumes across the city, killing as many as a thousand people. For her family, the information helped to fill out the mythic story of Marvin Feld, the father and grandfather they had never known, the charming war hero who had died too young and whose parents had never accepted the fact that their son had fallen in love with a penniless girl from Memphis. Goldie had never made a secret of her first marriage, though she chose not to mention Marvin's homosexuality, preferring instead to concoct an image of newlyweds who looked like Ginger Rogers and Fred Astaire. Sometimes, after a glass of wine or two, she would describe the romantic dinners the two had shared at a spot called Bill's Place, or the way he squeezed orange juice for her in their cozy apartment on the hill, or the day they fell in love, curled up together in the cabin of his parents' yacht, staring up through the porthole at Alcatraz. The information about Bari disturbed Goldie, of course, but she didn't find it "interesting" at all. Where was dear Marvin when the ship exploded? Had he felt any pain? Was it over quickly?

"It's too sad," she said, waving away the stack of pages that Sadie had printed out and offered to her to read. "I suffered enough from that already."

And she had. Two weeks after she received the news of her husband's death, her in-laws sent a notarized letter to Goldie. She had known the Felds for years already and knew how much they adored their only child. She could imagine the extent of their grief, and from the depths of her own despair, she felt for them. The letter, however, showed no hint of emotion. Rather, it informed her in the most legalistic language of "the financial dispensation" she could expect should she "agree to certain non-negotiable conditions." As Goldie knew already, Marvin had taken the time to update his will in New York, and that document left everything to his wife and their child. As heir to the Feld fortune, however, he did not actually have a lot of money of his own. Marvin's own estate contained about ten thousand dollars, hardly enough to pay her expenses for the next few years, much less provide for the future. The Feld's proposition, therefore, was something that Goldie had to consider seriously. In return for her promise to leave San Francisco and "permanently refrain from making any more appeals to their generosity," they agreed to deposit into her account one hundred thousand dollars, which they assumed would be sufficient to maintain the quality of life for both "Mrs. Goldie Rubin Feld and her child."

Goldie, of course, found the offer insulting. "*Her* child? What do they mean by *her* child?" she asked Mr. Blankenship. In Goldie's state of grief and confusion, she had lost her formality with her former boss. Mr. Blankenship didn't mind. The Felds' behavior infuriated him as well. In his opinion, Marvin had done everything that a homosexual man could do to satisfy the expectations of his parents. And now the Felds were punishing Goldie? Mr. Blankenship was so angry that he had accepted a longtime offer from Emporium-Capwell and planned to give notice the following week.

"Ignore the snub, my dear," he told her. She had, since receiving the letter, stopped appearing at Feld's. Most evenings, now, the two of them sat in the living room of her apartment, discussing Goldie's options. "You can't fight them," he said. He would, in truth, have liked to see her try it. He was an orderly and proper person, but he wasn't above getting satisfaction from observing a just revenge. On the other hand, he could see, in practical terms, that Goldie needed to accept the offer. "What about Memphis?" he said, trying to focus on the future, not the past.

Goldie shook her head miserably. "I'd rather die."

"Atlanta? That's also in the South."

Goldie rolled her eyes. "What a backwater."

"Would you like to stay in California? Should I suggest Los Angeles?"

Goldie shook her head. "I want to get as far away as possible."

"New York?"

Goldie considered this option. "My sister Eleanor lives in New Jersey, not far from Manhattan. She's been good to me."

"There you have it, then," said Mr. Blankenship. It gave him comfort to solve problems.

"But I can't live with her."

Mr. Blankenship squeezed her hand. He had a clearer sense of the purchasing power of one hundred thousand dollars than Goldie had. "Darling," he told her. "You don't have to."

And that was how, less than six weeks after hearing the news of Marvin's death, Goldie Feld, almost seven months pregnant, boarded a train for New York City.

February 22, 1944—San Francisco

Dearest Mayumi,

Everything bad has happened. Marvin was killed in the war. I have to leave San Francisco before I have my baby. Don't WORRY about me. I'll be FINE. Please know that I think of

you often with the deepest WISH that you can go home soon.
Please give my warmest regards to your mother and father and
Akemi. And Henry.

With all my love, Goldie

She never consciously intended that letter to be her last, but
something shifted in her mind as her train rumbled east toward New
York City. This time Goldie traveled in comfort. She had a fine set
of luggage (same style as Marvin's, though maroon) and her own private roomette. Four years earlier, traveling west, she had subsisted
on sandwich quarters and the hunks of bread she could grab surreptitiously while striding through the dining car. Now she had her own
bed and sofa, private toilet, writing table, and plenty of money to
buy herself meals. But Goldie had traveled west with hope, and she
was traveling east without it. For most of the journey she stared out
the window, watching the landscape shift from forested mountains,
to desert, to prairie, to rolling hills, and then cities. She kept her
hand on her belly then, following, too, the journeys of the baby—her
single companion now—stirring inside her. A whole new life. And it
was with a growing sense that she had to make something of that
life—her baby's and her own—that she resolved to leave her sadness behind and turn her face completely toward the future. This
effort demanded all her resources, and it took the entire journey to
coalesce. By the time the train arrived in New York City, however,
Goldie Rubin Feld was ready. Somehow, through the force of her will,
the past had grown smaller and smaller in her mind until, finally, it
disappeared.

Part Five

19

Henry Nakamura

Anna and Goldie approached San Francisco at dusk, driving in across the Bay Bridge and descending into the city like airplane co-pilots coming in for a landing. Nothing could ever render Goldie entirely speechless, but the change in the city after sixty years made her pause much longer than usual. The elegant skyscrapers she remembered from her youth were now lost among dozens of boxy high-rises that resembled one another in uniform dullness. "I simply can't believe my eyes," she said. Then, after a moment, she pointed to a small hill on the edge of downtown. "There's that pretty tower, though."

"Coit Tower," said Anna, who, having lived in the city for a few months after college, was experiencing her own nostalgia now.

"I climbed it once."

"Me, too."

By the time they arrived at the Hotel Senseki, it was after six o'clock. Despite their Japantown location, Goldie announced, "I'm not eating any Japanese food." She was too tired to venture far from the hotel, though, so they ended up going down to the East Meets West Steakhouse on the lower level, where she could get a rib eye and Anna could order sushi.

"I can't stand raw fish," Goldie said, looking with suspicion at her granddaughter's dinner. The design of the restaurant twisted the basic surf and turf theme into a kind of postmodern Kabuki, with woodblock prints of cows in kimonos and long-lashed koi hiding co-quettishly behind open fans.

"Did you ever try it?"

"Of course not. I'm not a caveman."

Anna had always found it interesting to watch her grandmother cultivate a cosmopolitan air while remaining, in so many ways, the poor Jewish girl from Memphis. She would not eat pork or shellfish, even though she refused any attempts to connect her taste in food to her religion. She had no appreciation for music, unless you could dance to it. Despite her extensive knowledge of fine antiques, she kept a collection of Japanese ceramic good luck cats (the kind you see in every sushi bar) in a shadow box in her bathroom.

The waiter came to the table and looked down at Goldie's plate with concern. "Was the steak all right?" he asked.

Goldie was tired, but not too tired to enjoy the attention. She put her hand on the edge of the plate and looked up at the waiter, a long-limbed young man with a tiny ruby stud in each ear. "At first it seemed a little too well done, but I really didn't want to send it back," she told him, "and then I cut into it and it was perfect. Pink and perfect."

He didn't seem convinced, because she'd eaten so little. "Be honest. You can send it back if you like."

This was the kind of service Goldie loved. "I'm always honest," she assured him. "I just can't eat much. When I'm in New York, I take my leftovers back to the doorman."

The waiter still hovered. "You sound like you're from the South."

"We're two Memphis girls," Goldie said, drawing out the vowels even more excessively than usual. Despite her aversion to her hometown, she liked the attention she drew with her accent.

"I'm from Little Rock."

"Just down the road," Goldie exclaimed, as if they'd discovered they were neighbors. Then she said, "You're a sweet boy. What's your name?"

"Milt."

"Milt, let me tell you. I haven't been in San Francisco in thirty years." She looked at Anna. "Is it thirty years?"

"Something like that." Anna smiled. More than sixty, actually, but did it matter?

"Thirty years," Goldie continued. "So it's something of a shock for me. A shock. I used to visit Japantown back then, and the shops were filled with things you'd never seen in your life. I tell you it was like going to the Orient."

Milt hugged his order pad. "Now it's all sushi bars and boutiques selling Japanese comic books and ceramics." He gazed down at Goldie as if she were the only person in the room, even though the restaurant was very crowded.

Goldie threw up her hands in mock exasperation. "I don't know a thing about it now! I have no idea, because we just got here this afternoon. But still, I'm cognizant of the fact that this is not the same city that I loved thirty years ago."

"You might love it," Milt offered.

"Love it? I'm going to adore it. I'm going to be wild about it, Milt." She looked at Anna, reached over, and squeezed her hand. "We made it!"

The look on Goldie's face—such a mix of joy and surprise and relief—made Anna laugh with pleasure, because she was relishing the same emotions. For so many years, she realized, she had focused on the things that drove her and her grandmother apart. Anna had not been wrong to wear a flapper dress or to marry Ford, but she could see now that those decisions had undermined Goldie's sense of security in some fundamental way. Each person becomes trapped by the experiences that form them, and Goldie's well-being depended on adherence to the values and behaviors that had helped her to survive. This realization did not compel Anna to think differently about the choices she had made—wasn't she governed by her own life experiences?—but it did stir within her a greater compassion for her grandmother.

Milt squatted down so that he was eye level with Goldie. "Can I just tell you that I work here six nights a week, and as you can see, we get a pretty sophisticated crowd—"

"I know that," Goldie cut in. "We're staying upstairs, and we were dying of hunger and exhaustion so we came down. This is marvelous."

"What I mean is, you're the most elegant person I've seen in a long time. You don't look like you're exhausted. You look like someone in *Vogue*. A lot of people buy expensive clothes, but they don't know how to wear them."

Goldie, who had been too tired to change clothes, still had on the black-and-white polka dot silk Yves Saint Laurent blouse she'd been wearing all day, and she did look better than anyone else in the restaurant. "I could tell you some stories, Milt," she said reaching out to pat his arm. "And let me give you a fashion tip."

The waiter leaned in closer.

"According to Gianfranco Ferre, you can mix a lot of colors you never would have thought of mixing. Try navy with dark brown. You wouldn't think so, but it works."

"Really?" Anna asked. This was news to her.

"Style takes imagination," said Milt, turning his attention to Goldie's blouse. "Speaking of which, I love those polka dots."

"People are scared to wear polka dots. But they make an outfit."

Milt said, "Most people couldn't pull it off."

Goldie looked humble and pleased, and certainly what he said had made her happy. She worked hard to keep up her appearance and refused to go out with even a smudge on her shoe. But still, the attention no longer mattered. She took his hand and squeezed it. "You are a sweet young man, Milt."

"I'm studying fashion." He turned his head and looked around the room. "Shoot. I have to get back to work." He added quietly in Goldie's ear, "I could sit here all night and talk with you, but I'd lose my job."

Goldie laughed. "We could sit here all night and talk to you, but I'll die right here if I don't get to bed. We'll just take the check, Milt."

"He's sweet," said Anna, when they were alone again.

Goldie opened her compact and checked her lipstick. "Don't turn your nose up at anybody. You can learn from a hobo on the street."

Anna rested her cheek on her palm and looked at her grandmother with wonder. "I'll keep that in mind," she said.

When Milt returned with the check, he carried a large plate of cookies. "I stole them from the pastry chef," he whispered. He looked at Anna and smiled. This was the first time they'd really acknowledged each other. "How are you two related?" he asked.

"She's my grandmother," Anna replied, experiencing a feeling of pride the possibility of which she would have absolutely rejected a few weeks earlier.

Goldie's cell phone rang a minute or two after they returned to the room. They were expecting a call from Sadie, who was supposed to have learned the gender of her baby that day. Goldie was in the bathroom, so Anna picked up the phone. "Hello?"

"Anna?" She recognized Naveen's voice immediately, and with that recognition came a sudden destabilization, as if she were no longer grounded to the carpet.

"Oh, hey."

"Is your grandmother okay?" Anna found the anxiety in his voice unexpectedly touching.

"She's fine. I just picked up the phone for her. We got to San Francisco this afternoon."

"That's good to hear."

If Goldie's time in the bathroom afforded Anna and Naveen any opportunity to speak honestly at last, they squandered it by engaging in such a long period of silence that Goldie reappeared without their having exchanged another word. "Well," Anna said, "I guess she's here right now." She handed Goldie the phone, ignoring the sense of loss that washed over her as she did it. "It's Dr. Choudary."

Goldie took the phone, sat down in a chair, and lifted it to her ear. "You really are an excellent doctor," she said. After a pause, she added, "I know exactly what you're saying. Blood clots are a dangerous thing, and I have every intention of getting up and walking around the airplane. Even if I'd rather be sleeping, I'm going to drag myself up and practically walk across the Pacific by myself. Blood clots can kill you. I'm cognizant of that fact."

Anna sat on the edge of the bed pretending to read through a brochure about shopping in the Japan Center, but she was actually listening to Goldie's conversation with Naveen. From his perspective, Anna's refusal to engage with him probably seemed skittish and silly. She considered herself prudent, though. The fact was that they had only known each other for a day. They had watched a movie, eaten dinner together, had sex. What did that prove about either one of them? Or both of them together? To Anna's thinking, it proved the value of the one-night stand. It had been fun, and important to her own process of healing, and it was also uncomplicated. It left them free from pain, unencumbered. Naveen could not ignore the value of that. Simply put, Anna did not want to suffer.

When Goldie's conversation finally concluded, she snapped shut the phone and set it back on the table. "I'm not even going to wash my teeth," she said. She looked so exhausted that Anna helped her get out of her clothes, then found her peach nightgown and let it slowly flutter down over her grandmother's head while Goldie held up her arms.

"Go to sleep now," Anna said.

"What are you going to do?"

Anna glanced at the clock. For once, she really didn't feel like drawing. "I think I'll go for a walk."

"Walk? Where are you going to walk? I don't want to be worrying about you. I'm dead here."

"We're next to a mall," Anna reminded her grandmother. The Senseki sat at one end of the Japan Center, she explained, showing Goldie the shopping brochure, which said that the stores stayed open until 10 P.M. Anna could remember wandering through Japantown years ago, and she suddenly felt the urge to look again at the heavy iron teapots, sushi sets, and silk kimonos she remembered loving then. Maybe she'd even find a store that sold *manga*. Aside from the few minutes when Naveen's call had thrown her off, their arrival in San Francisco had given her a new sense of possibility, a buoyancy, even though she was having trouble tracing that feeling back to any particular cause. She just felt happy. "Please don't worry."

Goldie sat on the edge of the bed, brushing her hair out. "I was all alone in this city. I managed. You'll manage. But I would have killed to have somebody worry about me the way I worry about you."

Anna sat down next to her grandmother and put her hand on Goldie's knee. "I'll stay here if you like, Nana. I really don't care."

Goldie lay down and let Anna pull the covers over her. "What am I going to do?" she asked, her eyes already beginning to close. "I leave in two days, and then I'm in Dubai and you're all alone again. You could be walking around town at 3 A.M. and I wouldn't know it."

"I guess you have to trust me."

"I trust you, darling. You go on and do whatever it is that you have to do."

It took a couple of minutes for Anna to leave the room, because Sadie finally called to inform them that Goldie's first great-grandchild would be a girl and that Sadie and Diane planned to name her Dakota Rose. After that, Goldie and Anna had to spend a few minutes discussing the merits of this name. (Anna thought it was pretty; Goldie, who had shown surprising restraint during the actual call, said, "If they wanted to name their child after a state, why not call her 'New Hampshire'?"). By the time Anna had found her back-pack and cell phone and put on her shoes, Goldie was curled up with her hands clasped below her chin, like a sleeping baby.

Anna picked up the napkin full of Milt's cookies. He had given them many more than she and Goldie could eat together, more than Anna, unrestrained by her grandmother's scrutiny, could even eat on her own. As she looked down at them—ginger lace cookies, biscotti, sugar cookies dipped in chocolate—a surge of romantic feeling welled inside her and she suddenly wanted to share them with Naveen. She wasn't willing to ask herself the obvious question: Had she been wrong to cut him off? Instead, she simply wondered: If she could wander alone through the city with him, where would they go?

Anna had pocketed the cookies and was about to walk out the door when the sound of movement in the bed made her turn around. Goldie, her face pale in the light from the lamp, was gazing at her. "I love you, darling," she said. "You take such good care of me."

Anna grinned. "I love you, too," she said, before shutting the door behind her.

The next morning, they argued. Anna had decided to call Nakamura Imports as soon as the office opened, but at breakfast Goldie announced, "I'm just going to relax in San Francisco. I'm not doing anything else." They were seated at a table by the window in the hotel restaurant. Outside on Post Street, the rush hour traffic sounded like a band warming up to parade downtown.

"What are you talking about?" Anna asked.

"I'm resting up before my cruise. I'll just enjoy this pretty hotel."

"But we drove all the way out here to return the prints."

Goldie was concentrating on buttering a slice of toast. "Do you want me to collapse on my cruise because I'm so exhausted?" she asked. "I arranged to bring them out here. Now you take over. Do you expect me to do everything in this family?"

Anna stared at her grandmother, who did not look exhausted at all. The devotion Anna had developed for the prints made her feel even more indebted to their rightful owners, and now she experienced a spasm of hurt on behalf of the long-lost Nakamuras. "Why are you acting this way?" she demanded. "Don't you want to see your friends?"

Goldie poured some milk over her Raisin Bran, then stirred it around. "Haven't you heard the phrase 'water under the bridge'? And anyway, I'm tired."

Anna leaned back, crossing her arms and trying generally to look as irritated as possible. "I can't believe I drove you all the way out here for this," she said, but Goldie merely took a bite of toast, looking up at Anna with the sweetest smile.

Back in their room, Anna picked up the phone to call Nakamura Imports. She was still irritated with her grandmother, but as Goldie showed no signs of budging, Anna equated her responsibility to that of a German descendant with a cache of stolen Nazi art. She had to return the portfolio herself. "I shouldn't be the one to do this," she muttered, but Goldie, filing her nails on a chair by the window, ignored her.

After a few rings, a receptionist answered. "Nakamura Imports."

"Hello," Anna said. "My name is Anna Rosenthal. I've got kind of a complicated situation here."

"What can I help you with?" The man sounded bored, but willing to listen.

"A really long time ago," she began, "like in the nineteen forties, my grandmother lived in San Francisco and she was friends with the Nakamura family."

Goldie seemed to have found a snag in the nail on her thumb. She held it up to the light from the window, then went at it again like some elderly woodsman sawing away at a very tiny tree.

"Yes?" the man replied, waiting.

"Well, she has some art that I think belongs to them and—"

"Hold, please."

A moment later, she heard a different voice, this one gravelly but alert. "Hello? Henry Nakamura here."

Though Anna had known, logically, that the man himself might pick up the phone, the sound of an actual person confounded her. She felt as if Rumplestiltskin or Peter Pan had suddenly come on the line. "Hello," she stammered. "My name is Anna Rosenthal. I have a kind of strange reason for calling."

"Anna Rosenthal?"

"Years and years ago, during the war, my grandmother Goldie Rosenthal—I mean, Goldie Feld, or Goldie Rubin—might have known you." He didn't respond. Anna added hurriedly, "I think she was friends with your wife."

Goldie looked up. "Not his wife. His *sister*!"

"My sister," Henry Nakamura said. "Not my wife."

"Sorry! Your sister. I'm sorry. So you remember?"

"Yes, of course." After a moment, he said, "She was a nice girl from Memphis."

Goldie had returned her focus to her nails now, but Anna could see, by the frequency with which Goldie looked up, that she was more interested in this conversation than she cared to admit. "Yes, that's right, from Memphis," Anna said. "I'm calling because she has some art that she'd like to return to your sister."

Henry Nakamura said, "My sister died a few years ago."

"Oh, dear. I'm so sorry."

"We miss her. But she was eighty and ill, so it was the right time."

"I see." Goldie was staring at Anna now, and Anna mouthed the words "She died" while holding her hand over the receiver. Goldie absorbed this information with a solemn nod but didn't seem surprised. In her world, people died quite regularly.

"My grandmother thought so highly of her," Anna told Henry Nakamura. What did Anna know? It sounded nice, though.

"She was a—I think the term you'd use today is *free spirit*. We all thought the world of her."

"I'm sure," said Anna. In the silence that followed, she remembered the pictures. "Could I maybe bring the portfolio by? We're in San Francisco."

"I suppose so," he said. He seemed to be considering the situation. After another pause, he said, "Why don't you meet me at the Japanese Tea Garden in Golden Gate Park? I go there often, and you might enjoy seeing the place yourself. Could you come to the tea pavilion tomorrow at about nine o'clock?"

"Um. Let me see." Anna thought that perhaps the novelty of the setting might serve as some enticement. Covering the mouthpiece again with her hand, she said to Goldie, "He wants us to meet him at the Japanese Tea Garden."

But Goldie seemed to have returned her attention to her nails. "You're free," she said. "You go."

Anna could have thrown a pillow at her grandmother at that moment. To Henry Nakamura, she said, "I'm not sure if my grandmother will be able to join us. She's very tired from our travels, so it may just be me."

Henry Nakamura took a moment to answer. "That's fine," he said. Anna could hear some feeling in his voice, but she couldn't decipher it at all.

Just before nine the next morning, Anna walked through the ornately carved entrance to the Japanese Tea Garden. As she began to climb the stairs to the tea pavilion inside, the sight of the little wooden chairs and tables scattered haphazardly under the eaves made her wonder if the place had even opened yet. Then she saw the old man, white haired and gently waving his hand, wearing a sport jacket, sunglasses, and a beret. He was sitting on a chair in a corner overlooking the stream, a knobby cane balanced between his knees. It wasn't until she had made her way across the floor and finally stopped in front of him that his mouth slowly eased into a smile.

"Mr. Nakamura?" she asked.

"Call me Henry," he said. It took him a moment to pull himself up, but once he did he stood solidly in front of her, full of good cheer. He held out his hand. "I would have known you anywhere," he told her. "You look just like your grandmother."

Anna laughed, pulling at the cuffs on her jacket. "That's probably because I'm wearing all her clothes." This morning, for the first time in years, Anna had let Goldie pick out an outfit for her to wear. She had on a dark green Armani pantsuit, Hermes scarf, and pair of hand-sewn Italian leather heels. Because Goldie's feet were half a size larger and extra wide around the toes, Anna had to walk with her toes pinched hard against the bottom of the shoes to keep herself from tripping out of them. "She wanted me to make a good impression."

Henry was gazing most intently, though, at Anna's face. He didn't say anything, and in the awkwardness that followed, she remembered the portfolio under her arm. "These are your pictures," she said, holding up the velvet case. It felt like a victory to finally hand them over to their rightful owner.

But Henry gave the portfolio only a perfunctory glance. "Oh, yes," he said. He took the parcel from her arms and set it on a table. "Shall we take a walk?" he asked.

Anna looked at the artwork. The entire garden was deserted, but she had just driven all the way across the country to return the prints to him. She didn't want to risk losing them to some thief in a park. "Is it safe?" she asked.

"Don't worry at all." He had already started across the tearoom and merely paused to call over his shoulder, "The waitress just stepped away for a minute. She'll keep an eye on it for us."

Anna trailed Henry back down the stairs and along a path that followed a stream. "We'll take a walk, drink some tea," he said. The morning was overcast, and though the fog had lifted, the garden seemed empty, the only other movement coming from a pair of birds darting between the lacy leaves of a maple tree. Henry moved easily here, and though he gripped his cane, he seemed to rely on it more to point at things than to keep his balance. After a couple of minutes, they reached a wooden structure shaped like an upside down U, which spanned the stream at a branch of the path.

"What do you think of that?" he asked.

"Is it supposed to be a bridge?"

He laughed. "It *is* a bridge. We call it the Moon Bridge." He looked at her more seriously then. "Did your grandmother tell you that my family used to live in the tea garden?"

Anna shook her head. "She's told me very little."

Some flash of feeling—was it hurt? nostalgia?—passed across the old man's face and then, just as quickly, disappeared. With the tip of his cane, he motioned back along the path in the direction from which they had come. "The pavilion, where you and I just met, stands on the footprint of the house I grew up in."

"I had no idea," Anna said. She had visited the tea garden during the brief few months after college that she lived in San Francisco, but Goldie had never mentioned having once had friends who lived there.

Henry leaned against the railing of the bridge, its wood worn smooth from years of use. "I liked to race over this bridge when I was a boy. My sister, Mayumi, would hold the stopwatch right here," he pointed with the tip of his cane to a small patch of grass surrounding a weathered-looking bonsai. "I had to make it over and back in fifteen seconds."

"Could you do it?"

He sighed. "Well, yes, but ultimately I had no chance for complete success. If I managed it in fifteen seconds, I had to do it again in fourteen seconds. And so on, until I failed."

"It's so disheartening," Anna said.

"Let's call it excellent training for later in life." He turned again toward the bridge, which despite its elegant line was ponderous and imposing. "It's not very convenient, is it?"

"Not at all."

"But the shape creates a reflection on the water that makes a perfect circle. Like the moon."

Anna said, "It's kind of lovely when you think of it like that."

They wandered farther into the garden, along paths that led past gnarled cherry trees that, Henry told her, had been trained into their shapes through years of careful attention. His family had been forced to leave when the Japanese were sent to internment camps during World War II, and they didn't return to San Francisco until 1945. Though the Nakamuras never lived inside the park again, Henry's father remained as caretaker until the end of his life. Henry made it clear to Anna that he was not a horticulturalist himself, but he had a vast knowledge of the place and displayed the kind of weary affection that people often have for beloved family members who are also overwhelmingly needy. "I walk along these paths," he told her, "and see the results of a hundred-year war against weeds."

Eventually they reached a small pond shaded by willow trees. From here, they could look down on a dozen or so koi, bright bursts of orange and white, fluttering through the water. A few of the fish were motionless under rocks, their heads hidden, their tails rhythmically beating the current in the only sign of life. "Do you see the eggs?" Henry asked. With the tip of his cane, he pointed to clusters of tiny white spheres floating in the water. "They're spawning. It's fortunate that you're here right now, because we only see this phenomenon as the weather turns warmer."

Anna squatted to look more closely. "The eggs look like pearls."

Henry walked around to the other side of the pond. "I'm searching for Miss Cho," he said, peering down into the water.

"They all have names?"

"I only know Miss Cho. Miss Butterfly. My father shipped her here in a barrel not long before the war. She was already twenty-five years old when she arrived. What does that make her now?"

Anna stood up and followed him to the other side of the pond. "More than ninety," she told him, though she suspected by the look on his face that he knew the fish's age already.

Henry resumed his study of the water. "She's usually easy to spot." When he didn't see her, he stepped out onto a set of jutting rocks so that he could get a better view of the deeper part of the pond.

Anna walked closer to where he was standing on the ledge. Here, the rocks seemed less stable, and his position struck her as precarious for a man in his eighties. When he leaned out to get a different angle, Anna resisted the urge to hold him.

"Oh, dear," Henry said after a while. "I was worried that this might happen."

"What?"

"That's Miss Cho, over there under that rock. She has a gash on her side."

Anna saw her now. The fish was slightly larger than the others, but it was her coloring, and not her size, that was most distinctive. The other fish were either orange or white, while a few white fish had large patches of orange spreading along their sides. Alone among all of them, Miss Cho was a perfect blend of both these colors, the effect of which created an almost translucent shade of peach. And there, on her side, Anna saw the bright red wound, perhaps half an inch thick and six inches long. "Oh, no," she said.

Henry was already walking away from the pond toward a cluster of bushes beyond the willows. "I can't tell you how often I've had to do this," he grumbled to Anna who tagged along behind. "The park is understaffed. Consequently, they forget to check the pond when the fish are spawning. It happens every year. I call and write letters, but they simply don't do it."

"What happened?" Anna asked.

Henry was leaning down, peering under the bushes, trying to jostle something free with the tip of his cane. "When they spawn, the male fish become aggressive—not surprising, right? Sometimes the females are pushed into the rocks at the side of the pond. They get cut. It happens all the time. People who *care* about their fish, they have protections for this sort of thing. They line the edges of their ponds with rubber to mitigate the impact. Golden Gate Park, though, doesn't do that. So a few of us have taken matters into our own hands. We're a kind of patrol."

He had by now managed to get his hands on the object under the bushes, which was covered by a tarp. It was a plastic tub with a back-pack inside it. He carried it back to the pond, not even bothering to use his cane now. Then he pulled from the backpack a large towel, some packets of medication, and a pair of thigh-high rubber boots. He looked up at Anna. "You must think I'm thoroughly crazy now."

"Not really," Anna said. She was too surprised to think at all, actually. "But you've got to let me help you at least."

He did. Over the next few minutes, they filled the tub with pond water, wetted the big towel and a wad of other smaller ones, and set up what amounted to a clinic right there on the grass. Anna, who had been expecting to spend the morning discussing Hiroshige and Kunisada with an expert in art and antiques, felt some disappointment that things were not unfolding as she'd hoped. On the other hand, she liked the idea of performing first aid on a wounded fish.

Then Henry sat down on the grass and started taking off his shoes.

Anna looked at the tall rubber boots and at the wobbly rocks that lined the water. Trying for a firm tone, she said, "You're going to have to let me do that."

He looked up at her. "Do what?"

Anna thought of her grandmother, lying in the suitcase. She thought of Ford in his bed facing the dogwoods, and she knew that she was beyond the point at which she could watch Henry put himself at risk. "I'm going to have to be the one to go into the water."

Henry stared up at her from where he had seated himself on the grass. He already had one shoe off, but none of these tasks were easy or comfortable for a man in his eighties. "Saving fish isn't your battle," he told her.

Anna sat down beside him and began to pull off Goldie's heels. She had no interest in discussing the life experiences that had led her to this point, but she knew that she could not allow Henry Nakamura to step into the water. "Actually, it is my battle," she said.

Somehow, they managed. Anna took off her jacket, rolled her sleeves far past her elbows, pulled on the boots, and tucked the legs of her trousers down into them. Despite these precautions, she had no illusions that the Armani suit would emerge undamaged. Sure enough, as soon as she stepped into the pond, she felt a splash of water crest the top of the boots and run down her leg. She kept walking anyway, making slow progress across the pond. Once she reached the rocky ledge, it took some maneuvering, amid the swirl of suddenly disoriented fish, to find the ailing Miss Cho. Surprisingly, the fish didn't put up a fight, though Anna did have to reach fairly deeply into the water to grasp her. Somehow she managed to haul the fish out of the water, walk it back across and out of the pond, and hold it on the wet towel while Henry spread some kind of salve across the wound. Then, gently, Anna carried the fish back down to the ledge, squatted down, and released her into the water.

As Anna pulled off the boots and rearranged her now-wet clothes, Henry repacked the supplies and prepared to hide the tub back under the tree with the wet towels draped on top of it. "She's awfully pretty," Anna said, looking down at Miss Cho, who had reassumed her place beneath the rocky overhang.

A couple of tourists, holding hands, ambled by and paused to look down into the koi pond. The now-placid water showed no hint of the disturbance that had taken place only minutes before. "She adored that fish," Henry said.

Anna looked at him. Was he one of those old people whose attention constantly drifted to the past? "Your wife?" she asked.

Henry threw his head back, laughing. "Oh, dear no. Not my wife. She played bridge. I'm talking about Goldie. She loved Miss Cho."

As Anna followed Henry back to the teahouse, she tried to imagine the circumstances in which her grandmother would love a fish, even one as beautiful as Miss Cho. Unfortunately, though, Anna could not imagine Goldie in any way at that moment, except in reaction to the state of her Armani suit. Patches of wet fabric clung to Anna's legs. She reeked of pond. Goldie would kill her.

It wasn't until they had returned to the pavilion that Anna, washing her hands at the small sink by the kitchen, realized that she had lost Ford's ring. The days of grasping Bridget's steering wheel in the blazing sun had browned the skin on her hands, except for one newly evident pink strip across her thumb, where the ring used to be.

She must have made some audible gasp of surprise, because Henry, seated at a table at the edge of the pavilion a few feet away, sounded alarmed. "Is everything all right, my dear?"

Anna stared down at her hand and thought of the slimy pond water, the slippery fish, the looseness of the gold band on her thumb. She pictured Ford's ring, slowly falling until it settled into the sand beneath the rocky ledge.

"I lost my ring," she said. She noticed a curious flatness to her voice, which didn't at all match the tumult inside her. "My husband's wedding ring."

When she turned from the sink and looked at Henry, his face was filled with concern. "He died," Anna explained. "My husband, Ford. He died two years ago. I've been wearing his ring." Her eyes scanned the teahouse, darting from the concrete floor to the wooden eaves to the little rattan chairs around the empty tables. Of course, she didn't see the ring in any of those places. "It's probably back at the pond." She was halfway across the pavilion already.

"Anna?"

The sound of Henry's voice made her stop. She looked back and saw that he had pulled himself up from his chair. "Why don't you have some tea first? You could use a rest. We could look at the artwork together. If it's possible to find your husband's ring now, I would think we could also find it in half an hour."

Anna wanted to say that waiting half an hour would do nothing to relieve the anxiety she felt at this moment, but she also noticed that Henry was using his cane for support now. Perhaps he had depleted his reserves saving that fish. She had come here, after all, to meet him.

She should at least sit with him for a few minutes before rushing off to dig in the sand at the bottom of the pond. Anna thought of Goldie and how fragile she looked at night, as if every ounce of stamina had been spent in the effort of getting through the day, and she realized that she could not abandon Henry now. "I guess you're right," she said. She walked back to their table, and they both sat down.

Henry glanced toward the kitchen, from which they could now hear the sounds of activity. "Our tea should be ready soon. It can fortify your search." When Anna didn't respond, he added, "Your grandmother was always a big fan of Japanese tea."

Anna remembered the Nightingale Palace, and she told him about the game she and Goldie used to play.

He seemed to like that. "I don't know if she cared more about the tea itself or the ceremony that went with it," he said. "I do know that your grandmother loved good manners more than anyone I ever met."

"That's so true." Despite her anxiety about the ring, Anna began to laugh, surprised that he would remember such a telling detail.

"How is she?" Henry asked. He was still smiling, but his expression had taken on a certain awkward formality, which seemed tender and self-conscious at the same time.

"She's great." The intensity of Henry's gaze made Anna suddenly protective of Goldie, but she also felt that, after all these years, he deserved some concrete information. "We had some problems when we drove through Indiana, but now she seems as good as new. Her life has been very full." It wasn't easy to summarize the past sixty years, so she detailed the various milestones—Goldie's husbands, her son, the family's business successes. "My grandfather was kind of a homebody, but my grandmother loves to travel. She still does, after all these years. She's leaving for a cruise out of Dubai tomorrow."

"Lovely," said Henry. His attention suddenly shifted to the waitress, to whom he offered a grateful smile for her appearance with the tea tray. Middle-aged and wearing a kimono, the woman tottered toward them on a pair of dangerous-looking wooden sandals, the tea tray in both hands and, over one arm, a wool blanket that she motioned for Anna to take and drape over her clammy body. She must have been a comrade on the fish patrol.

"Thank you, Yukiko," Henry said. Anna pulled the blanket over her legs, and they both watched as the waitress set a teapot, cups, saucers, and a bowl of rice crackers on the table in front of them. Then she silently went away again.

Henry leaned forward and peeked inside the teapot. "We'll let it steep for a few minutes."

"I'd like to hear about your family, too," Anna said. "I'm sure my grandmother will want to know."

"Of course," Henry said. He told her that his sister, Mayumi, had opened a boutique dress shop in Los Angeles and that Kim Novak and Audrey Hepburn had been ardent clients. Henry had remained in San Francisco, building his antiques business. These days, though he still went to the office most mornings, his two sons ran the daily operations. He and his wife, Akemi, had been married fifty years, but she had passed away in the 1990s. Since then, he had lived in an apartment on Russian Hill, not far from his boys.

"It's nice that your family lives nearby," Anna said.

Henry, leaning back in his chair, traced the tip of his cane along the low stone wall that separated the pavilion from the garden beyond. "My sons are devoted and I love them. But, you know, I've always been independent. I traveled so much with my business. Sometimes I'd be in Europe for months, purchasing antiques. I wasn't always attentive to my wife and children. My sons still feel angry sometimes. I wasn't a perfect father."

This revelation, spoken with a tinge of remorse, surprised Anna, and she felt honored that he would be so candid with her. Still, she took so long to respond that Henry began to laugh. "I'm such an old man, dear," he told her. "My children often treat me like a child, so you'll have to forgive me for taking the opportunity to have an adult conversation."

The tea, he decided, had steeped enough. He poured them each a cup, then jiggled the bowl of rice crackers, bringing some of the dried green peas to the surface. "I'm supposed to stay away from salt, but I cheat," he said, sliding the bowl toward Anna.

She tasted a few. "Delicious."

Henry said, "You really do have your grandmother's eyes."

Maybe his interest reflected nothing more than curiosity over similarities between family members, but his gaze was so piercing that Anna had to look away. "My sister and father have the dark circles under their eyes, too," she said, trying to hide a sudden surge of shame, because Henry was so kind and Goldie had abandoned these people. Was that Anna's responsibility now?

Henry said, "My sister adored Goldie. She loved everything about her."

It was, finally, this expression of unbounded devotion that gave Anna the impetus to address the issue directly. "I'm really sorry," she said, mustering the courage to look at him. "I'm sorry that my grandmother just left San Francisco, and I'm sorry that she took your portfolio and disappeared."

Henry stared at her, trying to piece together what Anna was saying. Then, figuring it out, he raised his hands in the air as if to stop her. "Not at all, dear. You have to understand that the war was going on. That meant everything." His face now filled with emotion, and it took him a moment to find the words to continue. "Goldie did nothing wrong. Ever. Anyway, we heard bits and pieces over the years. Our friend Eugene Blankenship always kept us posted."

Anna was stunned. "You knew Mr. Blankenship?" All through her childhood, Mr. Blankenship, the proprietor of a Palm Beach shop called Eugene's, had come by the house whenever the Rosenthal granddaughters came to visit. The very English Mr. Blankenship had never had a family of his own, and he brought odd and wonderful gifts—trains on roller coasters, banana-shaped telephones, picture frames with secret compartments. Sadie later said that it was Eugene Blankenship, rather than any of the Queer Theorists she met at Yale, who convinced her that one could be gay and lead a full, rich life. Mr. Blankenship had died a few months after his one hundred and second birthday.

"Of course," replied Henry. "We were friends for over fifty years."

The waitress brought them a plate of sweets—peach-shaped candies surrounded by pale green sugary leaves. A group of elderly men carrying cameras—maybe a photography club?—stood clustered around a maple tree that leaned out over the stream. Henry watched Anna. After a while he said, "Would you tell me about Ford?"

Anna kept her eyes on the photographers by the stream. Under other circumstances, she could not have managed to answer such a question, but something about Henry made her try. "Well, he was a university librarian," she said. "Super smart. When he was healthy, he probably read ten novels for every one I finished. And he was funny and very kind, too, at least until the end. He got pretty crabby then."

"People do," said Henry.

"They do. It's not fair, I guess, to blame him for that, though I often have. Anyway, he was diagnosed with leukemia about five years ago, and then he died the year before last. What else? He loved jazz, which doesn't do a thing for me."

Henry said, "Jazz doesn't do a thing for me, either."

Anna picked up one of the sugar leaves and set it on her tongue, where it began to melt. "Nobody's perfect."

Henry raised his cup as if to toast. "Nobody's perfect," he agreed.

Anna let her eyes settle on the strip of pink flesh on her thumb. "I've been in an in-between period since he died," she said.

"In-between what?"

"In-between that part of my life and whatever comes next." The sugar leaf had disappeared, and Anna dug around in the cracker bowl again, pulling out four or five little peas and popping them into her mouth rather manically.

Henry said, "I had a sort of in-between period at one point in my life, too."

Anna looked at him. "When was that?"

"Living in the camps, out in the desert," Henry said. "I was so lost. What did I know of the desert? I'd seen pictures of the dunes of the Sahara, but this place was ugly. Even the mountains were ugly, like animals stripped of their skin and left to die. My grandchildren go camping in the desert. They tell me it's so stark and beautiful and the nights are full of stars. I never saw it that way. I used to walk behind the barracks. It was just dirt and scrub brush out there. Going back there frightened me, but I went as often as I could. It gave me comfort to be alone. You know what I did?"

"What?"

He closed his eyes. "It's a cliché. I would walk out there, all alone, and I would squat down and dig my hands into the dirt and then lift up handfuls and let it sift through my fingers. My sister was an artist. She collected that dirt and found fossilized shells in it. She used the shells to make tiny, exquisite pieces of jewelry. But I wasn't like that at all. I carved wood, but I hated every minute of it. I felt so sorry for myself. I would just think, 'This is my life. This is my life passing by.'" He opened his eyes and looked at Anna. He looked terribly sad for a moment, but then he suddenly laughed and shook his head. "I was quite melodramatic as a young man. My emotions were always right on the edge."

"I feel that way sometimes," Anna said.

He poured them both more tea. "Grief is a kind of prison, too."

Anna thought about this for a few seconds. "I keep thinking I need a plan," she said.

"You don't need a plan. You just need to move through the day with the idea that something good could happen to you. It might not have happened yesterday, but it could happen today."

The waitress had brought the portfolio over from where she'd kept it for them in the kitchen, and Anna opened it now. Together, she and Henry went through every picture. She told him how, over the past few weeks, she had often copied Hiroshige's images into her sketchbook, and she told him that the work inspired her. He seemed to take pleasure from that, and pleasure, too, from paging through the book with her. "My father loved this one," he said, pointing to one of the Hiroshige images, a narrow road running up the side of a mountain with the ocean far below. Of another image, a village gate at night with a moon hanging over it, he said, "My mother used to sing songs about the moon."

Anna turned the book to the Kunisada prints and found, among the "lady pictures," the one of the girl in front of the screen. "This is my grandmother's favorite," she said. "She told me that it describes the emotions of her life back then."

Henry stared down at the picture. "I didn't know that," he said. "Really?"

When they reached the end of the book, Henry closed it and held it on his lap. "On the telephone, you mentioned that you planned to return these to me," he said.

"Your family gave them away under duress. They belong to you."

He shook his head. "We experienced duress, yes, but not in regard to these pictures. They're Goldie's."

"No. Your family should have them."

"Anna?"

"Yes?"

"They're Goldie's. If she doesn't want them, they're yours."

She could see in his face that the discussion was over. "Thank you," she said.

They finished their tea. Henry looked at his watch. "I suppose you want to go back to the pond now?"

Anna rubbed at the place on her hand where Ford's ring used to be. "It's not a bad spot, really."

"What?"

"The fish pond in the Japanese Tea Garden. I've been trying to find a place for it."

Henry gazed at her. "You're thinking of leaving the ring there?"

"Why not?"

The waitress came and cleared away the dishes. Henry seemed to be considering Anna's decision. After a while, he said, "It is a pretty place, under the willow trees."

They walked out toward the front gate of the garden together. "Did things get better for you, when you left the camp?" Anna asked.

Henry looked at her. "Are you wondering if I've remained miserable for the rest of my life?"

She shrugged. "I guess."

"No. My experience in Utah changed me completely. I became determined after that."

The clouds had parted and they stopped in the shade of a gingko tree near the front entrance. Anna's smelly clothes had dried stiffly and felt increasingly uncomfortable in the heat. She was not quite ready to say good-bye, though. "This may surprise you, given all that I said, but I'm actually kind of hopeful about the future," she told him.

Henry placed the tip of his cane between his feet, resting both hands on the knobby handle. He was looking at Anna more seriously now. "Hope is good," he said, "but hope is passive. You're responsible for yourself, you know."

Something in this advice made Anna think of Goldie. "My grandmother says, 'Make your own party.'"

At that moment, it seemed to Anna that Henry's eyes became infused with a different kind of light. His face relaxed and slowly eased into a smile. "That sounds just like Goldie," he told her. And then, though it was obviously time to go, they remained where they were for a few more seconds, looking up at the pale green leaves of the gingko, which spread over their heads like thousands and thousands of tiny fans.

20

The Heart of It All

*B*y eleven thirty the next morning, Anna was guiding Bridget toward the curb in front of the international terminal at SFO. Goldie had been checking her money and passport during the drive, and for that last stretch of freeway between South San Francisco and the airport exit, she sat with her hands folded on her purse, giving Anna last-minute instructions.

"You can talk to your father about where to sell the car, or like I said, you can keep it. It's nothing to me. I'm done with it." And then, a moment later, she drifted in another direction: "You could stay here for a week or so. Keep the hotel room and be a tourist. Put it on my credit card. I couldn't care less." As for the meeting with Henry Nakamura, Goldie had, over the past twenty-four hours, showed a single-minded indifference to that subject. She hadn't even cared about the ruined Armani suit, reacting to the sight of it with a sigh and a roll of the eyes. "That's why I pack plenty of clothes," she had grumbled, before stuffing it in the trash.

Even when Anna described Henry's gracious insistence that she keep the portfolio, Goldie's attention remained entirely focused on her granddaughter. "What's the good of having all this valuable art," she demanded, "if you don't know what you're doing with your life, or where you would put it?" It was dawning on Anna that returning the portfolio to the Nakamuras had been less important to Goldie than finding an excuse to get her granddaughter out of Memphis. Now, after more than two weeks on the road, Goldie considered the effort a failure. Anna had not made any decisions at all.

Of course, Anna could have helped relieve the stress with some confident promises: "I'm moving to New York! I'll become a painter! I'll get my teaching certificate!" She could even have simply announced, "I feel so much better now!" which, though perhaps a minimal consolation, would have amounted to something. Anna was Goldie's granddaughter, however, so she was stubborn, too. "It's not as clear as that," she said. "You can't solve every problem in two weeks."

"I'm not talking about every problem. Someone asks you, 'Where do you want to live?' and you can't even answer."

"You've got to trust me," Anna said. She felt disappointed that Goldie showed so little interest in Henry. If Anna could have described the encounter to her grandmother, then perhaps she could also have explained that she did, in fact, feel better. She had no clearer idea about the future than before, but she had become much happier over the past few weeks. *Something good,* she told herself, *might happen today.* That counted, too, but Goldie didn't seem interested in hearing it.

"Do whatever you want," Goldie had said. "I did my best. I'm giving up."

Now, as they pulled up in front of the terminal, a tall, broad-shouldered woman in a bright green Travcoa jacket stood on the curb with a clipboard in her hand. The sight of a Rolls-Royce must have indicated the arrival of one of her clients, because she took a step closer when she saw them. "I like that," Goldie said. "They are a very reliable company." She lifted her hand and fluttered her fingers. As the car stopped, the woman opened Goldie's door.

"Good morning!" she chirped.

"I'm Mrs. Rosenthal."

"I'm Heidi, Mrs. Rosenthal. It's great to meet you." Heidi held out a big hand to help Goldie get out of the car, but Goldie refused to take it. "I have to do these things myself, Heidi."

Anna jumped out of the car and hurried around to the other side. She and Heidi stood watching as Goldie put both legs on the ground, gripped the handle on the inside of the door, and pulled herself up. "I'm her granddaughter," Anna said.

Heidi shook her hand. "Don't worry about a thing. It's going to be a fabulous trip. Dubai is unbelievable."

Goldie was standing, balanced now, next to the car. "They say it's one of the Wonders of the World," she announced, breathing a little more heavily from the exertion of extracting herself from the car. "You can't miss it."

"Let's get your things," Heidi said, gesturing toward someone they couldn't see inside the building. Anna opened the trunk, and within seconds a porter had appeared and Goldie's suitcases lay piled on a luggage cart on the curb. Ever since they left New York, Anna had anticipated this moment with a sense of approaching relief. Goldie and her luggage would be someone else's responsibility now. Tonight, she told herself, she'd take the bus to the Mission, eat a burrito, maybe go to the movies. If she didn't get back to the hotel until after midnight, no one would care. No one risked falling into a suitcase. No one would get up at 7 A.M. and bombard her with comments about the weather. By 7 A.M. tomorrow morning, Goldie would be stretched out in business class somewhere over Asia, a satin sleep mask pulled over her eyes.

Anna moved closer to Goldie. "Are you sure you don't want me to come inside with you? I could make sure you get checked in."

Goldie had been digging through her purse, double-checking for her passport. "Are you insane? Heidi—that's your name, right?" Heidi nodded. "She's going to help me now. She knows more about this than you do."

Anna reached deep inside herself, searching for the fortitude that had helped her survive with Goldie over the past two weeks. If they had to say good-bye to each other under this cloud of aggravation, then there was nothing Anna could do to change that. "Well then," she said, "I guess I'll be going."

Goldie looked up then, and Anna saw, for what might have been the first time in her life, a surge of remorse cross her grandmother's face. In the flash of an instant, regret, sorrow, affection, and all the mixed-up feelings that one frustrated and addled eighty-five-year-old mind could produce overtook whatever front Goldie tried to project. She put her purse under her arm, then reached out and took her granddaughter's hand. "You have no idea, darling, how much I'm going to miss you," she said.

It seemed to Anna then that every emotion she had ever experienced in regard to Goldie—the childhood adoration, the resentment and fury over Ford, the frustration and amusement and tenderness she had lived with ever since they left New York—all collided into one great storm of feeling. "Saying good-bye is sort of awful," she told Goldie.

"Darling." Goldie's expression became firm and focused now. "You need to get on with your life. You don't need to have your old grandmother dragging you around." She swung their hands a little, as if they were two playmates at recess. "I'm sorry I didn't do better, setting you on the right track. But we had fun, didn't we?"

Anna nodded. She didn't want to cry.

"Give me a kiss." Anna leaned over and kissed her on the cheek, then put her arms around her. Goldie seemed so tiny now. "Remember, your grandmother loves you."

"I remember. I love you, too."

"Give yourself a happy life, all right?" Goldie had her hand on Anna's back.

"Okay."

"I gave myself a happy life. The happiest life imaginable. Do that for yourself, all right?"

"I will," Anna said.

They stepped back and looked at each other. "You're a beautiful girl, a gorgeous girl." Then Goldie slid her hands down her sides, smoothing down her sweater. She looked at Heidi and said, "I'm ready now."

Anna heard the first few notes of "Mack the Knife" just as she was steering the car away from the drop-off lane in front of the terminal. Realizing then that Goldie had left her cell phone on the seat, she said, "Shit," fumbled around to find the phone, then opened it with her lower lip. "Hold on," she barked, then dropped it back onto the cushion. She had been driving Bridget for weeks, and she now maneuvered the Rolls with such confidence that she could have been zipping around in a Mini. Still, airports present their own complex challenges of lanes and exits. Anna squinted to read the signs up ahead and figure out how to loop back to the terminal to find parking. "Just a second," she yelled toward the person on the phone.

Eventually she saw a sign that pointed her onto a ramp for short-term parking. Bridget dipped down out of the sunlight and into the dim maze of the garage. Anna paused to pull a ticket from the machine, then slid up the ramp into the darkness before picking the phone up off the seat. "Sorry about that. Hello?" She held it to her ear and, following the arrows leading her through the lot, found herself hoping that the caller was Naveen.

It was Sadie. "Where's Nana?" she asked.

"I dropped her off, but she left her phone, and I'm about to run back in and give it to her. Didn't you say good-bye already?"

"Yes," said Sadie, "but I'm at Ikea. I need her opinion about the color of a lamp."

"I'm driving. Call her in a little while, okay?" Anna snapped the phone shut and, still holding it in her hand, wound her way through the garage. Finally, on the far side, she found a parking place big enough to accommodate a Rolls-Royce and pulled in.

Anna glanced at her watch. Even though it was nearly three hours before Goldie's flight, her tour group could line up for security at any time. Anna knew she should hurry, but the phone in her hand held her back. She remembered what Henry Nakamura had said about becoming determined, and she remembered Goldie's advice: make your own party. Anna opened the clamshell, scrolled through RECEIVED CALLS until she found an unfamiliar area code that she decided was Indiana, and without another thought, called Naveen.

He answered after only a couple of rings. "Hello?"

"It's Anna. Did I catch you working? Can you talk?"

"It's okay," he said, but he didn't sound friendly. Now it was her turn to worry that he might hang up. For a long moment, he said nothing. Then he asked, "Is your grandmother all right?"

"She's fine. I dropped her off at the terminal a minute ago, and then I discovered that she left her phone in the car. I have to run inside and find her." The nervousness in her voice sounded so obvious. Did he hear it?

"What time is her flight?"

"Two-thirty."

He seemed to be calculating in his head. "She gives herself plenty of time."

They were both silent for a moment. Finally, Anna said, "I'm going to have to find my way through this parking garage while we talk. She's the type to race straight to the gate."

He still said nothing.

She picked up her bag, got out of the car, and locked the door, then followed a green line on the floor that promised to lead toward the international terminal. "I'm underground. I might disappear."

He said, "I'm prepared for you disappearing."

Anna let that one pass. She walked around a bank of elevators and crossed a couple of rows of cars on the other side. "So," she said, "how are you doing?"

"Why did you call?"

"To give you the recipe for the maharani's meatballs?"

He didn't laugh. He didn't say anything.

"I just needed to tell you something." The green line led in a zigzag route up a set of stairs, out onto another parking area, then across the building. She felt like a child traipsing through a fun house. "I'm sorry I hung up on you, but I wanted things to be simple," she said. "I didn't want to suffer."

Naveen was silent. Anna asked, "Are you still there?"

"Yes."

She skirted around a family loading a mountain of suitcases into a tiny van. She had made her apology to Naveen; she could hang up and be done with it, but she remembered Henry in the desert, watching dirt slip through his fingers, and she remembered that her life, too, was slipping by. "I'm just saying, you know, that that was my first time, for anything, after so much bad stuff happened. I wanted things to be clear and easy, so I liked the idea of a one-night stand." And then, mustering the remainder of her courage, she said, "The whole experience, though, turned out to be less clear than I'd expected, and less easy, because I like you too much. So I've realized that, one way or another, I'm going to suffer. I might as well call and get to hear your voice again."

When he still said nothing, she grew worried. "Are you mad? Did I lose you?"

"No." The single syllable sounded gentler this time, and then he asked, "Did you ever have a one-night stand before you spent the night with me?"

"Not really," she admitted. "Actually, no."

"You seem to have this idea about one-night stands. But that wasn't a one-night stand. For one thing, people don't talk like that."

"I guess you're right." She had stepped onto a moving sidewalk that led through a long tunnel decorated by a neon cityscape of San Francisco. A group of Asian teenagers—slick haired and full of bluster—moved past in the other direction, chattering together in a language that she couldn't understand.

"I'm just saying I liked it."

Anna remembered his description of her in the hospital waiting room that first morning, sleeping with piles of discarded sketches all around her. "Did I seem kind of crazy then?"

"No," he said.

She came to the end of the sidewalk, looked at her watch, and saw that it was nearly noon. "Now I'm scared I'll miss my grandmother." Up at the top of the escalator, she could see the bright sunlight flooding the terminal, and she thought of Goldie, moving toward the airplane without her cell phone. "Do you think she's really okay, traveling like this, after her injury?"

"She's fine."

"What if something goes wrong?"

"It seems to me that she understands the risks quite clearly. Something could go wrong in New York or Florida, too. She knows that the worst could happen, and she's prepared for that."

"But in Dubai she's really all alone."

"I'm sure her companion could help her."

Anna wasn't sure she heard him clearly. "Her companion?"

"She said she travels with a companion. She said that your grandfather never went anywhere with her, so she goes with a companion. She's been doing that for fifty years."

"My grandmother doesn't travel with a companion." And then, in an instant, everything that Anna had observed in the past twenty-four hours realigned and fell into place. "I have to go. Can I call you back?"

He sounded alarmed. "How do I know you'll call me back?"

"Trust me!" she said and then, just before snapping shut the phone, she gave him her cell number.

Anna ran up the stairs and into the great hall of the terminal. She stopped to get her bearings, then hurried across the building until she came to a large sign that gave the aisle information for each airline. Disconnected thoughts shot through her mind: the fluctuating importance of Marvin Feld; Goldie's refusal to hear anything at all about Henry Nakamura; her lack of interest in what happened to the Japanese prints. Had the entire journey been a ruse to shake Anna out of her torpor? Perhaps. Mostly, though, Anna thought of the seriousness with which Henry had addressed her the day before. If he were really so tangential to Goldie's life, why had he focused on Anna with such paternal warmth and care?

Above her, the sign said EMIRATES: AISLE 14. Twelve aisles lay between Anna and her grandmother. She turned and ran, her backpack flapping against her leg.

At Aisle 14, Heidi stood alone in front of the ticket desk, counting through a tower of passports stacked on the counter in front of her. "Hey," Anna said, breathless from running. "My grandmother left her phone in the car."

Heidi raised her fingers to hold Anna back. "Sixteen, seventeen, eighteen, nineteen. There!" she said, then turned with a look of satisfaction on her face. "I'm sorry, what did you say?"

"My grandmother, Goldie Rosenthal. She left her phone in the car. I brought it to her."

"Do you want me to give it to her or do you want to see her yourself? She's waiting over in the restaurant area. We're going to go through security in a few minutes, and then we'll head to the Emirates Lounge."

Anna asked, "Did her friend check in already?"

"Oh, sure. They checked in together."

"I'll walk over there with you."

Heidi picked up the passports, slid them into a carry-on bag, then led Anna across the terminal, slipping into tour guide mode as she pointed out the defining architectural features of the building.

Anna was having a hard time focusing. As they approached the concession area, she found herself hanging back. "Do you mind?" she asked. "I'm thinking I'll just get a look at her. If she seems happy and settled, I won't bother her again and you can take her the phone."

"I understand completely," Heidi said. "Oh, there they are! They insisted on wheelchairs. Very smart. Why wear yourself out at the airport?"

But Anna wasn't listening. There, alone at a table, Goldie Rosenthal sat with her companion. He was wearing his beret this morning, but not his sunglasses. He was dunking teabags into a pair of Styrofoam cups, while Goldie apparently offered the running commentary that she had given her granddaughter every day for the past two weeks. He nodded, half listening and half doing as he liked. Anyone passing by might have assumed they had been married for decades. Anna thought of all the summers Goldie had spent in Rome. The trips to Morocco. Lithuania. Machu Picchu. Japan. Safari after safari. For how many years had Goldie regaled the family with accounts of her solo adventures? Thirty? Forty? Fifty years? Even after Saul died, she kept it up, always claiming that she maintained her sanity by taking time alone. In all those years of telling her story, and for the entire drive with Anna across the continent, she had never slipped.

The companion pulled the teabags from the steaming cups and set them on a napkin. Then he secured the plastic tops. *We all have a chance to be happy here*, Anna thought.

Heidi mused, "Don't you just want that for yourself?"

Anna said, "Of course."

Henry Nakamura tipped his head to the side, smiled, and offered tea to his beloved.

Acknowledgments

This is a work of fiction, though much is based on actual events and people. It is true that San Francisco's Japanese Tea Garden was designed and maintained by the Hagiwara family, American citizens of Japanese descent who were forced to leave their home and live in an internment camp after the bombing of Pearl Harbor. I was moved by their experience, but the story of the Nakamura family in this novel grew from my imagination. Likewise, though I mined many details from the history of my own Jewish American family in writing this book, Goldie and Anna are purely my own creations. I feel deeply grateful to my Sachs, Gold, and Goodman relatives for sharing their stories with me.

Several years ago, on a visit to the Cameron Art Museum in Wilmington, North Carolina, I happened to see a book of prints by the artists Ando Hiroshige and Utagawa Kunisada II, which affected me so deeply that for months afterward I couldn't get it out of my mind. In part to satisfy my own fascination with these pictures, I used them as seeds for the story that eventually evolved into this book. Happily for me, the Cameron was wholly supportive of my efforts; I'm particularly appreciative of Holly Tripman, the registrar, who later indulged my curiosity by pulling the collection out of storage and allowing me to spend an entire morning examining it.

In order to give an accurate account of the medical issues addressed in this book, I relied on the guidance of several physicians. Thanks to Dr. Walt Laughlin, Dr. Robert Rotche, and Dr. Michael Moulton, who gracefully adapted their professional expertise to the service of fictional accuracy and plot development, for which, I am quite sure, medical school never trained them. Thanks, too, to Louisa Canady, a specialist in Japanese koi, who helped me to better understand the spawning habits of these fish.

I'm grateful to Judy Goldman, George Bishop, Diane Sachs, Ira Sachs, Jr., and Todd Berliner for reading early drafts of this manuscript and commenting on it so perceptively. Karen Bender, Rebecca Lee, Clyde Edgerton, Robert Siegel, Sarah Messer, John Jeremiah Sullivan, Celia Rivenbark, David Gessner, and Nina de Gramont provide the understanding and support that makes living in Wilmington, North Carolina, a source of comfort and creative inspiration for a writer. My agent, Douglas Stewart, has, as always, been a warm and wise guide through the serpentine paths of publishing, while my editor, Emily Krump, offered just the right insight at just the right moments. My family, including Rose Sachs, Ira Sachs, Sr., Lynne Sachs, Mark Street, Boris Torres, and all the Namerows, Berliners, Smiths, and Vidulichs are a constant source of inspiration, support, and good cheer. And, finally, thanks to Jesse and Sam Berliner-Sachs for all their love, which keeps me going.

Insights,
Interviews
& More . . .

Meet Dana Sachs

DANA SACHS's writing has appeared in *National Geographic*, the *Boston Globe*, and other publications. She is the author of *The House on Dream Street*, *The Life We Were Given*, and *If You Lived Here* (a novel) and she lives in Wilmington, North Carolina. ﹏

A Conversation with Dana Sachs

Many authors have quirky or distinct writing rituals. What is your writing process like? As someone who has written both fiction and nonfiction, do you find your process changes based on the book? How so?

Some writers insist that you have to write for a specific number of hours every day. I've never been able to do that. Especially since I've had children, I have to write whenever I get the chance. I don't want to sound like some Supermom, though. My kids are in school all day now, so if I can't find the time to write during their school day, I don't have anyone to blame but myself. As for the differences between fiction and nonfiction, yes, the differences are significant. But, at heart, I'm a storyteller. The main challenge is finding a way to tell that particular story.

Writing experts often advise people to "write what they know." In writing The Secret of the Nightingale Palace, *did you follow this rule? How did you follow this rule, and how did you break away from it?*

I can best answer this question by describing the process through which I created the character of Goldie. When I began the novel, I wanted to model Goldie on my paternal grandmother, Rose. In the finished book, the similarities between the two are clear: they both come from large, poor Southern Jewish families; they both married twice and, through shrewdness and hard work, became successful in business; they both developed a devotion to fashion and, from an early age, exhibited an innate sense of style. However, Goldie's story is, ultimately, very different from that of Rose, who never lived in San Francisco, never married the heir of a prominent family, and ▶

never (to my knowledge, at least!) fell in love with the "wrong" guy. Goldie's character and story changed with the evolution of the novel. Fiction creates its own demands, which are often unexpected, and I had to address those demands with my imagination, not from real life. In the end, Goldie still has a lot of Rose in her, but they're very different people.

In the cases where you were writing about something new, how did you go about researching those subjects?

As a former journalist, I love research. I had great fun, for example, figuring out popular salad dressings from the 1940s. Any history lover could, like me, lose hours reading about the mustard gas disaster that took place during World War II in the Italian port city of Bari, but a fiction writer gets to call those absorbing hours "working." Sometimes, though, our research comes in the form of simply experiencing life, which can be mysterious, intriguing, unsettling, and, occasionally, very painful. When I first began *The Secret of the Nightingale Palace*, a dear friend of mine was dying of cancer. She had always been a deeply engaging, charming person, but at the very end of her life she became angry, lashing out at the people who loved her best. The anger was shocking, and heartbreaking, because she had come to the end of her life and there was no way to resolve her anger or ease the pain it caused before she passed way. Though that experience for me was nothing like "research," it did inform my thinking as I tried to describe Ford's deterioration from leukemia and the ways in which Anna was left with emotions she couldn't resolve and questions she couldn't answer.

The historical portions of the book include accurate details about life in San Francisco leading up to the Second World War. Were there any interesting details that you wanted to include, but couldn't fit into the story?

Oh, many! Here's one I love. When Henry Nakamura tells Anna about his time in the internment camps during World War II, he describes the jewelry that his sister, Mayumi, made out of tiny shells that she found by digging in the dirt behind their barracks. I would have liked to describe in greater detail the artwork that Japanese internees created, because the items themselves are extraordinary—model ships and trains, tiny carved wooden birds, delicate embroidery, to name just a few. The art also serves as a testament to the ways in which humans find relief from suffering. For online pictures, see "The Art of Gaman: Arts and Crafts from the Japanese American Internment Camps, 1942–1946," a 2010 exhibition at Smithsonian: http://americanart.si.edu/exhibitions/archive/2010/gaman/.

Anna and Goldie bond over their shared love of art and aesthetics. Which artists or works of art inspire you?

At one point in the novel, Anna considers the difference between herself and Ford when it comes to art. She values work that touches her emotionally, while he always tried to understand it intellectually. I'm a little Anna and a little Ford. I like to understand, for example, why critics value a piece of art, but that won't mean I'm inspired by it. As a fiction writer, I'm drawn to art that hints at worlds, relationships, and conflicts that exist beyond the work itself. Japanese printmakers do that. So does Vermeer. Joseph Cornell does it, too. The contents of his boxes remind me of precious objects collected by mysterious people over many, many years. I can't think of any better description for his artwork than "novelistic."

What are you reading right now? Are there any books or authors that you continue to go back to?

I keep returning to the great storytellers, like Jane Austen, George Eliot, and Henry James. Their worlds seem so real, their characters so human, despite the fact that they inhabit societies and centuries very different from my own. Other writers I deeply admire are Somerset Maugham, Barbara Pym, Nancy Mitford, Raymond Chandler, and Flannery O'Connor. And, yes, of course, I love many contemporary writers, too, including Kiran Desai, Alice Munro, Alan Bennett, David Mitchell, Ann Patchett, Haruki Murakami, Rohinton Mistry, Toni Morrison, and Julian Barnes.

Questions for Discussion

1. A great deal of *The Secret of the Nightingale Palace* focuses on grace and poise. How do these themes interact with the concepts of death, dying, and love? Do you think that Goldie effectively taught Anna about grace and poise?

2. There are two sets of sisters in the novel (Goldie and her sisters; Anna and Sadie). How do these sisters serve as foils for one another? Do they motivate or discourage one another?

3. Anna has a lot of trouble deciding what to do with Ford's wedding ring. Is it fitting that she loses it in the tea garden? Do you think she should have tried harder to find it? Should she have handled this differently?

4. The narrative switches between Goldie's history and Anna's present. What are the parallels between the two women? What is the effect of the reader knowing more about Goldie's past than Anna does?

5. Goldie has had two seemingly unfulfilling marriages: the first to Marvin (who loved her but would never be attracted to her), and the second to Saul (their marriage was described as a business relationship). How does Goldie's past influence her judgment of Anna and Ford's marriage? How does it change the reader's opinion of Goldie to find out that she and Henry have been seeing each other for all these years? Do you like her more or less?

6. How do the concepts of nationality, ethnicity, religion, and class play into the plot? Did this story resonate at all with your own family's/ancestors' experiences coming to America or their attitudes now?

7. Goldie is an interesting combination of strength and traditional values. Do you think she could be seen as a feminist character? Why? Why not?

8. In the wake of Ford's death, Anna struggles to come to terms with her feelings for him. Though she remembers that they were once in love, his behavior was often cruel during his illness. Does Anna ever make peace with the bitter end to their relationship? Do you think Ford's slow death is well portrayed? How did it affect Anna's ability to move on?

9. Goldie and Anna rebuild their relationship over the course of their journey and manage to reestablish the closeness they enjoyed in the past, too. Would you say that they have a friendship that goes beyond the fact that they are family? How does their age difference impact their understanding of each other? Do you have friends who are significantly older or younger?

10. The art portfolio that Henry gives to Goldie seems to have a strong effect on her. Why is she so drawn to the pictures? What is the significance of Goldie passing on the portfolio to Anna? Is there a work of art that affects you in a similar way, or that you are particularly drawn to?

11. Do you think that Naveen and Anna have a future together? What is it that draws her to him? Is he similar to or different from Ford? Henry? Do you agree with Goldie that there can only be one love of your life? ❧

Have You Read?
More from Dana Sachs

IF YOU LIVED HERE

Forty-two-year-old Shelley Marino's desperate yearning for a child has led her to one of the only doors still open to her: foreign adoption. It is a decision that strains and ultimately shatters her relationship with her husband, Martin—the veteran of an Asian war who cannot reconcile what Shelley wants with what he knows about the world. But it unites her with Mai, who emigrated from Vietnam decades ago and has now acquired the accoutrements of the American dream in an effort to dull the memory of the tragedy that drove her from her homeland. As a powerful friendship is forged, two women embark on a life-altering journey to the world Mai left behind—to confront the stark realities of a painful past and embrace the promise of the future.

"Sachs is an expansive and generous writer who gives us, at all times, the pulse of life being lived. She's the real deal."
—Louis Bayard, author of
Mr. Timothy and *The Pale Blue Eye*